A Prairie
Christmas Collection

Books by Stephanie Grace Whitson

Historical Fiction
Love at First Light
Messenger by Moonlight
Daughter of the Regiment
A Captain for Laura Rose
A Basket Brigade Christmas (novella anthology)
A Patchwork Christmas (novella anthology)
Christmas Stitches (novella anthology)

The Quilt Chronicles Series (3 books)
The Message on the Quilt
The Shadow on the Quilt
The Key on the Quilt

Stand-alone Books (not part of a series)
A Most Unsuitable Match
Sixteen Brides
A Claim of Her Own
Belle of the Wild West

Pine Ridge Portraits Series (3 books)
Secrets on the Wind
Watchers on the Hill
Footprints on the Horizon

Dakota Moons Series (3 books)
Valley of the Shadow
Edge of the Wilderness
Heart of the Sandhills

Keepsake Legacies Series (3 books)
Sarah's Patchwork
Karyn's Memory Box
Nora's Ribbon of Memories

Prairie Winds Series (3 books)
Walks the Fire
Soaring Eagle
Red Bird

Contemporary Fiction *(3 books)*
Jacob's List
A Garden in Paris
A Hilltop in Tuscany

Nonfiction
How to Help a Grieving Friend: A Candid
Guide for Those Who Care
Home on the Plains: Quilts and the Sod House Experience
Ink: A Writing Life

A Prairie Christmas Collection

Three Historical Romances

STEPHANIE GRACE WHITSON

*Dedicated to the memory of
God's extraordinary women
in every place
in every time.*

About the Author

Award-winning novelist Stephanie Grace Whitson began writing her first novel when she was inspired by the lives of pioneers laid to rest in an abandoned cemetery near her home in southeast Nebraska. What began as a hands-on history lesson for her homeschooled children became a topic of personal study that eventually evolved into a story about an 1840s woman headed west across what would become the state of Nebraska. Creating her imaginary friend Jesse King led Stephanie to learning about the Great Plains women she came to think of as sod house homemakers. Researching their stories has inspired several novels. Her writing career has spanned nearly three decades, and her idea file is still brimming with book ideas—all of them inspired by the often nameless and anonymous women who pioneered in the western United States. Stephanie is a follower of Jesus Christ and student of the Bible, a lifelong learner (she earned her master's degree in history in 2012), a lover of antique quilts who enjoys hand quilting, an avid reader, mother to five grown and married children, and grandmother to thirteen. Learn more at www.stephaniewhitson.com.

A Picture Perfect Christmas

Chapter 1

September 19, 1886
North Platte, Nebraska

Not again.

The moment Lydia McCord stepped into the kitchen and saw Papa in the next room, dread clutched at her mid-section. Leaning back against the kitchen wall, she closed her eyes. He was sitting in his favorite chair reading the newspaper. Pipe smoke curled toward the ceiling. It was a peaceful enough scene—except for one thing. The newspaper wasn't the *Lincoln County Tribune*. Oh, no. Papa was studying *The Denver Post*. And what that probably meant was enough to tempt his only child to tears.

Taking a deep, calming breath, Lydia looked about the tidy kitchen. Her eyes wandered upward toward the beautiful floral wallpaper border she and her best friend, Alice Dillon, had hung a few weeks ago. The elegant design was the perfect complement to the red and white transferware dishes Lydia had purchased at Dillon Dry Goods.

To Lydia's mind, everything about this lovely house was perfect. Set in the middle of a large lot at the corner of Fourth and Vine, the Queen Anne style house was just far enough from the rowdy part of town frequented by cowboys and ne'er-do-wells and just close enough to stores, churches, and the homes of her growing circle of friends. It was large enough to serve not only as a home but also as Papa's medical office. His patients arrived via the wide gate set into the picket fence outlining the lot. They followed a brick path to the porch, mounted four steps, crossed to the door, and found welcome in the front hall. What had once been a formal parlor to the immediate right now served as Doctor McCord's waiting room. Heavy pocket doors closed it off from the examination room—formerly the dining room. The breakfast room at the far end of the entry hall had become a two-bed infirmary, available in the rare instances Papa kept a patient overnight. Beyond the rooms used for Papa's practice were a den and a large kitchen.

This house was so much better than the crowded apartment Papa had considered at first. That space had been along Front Street and so close to the Union Pacific Depot they would have heard every creak, every screech, every conductor's *All aboard!* Instead, the McCords had a real home—the first one Lydia had had in the five years since Mama's passing, when they'd begun the tumbleweed existence that had taken them from Chicago to Springfield, from Springfield to St. Louis, from St. Louis to Omaha, and, finally, from Omaha to North Platte. But now, if that infernal *Denver Post* was any indication, Papa was about to suggest they leave North Platte.

Lydia suppressed a frustrated sigh. He would raise the subject over supper. *I had great hopes for North Platte, but it just isn't measuring up.* He'd hold his hand up in anticipation of her protest. *Once we're settled in Denver, you'll see that I was right to move on.*

Unless. Lydia pressed her lips together. *Unless I do something to stop it.* She surveyed the kitchen. *Her* kitchen, with its beautiful border print and crisp white curtains. *Her* stove—the scene of countless tearful battles and, at last, hard-won success. Finally, Miss Lydia McCord could hold her own in the kitchen. She could bake flaky biscuits and good bread and decent pie—even if the latter could do with further improvement.

Thinking on her many pie failures, Lydia recalled Mrs. Dillon's encouraging words. *There's not a woman born who baked a blue-ribbon pie on her first attempt. It takes practice.* As she remembered Mrs. Dillon's kindness, Lydia gave a little nod. She had practiced and she would continue—right here in *this* kitchen in North Platte, Nebraska. She might even compete for a ribbon at the upcoming county fair.

Lydia's mind raced as she formulated her argument against another move. *You're fast becoming the most beloved and trusted doctor in town.* She would remind Papa of the grateful families he'd treated last month when diphtheria raged through a dozen homes. She would point out how well the arrangement of rooms served the medical practice. How comfortable the large, airy bedrooms upstairs were. *We can't move again, Papa.*

Lydia loved everything about North Platte. She loved the bustling streets frequented by hordes of businessmen and land seekers, loved singing in the church choir, loved the promise of putting down roots, and loved her new friends, among them Arta Cody, daughter of the famous William F. Cody, Buffalo Bill himself. Although she hadn't admitted it before now, the very notion of moving made her realize that she also might love Clint Davis, son of a prominent rancher. She'd forego mentioning Clint in the context of reasons not to move away. Papa wasn't exactly approving of Clint. Given time, though, Lydia was certain Papa would see the good heart that beat inside the handsome cowboy's broad chest. And Papa would have plenty of time for that because the McCords weren't going anywhere. In North Platte they lived, in North Platte they would stay, and that was that.

Lydia swallowed. This time, she would summon courage to say the words she'd always suppressed. *I won't. I love you, Papa, but I'm not moving again.* Merely thinking the words made her tremble, but she was going on twenty years old, and she had had enough. With a brisk nod, Lydia called out, "It's roast beef and potatoes tonight, Papa. Hope you're hungry."

Marching to the cupboard by the back door, Lydia reached for her red and white dishes, then decided to begin a new tradition. She would make evening meals special. Before retrieving the dishes, she spread a tablecloth over the oak table. At the center, she placed the blooming geranium Alice's mother had given her. She had added dishes and silverware and was tucking cloth napkins beneath each fork when Papa appeared in the doorway, newspaper in one hand, pipe in the other.

With a puzzled frown, he motioned toward the table. "Fancy. Don't tell me I forgot your birthday."

Lydia forced a chuckle as she lowered the oven door and took out the roasting pan. "I've decided it's high time we act more civilized. Dishing things onto our plates directly from the stove top might do the job, but this"—she gestured at the table—"is much nicer. More *homey*." She slid the roast onto a platter and spooned potatoes into a bowl. After setting both on the table, she handed Papa a large knife and the meat fork. While he sliced the roast, she bustled about, making a fresh pot of coffee and bringing butter and jelly, salt and pepper to the table. Once seated opposite Papa, she bowed her head and recited the table grace she'd heard at the Dillons' table. "For food that stays our hunger, for rest that brings us ease, for *homes where memories linger,* we give our thanks for these. Amen."

Papa joined in the *amen* without comment. As he drizzled gravy over his meat and potatoes, he indicated the newspaper he'd draped across the chairback between them. "There's something I've been wanting to talk to you about."

"In a minute," Lydia interrupted. She rose to her feet. "I forgot…" Snatching a pitcher off a shelf, she hurried out back to the well pump. Her heart pounded as water gushed into the pitcher. *I'm not leaving North Platte. I want a home where memories can linger.* Back inside, she filled two glasses with cold water, all the while preparing her speech. Her refusal to move. Once again seated at the table, she offered Papa a biscuit and pointed to the newly opened jar on the table.

"Quince preserves from Mrs. Keller," Lydia said. "Partial payment for stitching up Andy last week."

Papa sighed as he dipped a spoon into the rosy preserves and spread sweet onto his biscuit. "Poor child is going to have a nasty scar." He rose from the table and fetched the coffee pot.

As Papa poured them both coffee, Lydia hastened to reassure him. "Mrs. Keller didn't say a thing about scars. The only thing she mentioned was how grateful she is there's no sign of infection." She paused. "And Andy won't care about a little scar, Papa."

Papa traced a line along his cheekbone. "There's nothing little about it. The boy's lucky he still has an eye."

"Mrs. Keller knows that, and she's mighty grateful for what you did." Lydia rose and fetched a box from the back porch. "Here's proof." She held the box so Papa could see the dozen jars. "Elderberry, chokecherry, apple, wild plum and something called sand cherry." She paused. "What's a sand cherry, anyway?"

"Don't know," Papa said.

"I'll have to ask Clint." Lydia set the box aside and returned to the table.

Again, Papa tapped the newspaper. "Got something to talk to you about."

Lydia steeled herself for the inevitable even as Papa slid the paper toward her. He tapped the lower right corner of the page. "Read that," he said and took a bite of biscuit.

Lydia read, surprised when she realized Papa hadn't brought the *Denver Post* to the table. This was the local *Lincoln County Tribune.*

The Hansen Photo Car will arrive in North Platte on September 20 and remain for several weeks. Our arrangement of light combined with superior instruments and workmen enables Hansen to send out the finest art work that is done in the west. All work is made and finished in the car without delay. If you want superior photos this is your chance.

Prepared to debate the matter of moving, Lydia read the ad twice before looking up and asking, "Photo car?"

Papa nodded. "It's a special train car built to house a photography studio, a dark room, and living quarters. They travel the rails from town to town—mostly where there's no photographer in residence, although not always. When it arrives, it'll be put off on a siding near the depot. With the county fair coming up, they'll likely be very busy." He pointed into the small family parlor where a framed portrait of Mama hung above a bookshelf, then looked back at Lydia. "One of these days, when I'm an old bachelor living alone, I'll want your portrait hanging right next to your mama's."

Hearing Papa talk about being *an old bachelor living alone* caught Lydia by surprise. He'd thought about that? Was he softening toward Clint? *Best not bring that up.* Not knowing what to say, Lydia took a sip of coffee.

"I'm not blind, Lydia. You're not a girl anymore. You're a young woman. Young women have dreams, and yours shouldn't center on a life measuring out powders in your father's dispensary."

"You're hardly *old*," Lydia protested. *You could remarry. Be happy again.* More than one widow in town had given Papa special notice. In fact, Lydia very much doubted that sweet Andy Keller's mother handed out boxes of her award-winning preserves to just anyone. But this was not the time to bring it up. That notion might encourage him to flight. To Denver.

Papa dabbed his snow-white moustache with his napkin before speaking again. "When that photo car arrives in town, we'll sashay down to the depot, and if Hansen's work passes muster, I'll order up your portrait." He smiled. "And then, when you've gone off and married that knight in shining armor you've been dreaming about, I'll have your likeness right next to your mama's, the both of them to remind me of the two best things about my life." He sat back. His blue eyes twinkled as he peered at her over the top of his spectacles. "Took the wind out of your sails, didn't I?"

Lydia did her best to look innocent. "Wh-what?"

He chuckled. "You've been busy lining up arguments against another move."

Lydia gave a slight shrug.

Both she and Papa concentrated on eating supper for a few minutes, but then Papa said,

"Might be you should pay a visit to Mrs. Perkins. Order up a new dress for the occasion."

Lydia stared at him, disbelieving. Never had Papa paid one scintilla of attention to her wardrobe. How did he even know Mrs. Perkins's name? Did he realize she was the preferred seamstress with the most fashionable set in town? Lydia cleared her throat. "I don't um … think … a portrait requires …" She paused. "Mrs. Perkins charges quite a bit, Papa. We don't need to spend that much. I'll ask Alice's mother to recommend someone less expensive."

Papa shook his head. "A friend of mine used to say a young lady should feel pretty when she sits for a photographer." Papa winked. "Mrs. Perkins, Lyddie-girl. Take Alice's mother along if you think you need another woman's advice, but Mrs. Perkins is to be the maker."

Chapter 2

At the shriek of the train whistle, Gabriel Stamford startled. He'd been lulled to sleep by the familiar rhythm of the rails, but the harsh signal meant it would soon be time to go to work. Rising from where he'd been sitting at his desk in the studio portion of the photo car, he made his way toward the living quarters in the back.

Pa was already awake, sitting on the edge of the cot Gabe had lowered for him earlier in the day. He'd protested the idea of resting while the train clattered along. "I won't be treated like an invalid. Had a dizzy spell. Nothing to be worried about."

"More than one dizzy spell in recent days," Gabe reminded him. "There's nothing needs doing until we're on the siding in North Platte. No reason you shouldn't take it easy. There'll be plenty to keep us both busy once the car's in place."

Pa had grumbled but he'd settled back and slept deeply for hours. Gabe knew, because he'd checked several times, between bouts of selecting the best examples of their work to put up about town by way of advertising. Ads had been running in the North Platte newspapers for more than a week now, but there was nothing better than showing the actual work. They would target hotel lobbies and newspaper offices for that.

As the train slowed, Gabe stepped out onto the rear platform to watch the train crew guide the Stamford Palace Art Car into its place on a siding midway between the combination Union Pacific Depot/hotel and a separate freight depot. He admired the former, a two-story frame building boasting a cupola. At the rear of the passenger depot, a long wing of hotel rooms extended toward the east, all of it separated from the tracks by a board fence. Beyond the depot/hotel, he spied another hotel, a bank, two grocers, and a huge livery advertising feed and sales.

The photo car unhitched, the train slipped back onto the main track to take on water and passengers bound for points west. Gabe fished his pocket watch out of his vest pocket. *Three o'clock.* Plenty of time to distribute examples of the Stamford's photographic art about town. Ducking back inside the living quarters, he hurried into the studio to gather up the cabinet photos he'd selected, then returned to where Pa sat and held them out. "Want to give a last look at the work I'm proposing we put up? If the size of the commercial district and the number of folks on the streets are any indication, we're going to be busy, county fair or no."

Pa started to push to his feet, then sank back. "Reckon you know what you're doing," he said with a grimace.

"You still dizzy?"

Pa waved a hand in the air. "Not dizzy, but I've got a terrible headache."

Gabe set the stack of cabinet cards down on the little table behind him. "I'm going to rustle up a doctor and have him come check you over."

"You will do no such thing," Pa said. He waved toward the rear platform. "All I need is some fresh air. Put my chair out there before you leave to make the rounds. I'll be right as rain come morning."

Gabe tilted his head and studied his father, worry creasing his brow. "I don't like leaving you alone."

"And I don't like being fussed over." Pa cocked a shaggy white eyebrow. "Although I wouldn't call it 'fussing' if you were to bring home an apple pie once you've put those samples up in town."

Well, at least Pa had an appetite. That was something. Gabe retrieved his leather satchel and a stack of printed flyers from the other room. He took up the photos. "If you're sure."

"I'm sure," Pa said. Once again, he motioned toward the back platform. "Set my chair up and get along. Now that we've mentioned pie, I'm looking forward to it."

Gabe nodded. "I'll see what's to be had in the way of groceries, too, so we don't have to go anywhere to eat if you're not up to it."

"Don't overdo it," Pa said. "It may be a fast-growing town, but we'll still likely get paid in eggs and butter and such. Maybe just as often as cash."

Gabe nodded and set what Pa called his "campaign chair" on the back platform—a folding chair such as had accompanied many a military officer in the field. Then he hopped down from the car and set off across the tracks. Ducking through the largest of two gaps in the fence, Gabe smiled when he saw a bakery sign. Pa might get his wish for apple pie. First, though—the depot.

Inside the busy depot Gabe paused, considering which back-drop would be best for each person he met along the way. The landscape for the calico-clad woman clutching that carpetbag close. The same for the finely dressed lady with the parasol, although she'd look even more dignified with one hand braced against the edge of the cherrywood pillar, the other holding the ivory handle of that parasol. The parasol would be closed, of course, and held at a jaunty angle, its tip just touching the carpet. When three men about his own age jostled and shoved each other as they hurried into the depot from the hotel lobby, Gabe pictured a scene for them. A small table and a deck of cards. A cigar or two. Hats pushed back on their heads. Pa wouldn't approve of that, but Gabe believed the young men would like the notion.

After posting flyers in the depot waiting area and hotel lobby, Gabe asked directions to the newspaper offices. He stepped back outside. Based on his reading of more than one dime novel, he'd expected to encounter cowboys driving cattle down the street the moment he stepped off the train. Possibly an Indian or three. Instead, he saw suited gentlemen squiring ladies with parasols and buggies and carriages moving along at a reasonable pace. It was all a bit disappointing.

Ah, well. If the Omaha papers were right, Buffalo Bill himself planned to return to North Platte in time for the county fair. By then, he and Pa would have had a little over two weeks to prove their mettle with the citizens of Lincoln County. Perhaps Colonel Cody would need promotional photos. If he brought any of his performers back with him … *Stop daydreaming.*

That had been Pa's advice when Gabe said something about getting the great showman into the studio. *What if we just do the best work we can for the folks living their everyday lives?*

His hand on the satchel holding flyers and samples, Gabe crossed the street. A trio of cowboys galloped in from the north. He watched as they pulled up outside a rough board building with a wide porch jutting out over the entrance. A couple of ladies—probably not *ladies* per se, but females— lounged up there. When the cowboys dismounted, one of them must have called out a greeting because all three females stepped forward and leaned over the railing. One of the cowboys took his hat off and bowed low. Horses hitched, the trio hurried inside.

A farm wagon rattled in from the east, its seat occupied by an overall-clad driver and a woman sporting a yellow sunbonnet. As the wagon turned a corner to head south, the woman appeared to be studying the photo car. She nudged the driver and nodded that way. Gabe smiled when he caught sight of a gaggle of tow-headed children barely visible above the sideboards. Capturing a good image of a family with several young children could be a challenge, but when it worked well, there was nothing more satisfying.

Gabe loved everything about photography; loved reassuring bashful children and settling the nerves of self-conscious elders; loved the surprise that registered when they first saw their own images on a cabinet card and the joy when parents realized they finally had a way to keep their children with them. He didn't mind offering a second sitting when a subject was unhappy with an outcome, and he especially enjoyed doing what he could to help people relax in front of the camera—which was no small feat, given that a person had to remain still for at least twenty seconds for the process to work. It didn't sound like a very long time—until folks had to do it.

Gabe ducked into the bakery before distributing more flyers. The kindly owner agreed to reserve an apple pie until he'd made his rounds.

"I live in the back," she said. "If I've closed up, you come around and knock on the blue door. Your pie will be waiting."

Gabe thanked her, then went on his way with a smile. He and Pa were going to like North Platte.

Lydia had just swung the front door closed and hung *The Doctor is Out* sign when Alice Dillon charged up the front porch steps, yanked the screen door open, and rapped on the interior door. "I know you're in there, Lydia McCord. Open up!" The moment Lydia complied, Alice pushed her way into the foyer. "Have you seen it? At the depot! It's here! The photo car's here! It's amazing! Long and sleek and—they've a flag flying and portraits hanging outside and—" Alice reached for Lydia's hand and gave a tug. "Come on! Come see it!"

Lydia resisted. "I can't rush out the door right now." With a meaningful glance up the stairs, she lowered her voice and explained. "Papa's up there poring over his books about a difficult case. He's left me to mix some powders he intends to deliver yet this evening."

Alice gave a little stomp with one foot. "Well then, hurry. Get to mixing." She waved a hand toward the dispensary housed in a repurposed space beneath the front stairs. "I'll wait."

Ducking into the dispensary, Lydia reached for a small mortar and pestle. Taking down three clear glass containers from the single shelf above the counter, she carefully weighed ingredients, then combined them in the pestle and ground them down to a fine powder. As she worked, Alice jabbered.

"The newspaper ads said to look for the Hansen Photo Car, but that's not what we got. It's right there in fancy gilt lettering stretching the entire length of the car. Bradley Yost paced it off. It's fifty feet long! Fifty! And the name isn't Hansen. It's Stamford & Son." Alice raised an open palm and painted the air as she recited, "*I. G. Stamford & Son, Palace Art Car. Expert Photographers of Children. Cabinets, $3 per Dozen.*"

Papa's voice sounded from the front stairs, which he was descending with a large medical book in hand. "Did you say *Stamford?*"

With a little squeak of surprise, Alice whirled about. "Yes, sir. I. G. Stamford & Son. Wait until you see it! There's a glass window in the roof and a wall of glass on one side—like a plate glass window, only in sections. Panes. Big ones. Bradley says that's to make sure there's plenty of light for the camera."

As Alice babbled on, Lydia finished creating Papa's prescribed medication. Taking up an ivory-colored envelope, she printed the patient's name on the front. After pausing to double-check Papa's notes, she added instructions. *One teaspoon mixed with ½ cup water. Administer two droppers full after each feeding.* The instructions noted, Lydia spooned in the powders, sealed the envelope, and handed it over Alice's shoulder to Papa.

Papa looked it over and set the book he'd brought downstairs aside. With a smile and a *nicely done,* he addressed Alice. "Do I understand that you wish Lydia to accompany you to view the wonders of this train-car-turned-photographic-studio?"

Alice nodded.

"Would you object to an escort?"

"Of course not!" Alice enthused. "I bet half the town will be there. It's the first one ever to visit Lincoln County!"

Papa tucked the envelope into his coat pocket. "We'll need to stop by the Hawleys on the way. The name Stamford is probably a matter of coincidence, but I once knew a photographer by that name." He smiled at Alice. "I've never seen a railroad photo car, and after hearing your description, I'll admit to more than mild curiosity."

Lydia and Pa took bonnet and hat from the hall tree by the door. Once at the street, Papa offered an arm to each of the young ladies. "How delightful to stroll in the light of two bright stars."

Alice giggled then blushed. Lydia just shook her head.

From his position atop a ladder, Gabe hung the last of half a dozen framed portraits circling four rows of elegant gilt lettering.

Superior Work
The Finest Done Anywhere
Made & Finished on the Premises
Orders Filled Without Delay

He twisted about and called to Pa, who was standing a good distance away, one hand at his brow to shield his eyes from the late afternoon sun. "Look all right?"

Pa nodded, speaking around the pipe clenched between his teeth. "Looks fine."

At last. Gabe had been up and down the ladder at least a dozen times in the last hour, rearranging the portraits they always hung on the exterior of the car to lure customers. He'd have to climb it again the moment the sun set. They'd learned the hard way that in Nebraska, a clear horizon at sunset did not mean it wouldn't rain in the night. As soon as daylight waned and shadows obscured the portraits, Gabe would take them in, slipping each frame into a fabric sleeve and lining them up by the door for the next day when he'd hang them once again. The up and down was all part of the well-established routine between father and son.

What was not routine was Pa's indecision as to what should hang where. It wasn't like him, and it was yet another of Gabe's mounting concerns about his father. Headaches. Dizzy spells. And now, this unusual hesitation about something that had always been automatic for I. G. Stamford, a photographer with a keen eye for composition. One more headache, one more dizzy spell, and Gabe would insist Pa see a doctor. He already had a name. *A. B. McCord, M.D.,* practicing in North Platte for less than a year but already in possession of a sterling reputation according to both the editor of the *Lincoln County Tribune* and the desk clerk at the depot hotel.

"Looks as though putting up the samples is already doing some good," Pa said. He nodded toward the folks making their way toward the gap in the fence between the depot and the tracks. "Those pretty girls are more likely to want to hear what *you* have to say over an old codger like me." He wrested the ladder from Gabe's hands. "Be charming," he said and retreated toward the rear of the railroad car to stow the ladder.

As the group approached, Gabe called a greeting. He scanned faces, already considering backdrops and poses, wondering if the

two young women on either side of the bewhiskered older gentleman were sisters. It wouldn't require much in the way of cre-
ativity to show them in a good light. Both were lovely. Probably
not sisters, though, as he noted jawlines and eyes, mouths and
noses. One blond, one with dark hair. One with pale eyes, the
other hazel. And *have mercy, those full lips.* He tore his gaze away
from the dark-haired beauty and had just introduced himself to
the group when Pa called out.

"Doc?" Pa leaned the ladder against the rear platform and
hurried this way. The closer he got, the bigger his smile.

"As I live and breathe, it really is you!" Putting one hand on
Gabe's shoulder, Pa said, "Son, meet Doctor Algernon McCord,
the sole reason you still have a father able to drag you all over
kingdom come." Without pausing, Pa spoke to the doctor. "And
Doc, I present your namesake, Gabriel Algernon Stamford."

Chapter 3

*L*ydia had never seen Papa at a loss for words, but he was now. Alice spoke into the somewhat awkward silence. "We were expecting the *Hansen* photo car," she said. "They've been in all the papers for weeks now."

"Hansen had a personal emergency," Mr. Stamford the elder said. "He asked Gabe and me to fill in." He beamed at Papa. "I'm sure glad we did." He nodded from Lydia to Alice. "And these are your daughters, I presume?"

Lydia spoke up, introducing herself and then turning to Alice. "And this is my dear friend, Miss Alice Dillon. We've been looking forward to the arrival of the photo car although, as Alice said, we expected the photographer's name to be *Hansen*."

Alice had released Papa's arm and moved closer to the photo car. Pointing to a line of gilt lettering, she called out to one of the men in the crowd. "See that, Mr. Hawley? *Babies under two photographed free!* You and the Mrs. should bring the twins!" She looked at the younger Mr. Stamford. "Still free if they come in multiples?"

"As advertised." The younger Stamford nodded at Mr. Hawley. "Congratulations, sir, on your double blessing."

"Double-something," Hawley said, then gave a little shrug. "Not sure about the blessing part yet. They got the colic." He nodded at Papa. "Hoping what the doc dropped off earlier will give some relief. The wife's about wore out."

Andy Keller's mother had joined the group, and at the mention of the Hawley twins' colic, she spoke up. "You could take the twins for a stroll in that fancy perambulator parked on your porch, Carl. Give poor Mabel a few minutes peace and quiet." When the other women in the gathering murmured agreement, the hapless father of twins muttered something and retreated, ducking beneath the fence to make his escape.

Mr. Stamford senior waved a hand toward the train car. "Would you folks like a tour?" He indicated his son. "I'm sure Gabe would oblige while I catch up with my old friend." He spoke to Papa again. "Don't tell me you've forgotten B. D. Stamford, Doc."

Papa shook his head. "Haven't forgotten. Haven't forgotten *anything.*"

Mr. Stamford sobered a bit. "And don't we wish we could." With a deep sigh, he looked at Lydia. "I was what you might call a 'difficult case.' But your Pa pulled me through. Saved a leg that a lesser sawbones would have taken off." He put a hand on Papa's shoulder and gave it a squeeze. "Not something I'll ever be able to repay you for, Doc." He pointed toward the rear platform of the train car. "But if you'll join me while the others see the studio, I'll bring out the good stuff. We'll toast the past and catch up to the present."

Papa let himself be led away. As Lydia followed Alice and the others up the iron steps and into the photo studio, she worried. She'd learned long ago not to ask questions about Papa's service in the War of the Rebellion. He didn't want to talk about it. All right. But why this reaction to a past patient's gratitude? That didn't make sense.

The Stamford Palace Art Car housed a surprisingly roomy photographic studio. While Alice peppered the younger Mr. Stamford with questions, Lydia admired the efficient use of space. The glass in the roof. The panes forming a large window in one wall of the train car. The huge box camera perched on a tripod. The beautiful desk beneath a smaller window on the right, the space to the left hidden by a black curtain. When Lydia tried to peek through the crack in the curtain, Mr. Stamford noticed.

"The dark room, Miss McCord. Glass plates, collodion, silver nitrate and the like. We do all our own developing right here."

Lydia felt her cheeks color. Did Mr. Stamford think her nosy? Perhaps he did, for instead of explaining more about the dark room, he moved to demonstrate a tall case housing backdrops that could be lowered like so many window blinds.

Andy Keller's mother asked, "Do you have a backdrop suitable for a boy and his dog? My Andy would want Petey in the photo."

"Petey?" Stamford asked.

"Part dog, part whirling dervish," someone said.

"I'll say," another agreed. "I've never seen that dog but what he's in motion. In and out and around—sometimes between the wheels of a moving wagon. It's a wonder he hasn't been squashed a dozen times. Lives a charmed life, Petey does. Some days he's the sweetest dog you ever saw. Others he's a devil."

"He's *never* a devil," Mrs. Keller snapped, offense sounding in her tone.

Mr. Stamford rifled through a desk drawer and then handed a photo to the woman. "It took three separate sittings, but we finally got a good shot of this fellow. And you can see there's mischief in every ounce of him."

Lydia looked over Mrs. Keller's shoulder as the older woman studied the photograph. In it, a boy with a somewhat vague expression half reclined on a chaise. Perched beside him, a black and white mutt draped his forepaws over the boy's lap. The dog's ears were erect, the curly tail slightly blurred.

"That even looks like Petey," Mrs. Keller said.

Lydia nodded agreement. Most residents of North Platte were well familiar with the little dog who was, in Lydia's opinion, not only a whirling dervish but also quite possibly Andy Keller's fur-coated guardian angel.

Mr. Stamford pointed at the blurred tail in the photo. "We did have to concede when it came to the tail."

Mrs. Keller smiled as she handed the cabinet card back to the photographer. "I don't care if it takes *five* sittings, I'll pay the fees."

"There's only one fee," Stamford said. "That's what 'satisfaction guaranteed' means to my father and me." He glanced out the window. "But now, as I see shadows lengthening, I'll conclude the tour so I can bring in the portraits hanging outside. Please tell your friends about the Stamford Palace Art Car."

With agreeable murmurs, people filed out until only Lydia and Alice remained. Lydia glanced toward the rear platform. How was the reunion going? Had Papa finally relaxed?

Young Stamford followed her gaze. "I've heard plenty about your father."

Lydia could only reply with a vague nod. It felt rude not to say the same, but she didn't want to lie. She'd never heard the name Stamford. Papa seemed uncomfortable when greeted by someone from the past—even someone lauding his prowess as a physician.

"Can I offer you both a cup of tea?" the young Stamford asked. "And there's pie. Apple, from the bakery on Front Street."

"You learn fast if you've pie from Mrs. Mac," Alice said.

Stamford tilted his head. "Mrs. Mac?"

"Oh," Alice said with a grin. "Her full name's MacDonald—but we just call her Mrs. Mac. Best pie in town—except for my mother's, of course."

Stamford pointed toward the rear platform. "If you don't mind passing through the private part of the car, we can join Pa and Doctor McCord without taking on the stairs."

Alice chattered away as they filed through a tidy living area sporting a small stove, a table for two, and what Lydia assumed were narrow sleeping cots attached to the car wall, one above the other, by iron hinges. At the moment those cots were raised, revealing long, low shelves crowded with all manner of supplies. She saw biscuit tins and a coffee grinder, crocks and flour sacks, small crates and jars. Above the back door, a portrait of a woman looked down on them.

"My mother," Mr. Stamford said. "May she rest in peace."

Lydia glanced back at him. "I am so sorry." She looked back up at Mrs. Stamford's image. Both the line of the woman's gown and the style of her hair spoke to a bygone era. Did young Mr. Stamford even remember his mother? He couldn't have been very old when she died. Color photography was only a dream, but color wasn't necessary for one to know where Gabriel Stamford had gotten his exceptional long-lashed, pale blue eyes.

It took less than a week for Gabe to get his fill of swaggering cowboys who thought slouching was a good way to pose for a photo. Pa had kept his sense of humor about it all. Gabe had, too. At first. But about the ninetieth time a gun-toting subject said something about the "duded-up city-boy" who "helped folks play dress-up," Gabe almost knocked the guy on his ... attitude. Of course, the subjects hadn't really made snide comments ninety times, but still.

It had been a busy few days. Pa had been more himself and together, the two had printed dozens of cabinet cards. Word of mouth would hopefully enable them to print dozens more. For now, though, Gabe was ready for the break afforded by tomorrow's sabbath rest and more than ready for this evening, when the Stamfords were to dine at the McCords.

As Gabe took down the exterior displays and locked the studio door, he wondered at the strange coincidence that had brought the Stamford Palace Photo Car to North Platte, Nebraska, and an unexpected reunion between Pa and a friend from the past. Over twenty years ago Pa had been a young photographer trailing after the now-famous Matthew Brady. He'd taken hundreds of photos of men in uniform and hundreds more in the aftermath of battles. Pa had never talked much about the latter but seeing the silver-haired Doctor McCord seemed to have unleashed a flood of memory.

Every evening this past week Pa had regaled Gabe with stories from the past, including the one about a young photographer with a minor leg wound that would have resulted in amputation, except for the personal care of a stubborn physician named Algernon McCord. Gabe had always been a little embarrassed by what he considered an unwieldy and downright awful middle name. Meeting Doctor McCord and hearing Pa sing his praises tempted Gabe to reconsider. He smiled at the idea of spending an evening in Miss Lydia McCord's company. *Who wouldn't?*

Chapter 4

Lydia had just set the table for the Saturday evening meal when someone rapped on the back door. A glance out the kitchen window at the buckskin horse hitched to the garden gate had her sweeping palms over her hair to smooth errant strands back in place. Could there have been a worse moment for Clint to come calling? She was hardly in a state to welcome a beau, what with cleaning and cooking and—Clint knocked again.

Lydia closed her eyes for a moment. *Calm. Calm.* She inhaled the aromas filling the kitchen. Supper smelled good. It wouldn't hurt for Clint to take that in. She opened her eyes and glanced over at the table with its cheerful red and white dishes and the small vase of fresh flowers. While she'd initially taken the impending evening with dinner guests as a rare opportunity to show Papa how pleasant it could be to entertain friends in a gracious home, it might not hurt for Clint to see what awaited a man with whom she shared life.

Taking in another calming breath, Lydia went to the porch door. "Clint! What a nice surprise. Come in." When the tall cowboy snatched his hat off his head and followed her inside, Lydia's heart thudded.

"There's a dance over at the opera house tonight," Clint said.

"Is there?" Had Alice said something about that? Lydia couldn't remember. It had been one of those weeks—an over-full waiting room every day and someone banging on the door for the doctor every single night. She glanced toward the stove where the potatoes were in danger of boiling over. Stepping away from Clint, she took up a wooden spoon and shoved the pot toward the back of the stove top to cool.

"Pa sent me into town on an errand," Clint said. "It'll be a bit before I can get back to the ranch, dude up, and drive back into town. At least sundown, I expect." He looked over at the blue crockery bowl at the back of the stove, its contents hidden by a red checkered cloth. "If that's biscuits, I wouldn't mind a couple with butter and jelly when I get back. Ma's been down in her back this week. Probably won't have any supper cooked."

Lydia frowned a bit. "I beg your pardon?"

"Only if it's not too much trouble," Clint said. He traced a lazy line along her forearm as he murmured, "You wouldn't want a fella to keel over in the middle of a reel, would ya?"

His touch sent a shiver up her spine. "I—uh—of course not. But—"

"Good, then." He put his hat back on and turned to go. "See you a little after sundown."

Lydia crossed the back porch. Opening the screen door, she spoke to Clint's back as he headed toward the horse hitched at the gate. "Clint. I can't go to a dance tonight."

Clint wheeled about to face her, his expression a combination of surprise and suspicion. "Why not? Don't tell me you said *yes* to that storekeeper Bradley Yost." His lip curled in derision.

"I didn't say *yes* to anyone, since no one actually *asked* me to a dance." She let that set for a beat. "As it happens, Mr. Stamford—the photographer with the photo car parked down at the depot—is an old friend of Papa's. He's coming to supper." She paused. "That's why there's dinner rolls and potatoes atop the stove—not to mention a roast chicken in the oven." She forced humor into her voice. "And the fact you didn't notice the aroma in the air doesn't say much for my culinary gifts." She tilted her head. "Didn't you notice I'd set the table for guests?"

Clint flashed a glance in the direction of the kitchen and then back. "You'll have finished well before eight-thirty."

"It would be rude to desert company."

His lips pursed in an excellent imitation of a pout. "Guess I'll just have to give your dances to Alice Dillon."

Hurt but unwilling to show it, Lydia retorted, "Guess you will." Letting the screen door slam behind her, she retreated into the kitchen.

Again, there was a rap on the screen door. When Lydia didn't move, Clint called out.

"I'm sorry, Lyddie-Lou."

Lyddie-Lou. The pet name Clint had recently invented slithered beneath the hurt. He sounded repentant. Lydia stepped back to the open doorway. But she didn't cross the porch. "Give Alice my best," she said and folded her arms across her waist. "And have a good time."

"Can't have a good time. Not without you." Clint stared off toward the road. Finally, he ducked his head, grinning up at her from beneath the wide brim of his black hat. "Sure you won't come?"

"Certain I *can't*," Lydia said. "It's not the same thing."

With a dramatic sigh, Clint nodded. "Guess I'll have to understand." He took a few steps toward the road, then turned back and said, "Have a nice time with the geezers."

Lydia could hear him chuckling as he mounted up and rode away. *What on earth was a 'geezer'?* The man was always using terms Lydia didn't understand. He liked to tease her about her ignorance of ranch life. She took it as a challenge and was steadily expanding her knowledge of western terms and cowboy lore. *Geezer* was another chance for her to show Clint Davis that Lydia McCord might not have grown up in the West, but she was perfectly capable of learning everything required to make a good home there. A home with him. Someday.

As far as Gabe was concerned, the McCords lived in a palace. The grand house gleamed white behind a picket fence marking the perimeter of the huge corner lot. Pink and white roses rambled along the fence. They were almost finished blooming, but Gabe could well imagine the riot of beauty in the summer. And the aroma. North Platte and the surrounding grasslands were mostly treeless, but someone had planted three young shade trees in the yard, and they seemed to be thriving. Flower beds close to the house boasted purple asters and yellow mums, plants Gabe knew by name because of a Kansas City aunt who loved to garden. As he and his father made their way up the front walk, Gabe noticed a wicker porch swing off to the left. Everything about the place exuded welcome.

Pa gave the ringer set in the front door a twist, and in no time Doctor McCord was welcoming them into a wide foyer. Stairs on the left led up to the second story, with a landing graced by a small stained-glass window.

Directing his guests to hang their hats on the hall tree beside the front door, the doctor led the way past a room on the left set up as a two-bed infirmary and a small parlor on the right, and toward the mouth-watering aromas wafting from the back of the house. Once in the kitchen he set the pie the Stamfords had brought with them on a worktable by the back door, which opened onto a screened-in back porch. "Lydia and I live at the rear of the house—and upstairs, of course." The doctor looked hopefully toward the narrow back stairs rising from the kitchen. "I'm sure she'll be down soon."

"You've made the space work very well for you," Pa said.

Doctor McCord nodded. "Lydia's idea, actually. I've always been happy with quarters above an office in the business district. But when we came here last year—" He gestured about them. "Would you like a tour?"

"If you're willing to give one," Pa said.

The doctor led the way back out of the kitchen and into the hall. Just past the infirmary he opened a door to what had been a closet tucked beneath the stairs. "My dispensary," he said of the small space boasting a long counter atop which rested scales, several beakers of varying sizes, and a mortar and pestle. Above the counter a shelf lined with jars led all the way to the opposite wall and a tall narrow window.

"Quite an efficient use of space," Pa said.

Doctor McCord shrugged. "Patients appreciate being able to tote remedies home with them. I'm fortunate to have a daughter with an aptitude for science. Lydia's quite adept at mixing powders and such." They stepped across the hall into a good-sized room with a bay window set into one wall and bookshelves on another, the latter built around a fireplace framed with green tiles. An ominous looking table in the middle of the room identified it as the examination room. Gabe concentrated on the impressive library of reference books until the doctor slid open pocket doors, revealing more of the room at the front of the house. "My waiting room," he said and motioned to the two doors opposite the front door that stood open, revealing a side wing of the porch. "My daughter likes to keep those doors open as much as possible this time of year."

"All very well thought out." Pa smiled.

"Lydia keeps things running."

Pa inhaled with appreciation. "And she's a fine cook."

Miss McCord spoke as she descended the main stairs. "Please don't raise your expectations too high."

Gabe looked up, instantly aware of the way her gold ensemble complemented her sable hair and hazel eyes.

Miss McCord continued, "I'm a true novice with most cooking, but I'm enjoying learning"—she glanced at her father and smiled—"now that I have a real kitchen."

As he and Pa followed the McCords back into the kitchen, Gabe noted the smallness of Miss McCord's waist and the grace with which she moved. When she directed the men to be seated at the table set for four, Gabe protested. "Please. Put me to work." Smiling, Miss McCord handed him a large white pitcher. She pointed toward the back of the property.

"There's a pump at the base of the porch stairs."

The pitcher was only half full when a clatter from inside followed by the doctor shouting Pa's name had Gabe dropping the pitcher and charging back inside. Pa lay on the floor, the doctor kneeling on one side, Miss McCord on the other. She was working to loosen Pa's tie as her father felt for a pulse.

Gabe croaked, "Is he—?"

"No," Miss McCord said immediately.

When she got to her feet, Gabe took her place. One look at Pa and he knew. Still, he asked. "It's more than fainting. Isn't it?"

Doctor McCord nodded. "I'm afraid so."

Chapter 5

While Pa and Mr. Stamford's son carried the unconscious man into the examination room, Lydia busied herself in the kitchen. She returned food to the oven to keep it warm and was making a large pot of coffee when Gabriel Stamford stepped into the kitchen.

"Doc said—" His voice wavered. He shook his head. "Nothing I can do."

Lydia pulled a chair out from the table. "Please. Sit down. I'll have coffee ready in a moment."

The younger Stamford obeyed. He leaned back in his chair and closed his eyes for a moment. "He hasn't been himself. I've wanted him to see a doctor, but he's refused. I was going to insist." He opened his eyes and looked at her. "Especially when you came to the railroad car our first night here. An old friend, I thought. He'll agree to see his old friend. But then we got busy these past few days. He insisted he felt better."

Lydia poured coffee for them both and then joined him at the table.

Stamford took a sip of coffee, then gripped the mug between his palms as he continued. "I should have known it was all an act." He grimaced. "I should have insisted. Made him come sooner. I should have—"

Papa appeared in the doorway. Stamford leaped to his feet but Papa motioned for him to sit again. "Tell me exactly what you mean when you say he 'hasn't been himself.' Everything you can remember, no matter how small it may seem."

"Headaches. Trouble with his vision. Dizziness. Difficulty making decisions."

"But he hasn't consulted a doctor," Papa said.

The young man shook his head. "I should have—"

Papa's voice was stern when he interrupted. "Gabriel. There is nothing to be gained by taking blame for something that is *absolutely* not your fault." He glanced Lydia's way. "I was going to suggest you put the meal on hold and make a very large pot of coffee. But I see you've already done that." He looked back at his patient's son. "I'll know more in a bit. I'll also contact a couple of colleagues in Chicago. In the meantime, I leave you in my daughter's capable hands." He returned to the examination room.

Young Stamford continued to mutter regret. "I should have insisted he see a doctor weeks ago. I just let him—" Breaking off, he put his elbows on the table and hid his face in his hands.

It tore at Lydia's heart to see the young man so broken up. She longed to reassure him—to promise that things would be all right. But she knew better. The laxness on the right side of his father's face was undeniable. The poor man had suffered a stroke. He was in a coma. There was no cure and no way to know if he would ever wake up or, if he did, what limitations he might face. Would he be able to walk? To talk? Knowing what she did, Lydia could not promise a bright future. She could, however, remind young Mr. Stamford that he was not alone. With that in mind, she reached over, grasped his forearm, and gave it a squeeze.

A familiar voice rumbled, "Guess I can see the real reason you didn't want to go to the dance with me."

Lydia jumped and whirled about. Clint loomed in the kitchen doorway, scowling at Gabriel Stamford.

Miss McCord leaped from her chair and rushed across to where the stranger stood. "I didn't expect to see you tonight."

"Guess I know that. *Now.*" The boot-clad stranger emphasized the last word. He threw his shoulders back and jutted out his chin. "Thought I'd surprise my girl and see if she'd be able to come out for at least one dance." He scowled at Gabe.

Intending to introduce himself, Gabe rose to his feet. He had no chance to speak, for at that moment, Doctor McCord returned to the kitchen. One look at the older man's expression, and Gabe steeled himself to receive the news. *Pa's dead.*

The doctor greeted the stranger with a nod. "Clint." Then he spoke to Gabe. "Still unconscious, but his breathing is steady. That's a good sign." He paused. "It's a stroke. I'll want to keep him here in the infirmary for now."

Gabe nodded. "Can I stay with him?"

"Of course," the doctor said. "Come help me get him settled. Then we'll talk." He spoke to the stranger. "Lydia's needed here, Clint, and will be for the rest of the night."

"It was sweet of you to stop by," Lydia said, "but you heard what Pa said. I can't leave. Not tonight."

"I got that," Clint snapped. "What I don't know is what's going on."

"Papa's friend—"

"*Papa's* friend?" Clint said with a snort. His gaze flicked toward the hall and then back to her. "More about our age, I'd say. More than a *friend*, too, from what I saw."

Lydia frowned. What on earth was he talking about? What did he think he'd seen? *My hand on Mr. Stamford's arm.* She huffed.

"What you *saw* was me trying to reassure a boy in danger of losing his father."

"Hardly a boy," Clint muttered. "And you didn't say anything about *two* coming for supper when you said you were having company."

For goodness' sake. "Well, excuse *me.* Guess I didn't realize I'm required to clear the guest list with you when Papa wants to reminisce with an old friend. A friend who says Papa saved his life. Who rides the rails plying his trade aboard a railroad photo car. With his *son,* Gabriel. A friend who suffered a stroke moments ago and to whom we'll give care as long as required. Right here. In this house. Papa and I are both determined to do all we can for him. And for Gabriel, for that matter."

Lydia's ire had risen as her explanation lengthened. She felt her face flush with emotion. *And yes, I'm calling him* <u>Gabriel</u>. *He needs a friend. I'm going to be one.* She took up Gabriel's coffee mug and proceeded to refill it. "I have a great deal to do right now, Clint, and none of it includes soothing your prodigious ego." Setting the coffee mug down, she marched toward the front hall. Clint called after her, apologizing for the second time tonight.

"I'm sorry, Lyddie-Lou."

Lydia turned about to face him. She waited.

He shrugged and gave something of a sheepish grin. "Don't be mad." He took his hat off and raked his hand through his abundant dark hair. "Shucks. I don't wanna dance with Alice. I want *you.*" He smoothed the feathered hatband.

Somewhat mollified but not willing to give ground, Lydia gestured toward the still-warm stove. "I've got a couple of hungry men here who didn't get a chance to eat before poor Mr. Stamford collapsed."

Clint gazed over at the table, then back. Nodded. "I'll go. But not until you say you'll forgive me. I thought—" He gave a little shrug. "Wrong. I thought wrong."

"You certainly did."

Clint nodded. "Forgiven?"

"Forgiven."

With a nod, Clint put the hat back on his head. He tugged on the brim to settle it in place, and then he smiled that smile—the one that spoke a promise that thrilled Lydia all the way down to her toes.

After a restless night by Pa's side in Doctor McCord's infirmary, Gabe spent the better part of the Sabbath keeping watch and poring over the medical books the doctor was kind enough to let him read. As far as Gabe could tell, Pa's condition could be summarized with one word: *unknown.* There was no way to look inside Pa's head, but the obvious lack of muscle tone on the right side of his face indicated damage. Neither the extent nor the result could be predicted. But the possibilities ran a terrifying gamut beginning with various levels of muscle weakness and ending with what the medical world termed *cognitive impairment.* And that was assuming Pa woke up. There was no guarantee he would.

By early evening on Sunday, Gabe gave up asking questions. Doc McCord was patient, but the poor man must be weary of trying to come up with new ways to say *I don't know* and *we must wait and hope for the best.* Lydia McCord prepared a light supper, but Gabe couldn't eat and excused himself to keep his vigil over Pa.

Not long after sundown, Doc did another cursory examination. "His breathing is regular. He doesn't appear to be in any distress." When Lydia McCord appeared in the doorway, the doctor said, "If you'd step out for a moment, Lydia can keep watch while we discuss the next few days."

Gabe vacated his chair. He followed the doctor into the small parlor across the hall. Doc asked a question as soon as they were both seated. "Absent my old friend's misfortune, how long would you have stayed here in North Platte?"

"Until after the county fair early next month," Gabe said. "We planned to set up a photo booth at the fairgrounds. Once we'd finished developing and printing orders from the fair, we'd depart for Ogallala. By October 12 at the latest."

Doc nodded. "And then what? Home for the winter?"

"The train car's home."

"Is it really?"

"You sound surprised."

"I'm imagining that little stove trying to keep up with winter winds."

Gabe smiled. "We're down south by the time the snow flies."

"Ah." Doc sat back, thinking.

"Is it possible for you to make any kind of prediction—" Gabe broke off. Shook his head. "I'm sorry. I keep asking the same thing. I just—" He rubbed at his forehead and the pounding headache that had begun late that afternoon. "I can't think what to do. There's a great deal of value in the glass plates and developing supplies, the camera and other equipment. Not to mention a locked strongbox. I don't dare leave the car unattended for long." He drew in a long breath that was, try as he might, more like a sob. "What should I do?"

The doctor leaned forward and put a comforting hand on Gabe's shoulder. "That first evening, when your father and I sat outside your living quarters getting reacquainted, one thing was very clear. He's quite proud of you. But it's more than fatherly pride. He respects your skill as a photographer. He praised you up and down—in terms I admit I didn't completely understand because I don't know the vocabulary of the work you do. But thinking back to that conversation, I think he'd want you to carry on as best you can—with the business."

After a moment, Gabe said, "You're probably right, but I can't see how it's possible. Pa needs constant care." He paused. "Kind as you and your daughter have been, I can't expect—"

The doctor interrupted. "I'm glad to hear you acknowledge the need. Not everyone is realistic about that after a serious incident like this. And not everyone accepts their own limitations when it comes to providing the best care for a loved one."

As the doctor strung together terms like *acknowledge the need, serious incident,* and *limitations,* Gabe's stomach clenched. Pa was in dire straits. That meant the business was, too.

But then Doc proposed a partial solution.

"I'd like your permission to call in a local woman acclaimed for her nursing skill. Mrs. O'Brien has provided sickbed care for many of my patients. She's not only a fine nurse but also very affordable."

Hope glimmered. "I'd like to say the money doesn't matter," Gabe said, "but of course it always does in some measure."

"She charges seventy-five cents a day—and her days are usually ten hours or so, because she cares more about the patient than the clock."

"She sounds like a saint," Gabe said.

"Having observed her giving care, I won't disagree with the possibility," the doctor said.

Gabe forced a smile. "North Platte has given us a strong welcome. We can afford Mrs. O'Brien."

Doc nodded and rose to his feet. "After we eat, Lydia can walk with you to Mrs. O'Brien's. I'll stay here and see to my friend."

Gabe shook his head. "You go, Doc. I'll stay with Pa."

"First, a meal. Then a walk and some fresh air." The doctor smiled. "My prescription for that headache you've been fighting."

Gabe looked at him in surprise, then rubbed his forehead. "How'd you know?"

"It's my job to know." Doc looked up at the portrait of his wife. "Just as it's yours to be about the important business of preserving beautiful memories."

Chapter 6

As Lydia led the way to Mrs. O'Brien's, she did her best to distract Gabriel Stamford from his father's dire condition. "Do you really live on the train car year 'round? You don't have another place—an apartment or even a small house?"

"We did before we had the photo car built."

"Don't you miss having a home?"

Gabriel didn't answer right away. Finally, he said, "We do have a home. You toured it. It's actually quite comfortable."

"Until it snows." Lydia shivered.

"By the time it snows, we're down south enjoying sunny skies and warm breezes."

"I should have thought of that," Lydia said. They hadn't walked far when she added, "You've made me think of my friend, Irmagard Friedrich."

Gabriel tilted his head. "I don't remember meeting an Irmagard."

"You haven't. She's traveling around the country, too. A combination of train cars and tents, depending on how long the Wild West spends in any given place."

"*She?*" Gabriel looked over at her. "Tell me more."

"Her father is friends with Colonel Cody. He wrangled Irmagard an audition this past spring. Now, she's a trick rider, living in a New York hotel and preparing for the winter at

Madison Square Garden." Lydia grinned. "She even has a show name. Liberty Belle."

"That's—amazing."

"She is. Amazing and brave and—a little crazy, if you ask me, to do the things she does in the ring." She paused before saying, "All Irma ever wanted was to travel. And all I ever wanted was to stay put."

"Your father said you came to North Platte last year?"

He'd paid attention. With everything that was happening, he'd paid attention. "We've been tumbleweeds since my mother passed away a few years ago. Chicago to St. Louis. St. Louis to Kansas City. Kansas City to Omaha … and so on. And, as Papa told you, we landed here in North Platte last year." She blurted out the question. "Don't you find it lonely, moving about all the time?"

Gabriel shrugged. "Seems to me a person can be lonely anywhere. It's not really a matter of location. But there's one big difference between your experience and what Pa and I do."

"What's that?"

"Am I right that you and your father didn't know anyone when you first arrived in all those places you listed?"

Lydia nodded.

"Well, the photo car travels a regular route from season to season. When we arrive in a place, we're reconnecting with old friends. When we leave, we aren't saying *good-bye* as much as *until next time.*" He grinned. "And, speaking of familiar faces, thanks to Pa's weakness for apple pie, we know the best bakeries in most of the towns along the way."

Lydia decided to test him. "Best bakery in Arkansas."

"Mama's on Main Street in Hot Springs. Closed Sunday and Monday."

"Dallas, Texas."

"The Chess Pie Emporium."

"Fort Worth?"

"Mamo's Chicken Palace."

Lydia laughed. "You made that last one up."

"Not only the best pie. Also the best fried chicken. And grits. Although I'm partial to the biscuits with molasses." He smiled. "Thank you."

"For what?"

"For the distraction. For making me smile."

He did have a beautiful smile. And those pale eyes combined with that mop of curly blond hair? Very striking. So different from Clint's dark—*different. Not Clint.* Lydia looked away and pointed at the house up ahead. "That's the Kellers'. On the corner. Mrs. O'Brien lives in a tiny little place on the alley."

Gabe's introduction to Mrs. O'Brien did not go as planned. As he and Lydia traversed the yard on their way to her front door, a small brown and white dog tore off the back stoop of the larger house and launched itself at him.

Lydia took Gabe's arm. "Stay still. Petey won't bite if you stay still." With a snarl the little dog latched onto the cuff of Gabe's trouser leg, dug in with all four paws, and did its best to drag him toward the street.

The top of a boy's blond head appeared above the porch railing. The child shouted, "Don't hurt him, mister. Please don't hurt him." He scrabbled down the stairs and hurried as best he could to where Gabe and Lydia stood.

Gabe's heart went out to the child, with his over-large head, spindly body, and a foot that dragged a bit.

"He don't bite," the boy said as he forced the dog to release Gabe's pant leg.

A stern voice sounded from the porch. "Andrew Jackson Keller IV, you and that dog were supposed to be inside this house nearly an hour ago." As the boy took the little dog into his arms, the woman rushed up. She peered down at Gabe's trouser leg. "If there's damage, I'll pay to have it repaired. Just please don't report it." She lowered her voice as she looked down at the little dog. "There's them as would say a nuisance should be eliminated."

"Petey isn't a noose-uns," the boy said, frowning. "And he don't need lin-ment. He isn't hurt."

The woman rested a hand on the boy's shoulder as she introduced him. "This is my son, Andrew."

"Andy," the boy corrected, then indicated the dog tucked beneath his arm. "And Petey. He don't stay still much. But he don't bite. Hardly ever."

"As for the trousers," Gabe said, "it's an easy enough repair and nothing worth causing a ruckus about." When Lydia let go of his arm, he added, "Fact is, I should be thanking Petey. For a moment, there, a beautiful girl took my arm." Studiously avoiding looking at the beautiful girl in question, he addressed Mrs. Keller. "You were going to bring Andy and Petey to the photo car."

Andy responded before his mother could. "Ma said he gots to stay still or the pitcher won't be good. Petey don't stay still."

Gabe thought back to what Pa had done to get the photo of the boy and dog that he'd shown Mrs. Keller. "I've a way to work that out."

"I can't work too good," Andy said as he stroked his little dog's head. "I'm not strong."

"As it happens," Gabe said, crouching down to look Andy in the eye, "strength isn't exactly what's needed." He put a tentative hand out as if to pet the dog. Petey licked his fingers. Gabe laughed before asking Andy, "Can you count to twenty?"

"I'm *slow*," Andy said, "not *stupid*. I can count far as you want."

"You only need to count to twenty," Gabe said. "Like this: one-one-twenty, two-one-twenty, three-one twenty, four-one twenty and so on."

Andy looked suspicious. "Nobody adds one-twenties when they count."

"It's a special kind of counting," Gabe explained. "The kind photographers use. If I were taking your photo, I'd use that special kind of counting. And I'd need you and Petey to hold very still while I counted from one-one-twenty all the way up to twenty-one-twenty." Gabe paused. "Let's do it together."

When the twenty seconds required to expose a treated glass plate had elapsed, Andy shook his head. "Petey won't hold still for all that."

"Does he know any tricks?"

"Plenty. He's smarter 'n me."

"Does he like treats?"

"What d'ya think?" Andy said with disgust.

"Andrew," Mrs. Keller scolded, "Mr. Stamford is being kind. You should be kind, too."

Andy grimaced, then apologized, adding, "Petey likes treats awful much. 'Specially bacon."

"Then bacon it shall be." Gabe stood and addressed Mrs. Keller. "If you could bring Andy and Petey to the photo car tomorrow—along with a generous supply of bacon—I'll explain how we're going to get a good photo. Right now, though—" He looked over at Lydia.

"Gabriel's father isn't well," she explained. "We're hoping Mrs. O'Brien might be available to do some nursing."

"And here we've delayed you," Mrs. Keller said. She spoke to her son. "Mr. Stamford has been very patient with us, young man. What do we say when people are kind?"

"Thank you, Mr. Stammer."

As the boy limped away, Mrs. Keller said, "You can't do better than Mary O'Brien when it comes to nursing." She turned to go, then added, "Andy and I will be praying for your father. And for you. About tomorrow—is there a time you'd prefer?"

"Lord willing," Gabe replied, "I'll be there all day. I'll work you in whenever you stop by."

On Monday morning before she flipped over *The Doctor is In* sign on the front door, Lydia paused in the doorway to the infirmary watching as Mr. Stamford struggled, albeit weakly, against the firm hand on his shoulder. "You're to lay back, now, dearie," Mrs. O'Brien said as she glanced at Lydia. "Our sweet Miss McCord will be fetching your boy-o, and won't we have a lovely surprise waiting for him, with his da awake and feeling right enough to fight them that's giving him care."

Taking her cue from Mrs. O'Brien, Lydia said, "I'll fetch Gabriel right now, Mr. Stamford. He'll be here in no time."

Papa followed her to the hall tree where she fetched her bonnet. "Do your best to prepare the boy," he said, looking back toward the infirmary. "He can't speak, and I doubt he's going to be able to walk until he regains some strength. He may always require some assistance."

Lydia nodded, then pointed at the sign on the door. "Is the doctor *out* or *in?*"

Papa considered, then flipped the sign over to read *The Doctor is In.* "Between me and Mrs. O'Brien, we should be able to handle things."

Lydia suppressed a knowing smile and hurried off. Mrs. O'Brien would love nothing more than the chance to show Papa how capable a combination nurse/office manager she could be. Difficult as was the Stamford's situation, something good could come of it. The moment the thought emerged Lydia scolded herself. *What a selfish thing to think.* She glanced behind her at the Presbyterian Church spire. *I'm sorry, Lord. You know I didn't mean that the way it came together. Please let Mr. Stamford get well soon. Help Gabriel, too. He's worried about—* The prayer ended abruptly the moment Lydia rounded the corner of Spruce and Front Street. A very long line of people was waiting to have their photo taken. She hurried toward the photo car, counting as she went. *Thirty people.*

Alice Dillon and her family were second in line. "Can you believe this?" she said as Lydia approached. "Do you know why there's only one Stamford working this morning?"

Lydia nodded. Lowering her voice, she said, "The elder Mr. Stamford suffered a stroke Saturday evening. He's regained consciousness, so Papa sent me to fetch his son." She looked down the line. What would all these people do if Gabriel left?

A train whistle blew, and the nine o'clock chugged into view. *Right on schedule.* Ah. That was the answer. The Stamford's first-come-first-served way of doing things must give way to a schedule. While Papa operated his office the former way, if Gabriel was going to work alone, he must see reason and begin the latter. Making her way to the head of the line, Lydia spoke to the couple waiting at the base of the iron stairs. "If you'll excuse me, I'm here to assist the photographer." *It wasn't exactly a lie.*

The burly man moved aside even as he pointed at a scrawled warning hanging on the door. *Under no circumstances is this door to be opened.* "Might be the young man would forgive a pretty young lady for ignoring that," he said. "But consider yourself warned. He's not in the best humor."

Perhaps some good news would help. Lydia reached up and knocked.

"Busy!"

Not in the best humor was a kind way to put it. "Waiting for twenty-one-twenty," Lydia called back. Hopefully echoing the count Gabriel had demonstrated for Andy Keller would let him know who'd knocked. And cheer him up a little. But when Gabriel yanked open the door and saw Lydia, anger transformed to fear. He stepped back.

"He's awake," Lydia said. "You should go."

Gabriel gestured at the line. "I can't."

"I'll take care of it." Lydia stepped into the studio. She'd expected to see at least one person posed before a backdrop, but the car was empty.

Noticing her confusion, Gabriel explained. "I was in the dark room. Just finished the first sitting. Printing can wait, but developing can't. That has to be done as soon as the glass plates come out of the camera. Which reminds me—" He ducked back into the dark room. Pulling the curtain closed, he said, "You said Pa's awake. Is he going to be all right?"

In her most encouraging tone, Lydia said, "Papa is very hopeful."

After a moment, Gabriel opened the curtain. "But?"

"Some difficulty with the right side. And with speech. But it's clear he *understands* what's being said." Lydia nodded toward the door. "He'll like hearing that business is booming."

Gabriel's shoulders slumped. He shook his head. "It won't be after today. Folks aren't going to be willing to wait."

"I have an idea to help with that." Lydia strode to the desk and began opening drawers. "Paper. Pen. Where—?" She found what she needed. "You'll reserve time slots. How long should they be?"

Gabriel hesitated. "I can't ask you—"

"You didn't ask. I offered." Lydia poised pen over paper. "We just heard the nine o'clock train arrive. You'll go see your father, and then you'll return to serve the couple who are first in line. I'll have them return at 10:00."

"Return? But—"

"Leave that to me," Lydia said. "How long will it take for that first appointment?"

"Could be as much as an hour."

Paper in hand, Lydia headed for the studio door. She opened it and took down the warning notice, then motioned toward the back door as if propelling Gabriel in that direction. When he hesitated, she jabbed a finger in the air, insisting. As Gabriel obeyed and moved toward the back door, Lydia addressed the long line of potential customers. "For those of you who don't know me, I'm Miss Lydia McCord. My father is Dr. Algernon McCord, and the Stamfords are our friends. Unfortunately, the elder Mr. Stamford has taken ill. He is under my father's care."

"The other one's leaving," someone toward the end of the line called out.

As one, heads turned to watch Gabriel hurrying away from the photo car.

"He'll return within the hour," Lydia said. "I'm going to give each of you an appointment time so you aren't forced to wait in this long line." She raised her voice as the line dissolved into a group crowded around the steps. "Mr. Stamford wishes me to thank each of you for your patience. It's my hope that you will all demonstrate the kindness my father and I have had opportunity to witness in this community we've come to love." As Lydia looked over the crowd, she wondered if she might be assuming too much.

The woman accompanying the burly man who'd been at the head of the line moments ago made a face. "Another hour?" she whined.

Alice's mother, God bless her, spoke up. "That's enough time for your husband to treat you to a late breakfast," she said and looked about her at the waiting crowd. "Time for us all to enjoy an unexpected visit to a favorite establishment."

"I choose Guy Laing's," someone joked, referring to a popular combination bar and pool hall.

Another man retorted, "Mrs. Dillon was talking about an *unexpected* visit, Hugo."

As laughter rolled through the crowd, the burly man smiled and pointed at the paper in Lydia's hand. "Anson and Ethel Miles. Returning at ten o'clock."

Chapter 7

*G*abe had never thought of his father as *old* until this moment sitting next to Pa's cot in Doc McCord's infirmary. He still wasn't old in years. He was, however, a weakened, battered, shadow of himself. Pa's useless right arm curled next to his body. When his efforts to speak resulted in unintelligible sounds, he clamped his lips shut and looked away.

Gabe did his best to sound hopeful. "It's going to be all right, Pa. We'll work it out."

Pa shook his head.

"We can stay in North Platte until you're better. I'll go by the telegraph office in the morning and send notice to the papers in Ogallala. There's no harm in postponing our arrival."

Although November loomed. There might be some shivering around the little stove after all.

Think of good news to share.

"You should have seen the line at the car this morning. Plenty more folks eager to have their photo taken. Lydia came up with the idea of taking appointments. She's there now, doing just that. We're allowing extra time for me to do the developing before the next client arrives. Like I said, it'll work out."

Pa had closed his eyes. Was he feigning sleep or had he dozed off? Either way, Gabe needed to get back to the photo car. "I'll be back this evening." When Pa didn't acknowledge the promise,

Gabe retreated to the kitchen where Mrs. O'Brien was just setting a teacup and saucer in the sink. "He's asleep," Gabe said, "or
pretending to sleep so I'll leave." He swallowed, tamping down
the fear as best he could.

"Don't you be giving up, now," the nurse said. "I've seen
much worse make a full recovery."

"Have you really?" Gabe couldn't hide the doubt.

"I'm not for telling tales, boy-o," Mrs. O'Brien said. "We'll
likely have him up in a chair for a bit yet this afternoon." As Doc
McCord came into the kitchen, she looked to him for confirma-
tion. "Isn't that right?"

"It is," the doctor agreed. "I'll be moving a comfortable
armchair next to the bed in a moment."

"Let me do that for you before I leave," Gabe offered.

"No need," Doc said. "You'll be wanting to get back to the
photo car. When your pa wakes up, Mrs. O'Brien and I will help
him learn how to transfer from his cot to a chair. Once I know
he can do that safely, I'll bring a better lamp down from my
upstairs office, and we'll see how his eyes manage. Has he ever
worn spectacles?" The doctor tapped his own.

Gabe shook his head. "You're thinking he might need them
now?" *What else could be wrong the doctor hasn't mentioned.*

"I'm thinking we'll take it one day at a time and respond
as required. Now, what kind of reading material would you
suggest?"

"His Bible," Gabe said without hesitation. "He reads from it
every day. Never misses."

Doc nodded. "Have Lydia bring it back with her."

Gabe turned to go, but the doc wasn't finished. "I imagine
Mrs. O'Brien mentioned that she's seen stroke patients make a
full recovery. I have, too."

Gabe nodded. "Thank you." He looked toward the infirmary. "He's all the family I have."

"Not anymore," the doctor said. "Now you have the McCords."

"And an O'Brien," Mrs. O'Brien chimed in.

"I appreciate that," Gabe said.

"But?"

Gabe shrugged.

"I'd tell you if I didn't have great hope."

"It's not that," Gabe said.

"What, then?"

Might as well be honest about it. He took a deep breath. "We still owe the Missouri Car and Foundry Company a hefty slice of this season's estimated income for building the photo car." He hurried to explain. "Don't misunderstand. We consulted with a banker and prepared a sound business plan. All our advisors agreed we could afford to have a car built to our own specifications. Several banks said they'd be happy to make the loan. All offered excellent terms. We didn't knowingly overreach."

"But you based your plans on *two* photographers working in partnership."

"Exactly," Gabe said. "I'm good at what I do, Doc, but there aren't enough hours in the day for me to do enough of it."

"We'll think of a solution."

Gabe allowed a low, sad laugh. "You have a secret concoction in your dispensary that'll replicate me until Pa recovers?"

"What if we found an assistant?"

"Easier said than done."

"Because there's an art to doing what you do well."

Gabe nodded. "Hence, the Palace *Art* Car. It's more than plopping someone in a chair and removing a lens cap." He shook his head. "It's not for everyone."

"Don't count your father out," Doc said. "He may progress faster than expected. Try not to panic."

Gabe thanked him and retreated toward the back door where he'd hung his hat on a peg.

"We'll expect you to dine with us this evening," Doc said.

"That's very kind, but you don't have to add feeding Gabriel Stamford to your list of duties."

"Having a friend join us at the table isn't duty, young man. It's a pleasure." Doc grinned. "And will be an even greater pleasure if said young friend were to visit Mrs. Mac's Bakery on his way."

Gabe agreed to do just that. When his walk back to the photo car took him past both Baptist and Presbyterian churches, Gabe's thoughts turned to Doctor McCord's question about what Pa liked to read. *His Bible.* Gabe hadn't hesitated. He knew the answer. Feeling chastised a bit, he remembered the proverb about trusting the Lord. *Trust in the Lord with all thine heart; and lean not unto thine own understanding. In all thy ways acknowledge him, and he shall direct thy paths.* Another of Pa's favorites came to mind. *Wait on the Lord; be of good courage, and he shall strengthen thine heart; wait, I say, on the Lord.*

Gabe blew out a breath. If only waiting and trusting were easy.

Gabe decided to stop at Mrs. Mac's on his way back to the photo car. If he bought dessert now, Lydia could take both dessert and Pa's Bible back to the house. Then, no matter how late he worked, everyone at the McCord's could enjoy dessert. He'd just made the purchase and stepped onto the boardwalk when Petey came tearing around the corner. Gabe managed to avoid the little dog, but he was not so lucky when it came to the huge canine in pursuit of Petey. The larger dog nearly swept Gabe off his feet. While he managed to stay upright, he did not manage to save the pie. It landed top down, splattering pie crust and filling onto Gabe's shoes. Handkerchief in hand, he bent down to wipe the worst of it away. Derisive laughter sounded from the street. Gabe looked up. *Great.* The jealous cowboy. Astride a horse. Which made him a towering presence.

At that moment, Petey came trotting back. Sniffing the mess on the boardwalk, he wagged his tail and began to eat.

"Beware the demon dog," Davis said, then nodded in the direction of Andy Keller, who was hurrying their way. "And owner. Known to cause trouble wherever they go." Davis spoke to Andy. "You owe this gent for that pie. And be glad that dog of yours didn't knock him down and break his leg or worse. Didn't the sheriff tell you to keep that mutt of yours on a leash?"

Andy spoke to Gabe. "I'm sorry, Mister Stammer. Honest. Petey got chased out of the yard by that big dog. You saw. It was a *giant.* Petey had to run. He might-a been kilt."

Gabe motioned at the pie. "Petey didn't do this. That honor goes to the stray 'giant.'" He smiled at the boy. "No harm done. I can buy another pie."

A relieved Andy scooped up his dog and trotted off.

Davis raised his voice to prevent Gabe's stepping back into the bakery. "Might bring you some business. My ma's got her heart set on a family portrait. Told her I'd check in with the photo car before calling on my girl today."

Everything about the man rubbed Gabe the wrong way. The presumptuous way he spoke of Lydia as *my girl.* The veiled threat he'd made to Andy Keller about Petey. And was it an innocent lapse or a deliberate snub that he hadn't asked how Pa was doing? Whichever it was, Gabe took the opportunity to slap back. "I'm working solo until my father recovers, so you'll need to make an appointment. Lydia's been kind enough to assist in the photo car today. You can kill two birds with one stone—reserve a time to have the portrait made and call on her all at the same time." *And yes, she's Lydia to me, too.*

He turned his back on Davis and reentered the bakery.

By the time Gabe had purchased another pie and returned to the photo car, Clint Davis had come and gone. The Bartlett Davis family would come to town late Friday afternoon to have a family portrait taken. It would be interesting to meet that family. Hopefully only *interesting*.

Lydia was about to take her leave when Mrs. Keller arrived with Andy, Petey, cooked bacon wrapped in brown paper, and an apple pie. As she set the pie on the studio desk, the older woman offered an apology for the collision that had taken place outside Mrs. Mac's. "Now, I know you've been busy today," she said, "and I want you to know that Andy and I can come back any time. But I wanted you to have the pie by way of apology and the bacon so we're prepared whenever you do have a moment."

Gabe pulled his pocket watch out and checked the time. "It'll be all right. This won't take long." He untied the string securing the cooked bacon. "I'm simply mimicking what my father did when he took the photo I showed you last Monday evening." He spoke to Andy. "Set Petey down and have him stay."

Petey obeyed. Ears erect, he focused every ounce of attention on the desktop. Gabe offered praise and a crumb of the cooked bacon. "That's a good dog."

Petey's tail wagged.

"Now comes the hard part," Gabe said. "We have to teach him he doesn't get the b-a-c-o-n until I say the word. He has to learn to wait." Gabe waited, then said "Bacon!" and tossed a crumb to the dog. Petey caught it in mid-air. Over the next few minutes, Gabe and Andy worked together to get Petey to stay put, waiting until Gabe said the magic word *bacon*.

"He won't never wait for twenty-one-twenty," Andy said after several failures.

"I think you'll be surprised," Gabe said. "He's a smart little dog. If I'm right, he'll want b-a-c-o-n badly enough that once he understands the game, he'll play it. He'll even like it. Every day, you'll count a little farther before you say the magic word and give Petey the treat." He paused a moment and spoke to Andy. "What's the magic word?"

"Bacon!" Andy said.

The moment the boy said the word, Gabe tossed the dog a bit of meat. "You'll work your way all the way up until Petey is waiting until you've counted to twenty-one-twenty and then—"

"Bacon!" Andy said and tossed the reward to his dog.

Gabe glanced at Andy's mother. "It worked for the dog in the photo. Once Petey's learned to wait a full twenty seconds for the reward, we'll schedule a sitting."

Mrs. Keller spoke to her son. "We'll work on it together. As Mr. Stamford said, Petey's a smart little dog. I expect it won't be long until he's getting his fair share of bacon." The moment the dog heard the word, he leaped to attention in front of Andy's mother.

"He's already doing it," Andy said with delight. "We just gotta teach him to wait for it."

The studio door opened and the couple who'd made the first appointment of the day entered. Andy scooped up his little dog as Gabe greeted them.

"Thank you, Mr. Stamford," Mrs. Keller said as she turned to go. "You've warmed this mother's heart."

"You might want to wait with your thanks until we see if it works," Gabe said.

"The photo, should it be realized, is merely a bonus," the woman said. "It's the kindness and the patience that's warmed my heart." Andy had already exited the car. "Not many take time for my boy," she said. Her voice wavered. "They assume there's no point."

"Then that is their loss," Gabe said.

Intending to depart with the Kellers, Lydia scooped up the now-empty butcher paper and reached for the pie Andy's mother had delivered. But Mrs. Miles wanted Lydia's opinion as to whether or not she should wear her hat for the photo.

Mr. Miles huffed impatience. "Now, Ethel, there's no need to bother the lady. You look fine."

Lydia tossed the crumpled butcher paper in a wastebasket beneath the desk. Then she directed Mrs. Miles to remove her hat. Put it back on. Take it off. Smooth the sides of her hair. "I think," she finally said, "that while it's a lovely hat, you will be happier with the result if you both pose hatless. Although—" she glanced at Gabe. "Mr. Stamford would be willing to take more than one view. Then you'd have options."

Gabe nodded. "Happy to do that."

Mrs. Miles reached up and removed the hat, then thrust it at Lydia. Lydia took it, set it down, and wished them both well as she once more prepared to leave.

"Aren't you staying?" Mr. Miles asked.

"I didn't plan to," Lydia said. "I was only—"

"You need to stay. Ethel likes you."

Chapter 8

"Ethel likes you," Mr. Miles said. "Besides that, there's no mirror, and she'll want to know the hat's right when she puts it back on." He looked at Lydia. "You can help with that, too." Next, he glanced behind him at the backdrop Gabe had selected. "Don't like being all closed up in the woods. What else you got?"

Gabe sent an unspoken plea in Lydia's direction. *Please stay.* He described the other backdrops to the couple.

"The arbor sounds pretty," Mrs. Miles said.

"She likes flowers, Ethel does," Mr. Miles said. "Let's see the arbor."

Gabe lowered the backdrop featuring a latticework archway set at an angle that emphasized the climbing roses rambling up the side and across the arch. Mrs. Miles pronounced it beautiful. Her husband nodded.

"That'll do," he said.

Gabe had anchored the bottom of the garden backdrop when doubt clouded Mrs. Miles's face. "But if I was outside, I'd have my hat on." She looked at Lydia. "Don't you think?"

"Not necessarily. A lady in her private garden might simply be relaxing for a few moments with her beau, recently become her husband." Lydia sent a charming smile in the direction of Mr. Miles.

Mrs. Miles blushed. Then she nodded. "But I'll want one with my hat on, too," she said to Gabe. "Just to be sure."

"As you wish," Gabe said. "I'll only be a moment." He slipped behind the black curtain, prepared the first plate, inserted it into the light-proof holder, and then stepped back into the studio. After sliding the plate holder into place in the camera, he posed the couple. Before removing the lens cap, he asked if this was their first time to be photographed. It was, and so he explained that once he removed the lens cap, they must remain absolutely still for a full twenty seconds. "I'll count it off for you. And it's not as easy as it sounds," he cautioned. "Once I've replaced the lens cap, you can relax a bit. Then I'll duck back into the dark room and prepare another glass plate for the next photo."

"And that will be Mrs. Miles's cue to don her hat," Lydia said.

The second photo did not go as well. After fifteen seconds Mr. Miles sneezed. At last, the couple departed with a promise to return the next day to see the prints from which they could order. Gabe wasn't quite sure how he'd manage having folks review prints while he took photos, but he'd find a way. As soon as the Mileses were gone, he said to Lydia, "I can't thank you enough for staying." He motioned at the black curtain. "I need to develop those two plates without delay."

Lydia waved him on his way. "I didn't think about people returning to approve prints and order more. I should have spaced appointments farther apart. And I never should have suggested two poses at the same sitting to the Mileses."

Gabe spoke from behind the curtain. "Neither of us could have known Mr. Miles was going to sneeze."

"The fact remains I could be more help if I understood the process."

"You've been a lifesaver," Gabe said as he poured developer over the first glass plate, then rinsed it with water. He opened the curtain. "I don't know how I'll ever thank you."

Lydia looked past him and into the dark room. "Explain the mystery behind what you've been doing in there."

Gabe glanced behind him. "There's no more mystery to this than there is to your mixing powders for your father. It's science, not mystery."

"You're capturing light," Lydia said. "That's more than mysterious. It's magical."

"Not when you understand the process."

Still, Lydia disagreed. "A prism can separate light and throw a rainbow onto a wall. But you begin with a flat rectangle of glass. Then you capture the light in this studio and send it to that rectangle. Somehow, you take what the light left on that bit of glass and print it onto a piece of paper and hand it to people. And you tell me that's not magic?"

Gabe grinned at her. "You make me disinclined to ruin the illusion."

She rolled her eyes. "Please. Ruin it. I want to understand. What you do is something special."

"You're making me blush." Gabe reached for the glass plate he'd just developed. "To prepare a glass plate to be exposed, I first apply a thin coat of collodion. Next, I dip the plate into silver nitrate. That binds with chemicals in the collodion to create a silver halide coating. That coating is sensitive to light."

"Hence, the light-proof holder," Lydia said.

"Exactly."

"And the light-proof holder is what you slid into place in the camera before posing the Mileses."

"Right again," Gabe said. "Once they were posed, you saw me pull one side of the holder out of the camera. That was so the light coming through the lens could reach the glass plate. Next, I removed the lens cap."

"To capture the light," Lydia said with a smile. "And after you'd counted off the twenty seconds, you put that lens cap back on to halt the process. Because you'd captured enough of the light—thanks to that—" She pointed to the glass panes in the ceiling. "And those—" she indicated the large expanse of glass in the side of the car opposite the door.

"Yes."

"Just now you removed the plate from the plate holder. You had to be in the dark for that because of that light sensitive coating."

"Yes," Gabe said. "Until I'd poured developer on the plate, rinsed it with water, and put it in the tray with a fixing agent." He paused. "It *is* chemistry."

"What *sort* of chemistry? Tell me the names of the chemicals."

"At the moment, I don't recall them all." When Lydia frowned, Gabe said, "Just watch." He manipulated the tray holding the fixing agent before washing the plate again with water and holding it up. "The fixing agent has removed what *hasn't* been exposed to light. And voilà. A negative image." Lydia leaned close to study the image on the plate, her head nearly resting on Gabe's shoulder.

"That's amazing," she murmured.

Gabe took a step away. "It is. But it's also—"

"—science."

They said the word at the same time, laughing over the unplanned duet. "Once the plates are dry," Gabe said, "there's still more chemistry. Varnish, albumen, specially treated paper, silver nitrate, sunlight, gold chloride, and more. Finally, though, I'll have a print ready for mounting. Pa and I usually do up a dozen cabinet cards but given *Mrs.* Miles's uncertainty, I won't make more than one print of each pose until they have a chance to see them."

"And until they've paid you," Lydia said. "A dozen prints require a lot of work. And you only charge three dollars?"

Gabe shrugged. "It sounds more complex than it is. You get to where the printing process is more or less automatic."

He remembered the second plate waiting to be developed and ducked back into the dark room. A female voice called a greeting.

"Lydia! What are you doing here?"

"Witnessing magic and mystery," Lydia said. "Although Gabriel insists it's only science."

While Lydia chatted with the Dillon family, Gabe finished in the dark room. He smiled as he worked, listening while Lydia suggested a backdrop and then recruited Alice Dillon's brother to move a chaise into place. She had pronounced the setting perfect, and when Gabe stepped out from the darkroom and took it all in, he agreed.

Everything was perfect. Perhaps even magical.

The day raced by, and as the last photo session concluded, Gabriel said, "I can't thank you enough for staying today. I hope your father didn't suffer too much for your absence."

"He probably didn't even notice I wasn't there," Lydia said. When Gabriel looked doubtful, she laughed. "The last time Mrs. O'Brien tended a patient in the infirmary, I spent an entire Saturday with Alice's family. When I returned home, Mrs. O'Brien had not only cared for her patient but also prepared my father's favorite meal." She paused. "And if I'd been a bit more discerning, I'd have sensed the poor woman's disappointment when I showed up to eat with them."

"I see," Gabriel said.

"If only Papa would," Lydia replied. "He admires her efficiency and her nursing skills but has yet to notice the attention she gives to such things as his favorite meals and preferred desserts."

"Obviously you don't mind the notion of their becoming… close."

"Papa's barely fifty years old. He deserves to be happy again," Lydia said. "After all, I'm not going to live beneath his roof forever."

They locked the studio and walked along in companionable silence until they passed Lloyd's Opera House. Gabriel commented that he hadn't realized North Platte had such a fine theater.

"It *is* fine," Lydia said. She rattled off a number of things about it that began with the movable stage and ended with the Rochester lamps that pulled up and down on chains. "You should see the scenery," she said. "Productions have street scenes, forests, rocky landscapes—there's even a prison. The artist who painted the curtain did a fine job, too. There's a seacoast in the center." She paused. "Well, I suppose it's a fine rendering. I haven't ever seen a real seacoast."

"But you've seen the prairie grasses on a windy day. That reminds me of the waves."

"You've seen the ocean?"

"Technically, I should say *no*. Pa and I spent last Christmas at a resort in Galveston, Texas. That's the Gulf of Mexico. But I was still impressed, and there were plenty of waves."

Lydia thought about that for a moment. They'd rounded the corner and were nearly home when she murmured, "Seeing the ocean is about the only thing that would tempt me to travel that far away."

Gabriel looked surprised. "The only thing?"

"As I said before, I'm tired of being a tumbleweed. I want to put down roots in Lincoln County. Deep ones."

Together, they walked to the back gate and from there up onto the back porch where an inviting aroma made Lydia smile. She looked back at Gabriel. "As I predicted. Papa's favorite meal."

Gabe hurried toward the infirmary, but he didn't step into the hall. Instead, he paused in the kitchen, listening as Doc McCord read. "'O taste and see that the Lord is good; blessed is the man that trusteth in him. O fear the Lord, ye his saints: for there is no want to them that fear him...'" He glanced at Lydia with a smile and a nod. Lydia frowned a question. Motioning for her to follow him, he retreated to the back porch.

"If Pa's asked for Psalm 34, he's going to be all right, whether he recovers completely or not."

"What makes you say that?"

"It's one of Pa's favorite passages of Scripture. He read it aloud almost every evening after my mother died. At that lonely supper table, looking at her empty chair, Pa still insisted that God was good." *And God is.* The truth of it washed over Gabe. Pa had had the stroke in the presence of a man who was not only an excellent doctor but a good friend. They had money enough to hire Mrs. O'Brien. And Lydia... Mrs. O'Brien stepped into the kitchen from the front hall. Bustling to where Gabe and Lydia stood, she spoke first to Gabe.

"He's been asking for you."

Gabe didn't hide his surprise as he looked toward the infirmary. "He's talking?"

Mrs. O'Brien shook her head. "Only a word here and there." She smiled. "But he chooses each one very well. There's no mystery to what the dear man asks. He's been up for much of the day, and he'll be wanting to hear how you fared."

Gabe hurried into the infirmary. Pa may have been up for much of the day, but now he was abed, pillows all about for support. His eyes lit with joy at sight of Gabe.

"He'll want a full report, young man," the doctor said as he closed Pa's Bible and rose to leave.

Pa grunted agreement, not intelligible insofar as the exact words but absolutely clear in their intent as he bobbed his head up and down. *Yes.*

Gabe took a seat and gave a spirited account of the apple pie incident. "I not only purchased another pie, Andy's mother delivered one to apologize." He smiled. "I suppose a day that begins and ends with apple pie is a good one." So was a day spent with Lydia, but Gabe didn't say that. She was somebody else's girl. For now.

Chapter 9

Lydia didn't exactly plan to become Gabriel's assistant. It just happened. Gabriel needed help, and she was good at helping. She made appointments and calmed nerves, selected backdrops and posed subjects. Orders came pouring in, and she convinced Gabriel to teach her how to make prints from glass plate negatives.

The work was fascinating. When Gabriel expressed reluctance to "presume upon Lydia's time," she reminded him that Mrs. O'Brien neither needed nor, when it came right down to it, wanted her assistance. There was something to be said for giving Papa a few days to notice the woman's efficiency. Her good cooking. Her good humor. Her blue eyes. Saying that made Gabriel laugh. It was very good to hear him laugh.

When her first Friday assisting in the photo car arrived, Lydia prepared for the day with a combination of happy anticipation and cautionary dread. Happy anticipation came from the knowledge that Andy Keller, Petey, and Andy's mother would be in to have their photo taken. As Gabriel had predicted, Petey was a smart little dog who'd quickly learned to wait for his bacon. How wonderful it would be to capture a happy moment in lives that had known more than their share of difficulties.

There was, however, one thing about Friday that gave Lydia a glimmer of cautionary dread. The Bartlett Davis family would be in to have their photo taken. Clint might not have made his and Lydia's relationship official, but after his misinterpreting her hand on Gabriel's arm—*well.* He wasn't going to be happy to learn that she'd spent much of the past few days with handsome, blond-haired, blue-eyed Gabriel Stamford.

As she dressed for the day, Lydia prepared the explanation that would, *please God,* smooth Clint's ruffled feathers. *Gabriel's father—* She hesitated. Clint would undoubtedly hone in on her calling him *Gabriel.* It was one thing to have done that in the wake of the elder Mr. Stamford's stroke and another to continue the practice at the photo car. She could just see the expression on his face. Ah, well. *Being less formal helps customers relax and that, in turn, helps capture a better photo.* Clint would have to accept that. It was the truth, after all. She and Gabriel had simply slipped into using their given names. There was no hidden meaning to it.

With a nod, Lydia continued to formulate her reasonable explanation to Clint's expected objections to her being the photographer's assistant. *It's only right to help when it's within one's power to do so. Mrs. O'Brien is an excellent private nurse, but her talents do not end there. She is supremely efficient, and she's a good cook. Logic dictates that while Mrs. O'Brien assists at the house, I assist Mr. Stamford's son. They'd have to hire someone if I didn't help. Why shouldn't I spare them the expense?*

Lydia frowned at herself in the mirror. The real reason she was helping Gabriel was that she enjoyed it. She enjoyed him—and what was wrong with that? Friends helped friends.

You just go on thinking that this is all about friendship. Alice Dillon had said those very words only yesterday. But Alice spent an undue amount of time reading romance novels. She'd read each of Jane Austen's at least three times each. She claimed that Bradley Yost was her Mr. Darcy. What's more, Alice didn't like Clint. Of course she'd make wrong assumptions and draw wrong conclusions about Lydia's spending time with Gabriel.

Lydia said the words aloud. "Wrong assumptions. Wrong conclusions." With a last glance in the mirror, she descended the back stairs. And heard Gabriel's voice as he read to his father. The Bible again.

"'I laid down and slept; I awaked; for the Lord sustained me. I will not be afraid of ten thousands of people...'"

From where she stood at the kitchen stove, Mrs. O'Brien listened. As Lydia approached and poured herself a cup of coffee, the older woman said, "'Tis a soothing voice the lad has, is it not?"

Lydia nodded agreement. "That voice serves him well in the photo car, too. He has a talent for calming those who are especially nervous in front of the camera." She paused. "I hope it holds true this morning."

"And what's to happen this morning?"

"The Kellers and Petey."

Mrs. O'Brien chuckled. "Ah, the infamous Petey."

Lydia smiled. "Andy was waiting for us when we walked past the Keller house on our way home last night. 'Petey's learned it, Mr. Stammer! He's learned to stay still all the way to twenty-one-twenty.'"

Mrs. O'Brien's confused expression transformed into a smile. "Ah, the timin' of things. The wee pup's got to stay still."

Lydia nodded. "Andy says the dog can do it. The question is, *will* he."

"And here's the talented Mr. Stamford after coffee."

"I'd already drunk my quota before walking over here." He glanced toward the infirmary. "Pa's nodded off."

"Let the dear man rest. Be assured I'll see that he doesn't go hungry." Mrs. O'Brien pointed Gabriel to the table, which was already set for breakfast for four. "You can take your father's place and join us for a bit of breakfast."

"Thank you, but I've had breakfast, as well."

The nurse feigned anger. "Am I that bad a cook, then, that you'd rather pay Maggie MacDonald than enjoy the company of friends?"

"I didn't pay anyone," Gabriel said. "I cooked. But rest assured, my flapjacks aren't nearly as good as yours."

Mrs. O'Brien calmed a bit. "Indeed, and that's no surprise, but it's good to hear you admit as much." She pulled a pan of biscuits from the oven and plopped it atop the stove. "You'll have a sit down and eat a biscuit with some of Mrs. Keller's quince butter or I'll be taking it a personal insult."

Raising his hands in surrender, Gabriel plopped into a chair at the kitchen table.

Mrs. O'Brien snatched up a butter knife and used it first to point at Lydia and then to an empty chair. "Have yourself a seat, dearie. It's biscuits with my sausage gravy this morning."

"May the saints be praised," Papa said as he strode into the kitchen. Sitting at the table, he reached for a biscuit. After tearing it in half, he smothered both halves with sausage gravy spiced with plenty of pepper. He pointed at the biscuit Gabriel had slathered with butter. "Quince preserves are good, but you're missing out if you don't partake of Mrs. O'Brien's biscuits and gravy."

The nurse muttered something about the doctor being full of blarney. But Lydia noted that the woman's blue eyes twinkled with happiness when she said it.

As Gabe pulled the plate holder from its slot at the back of his camera, Andy wrapped an arm about his wriggling little dog. He planted a kiss right on the pup's nose. "You did good." He looked from Gabe to Lydia and back again. "Isn't that right, Mr. Stammer? Didn't he did good?'

"He did," Gabe agreed as he ducked into the dark room. He raised his voice so he'd be heard. "You did an excellent job of training him. You should be proud. I'll be ready in just a moment to take one of you and your mother. Lydia will help you decide which backdrop you'd like us to use." While he spoke, he was developing the first plate and moving on to prepare another. By the time he stepped out of the dark room to slide the plate holder back into the camera, a new backdrop was in place. Mrs. Keller sat in an armchair with Andy standing at her side. When Lydia plopped Petey into the woman's lap, she startled, laughed, and looked at Andy.

"That's perfect," Gabe said. "Look at your son."

"But Petey—"

"Don't worry about Petey," Gabe said and removed the lens cap. "Keep your gaze fixed on your son."

As he counted, Lydia said quietly, "The dog recognizes the counting. I hope you have more bac—"

Gabe looked a warning her way, but he kept counting.

"Sorry," Lydia said. "I hope I didn't ruin the shot."

Gabe slapped the cap onto the lens. "Let's find out." He removed the plate holder and slipped into the dark room. Working quickly, he developed the glass plate, then stepped back into the studio and held up the plate to view it. He smiled at Andy. "You did a very good job of training Petey. He stayed still for this one, too." It was going to be a wonderful portrait of mother and son—plus dog. He'd handed Mrs. Keller a price sheet and made arrangements for them to come back to view the prints, when someone rapped on the studio door.

"Lydia?"

An older bearded man stepped into the studio. It had to be Clint Davis's father, and from the way he tensed and stepped back when Petey barked at him, Mr. Davis was not a dog lover. Petey knew it, too, and took it as a reason to snag the cuff of one pant leg and try to draw the man away from Andy.

"Petey don't!" Andy moved to grab his dog, but the little animal refused to let go.

Clint Davis bent down, encircled the dog's midsection with huge hands, and squeezed. Hard. With a yelp, Petey let go of Mr. Davis's pant leg, snarled, and snapped at the hands holding him. Clint flung the dog away from him. Petey landed with a yelp and for a moment, chaos reigned.

At last the Kellers departed. Gabe introduced himself to the Bartlett family before stepping into the dark room to prepare a couple of glass plates for their session. While he worked, Lydia showed the family the various backdrops.

It didn't take long for Gabe's dislike for Clint Davis to spread to the man's mother, as she questioned her husband to make certain "that little cur" hadn't ripped the hem of "an expensive pair of suit pants especially ordered from Chicago." Reassured by Mr. Davis that no real harm had been done, Mrs. Davis went on to wonder aloud at the idea of a woman wanting to preserve the image of a child who was so obviously not normal. She then segued from unkind commentary about Andy Keller to sneering about Lydia's presence in the photo car.

"Clint didn't tell us you'd taken a job. Isn't that quaint, Bart?"

"I imagine Clint told you that Gabriel's father suffered a stroke a few days ago," Lydia said.

"I don't believe he mentioned that about *Gabriel's* father."

"Well, I'm helping out until he's able to return to the work."

Plate holder in hand, Gabe stepped back into the studio. As he slid the plate holder into its slot in the camera, he said, "It happened last Saturday evening. As it happens, my father and Lydia's know one another from the war. I'm very thankful we'd been invited to dine with the McCords that evening. Doc McCord was there to provide immediate care. And Lydia's been wonderful to help here in the photo car. I don't know what I'd have done without her these past few days."

Mrs. Davis's lips smiled, but her eyes did not. "How fortunate for you."

Gabe noted the resemblance between mother and son—more than eye and hair color. Both held their heads in a way that gave the impression they were looking down on lesser beings. Both had mouths that curved downward at the corners in what seemed a perpetual expression of disapproval. In contrast with his wife and son, Mr. Davis had a ruddy complexion and kindly eyes. It was he who offered sympathy for Pa's illness and wished him a quick recovery.

"Let's get on with this," Mrs. Davis said and dropped onto the chair her son had positioned at Lydia's request. When Lydia suggested that Mrs. Davis might wish to straighten the bow at her neckline, the older woman lifted her chin and snapped, "You do it." She glared at Gabe. "Most photographers would have a mirror at the ready."

"An excellent suggestion," Gabe said. He directed Mr. Davis and Clint to stand behind Mrs. Davis.

"This won't do," the woman said, looking up first at her husband and then at her son. "Bart should sit next to me. Clint should stand behind us, a hand on each of our shoulders."

Just do what she wants. Gabe changed the seating from a single chair to a padded bench. Clint stood behind his parents. The first glass plate exposed, Gabe slipped the plate holder out and ducked into the dark room. Surprised to hear the Bartletts saying goodbye to Lydia, he stepped back into the studio. "We can do another pose."

"No need," Mrs. Bartlett said.

"But—"

"Do you not trust your own work, Mr. Stamford?"

"Of course I do," Gabe said. "But we always offer—"

The woman didn't wait for him to finish. "We've other business in town," she snapped. "Our son will be by on the morrow to approve the first print. We'll want at least three dozen cabinet cards." She pointed at the large framed portrait hanging above the window over Gabe's desk. "You do offer large portraits like that?"

"Yes, ma'am. Satisfaction guaranteed."

"We'll want one of those, then. In a simpler frame. That one's far too gaudy." She brushed her dark skirt with a gloved hand, commented on the white hairs left behind by *that pathetic child's cur* and swept out. With an apologetic smile, the elder Mr. Davis followed.

Clint Davis lingered. He looked about the space before speaking to Lydia. "You've been here all day every day this week?"

"It's fascinating," Lydia replied. "Gabriel needs the help."

He directed his next question to Gabe. "How long are you staying in North Platte?"

"We're due in Ogallala the evening of October 13," Gabe replied. "Of course everything depends on my father's recovery."

Davis frowned, then turned his dark expression on Lydia. "You plan to play at this until they leave?"

Gabe answered before Lydia had time to respond. "It's not *playing*," he snapped, then continued in a calmer voice. "Lydia's been a lifesaver. She's efficient, organized, personable, and an entire long list of wonderful things. I'd hire her in a heartbeat if I thought she'd take the job." He dared a look at the woman in question. She was blushing.

"She doesn't need a job," Clint sneered. "She wants to put down roots right here in Lincoln County." He looked over at Lydia. "Isn't that right, Lyddie-lou?"

Gabe balled up his fists until his fingers dug into his palms. *Who do you think you are? How dare you—*

Lydia's hazel eyes smoldered with rage. "In case you didn't notice, Clint Davis, I'm *right here*. I'd appreciate it if you'd stop talking about 'what she doesn't need' and 'what she wants' as if I'm not capable of speaking for myself." She glanced at Gabe. "And Gabriel's right. It isn't *playing* to preserve moments in time for people." She lifted her chin. "And yes, I'm going to be helping him do that for as long as he wants the help. Because he's my friend, and that's what friends do. They help one another."

Davis studied her for a moment. His expression transformed from proud dictator to repentant scallywag. "You can't blame me for being a little bit jealous." He nodded at Gabe. "He might be shorter than me and he might not be heir to the biggest ranch in the state, but he's not bad looking."

Gabe's temper flared again. Being talked about as if he wasn't even present illuminated why Lydia was so upset. Except she wasn't upset anymore. Amazed, Gabe saw Lydia's anger melt away. A blush blossomed on her cheeks. She'd just opened her mouth to say something when three young women stepped into the photo car.

Lydia called out a welcome, then crossed to the door, which she held open for Clint. He donned his hat. As he prepared to exit the photo car, she looked up at him and said in a low voice, "You've no need to be jealous."

Davis tugged on one of the dark curls framing her face. And Gabe Stamford realized that if he wasn't careful, he was going to fall in love with Lydia McCord.

Chapter 10

A sound snatched Gabe from sleep. He sat up. Cocked his head. Listened. First, the rattle of the door handle. Now, a creak. And the squeak of the hinge he'd forgotten to oil before retiring last night. Someone was opening the studio door at the opposite end of the photo car. Apparently, at least one citizen of North Platte knew how to pick a lock. *Please let it be just one.* He rose and reached for the shotgun mounted above the door between the living quarters and the studio.

It wasn't the first time some enterprising thief had plotted to free the Stamfords of their earnings. Neither Gabe nor Pa cared much for guns, but after losing a full week's income to an enterprising thief two years earlier, they'd agreed to protect themselves against future victimhood. Shotgun in hand, his heart hammering so hard he wondered the thief didn't hear it, Gabe barked, "Leave now and I won't pull the trigger." He cocked the shotgun and charged through the dark curtain and into the studio.

Hand clamped over her mouth, hazel eyes wide with terror, Lydia stood motionless.

"You—I—" Gabe's mouth went dry. He uncocked the shotgun. Stared past Lydia at the door she'd come through. "How?"

"I wanted to surprise you. Your father loaned me his key."

Gabe stared down at the shotgun. Had Pa's stroke done more damage than they'd realized? Had he forgotten about the gun? "Pa didn't warn you not to sneak up on me?"

"I didn't expect you to be here."

"Why wouldn't I be here? I live here."

"You said you were going out to the fairgrounds first thing this morning. To see about where you might set up a photo booth." Lydia shrugged. "You said you were going early. It's almost ten o'clock."

Ten o'clock? It couldn't be that late. Intending to withdraw his pocket watch, Gabe reached into—nothing. No pocket watch because no pocket on his night shirt. He was suddenly aware of standing barelegged and shoeless in front of Lydia McCord, whose expression had changed from terror to humor. Those hazel eyes shone with mirth. She was biting her lower lip in an admirable attempt to resist laughing out loud. He could feel his cheeks burning with embarrassment. He lurched through the curtain and out of sight, even more embarrassed when he realized he'd ducked into the dark room instead of the living quarters.

Through choked laughter, Lydia said, "I thought to have everything organized and laid out so that when you returned from the fairgrounds we could get right to the printing." She paused. "We missed you at breakfast. Your father managed to walk from the infirmary to the table—with help, of course. Papa says he's never seen someone so determined to recover."

As Lydia talked, Gabe stood in the darkroom with his head down, listening and feeling guilty for missing his first chance to have breakfast with Pa since the stroke. He should have been there.

"Are you feeling unwell?"

"No!" Gabe blurted it out. He wasn't sick. He was just—he took a deep breath.

"But you *are* exhausted," Lydia said.

"I'm tired," Gabe countered. "Apparently more tired than I realized."

Lydia's voice was gentle as she said, "I'm going to step out-side—in fact, I'm going to make my way to Mrs. Mac's bakery. You make coffee. We'll have a late breakfast and then work on printing this week's orders together. You can visit the fairgrounds later today or even tomorrow after church."

"I'll get dressed," Gabe said, again feeling heat crawl up his neck and bloom on his cheeks. *Stupid.* He hardly needed to say that.

Lydia chuckled. "An excellent plan."

Only after Lydia had departed did Gabe realize he should have promised to reimburse her for buying breakfast. He dressed and drew aside the drapes, then opened the back door and stepped out onto the platform. It was a beautiful, crisp, sunny day. Standing at the railing, he repeated the prayer Ma had taught him to recite every morning. "Cause me to hear thy loving-kindess in the morning; for in thee do I trust. Cause me to know the way wherein I should walk; for I lift my soul unto thee."

He looked southward toward town and then northward across the rails. To the north, few structures impeded the view of treeless grasslands stretching toward the horizon. Somewhere out there was the ranch where Clint Davis lived. The man who called Lydia *my girl.* Or that ridiculous nickname. *Lyddie-Lou.* It grated Gabe every time he heard it.

On a whim he stepped back into the train car. He'd given Lydia a very bad surprise moments ago. Maybe he could replace it with a good one.

Coffee cake in hand, Lydia looked up at Gabriel, who waited for her on the rear platform of the photo car. He'd donned the usual white shirt and dark pants but had yet to add tie and jacket. "You've been busy," she said as she handed the coffee cake up and then ascended to stand beside him. She gestured at the table and chairs he'd pulled onto the platform. "Above and beyond, Mr. Stamford."

"The least I could do," Gabriel said. Setting the coffee cake on the table, he pulled out a chair and motioned for Lydia to take a seat. While he poured coffee, she unwrapped the coffee cake, took up a table knife, and put generous squares of cake on each plate. She'd already raised the coffee mug to her lips when Gabriel bowed his head and recited a short table grace. Embarrassed, Lydia swallowed. Always the gentleman, Gabriel pretended not to notice. Instead, he asked a few more questions about his father, then surprised Lydia with an invitation for her to accompany him to the fairgrounds later in the day.

"I'd value your opinion as to where we locate during the festivities. Now that you understand developing and printing, you can help me think through how things should run during the fair."

"How they should run?"

Gabriel nodded. "I'll have to set up a portable dark room to develop the plates."

Lydia dabbed at her mouth with a napkin. "Dust is going to be a very big challenge."

"You're right. To be honest, I'm not certain I should even attempt a photo booth on the grounds. It would have been hard enough with Pa partnering in the effort."

Lydia scowled at him. Put a hand on one hip. "Are you implying, Mr. Stamford, that your current assistant is not up to the task?"

"Not at all." He stabbed at a piece of coffee cake. "But I imagine others will lay claim to her time and attention during the fair." He shrugged. "I saw the announcement in the *Tribune*.

Local ranchers challenged to enter their best horses in a 25-mile race. Can't imagine Clint Davis won't enter."

"That race is one brief part of a four-day event," Lydia said. "Of course I'll want to cheer him on, but that doesn't mean I don't also want to help you. To that end, I'd be pleased to drive out to the fairgrounds later today."

"Glad to hear it," Gabriel said. He was smiling when he refilled their coffee mugs. Smiling when, a little while later, he cleared the table. Smiling when he said they'd leave the table in place for now. Smiling as he led the way inside and into the studio to begin printing photos. But the smile faded as he stood at the desk looking down at the next glass plate negative.

"Something wrong?" Lydia stepped close to look over Gabriel's shoulder. She studied the plate. "It looks fine," she said. "I think they'll be very pleased." Later in the day, when Gabriel had fixed the print of the Davises and given it a final wash, Lydia mounted it.

"I hope you're right," he said. "It's been a while since I dealt with a subject as opinionated as Mrs. Davis. But the truth is, she should have listened to me about the pose."

Lydia held up the image. She studied the proud son, his kindly father, and the stern-faced mother. Gabriel had captured the three exactly as they were. Looking at the stern expression on Clint's mother's face, she resisted a shiver. *Make her son happy, and she'll love you.*

On Sunday morning Doc McCord kept Pa company while Gabe escorted Lydia and Mrs. O'Brien to church. The nurse sat with friends of hers, leaving Gabe to follow Lydia up the aisle to her usual place near the front. Was it his imagination or were a few eyebrows raised when they sat together? It was not his imagination that his and Lydia's voices blended well when they sang. It was a beautiful start to the day. And then, after lunch, Clint Davis arrived.

He strode up to the house—Gabe had helped Pa onto the porch for some fresh air after lunch—and the moment Lydia stepped out, he called, "How's my girl?" He didn't wait for Lydia to respond. Instead, he looked over at Gabe. "Taking her out to see Colonel Cody's new place, then on to the ranch." When he held out his hand, Lydia took it. "Don't you look pretty." Tucking her hand beneath his arm, he piloted her across the lawn and through the gate. In one sweeping motion he encircled her waist and lifted her up to the buggy seat. Climbing up beside her, he snapped the buggy whip above the horse's head and the horse leaped into action.

Gabe reached for yesterday's *Tribune* and made a show of seeking out news of the coming fair. Finding some, he read aloud. "'Let everybody pull together and give Buffalo Bill the handsomest reception ever known in the city. North Platte has reason to feel proud of the world-wide reputation her honored citizen has received and should show her appreciation of him.'" Gabe looked over at Pa. "The man's a phenomenon, and he'll be here Wednesday." He paused long enough to look in the direction Lydia had just gone. "Did you know a friend of Lydia's is part of the Wild West troupe? A trick rider, she says."

Pa responded with the word *dangerous,* although it sounded more like *dane-rush.*

"Agreed." Gabe nudged Pa with an elbow. "Reason for you to be thankful the only danger I face is the occasional ire of an unsatisfied client." At Pa's questioning look, Gabe grimaced. "Clint Davis's mother wasn't pleased. They'll be in tomorrow for another session. I'm hoping Mrs. Davis will be more willing to listen to the photographer this time." *Although I'm not counting on it.*

He returned to the newspaper and summarized the column outlining the county fair events. "Races of every imaginable type beginning on Thursday, culminating in a twenty-five-mile race on Saturday. Shooting contests, agricultural produce, ladies' fancy work and more. It promises to be quite the event." Again, he looked away from the paper. "You could have a ring-side seat for Colonel Cody's arrival if we set you up at the photo car."

Pa looked to be pondering the possibility. He shrugged.

"It's *not* too much trouble."

Pa smiled.

"All right, then. It's settled. I'll reserve a buggy and fetch you first thing Wednesday morning."

"There's no need for you to reserve a buggy." Doc McCord stepped out onto the porch. He glanced at Gabe. "I wasn't eavesdropping. Mrs. O'Brien is about to serve coffee out here, and as I came to join you, I overheard. The thing is, I imagine every available conveyance in the county is already reserved for Wednesday." He took a seat in a wicker chair. "Happily, you know someone willing to convey you to the depot in exchange for a place on your photo car platform overlooking the festivities."

Mrs. O'Brien stepped out onto the porch with a coffee service. Shortly thereafter, Pa indicated a desire to retire. With Gabe's help, he made his way back inside. Gabe perched on the edge of the armchair in the infirmary to discuss the coming week. "There's something I need to talk over with you."

Pa waved his good hand in the air by way of invitation. *Let's hear it.*

"At the rate you're improving, we'll be able to leave on schedule a few days after the fair. Lydia's been an excellent help and she's promised to help me finish up the work we take in during the fair. The thing is, I don't see a way to set up *at the* fair." He paused. "I'd have to haul some of our props out there along with at least one backdrop. We'd need to rent a tent. Set up a dark room. The dark room is the biggest challenge because of the dust."

"Hunh-unh." Pa grunted to get Gabe's attention. When Gabe looked over, the older man smiled. He reached out and patted Gabe's arm. "K."

"It's okay to forego the tent?"

Pa nodded. "Too mush."

He agreed. It was too much. "If it's any consolation, Lydia said most people who come to the fair will have plenty of opportunity to visit the photo car right here in town. The fairgrounds aren't that far away, and I checked with the powers that be and have permission to set up a display. I can show off our work and invite business." Gabe shrugged. "I'm sorry to disappoint you, though."

"No dish-oink." Pursing his lips in frustration, Pa gripped Gabe's arm. "Good boy."

"Thanks, Pa." No matter Pa's denial, Gabe knew the man was disappointed. They'd had many a conversation about how to run a portable photo booth. How it might lead to expansion in the future. But Pa understood that now was not the time. Thank God for that. Forcing a smile, Gabe said, "I'll let you rest, and see you in the morning."

Pa shook his head. "Later. You work. I fine."

"You sure?"

"Sure."

"All right, then. I'll see you tomorrow for supper."

As Gabe took his leave, Mrs. O'Brien patted his arm. "You're a good lad, Gabriel Stamford. You have yourself a nice long rest." She paused before adding, "And don't let the Margaret Davises of the world be a bother. She's not known for bein' agreeable. Not to anyone."

Gabe could have hugged her. He exited the house by way of the back door and stepped out onto the porch, looking in the direction of Scout's Rest, Buffalo Bill Cody's ranch. The construction of the Cody mansion out there was the talk of the town. Passengers aboard trains traveling along the Union Pacific rails could see the show place and its massive barns, with *Scouts Rest Ranch* emblazoned across one roof in huge letters. Gabe would have loved to see the place for himself. He would have loved even more to be the one taking Lydia for a drive this afternoon.

As he trudged toward the photo car, he shoved his hands in his pockets. The evening service was underway as he passed by the Baptist Church. They were singing a familiar hymn. *Blessed assurance, Jesus is mine.* Conviction pricked.

For a few moments, Gabe lingered in the street, listening to the song, convicted by the reminder of what was most important in life and apologizing to the Lord for letting himself be buried under worry and work. *Not to mention jealousy.* He glanced back toward the McCords. Lydia had made her opinion of the life Gabe lived very clear. A train car—even a well-outfitted one—wasn't any kind of home. She'd hated the tumbleweed existence she'd lived in recent years. She wanted to put down roots in one place.

She'd also like to see the ocean.

Chapter 11

As expected, the Davis family returned to the photo car early Monday morning. Despite Lydia's best hopes, tea with Clint's mother the previous afternoon did not seem to have changed the woman's opinion either about Gabriel's skill or Lydia's assisting him. Ah well. At least they posed as Gabriel had originally suggested, with Mrs. Davis seated and Mr. Davis and Clint standing behind her. It was a pose intended to reflect not only the men's protective instincts but also their affection for the woman in their lives. Best intentions, however, did not always produce the intended result. When Lydia saw the first print later that day, she withheld comment until Gabriel gave a low half-laugh.

"So much for magic," he said as he held up the print. "This isn't going to please, either."

"You can't capture what isn't there," Lydia said.

"Then where's the magic?" Gabriel teased.

"I mean it. No photographer in the world can capture affection or contentment or joy when it does not reside within a subject." Goosebumps prickled as Lydia realized what she'd just said about the woman who might become her mother-in-law one day. She shrugged. "I'm sorry, but it's the truth. She's a difficult woman."

Gabriel nodded. "If it's any comfort, Mrs. O'Brien said same." He sighed. "I do apologize, though, for making you a target of her disapproval."

"And how, pray tell, did you do that?"

"I roped you into this." Gabriel gestured at the prints they were making. Rows of printing frames aligned glass plate negatives poised over specially treated paper. The sun shining in from the windows in the roof of the train car would soon create the prints Lydia had learned to mount on cards engraved with the words *Stamford Palace Art Car.*

Lydia shook her head. "I wasn't roped into anything. I've loved every minute of helping you. Well—almost every minute." She looked at the print of the Davises with a sigh.

"Do you think they'll still want three dozen prints and an enlargement?"

Lydia shrugged. "Far be it from me to say." She would never dare to speak for Clint's mother. Thinking that could be her reality for the rest of her life made her want to change the subject. She looked toward the rear of the car. "Are you hungry yet?"

"Very." He reached for the box of sandwiches Mrs. O'Brien had prepared for them that morning. As soon as Lydia settled at the table he'd left out on the rear platform, Gabriel said, "I'll be working as long as the light holds. Don't feel obligated to stay."

"I won't," Lydia said, "but I will. Stay."

"You don't need to do that."

"I know." She took a bite out of the sandwich.

"Obviously I welcome the help. But please. When you're tired, head for home."

Home. Nodding assent, Lydia looked southward toward the home she'd fought for. She'd begun to realize that it wasn't the house, lovely as it was, that made her feel at *home.* It was Papa's love and Mrs. O'Brien's personality and even the elder Mr. Stamford's kindness. It was Alice and the rest of the Dillons. It was getting to know Mrs. Keller, Andy, and Petey.

After a moment, she turned her gaze north, toward the Davises'. All Clint had talked about yesterday was the changes he would make as soon as he was in charge. Someday there'd be a better house—one that dwarfed even Buffalo Bill's new mansion. Clint thought his father old-fashioned. When his time came, he would build an empire.

With a deep sigh, Lydia turned her gaze on Gabriel.

"What?"

She gave a little shake of her head. "Just thinking about that word *home*. How it means different things to different people."

"What things? Which people?"

Lydia set the rest of her sandwich back in the box. "We should get back to work so you don't have to walk me to mine because it's gotten dark." She could of course find her own way home after dark. But Gabriel would never allow such a thing. Not because he thought of her as his girl—a possession over which he ruled. But because a gentleman walked a lady home.

Home.

Wednesday! Colonel Cody was arriving at the depot later this morning. Thanks to the Stamford Palace Art Car, Lydia and Papa had the perfect spot from which to view the festivities. She had risen before daybreak and donned one of her favorite ensembles. The deep green walking suit made her hazel eyes especially captivating. At least according to Clint.

As a friend of W. F. Cody, Clint's father would be on hand not only to welcome the great man home but also to join him for breakfast at the Depot Hotel. Clint would attend the breakfast as well. He'd be far too busy to pay Lydia any mind. However, should he look for her in the crowd...well. It wouldn't hurt for her to be wearing his favorite color.

After the crowd dispersed, Papa would drive them all out to the fairgrounds, where Gabriel and his father would set up a Stamford Photo Car display. Fair organizers had wanted Gabriel to do that earlier in the week, but he'd said no. He wanted to wait in hopes his father would feel up to helping on Wednesday afternoon. When she'd heard about that, Lydia had said, "Clearly, you have a plan for helping Pa Stamford into the buggy."

"*Pa* Stamford?"

Lydia blushed. "Sorry. I—I think of him that way sometimes. He's so kind. So patient. Like my own father, when it comes down to it."

"Don't apologize. He'd love knowing you think of him that way. As do I." Gabriel's smile deepened Lydia's blush. He explained his plan to help Pa Stamford navigate the world. "A standard mounting block won't do the trick, but Alice Dillon's father put one together with shallower steps. I think it'll solve the problem both here and at the photo car."

Lydia nodded. She shouldn't be surprised. If she'd learned anything about Gabriel it was that he cared deeply about others. There was more to the work than earning money. He'd shown that when he took the time to help Andy Keller teach Petey how to stay still. And countless other times in recent days. The photo car being closed today meant missed income. But for Gabriel, enabling his father to participate in life again was more important.

It was barely dawn when Lydia descended to the kitchen, but Mrs. O'Brien had already arrived. Both women assumed their patient still slept, and so Mrs. O'Brien merely nodded a greeting as she slipped a pan of biscuits into the oven. Lydia stepped to the door of the infirmary to check on Pa Stamford, amazed to see him dressed and sitting in his armchair, his Bible opened across his lap.

"Goo-*d* more," he said.

"And good morning to you. Obviously, you feel well enough to join us at the depot."

"Lit-l while."

Mrs. O'Brien appeared in the doorway. "The doctor is about hitching the buggy," she said. "I'll have breakfast on the table in a few minutes."

Lydia followed her back into the kitchen. "I've been spoiled these days you've been nursing Pa Stamford. It's going to be hard on Papa and me to see you go."

"Won't be for another week yet," Mrs. O'Brien replied. She glanced toward the infirmary. "Although it's good to see how our patient's improved." The patient had made his way across the threshold and into the kitchen, assisted only by a cane. Seeing him, Mrs. O'Brien smiled. "And here's your *Pa Stamford* as we speak, proving he'll be ready to depart with his boy."

Lydia blushed and stammered an explanation to the elderly gentleman. "I realized I've been *thinking* of you as Pa Stamford. I don't mean any disrespect."

Gabriel's father motioned for her to come close. When she did, he switched his cane from the left hand to the curled right, bussed the tips of his extended fingers, and transferred the kiss to her cheek.

When tears threatened at the dear man's sweet response, Lydia croaked. "Pa Stamford it is, then."

"Is." With a nod, the kindly man transferred the cane back to his good hand and made his way toward the table.

Lydia and Pa Stamford were seated and Mrs. O'Brien was pouring coffee for them both when Pa came back inside. "Buggy's waiting out front," he said as he took his place at the table. He smiled at Pa Stamford. "It'll be easier to negotiate those steps. Once you've reached the buggy—well. Gabriel's bringing a little surprise. He swore me to secrecy, so I can't say anymore."

Lydia smiled across the table. "You'll like it, Pa Stamford."

"Pa?" Papa said in mock horror. "Have I been demoted?"

"Never!" Lydia said.

Pa Stamford pointed at her and then to himself. "Adotted."

"That's it," Lydia agreed. "We've adopted one another."

Table talk bounced about from the photo car to Buffalo Bill's arrival to the county fair.

Yes, Lydia said when Papa asked about it, Clint planned to enter Saturday's race.

"According to the paper," Papa said, "riders have to change horses at the end of every mile. They're allowed two assistants but must dismount and mount the fresh horse without help."

Pa Stamford looked interested. "Pony Exprus," he said.

"You're right," Papa nodded. "It'll probably remind everyone of that. And bring out stories of same." He took a forkful of eggs. "There's a $75 purse." He glanced at Lydia. "How many horses do you think Clint will use?"

"No idea," Lydia said. "He didn't have much to say about it Monday when he and his parents came in to have their photo retaken."

"And?"

"And what?'

"Did the second portrait suit the missus?"

"Remains to be seen," Lydia said.

"Not to complain," Papa said, "but I'd hoped to see *your* portrait by now."

"We haven't done that yet," Lydia replied with a little frown. "We've been a little busy."

Gabriel stepped in the back door. He sent a conspiratorial grin in Papa's direction and muttered *perfection* before settling at the table.

Pa Stamford greeted his son then pointed from Lydia to the portrait of her mother in the next room and finally at Gabriel.

"I know, Pa," Gabriel said. "I'm waiting for the right moment. It has to be perfect."

Pa Stamford raised both eyebrows. "Seven day."

"I'm aware," Gabriel said.

Seven days. That was all the time they had. Conversation continued, but Lydia hardly paid it any mind. She caught snippets here and there, but every time she tried to pay better attention, her brain returned to the words *seven days.* A week before Nurse O'Brien returned home. Life would go on. Lydia would once again manage Papa's appointments, and Gabriel would keep right on capturing light. Without her.

It made her want to weep.

Chapter 12

ive more days. After the last client of the day departed on Friday, Gabe locked the photo car door behind them and looked about the studio. *Five more days.* And then Doc McCord would bring Pa to the station and that would be that. On to Ogallala. On to Denver. On to warmer climates and Christmas in Galveston, where he'd wish Lydia were there to watch the waves with them.

He crossed the studio, intending to develop the exposed plate waiting inside the camera. "I'll develop this one," he said to Lydia. But then he paused and looked about them.

"What is it?" Lydia asked. "Is something wrong? Did I make a mistake preparing the plate?"

"No mistakes. I'll—wait a minute." He snatched the plate holder from the camera and ducked into the dark room. Working quickly, he poured developer over the plate, rinsed it, and set it aside. Fixing would have to wait. As he poured collodion onto a fresh plate and tilted it to coat it, he called to Lydia. "Whatever backdrop you want. Whatever chair. Just—hurry."

"What?"

"I said I wanted perfect light. Look around you. It's perfect right now. Golden. Hurry so we can capture it." Pouring the excess collodion back into its bottle, Gabe dipped it into the next solution, wiped it with a clean cloth, and inserted it into the light-proof holder. He ducked out of the darkroom and slid the holder into place in the camera. Lydia hadn't moved. "You're not ready." He rushed over to the wall of backdrops. "Which one? Hurry! Decide!"

"I'm not having my portrait taken when I look like this." She put her hands up to her hair. "With my hair like this."

"You're perfect," Gabe said.

She hesitated. "I'll admit the light's—"

"Perfect," he repeated as he lugged a chair over. "This one. I've always liked the high back. Your mother's sitting in a high-backed chair in hers. They'll match nicely." Taking Lydia's hand, he led her to the chair. "Angle this way," he said, motioning with both hands for Lydia to shift her position. "You'll be facing your mother when your father hangs the two portraits together. He'll like that."

"But—I look—"

"Beautiful. You've looked beautiful every day since the first day I saw you." He stepped to the backdrop case. "Now which one do you want?"

"If you want to match my mother's, use the plain one."

Nodding, Gabe pulled it down, then stepped back. She was right. The plain backdrop. He was right, too. The light was perfect and she should— "Look to your left. Too much. There. Exactly there. Yes." He moved to the camera and put his hand over the lens cap. "Now look at me. Pretend you're my girl." It worked. Referring to Clint Davis had done the trick. The expression on her face transformed. "All right. Here we go. Hold that thought." Removing the lens cap, he counted off the twenty seconds. At twenty-one-twenty he replaced it.

Lydia ran her palms over her hair. "I can't believe I just let you take my photo."

Gabe chuckled. "I told you the light was perfect." He moved toward the dark room. "I'll print it first thing tomorrow. As soon as there's enough sun to do the job."

"And I'll print the sisters MacKenzie," Lydia said, referring to the clients who'd departed a few minutes earlier.

"You'll be at the fairgrounds tomorrow with our fathers. Watching a certain race, among other things."

Lydia pursed her lips. It was almost as if she regretted that. But then she shrugged and said, "I wish you were coming with us. You know Pa Stamford would love having you there."

"I know you're right," Gabe said, "but I missed a lot of business by not being available on Wednesday when Colonel Cody arrived. It's best I don't miss any more. When I mentioned it to Pa, he understood." Pa had also understood Gabe's reluctance to witness Clint Davis's moment of glory with *his girl*, but Lydia didn't need to know about that. She glanced up at the early evening sky.

"We've lost the light now," she said. "Let's go to supper. Mrs. O'Brien promised meatloaf, and no one makes it better."

They'd left the photo car and were waiting to cross Front Street when Lydia took Gabe's arm.

"So much traffic," she said, motioning at the wagons and buggies crowding the dusty street. It was true that the county fair had the town bustling. But that didn't explain why, once they'd traversed the busy street, Lydia kept hold of Gabe's arm. He decided to take a chance and covered her hand with his.

She didn't pull away.

With Papa and Pa Stamford in the front and Lydia and Mrs. O'Brien in the back—after all, Papa said, one never knew when a patient might relapse—the buggy pulled up to the far side of the racetrack. From this vantage point, no one—least of all Pa Stamford—would have to navigate the crowds.

"We'll be right here," Papa said as he tied off the reins and adjusted his hat to shade his eyes. "If we take Ira back to the house, just wait near this spot. I'll return in the buggy to fetch you."

"I could ask Clint to bring me home." Lydia said, albeit without enthusiasm.

"You never know what demands will be made on him after the race. If one of his horses turns up lame or some such, he'll want to see to it. I don't want you stranded waiting on Clint."

Stranded waiting on Clint. Lydia knew how that felt. She'd learned it just last Sunday when Clint left her alone with his mother while he went out to the barn to check on one of the horses he'd hoped to ride in today's race. Thinking back on it, Lydia realized she didn't ever want to feel that way again. In fact, part of her wished she were back at the photo car today helping Gabriel fix glass plates and print photographs. What did that mean? *Think about it later. Find Clint and wish him luck.*

The Dillon family was just exiting one of the exhibit tents as Lydia made her way across the dry prairie in the direction of several strings of horses preparing for the race. Alice hurried over and looped her arm through Lydia's. She looked pointedly about. "Where's Gabriel?"

"At the photo car," Lydia said. "After being closed all day Wednesday, he didn't want to miss another day."

Alice gave a knowing laugh. "Maybe he doesn't want to watch Clint squire you about."

"There's no *squiring* going on," Lydia groused. "I only came to wish him good luck. After the race, I'm going home the same way I got here—in my father's buggy." Although she might have Papa drop her at the photo car. She could help ... and see the portrait Gabriel had taken in that perfect light he'd raved about. *When he called me beautiful.* No one had ever called her that. Why hadn't Clint?

"Hey." Alice nudged her. "I'm over here. Your best friend. Remember me?" Lydia looked over, and Alice pointed to where

Clint stood at the head of a string of fine-looking horses. Most of the horses entered in the race were cow ponies. Clint's were taller and heavier. He sauntered over.

"What kind of horses are those?" Alice asked.

"The kind it takes to win this race," he said. "Strong and faster than anything else you'll see running today." He tugged on an errant curl at the nape of Lydia's neck. "How's my girl?"

She barely resisted pulling away. "Came to wish you luck," she said and pointed to Papa's buggy on the far side of the track. "I'll be watching from over there."

Clint peered into the distance. "All I see is white hair. No photo-boy today?"

"If you mean Gabriel," Lydia said, "he's at the photo car. I promised to check in with him after the race." *And why did I say that? Gabriel made a point of telling me to enjoy the fair.*

At mention of Gabriel, Clint's expression changed. He looked away. "Guess I'll be going, then." He'd taken two steps when he wheeled back around, swept off his hat, leaned in, and pecked her on the lips. He grinned as he put his hat back on. "For luck."

"Are you blushing or angry?" Alice asked. "You're bright red."

Lydia wasn't sure how to answer that, and so she didn't.

"The photo car display looks nice," Alice said. "Plenty of great photos to impress. I've seen a lot of people take price lists."

"That's good to hear," Lydia said. "I'll be sure to tell Gabriel when I see him." *Right after this infernal race.* After what Clint had just done to embarrass her in public, she was not about to wait around to congratulate him, even if he did win. Which, from the look of those horses, he probably would.

A blast of a horn signaled the riders to approach the starting line. Clint leaped into the saddle. He did look fine astride that spirited animal, as it spun about before dancing its way onto the track.

"Come with me," Lydia said. "We've got a front row seat." Together, she and Alice hurried toward the McCord's buggy. As they wove through the crowd, Andy Keller hollered a hello. He was coming out of one of the exhibit tents with Petey in tow. But the little dog wasn't happy about being on the makeshift leash created from a length of rope. Every few feet, he'd balk and toss his head in a futile attempt to free himself. Then he did free himself and in no time was tearing through the crowd with Andy in pursuit.

Petey didn't actually go after any of the horses in his flight path, but he did run around and under them. As horses are wont to do, the animals protested. While handlers scrambled to calm their strings of animals, Petey charged onto the track—at the very instant a shot signaled the start of the race. Instead of leaping off the starting line, Clint's bay reared up and began to buck. Suddenly, the crowd was enjoying an unexpected rodeo.

Clint finally got the animal under control, but the rest of the field was half a lap around the track. He finished the first mile, but instead of remounting and trying to catch up, he ripped his hat off, threw it in the dirt, and stomped on it. Shouting something at the two cowboys handling his string of horses, he stormed off.

Lydia was more concerned for Petey than anything. She and Alice clung to each other, watching with horror as the little dog tore about the infield like a lunatic. Finally, he tore across the backstretch and onto the prairie, then dropped to the earth, panting. In moments Andy had scooped him up and made for the shade of a refreshment tent. And that was where Clint found them.

Alice saw Clint first. She nudged Lydia and nodded toward the tent. The race was still going on. Thundering hooves combined with shouts and whistles made it impossible to hear the words, but Clint had obviously lost his temper yet again. He'd even dragged one of the race officials over with him, for poor Bertram Rogers was standing by, looking not unlike a drowning man hoping for someone to throw him a rope.

Lydia decided to do just that. Jumping down from the buggy and adjusting her bonnet, she hurried over to the tent. As she drew near, Clint's invective came clear. Poor Andy cowered beneath the man's rage, clinging to Petey.

"Clint!"

Clint ignored her. He kept swearing.

"Clint!" Lydia repeated a little louder.

Still, he ignored her. As he raised an arm—Lydia hoped it was only to illustrate a point and not to strike out at the boy—she grabbed Clint's arm. He pushed back, trying to shake off whoever had intervened. The force of the gesture brought his elbow to her jaw. Lydia staggered back. Onlookers gasped. The back of her hand against her stinging jaw, Lydia once again called his name. "Clint Davis, stop it! Settle down!" Clint wheeled about. Rage flickered in his eyes. Spittle flew. Then he saw Lydia, and the rage melted away.

Lydia moved closer to a sobbing Andy and put an arm about him. "It's all right. It'll be all right now."

"But he said he was gonna *kill* Petey!" the child wailed.

Lydia scowled. "Is that right, Clint? Did you say you were going to kill Petey?"

His emotions might have cooled a bit, but Clint was still angry. "That stunt he pulled could have killed *me*!"

Lydia stared up at him. "Seems as if I remember your riding broncos out at Cody's this past spring." She glanced at Alice, who had finally caught up with them. "Do I have that right, Alice? You remember. We were with Irmagard. It was right before she auditioned for Colonel Cody. Wasn't that Clint saying something about how he liked them 'as wild as they come'?"

Alice cleared her throat. "I do believe it was."

Lydia looked at Bertram Rogers. "If it's all right with you, Mr. Rogers, Andy and Petey can ride with me in my father's buggy until we find Mrs. Keller."

A relieved Mr. Rogers nodded. "That'll be fine, Miss McCord." He pointed at her jaw. "You going to be all right?"

"Nothing a little ice won't take care of."

Clint seemed not to have realized he'd landed the blow. He stared at her now. Instead of paying him any mind, Lydia concentrated on tying the rope back onto Petey's collar. She made certain to secure the knot. Without so much as another glance at Clint, she took Andy's hand and started off.

"Lyddie," Clint said.

She ignored him.

"Please, Lyddie. I didn't mean it. Please let me—"

Lydia thrust her free hand into the air. *Don't.* She sensed Clint's yielding to the raised hand. She and Alice, Andy and Petey hadn't gotten far when Alice looked over.

"That's gonna bruise," she murmured. "Where his elbow caught you. I know he didn't mean it, but—"

Lydia moved her jaw back and forth. She winced a bit. And she kept walking.

Chapter 13

As Saturday unfolded, Gabe prepared glass plates and posed people. He developed plates and handed out price lists all the while haunted by four photographs that didn't even exist. First, the image of Lydia at the fair—on Clint Davis's arm. Next, Davis strutting about to show her off. Finally, a group of fairgoers admiring the handsome couple. And then there was the fourth image, the one Gabe had actually taken yesterday, the close-up of Lydia smiling up at her cowboy. *Pretend you're my girl.* That was the one that broke Gabe's heart. In a quiet moment with no customers waiting, he decided to print it. *Get it over with. Get on with your life.*

As Lydia's image emerged on the photo paper, a pang of emotion jolted through him. Staring down at the photo, Gabe allowed a low, bitter laugh. *Leave it to you to fall in love with the one girl in all of Lincoln County you can't have. She might call what you do <u>magical</u>. She might love capturing light and preserving moments. But none of that is going to matter if you declare your love. She's already told you she's had her fill of moving about. Remember what she called it? A tumbleweed existence. She wants to put down roots.*

Gabe glowered at the photo. So determined was she to put down those roots, she was at this very moment being squired about the county fairgrounds by an arrogant cowboy who cared more about possessing the biggest ranch, the fanciest saddle, the fastest horse, and the prettiest girl in town than anything else.

It was all about Clint Davis. She was *his girl*. Gabe could kick himself for having said *you're my girl* to her when he was taking the photo. If only that could have meant something else to her. He glared down at the image. At least Doc McCord would be pleased. It was an excellent likeness of his beautiful daughter.

A couple stepped into the studio, and Gabe forced himself to smile a greeting. As the afternoon progressed, he formulated a plan that would carry him through the next three days. He must accept the way things were. Pa needed him. Lydia did not. Would not, because she wanted no part of the life he lived.

As directed, Lydia sat at the kitchen table while Mrs. O'Brien attacked the chunk of ice in the sink. *Attacked* was certainly the right word. The furious woman muttered—just loud enough for Lydia to hear every word—as she wielded an ice pick. "Time somebody showed that no-count strutting rooster how to behave." Mrs. O'Brien glanced Lydia's way before going back at the ice. "Thinks just because he's a Davis he gets everything he wants. Win the race. Get the girl." Again, she glanced at the table where Lydia sat. "Ask me and I'd say same as me own mother once said to me. 'Mary,' said she, 'that boy doesn't deserve you and you'll be showin' him the door or I will.'" With a final savage stab at the chunk of ice, Mrs. O'Brien spread out a kitchen towel, plopped bits of it into the center, and expertly bound it up with a few folds. When she turned to face Lydia, her mood and manner transformed.

"Now, then, dearie," she said, all sweetness and light, "we'll just snug this right here." She put the cool cloth against Lydia's jaw. "Wouldn't you prefer a lie-down? A pillow to hold it in place, and I'm thinkin' a bit of a rest wouldn't do ya any harm."

Lydia lowered the cooling bundle to invite the nurse's inspection. "It's going to get worse, isn't it?"

Mrs. O'Brien looked it over. With a deep sigh she said, "Could be I've a help for that." She nodded toward the dispensary. "Would your father be having any arnica salve?"

Arnica. Of course. Lydia shook her head. "Papa used the last of ours the week before Pa Stamford's stroke. I forgot about it. We haven't restocked."

"Well, I've a brand-new tin at home. I'll fetch it and be back before you know it."

She grabbed her bonnet off its peg on the back porch. "You take that lie-down. I'll leave by way of the barn and let the gents know." She paused, smiling. "Isn't it wonderful that Mr. Stamford felt strong enough to insist on helping with the buggy? When I'm back I'll make a pot of tea. You'll feel better in no time." She looked Lydia in the eye. "You will, dearie. I'm not just prattling on."

Lydia managed a weak smile even as her eyes filled with tears. "I know. I just—" Her voice wavered. "I feel so stupid."

"You're anything but."

Lydia cleared her throat. "Please tell Pa that if Clint comes to the door—I won't see him. Not today." She swiped at the tears. "How could I have been so stupid as to think I wanted anything to do with him?" She looked off toward the part of town where the photo car stood on the siding near the depot. What was it she'd told Gabriel when he looked at the second photo of the Davises? *You can't capture what isn't there.* Clint's mother had shrugged her own husband's hand off her shoulder when Gabriel posed them that second time. Why hadn't she realized that Clint would never give her the respect and affection she needed? He didn't have it to give.

As more of Lydia's tears fell, Mrs. O'Brien stepped back into the kitchen, crossed to the table, and sat down. She reached for

Lydia's free hand and gave it a squeeze. "You're not the first lass to be drawn to a pretty face and you'll not be the last."

"I know you're right," Lydia said. "But I still feel like an idiot." With a sigh, she said, "I believe I'll follow your advice and take that lie-down." She rose and headed for the stairs.

Mrs. O'Brien called after her. "There's a proverb comes to mind. 'The mouth of fools poureth out foolishness.' That Davis boy might be pretty, but he's a fool. Be thankful the Lord gave you eyes to see it."

By Saturday afternoon, Gabe believed he had successfully argued himself toward accepting the way things were between him and Lydia. She was Clint Davis's girl. She would never be his. In his remaining time in North Platte, he would focus on being a good son. Tomorrow he would ask to borrow the doctor's buggy so he could take Pa for a drive. They would come here to the photo car, where Pa could oversee the enlarging and framing of Lydia's portrait. They could make adjustments to the dark room to accommodate Pa's needs. Later, they would present the framed portrait to Doc. Gabe would make his case for Pa's taking up residence in the photo car on Monday. They could have a couple of days to adjust things to his limitations before departing for Ogallala.

Moving to the doorway leading into the private quarters, he peered at the single cots bolted to the wall. He retreated into the studio and eyed the wall that closed off the dark room. This evening, he'd ask Doc to recommend a furniture store that might have a wall bed in stock. He could make the purchase over the lunch break on Monday and pay for delivery that same day. Closed up against that dark room wall, it would just be a nice piece of furniture when the studio was open for business. At night, it would lower to provide Pa a comfortable bed.

Toward the end of the day, Gabe stepped out onto the rear platform and took a deep breath. He'd done good work for photo car customers today. He had a plan for navigating the next three days. With God's help, he'd focus on something besides what would never happen between Lydia McCord and him. He would learn to accept it.

About the time Gabe was preparing to retreat inside, lock up for the day, and proceed to the McCords, Lydia rounded the corner of the depot and hurried this way. Gabe looked away. *Three days. You only have to manage three days.* He closed his eyes and sent a prayer for help. When he opened them, Lydia stood at the bottom of the platform steps looking up at him. *With a bruised jaw.*

Chapter 14

*L*ydia saw the question in Gabriel's pale eyes the second he noticed the bruise. Her gloved hand moved to cover it. A reflex, more than anything. "It doesn't hurt," she said. "Nurse O'Brien saw to it." When Gabriel jumped down to stand beside her, when his hand came up to cover hers, the tears she'd been holding back flooded down her cheeks. It was no use. She had to let them out.

"I'm all right," she sobbed. "I am. It's just—I just—Clint—" Gabriel took a step back. Rage flashed in his blue eyes.

"Clint?! Clint did this?!"

"It's not what you think," Lydia said. "He didn't mean it. Didn't even know I was standing there." She motioned toward the photo car. "Can we go inside?"

Gabriel climbed up and extended his hand. Lydia willingly took it. There was something comforting in that hand. The chilly breeze coursed through her. When she looked through the glass in the door toward the little stove he asked, "Would you like coffee?"

Lydia nodded. Once inside, she felt restless. While Gabriel brought in the table and chairs, she paced. He'd left a backdrop and a couple of props in place. Forcing a lighter tone into her voice, she called over her shoulder. "Did you miss me today?"

He appeared in the doorway between the living quarters and the studio, but he didn't respond to her attempt at banter. Instead, he leaned against the door jamb. "Coffee's on." He tapped his jaw. "You were going to tell me about this."

"You didn't hear?"

"How would I? I was here all day."

"I thought people might have talked about—the race."

"They did. A bit." He looked toward the dark room. "I'll admit to doing my best not to pay attention. And I avoided asking a lot of questions."

"Didn't you want to know who won?" She let bitterness sound in her tone.

"I imagined I already knew."

A fresh crop of tears threatened. She cleared her throat. Looked at the prints on the desk and saw her own image. Her hand went to her mouth.

"That was supposed to be a surprise," Gabriel said. "Enlargements are something of a specialty for my father. If you approve that, I'll bring him over here tomorrow and we'll finish the portrait for Doc." He pulled one of the large frames tucked between the desk and the private quarters out of its protective fabric sleeve. "I thought this one. But you can have any one you want."

"You made me look pretty."

Gabriel snorted softly. "You're not pretty, Lydia. You're *beautiful*." He stepped back into the private quarters.

Lydia watched as he took a small pot off the little stove, took two mugs down from a shelf, and poured coffee. He handed one to her, set his own down in the living quarters, and then moved about the compartment lighting the lamps she'd never paid much attention to. As the sun set and the light faded, the car interior took on a golden glow. She sat at the desk, looking out the window, watching pinpricks of light appear as townspeople lit lamps. She fingered the edge of the photo Gabriel had taken. "You said *you're my girl* before you took off the lens cap."

She saw the muscle working in his jaw before Gabriel responded. "I figured if you pretended to be looking at Davis—" Shrugging, he shoved out of the room, returning with his own coffee in hand.

"I wasn't imagining Clint." She felt her cheeks warming with a blush. "I was pretending to be *your* girl."

He blew out a breath. Shook his head. "Don't say that."

"It's true." *But he doesn't want to hear it.* She put her hand to her jaw. "Mrs. O'Brien tended this and said I should take a lie-down."

"Mrs. O'Brien's a good nurse."

"And a wise woman." She met his gaze. "It was a long, hard afternoon." He wasn't making this any easier. Just stood there, listening, those pale blue eyes fixed on her. She gave a little shrug. "Clint and I just—happened. I think I knew he wasn't—" She broke off. "Pa's never approved of Clint but he didn't intervene. Probably because he felt sorry about the way he's made us move around."

"The tumbleweed thing again."

Lydia nodded. "And so, when someone from a family who'd put down roots showed an interest, Pa didn't have the heart to stand in the way."

"Roots," Gabriel said, his tone bitter. "Down deep. Right here in Lincoln County." Shoving off from where he'd been leaning against the door jamb, he set his coffee mug down on the desk. Almost *slammed* it down. "You don't have to explain." He crossed the studio to blow out the lamp nearest the door. "I need to be checking in with my father. See how he fared today. Make plans toward leaving on Wednesday." He turned around. "Which brings me to something I decided earlier today. I'm going to see if Pa will come back to work on Monday."

"Monday? But—" Lydia looked about the studio. Frowned. She pointed at her jaw. "This is nothing. I can help on Monday."

Gabriel shook his head. "I don't think that's a good idea."

"But—why?" Hadn't he been listening? She was finished with Clint.

For a long moment, Gabriel said nothing. When he finally spoke, his voice trembled. "Because I love you, Lydia. I think I've loved you since the first moment I saw you. But—" he motioned about him. "This is my life. And you've made it very clear you wouldn't want it." He crossed the studio to another lamp and blew it out. "It's best this way."

"It isn't!" Now it was her turn to slam a coffee mug down. "You didn't let me finish. About Clint."

"Truth be told, I'd be just fine never hearing that name again."

"Then I won't say his name," Lydia said. "But you have to listen. Please just listen."

He stood across the studio from her, his arms folded across his body. She couldn't read his expression, but at least he was listening. She swallowed. "He never *courted* me. Not really. He just kept making assumptions and I kept allowing it, all the while smothering a multitude of doubts because of my wrong-headed ideas about that word *home*." She began to cry.

Gabriel produced a handkerchief.

She blew her nose. "Can I please tell you what finally brought me to my senses?"

He shrugged. Returned to the doorway between studio and living quarters. Waited.

She did her best to describe the scene between Clint and a terrified Andy Keller earlier today. Just the telling of it stirred anger to the point she had to get up and pace about the studio as she talked. "I told Mrs. O'Brien I'd been a fool, and I spent the entire afternoon telling myself that. Now I'm telling you.

I've been a fool." She swiped at her tears. "You know who has a *home*? Nurse O'Brien. Those two tiny rooms on an alley are more of a home than that big ranch house could ever be. You know why? Because a warm-hearted woman lives in those two rooms." She gestured about her. "And this is a home, because you and Pa Stamford have made it one." She started to cry again. "I said I don't want to be a tumbleweed and you said I had some wrong ideas about that, and you were right. Home isn't a place. It's the people you love."

"I don't blame you for doubting everything I've just said," she murmured, "but if you'll give me a chance, I'll prove that I mean it. You and Pa Stamford will leave on Wednesday. You'll go to Ogallala and on to Denver and wherever else the photo car needs to go. But when the schedule brings you back to North Platte, I'll be here. Waiting. Because I love you, Gabriel Stamford." She repeated it. "I love you."

He was silent for so long she thought he was going to reject everything she'd said. She glanced down, worrying the hand-kerchief still clutched in her hand. Finally, she dared to look at him. "You did say you love me."

Those blue eyes smoldered. "You have no idea." He raked his hands through his hair. Shook his head. "You've just made things very complicated for the Stamford Photo Car." He paused. "Pa and I only came to North Platte as a favor to our friends, the Hansens. We're not actually scheduled to come back to North Platte."

"At all?"

He shook his head.

Lydia slumped against the desk. "I didn't think."

"And I didn't dare hope," Gabriel said and drew her into his arms. After a moment, he mused, "What do you suppose Doctor McCord will have to say about my potentially taking his daughter off into the hinterlands?"

Lydia closed her eyes and savored the warmth of his arms. "He'll barely notice I'm gone if he hires Mrs. O'Brien. Or marries her." Her eyes flew open. "That could actually happen." She looked up at him. "And what do you mean, *potentially?*"

"You haven't said *yes.*"

Her heart racing, Lydia looked up at him. "You haven't asked a question."

Emotion flickered in the blue eyes. "I love you, Lydia McCord. With all the rambling and in spite of the unknowns ... will you marry me?"

Taking his handsome face in her gloved hands, Lydia kissed him lightly. "I will." And with the next kiss, which was not nearly so light, Lydia McCord finally understood the meaning of that word *home.*

Epilogue

Christmas, 1886
The Beach Hotel
Galveston, Texas

"Coffee. Two sugars, light cream."

My husband. Even after all these weeks, sometimes just the sound of Gabriel's voice took Lydia Stamford's breath away. She looked up at the man who'd just brought her coffee. When he bent to kiss her on the cheek, she stole his lips instead.

"Any more of that," Gabriel said, "and there'll be a hasty conclusion to your enjoying the last morning out here staring at the water." He traced a line from her collar, along her jaw, to the corner of her mouth.

"You're making me blush," Lydia said, glancing toward another couple seated at the far end of this, the third-floor balcony of the Beach Hotel.

"I can do better than that," Gabriel said.

How well I know it. Lydia just laughed. "Drink your coffee, Mr. Stamford."

"Yes, Mrs. Stamford." He took the chair beside her.

"In my wildest dreams, I wouldn't have imagined this," Lydia said, nodding toward the blue water, the clear sky.

Gabriel glowered at her. "Your wildest dreams are supposed to be about me."

"They were," Lydia teased. "All of the forty-two days and forty-three nights until Thanksgiving Day when you married me. But then you carried me across the threshold and into the photo car and made them all come true." She took a sip of coffee. "Remember?"

"And now it's my turn to blush," Gabriel said. He sat back and sipped his own coffee. "Speaking of dreams coming true, I didn't expect to be able to bring you here until we'd saved up for it."

"Those two old men," Lydia said, shaking her head as if scolding their fathers from afar. "We'll never be able to thank them properly." Pa Stamford and Papa had joined forces to unravel the plans Lydia and Gabriel had made for a wedding trip. The couple's plan had involved a working trip along the rails. Their fathers wouldn't hear of it. *No,* they said, *you'll take the photo car to Kansas City and leave it safely stowed with the Hansens. We've reserved a private berth on the train to Galveston and rooms at the Beach Hotel.*

Gabriel finished his coffee. "Exactly how long do you think it will be before your father breaks the news that he and Mrs. O'Brien are to be married?"

"Seeing as how he welcomed her back to work with a bouquet of flowers, I wouldn't imagine it'll be long." Lydia leaned back and closed her eyes. Papa was finally beginning to appreciate all of Nurse O'Brien's wonderful qualities. Pa Stamford had purchased his own little house in North Platte and improved to the point he'd begun to consider opening a photography studio on Front Street. At times, happiness welled up so much, Lydia thought she might burst. When something tickled her cheek, she brushed at it. Gabriel caught her hand, and she opened her eyes to look over at him.

"I almost hate to say it, but..."

"I know. Last morning watching the sea. And it's time to pack."

With a nod, Gabriel carried their cups and saucers to the tray where thoughtful hotel patrons deposited such things for staff to clear away. "All good things must come to an end."

When he reached for her hand, Lydia shot up out of the chair and into his arms. "Except it isn't ending. We're going *home*."

Mended Hearts

Chapter 1

York County, Nebraska
January 1890

When the far-off dot on the road finally transformed itself into a bay mare with a splash of white between her eyes, a surge of hope lapped at the edges of Adam Friesen's fear. He turned away from the bedroom window, forcing a smile as he spoke to his wife. "The storm's staying to the west. And I see Aunt Jennie's buggy. She's almost here."

Esther's knuckles went white. She clutched the top of the patchwork quilt covering her pregnant body. Terror shone in her dark eyes as she gasped, "I cannot be having a baby today. It's too soon."

"Aunt Jennie will know what to do." Adam hoped that was true. Esther had suffered horribly bringing four-year-old Anna into the world. Things had to be different this time.

"Go," Esther said. "Tell her—" She bit the words off as she moaned, "Tell her to hurry."

Adam fled the room. He rushed through the kitchen, grabbed his coat off the hook by the door, and loped toward the drive, pulling on his coat as he went. The moment Aunt Jennie pulled the horse to a halt, Adam rushed forward. "It's too soon," he said.

Aunt Jennie didn't reply right away. Instead, she handed her bag and cane over and climbed down. Once she'd shaken her heavy cape into place and recaptured her cane and bag, she said, "You were right to send Anna with Wyatt to fetch me. Lizzie will keep her occupied." She paused. "Wyatt has gone after Molly and Mrs. Rhodes. They'll be here soon enough." She glanced toward the dark clouds gathering in the west. "I only hope they get here before that storm." Clucking her tongue as if to scold the weather into obedience, she hurried across the yard toward the house, turning back just long enough to call out, "You must pray, Adam."

Adam nodded. Only when the plump old woman had disappeared inside and closed the door behind her did he lead Aunt Jennie's fine little mare toward the barn, grateful to be out of the cold wind, grateful for the work of unhitching her and turning her into a stall, thankful Anna was safe with Aunt Lizzie, glad he'd hired Wyatt Dahl last fall. Thanks to that, he hadn't had to leave Esther alone to go for the midwife.

Esther had had a hard time bringing Anna into the world. As he leaned against a stall door, Adam obeyed Aunt Jennie and prayed, thankful the devout midwife couldn't know what he was saying. *Lord God in heaven, I ask forgiveness. I have not loved her as I should.*

At the sound of approaching hoofbeats, Adam went to stand just inside the open barn door. Snow had begun to fall. Wyatt was returning with Molly and Mrs. Rhodes. *Thanks be to God.* Before Adam reached the buggy, the women had climbed down and run for the house.

Wyatt worked quickly to unhitch the buggy horse and lead it inside, encouraging Adam to leave the chores to him. But Adam shook his head. Esther was in good hands, he said. And yet, the moment his sturdy mare was in its stall, Adam hurried to the house. Oddly, Molly was donning her coat when he stepped inside.

At sight of Adam, she pulled her coat off and hung it up. She gestured toward the empty bucket sitting on the table. "Aunt Jennie says we need more water. When you get back inside, put it on to heat. I'll stoke the fire before I go back to—"

An unearthly wail interrupted her. Adam took a step toward the bedroom, but Molly stopped him. "Water first. And more firewood." She nodded toward the kitchen window. "It seems the snow will last."

Adam looked outside. Clumps of white gathered at the base of the tall grass growing alongside the corral fence. Esther's flower garden was little more than a plot of uneven lumps hidden beneath a layer of white. Another wail sounded from the bedroom, and Molly hurried away. The wail ascended to new heights.

I have not loved her as I should. Please, Lord. Esther screamed. His mouth went dry, and he headed into the swirling snow. *Please—if only You will help her, I will*—he broke off. He supposed it was a sin to bargain with the Almighty. Surely Deacon Lynch, who spoke of a God who was a consuming fire, would say so. *A consuming fire.* He pondered the concept as he lowered the bucket into the well.

As he drew the bucket up, he prayed. *Please do not consume us. She is a good wife, strong and true. We have come a long road, bound together by vows spoken out of duty. Give us time together, and I will praise You at every opportunity for the rest of my life. I will build the pews for the new church. And I will love her. I will.*

Returning to the house with the bucket of water, Adam poured it into a pot atop the stove. No sounds escaped from the bedroom. He went back outside for more wood. *I will prove my devotion. And give thanks.* He began to list blessings. *Anna*— not the child of his loins but surely the child of his heart. *Good friends*—not the least of them the women helping to usher Esther's second and Adam's first child into the world. *Esther—who loves me. At last, she loves me.*

It had not been an easy road for Adam and Esther Friesen. Nearly four years ago, a wicked stranger had taken Esther's innocence, leaving her bruised and alone. She would never say who had committed that horrible act. It didn't matter, she said, when she confided in Molly. It was done and he was gone. But Esther was with child. When she finally told her best friend, Molly—who was also Adam's sister—Esther also confided her plans to run away.

When his weeping sister told Adam what had happened, Adam offered a brash solution. "If she'll have me, I'll marry her. No one need ever know."

Esther resisted at first. After all, Adam was several years younger than she. But his hazel eyes were pools of caring, his deep voice convincing. "You don't want to be with strangers when—you know. You'll be wanting your mother when it's time. Molly too." He stopped short, his face burning with embarrassment at the mere mention of something so intimate as a birthing. Finally, he croaked. "I can provide for you. For both of you."

It was true. Adam Friesen had inherited his parents' farm. He was hardworking. A solid member of the community. Dependable. Finally, Esther murmured, "You—you'd do that? For me?"

There was disbelief in her voice, but just beneath the disbelief Adam detected the faintest note of hope. And relief. The import of what he'd said clutched at his midsection, but Adam Friesen was not one to back down. Besides that, he'd be a hero to Molly and Esther, an attractive prospect.

"I would," Adam said. "I will."

Tears came to Esther's eyes. She put her hand on his arm and murmured, "God bless you, Adam Friesen."

Seven months later, Anna tore her way into the world. By then, Adam had learned to be Esther's friend. It was quite some time before the rest came. But it did. Eventually. And so, as he carried an armful of wood through the falling snow toward the house, Adam Friesen prayed. *God in heaven, save my wife. Our child. Our love.*

April 1890
St. Louis, Missouri

Mere words shouldn't have the power to suck the air out of a room. Seventeen-year-old Rachel Ellsworth knew that. And yet, all she could manage was a little gasp. Pressing one gloved hand to her corseted midsection, she concentrated. *In...out. In...out.*

Paying the undertaker had emptied Papa's account—his *only* account. The pastor assigned to take Papa's place would arrive in ten days, and Rachel must vacate her home. She'd expected that, of course. The church owned the parsonage and its furnishings. What she did not realize was that there was no money. None.

She clutched the arms of the upholstered chair. *In...out. In...out.*

The middle-aged woman seated to her right put a comforting hand on Rachel's arm. Next, she scowled at the young man standing behind them and scolded, "Don't just *stand* there, Landis. Get the dear girl a glass of water."

Landis Grove obeyed his mother, striding across the room to a side table. Everything seemed to slow down. Rachel watched as he lifted a crystal pitcher, poured water into one of the half-dozen tumblers arranged on a silver tray, and then crossed back to where she sat.

"Just a sip, dear," Landis's mother said. "I know it's a shock, but you're going to be all right."

Rachel took the glass and gulped water. She drew an almost normal breath before murmuring, "Thank you."

"You must listen to Mother," Landis said. He was still standing behind her, and his voice came as if from on high. "You're going to be all right. We'll take care of you. In fact, we've already taken steps to do just that."

Rachel's pulse quickened. *The Groves have made plans.* Landis was going to propose! She'd promised Father she wouldn't marry until she was eighteen, but he would understand. Crisis sometimes forced adjustments, and Rachel could think of no greater crisis than the news the attorney had just delivered. Reverend John Ellsworth had left his only child both homeless and penniless.

"Mother's taken everything in hand," Landis said. "You won't have to worry about a thing."

Mrs. Grove leaned forward and spoke to her husband, seated on Rachel's left. At his wife's encouragement, Mr. Grove reached inside his suit coat, withdrew an envelope, and handed it over. "It's addressed to Mrs. Grove and me because Mrs. Grove made the contact. But the note is to you."

"It will warm your heart, dear," Mrs. Grove said. "Your aunts sound delightful."

My aunts? Rachel took the envelope. Pulling out a single sheet of notepaper, she read.

April 10, 1890
Lost Creek, Nebraska

Dearest Rachel,

Please forgive us for not coming to you the moment we heard the news. A late spring storm laid down a sheet of ice last week, and one night after attending a particularly difficult lying-in, I slipped and fell. While no bones were broken, I currently need a cane to navigate. Lizzie finally convinced me that our attending John's service would only complicate matters for you.

It has pained us greatly to leave you alone to bear the burden of your beloved father's passing. Please know that while we have not been with you in person, your name has been on our

hearts and in our prayers several times a day since we received the news.

Mr. and Mrs. Grove have kindly informed us of the difficulties arising regarding your father's earthly estate. Remember that such things are mere trifles in light of the eternal treasures John and Katie laid up in heaven. Do not forget that your heavenly Father knows what you have need of. Lizzie and I both hope that you will see His provision in this letter.

Please, Rachel, come to us at your first opportunity. Our way of life is simple, but we have prepared a room for you—both in our home and in our hearts. We hope soon to receive word that you have accepted our invitation.

In the Love of the Lamb,
Your aunts Lizzie & Jennie Meeker

The moment Rachel lowered the letter, Mrs. Grove reached over and squeezed her arm. "Now isn't that wonderful? Such a sure testimony to the heavenly Father's promise to provide for His own." She paused. "I can't say I'd have the kind of faith Reverend Ellsworth did in that regard. I'd never be able to leave my own child penniless, but—"

"Martha!" Mr. Grove scolded.

"Rachel knows I don't mean to criticize," Mrs. Grove retorted. "No one supported Reverend Ellsworth more faithfully than I. I'm just saying—"

"Yes," Mr. Grove said quickly. "We know." His voice was warm when he spoke to Rachel. "Your father was one of the best men I've ever known. And he raised a fine daughter."

"Indeed," Mrs. Grove said. With a forced little laugh, she added, "I wouldn't be surprised if we have to do battle with your aunts when the time comes for you to return to us. But it's obvious they are very keen on having you accept their invitation. Now, we've discussed it with Landis, and while he's reluctant to let you go, he understands how important it is for us to honor your father's wishes regarding your future plans." She looked up at Landis again. "Don't you, dear?"

Landis cleared his throat. "We did promise to wait until you're eighteen. And it's less than a year away."

He wasn't going to propose, after all. Feeling numb, Rachel nodded. *Never mind. He will soon enough. You'll be eighteen in November.* She glanced down at the letter again. The invitation did sound sincere. *Jennie and Lizzie.* Rachel had only faint memories of the two spinsters. She'd never met them before they arrived on the Ellsworths' doorstep soon after Papa sent the telegram informing them of their sister Katie's death—a terrible shock, for Mama hadn't been ill. She simply did not wake up one morning.

In the days following their arrival in St. Louis, Jennie and Lizzie moved quietly in the background, cleaning, arranging things for Mama's wake, managing the kitchen with amazing efficiency—essentially doing everything they could to help Rachel and her father navigate the first few days. Then, one morning a week after Mama's funeral, Aunt Lizzie said it was time for them to be going home.

Regret coursed through Rachel for not making the effort to stay in touch with her aunts since then. She'd been too lost in a fog of grief and too overwhelmed by the effort to keep Papa going to maintain a correspondence. Letters arrived weekly for the first year and then less often as time went on. After all, she didn't really know Mama's family.

The Meekers of Pennsylvania had been headed west when Mama met and fell in love with a young minister named John Ellsworth. Mama married and the rest of her family left her behind in Missouri. Rachel knew very little of what had happened to the family after that, beyond the fact that they'd finally settled in some far-off Nebraska town. She skimmed her aunts' letter again. *We have prepared a room for you—both in our home and in our hearts.*

Rachel remembered Aunt Jennie's round smiling face and kind voice. Tall, willowy Aunt Lizzie resembled Mama more—except where Mama's voice was mellow, Aunt Lizzie's was terse in a way that bordered on stern. Still, the invitation seemed sincere. And the Groves, Landis included, were clearly not going to invite Rachel into their family. Yet. What choice did she have?

"It's for the best," Mrs. Grove said.

"It's just for a little while," Landis croaked.

"But—my paintings." Just hearing the words made Rachel feel small-minded. With everything that had happened, surely she must sound foolish asking about her paintings. Her cheeks grew warm as she blushed with embarrassment.

But Landis understood. He reassured her. "Mother says we'll have them wrapped for safekeeping and stored at the bank."

"In the vault," Mrs. Grove said. "We know how much they mean to you."

Leave them? All of them? Rachel protested. "But I can't just—leave them." She looked up at Landis. "You understand—don't you?" He had to understand. After all, wasn't the Grand Tour part of their wedding trip plans? He was going to take her to the Louvre in Paris. They were going to attend the next Exhibition.

"Of course we understand," Mrs. Grove said. "Which is why you must select two or three pieces to take with you. To help you feel at home." She paused. "Now, I know it's been a lot to digest, dear, but with the subject of your paintings, I believe we've found a pleasant way to conclude an unpleasant meeting. Shall we give Mr. Carpenter his office back?" She didn't wait for Rachel to respond before rising from her chair.

Rachel tucked her aunts' letter in the beaded bag at her wrist and took Landis's arm. As they left Mr. Carpenter's office and stepped into the midmorning sunlight, Mrs. Grove suggested they all proceed to the parsonage so that Rachel could choose the paintings she wanted to take with her on the train. "That will give the movers plenty of time to properly wrap the rest of your things for their removal." She gave a deep sigh. "I know it seems that everything is happening very quickly, but it is an unfortunate fact of life that the world continues to revolve and we are expected to spin with it."

Rachel fought back tears as Landis helped her into the Groves' carriage. It was only right to accept her aunts' invitation. Papa wouldn't have wanted the church he loved to go without a shepherd for long. Still, as the carriage pulled away from the curb and Landis's mother chattered away about the building of crates to protect her art and the packing of her easel and canvases, Rachel's sense of foreboding grew.

What was it Mrs. Grove had just said? Something about the world continuing to revolve . . . *and we are expected to spin with it.* Spinning, indeed. Her world was spinning out of control.

Chapter 2

As the train car slowed, black letters on a faded board sign appeared just beyond the windows across from Rachel's seat. LOST CREEK. The name of the town only emphasized how Rachel felt after looking out at miles and miles of bleak, open prairie where the remnants of snowdrifts still clung to the edges of creek beds. As far as Rachel could see, Nebraska was vast, colorless, and empty—save for the people who lived in Omaha and a couple of other towns where the train had stopped along the way. But those small towns were mere dots of humanity on an empty canvas of land and sky, and the farther west she'd come, the more lost Rachel felt.

She leaned forward, hoping to catch a glimpse of her aunts. Had it really been less than two days since she'd boarded the train to her new home? Two days since she'd folded her wool cape and settled it into the rack above her seat back? After helping her board, Landis had walked along the platform until he found her car. He'd walked up to the window and pressed his open hand against the glass. She'd done the same even as tears streamed down her cheeks. *Only seven months.* Landis mouthed the words, touching the edges of his own mouth to encourage Rachel to force hers to curve upward.

Pushing down a wave of homesickness, Rachel stood to retrieve her cape. An elderly gentleman with a mane of white hair had been making his way up the aisle, but when Rachel picked up her carpetbag, he motioned for her to go before him. With a nod, she bustled through the door and down the iron steps leading to the depot platform. But there was no sign of the aunts. There was, in fact, not much of anything happening at the small clapboard depot.

She hesitated, looking toward the pathetic little town clustered just across the tracks. Finally, Aunts Jennie and Lizzie rounded the far corner of the depot. Short, round Aunt Jennie was still walking with a cane. Tall, slim Aunt Lizzie had a ruddy-cheeked, blue-eyed little girl in tow.

Aunt Jennie drew Rachel into a hug. "I am sorry we made you wait even one second. I am so slow these days. We're delighted you've come to us." She spoke to the little girl clinging to Aunt Lizzie. "This is her, Anna—Rachel, our niece."

The child gave Rachel a quick glance before thrusting the thumb of her free hand into her mouth and hiding her face in the folds of Aunt Lizzie's black cape. With a disapproving cluck of her tongue, Aunt Lizzie tugged on the child's hand, forcing her to stop sucking her thumb. "Say hello to Rachel," she demanded. The little girl turned her head just enough to peek at Rachel, but she did not speak. With a sigh, Aunt Lizzie crouched down to settle the bonnet dangling about the child's shoulders back on her head and tie it securely in place.

While Aunt Lizzie fussed with the bonnet, Aunt Jennie leaned close and murmured, "I delivered Anna's baby brother back in January. Sadly, her mother—" Jennie's voice wavered. She shook her head. "We've been helping their poor father with the children."

With the bonnet tied, Aunt Lizzie stood and handed the child off to Aunt Jennie. "I'll fetch the baby home from Molly's after I arrange for someone to bring Rachel's trunk to the house."

"Trunks," Rachel said. "And three bandboxes. For my hats." Landis's mother might have been willing to store paintings, but she had insisted Rachel would want every other earthly thing she owned with her. "And a crate protecting my easel and two of my paintings. Landis had it specially constructed to protect them." She paused. "Landis is my..."

"Yes," Aunt Lizzie said. "We remember Landis." She paused. "Two trunks, one crate, and three bandboxes. Do I have that right?"

"Actually, it's three trunks."

"Three."

Aunt Lizzie sounded incredulous, and Rachel rushed to explain. "I—I know it's a lot. It's just—I couldn't bear to leave Papa's books behind. And Mama's quilts. Only two, but—" Rachel's voice wavered. She swallowed. "Papa donated nearly everything to the poor."

When Aunt Lizzie next spoke, her tone was gentler. "Three trunks, three bandboxes, and one crate."

Rachel nodded.

"I'll see to it." Aunt Lizzie hurried into the depot.

Rachel watched her go, newly reminded of Aunt Lizzie's abrupt nature. She should have begged Landis to intervene with his parents. Surely they could have found room in that mansion of theirs for the books. She'd just assumed the aunts would have room. But they were already sheltering two children. Again, she apologized. "I hope I won't be in the way."

"In the way?" Aunt Jennie protested. "Dear child, we're delighted to have you. The truth is, we can use the help. We have plenty of room, and we've had great fun preparing for you." She looked down at the little girl. "Anna's helped us get your room ready. Wait until you see it!" Aunt Jennie led the way toward the road separating the train tracks from the edge of town, chattering as she walked. "Your room faces west. Lost Creek may not be much compared to St. Louis, but no one can match our sunsets!" They crossed the road while Aunt Jennie talked, making their way along a street lined with clapboard houses, most of them only one level.

Rachel was admiring the green shutters and window boxes on one when a young woman burst out the front door and trotted toward the street, leaving the screen door to slam shut behind her. "Aunt Jennie! Hello! Is this her?" The girl didn't wait for a reply before introducing herself. "I'm Nel. Nel Berkey. I've been watching for you! Welcome. I hope you quilt. You should come to Mama's quilting bee tomorrow. It's the perfect place to meet everyone—well, not everyone exactly, but at least ten someones—if everyone comes. Goodness but you're tall." She looked back at Aunt Jennie. "You were right. She's tall." Again, she smiled up at Rachel. "Aunt Jennie said you were like your mother that way. Tall."

A woman called from the house. "Nel Berkey! You've scorched the applesauce!"

The girl glanced back at the house. "Oh bother. Now I've done it." She raised her voice. "Coming, Mother." Again, she spoke to Rachel. "Don't forget. Quilting tomorrow. Right here." She trotted away, the hem of her pale blue dress brushing the earth as she retreated.

Aunt Jennie chuckled as the screen door slammed behind the girl. "And now you've met Nel, the unofficial social director for the young people of Lost Creek."

With Anna in tow, Aunt Jennie led the way up the tree-lined street, around one corner to the right and another to the left.

Aunt Lizzie caught up with them. She spoke first to Jennie. "Wyatt Dahl's loading the trunks and bandboxes. But there was no crate. Let's hope it's on the next train."

Rachel's stomach clenched. "I don't understand how it could have gotten separated from everything else. Landis promised to see to things personally."

"I'm sure everything will be just fine," Aunt Jennie said. "Let's get you home and get some lunch. You must be hungry after such a long trip."

Adam Friesen perched on his farm wagon seat, his feet braced against the toe board, his head bowed. From beneath the wide brim of his hat, he stared at the daffodils he'd just placed at Esther's grave. *Her daffodils.* The ones they'd planted together only last fall. He visited the cemetery every day, hoping that at some point there would be a moment of clarity. A glimmer of understanding as to why God had refused to answer his prayers. A hint that one day in the far distant future he might come to accept what had happened. But today was like all the others—silence occasionally broken by the rattle of harness as someone drove past. No one ever turned in to offer comfort. He was glad.

He closed his eyes and settled back, once again working his way through the day his son was born, reliving the fall from euphoric joy to disbelief to denial to bottomless sorrow, remembering the sound of a baby's cry, seeing the expression on Aunt Jennie's face, hearing those horrible words. *I am so sorry, Adam. So very sorry.*

Esther didn't die right away. Life drained out of her because of the hideous word *hemorrhage.* Esther whispered her love just before closing her eyes for eternity. And that was all. *That was all.*

As he sat in the wagon and slogged through it all again, moment by moment, tears leaked down his face and moistened his red beard. He brushed them away with the back of his hand and blew his nose into his red kerchief. And all the while he was yelling at God. *I've always loved Anna, but Esther...that took some time. How could You take her? We were just getting started.*

He flung protests and questions at heaven until finally—his emotions spent for the moment—Adam stuffed the kerchief back in his pocket, slapped the reins against the backside of his team of grays, and guided the wagon out of the graveyard. He turned toward town, mindful of a glimmer of—what? He wouldn't quite call it joy, but he did feel something that didn't seem to come from the pit of despair. Two reasons to keep going. Anna. The baby.

The baby. Nameless, so far, because he didn't know what Esther wanted. The easiest thing was to just name the little mite for his two grandfathers, but Adam did not relish the idea of the constant reminder of either man, for neither he nor Esther had had a good relationship with their fathers. Growing up in families where faith was only pretense had been one of the first things to bring Adam and Esther together. Their home would not be that way.

Home. Would it ever feel like home again? Adam scolded himself at the thought. How it *felt* didn't matter. He had children to raise. Crops to plant. Livestock to tend. Esther's chickens. Esther's garden. All of it fell to him, now. All the work.

Thank God for Aunts Jennie and Lizzie. What would he have done without their kindness these last weeks? Anna was only four, and the baby—he had to name the baby. He glanced upward. *What was the name, Esther? The name you wanted?* With a shuddering sob, Adam reined the horses in just long enough to regain control of his emotions. When he felt he could face the dear women caring for his children, he clucked his tongue against the roof of his mouth to get the team moving again. Nearing the Meeker house, he heard Anna's voice before he saw her.

"There he is! That's my papa!"

How could another's joy cause a fresh stab of pain? And yet, it did. Still, when Anna came bouncing down the front steps,

Adam hurried to pull up and climb down. When he crouched low and opened his arms, Anna flung herself at him, circling his neck with her thin arms and snuggling close. Adam closed his eyes and inhaled the scent of her, a mixture of clean clothes dried in the sun and sweaty blond hair.

"You've been playing hard," he croaked and reached up to push her hair away from her moist temples.

Anna nodded. "I hided from Rachel, but she found me and I ran fast so she couldn't tag me."

"And who is Rachel?"

A mellow voice answered from the top of the porch steps. "I'm Rachel. Rachel Ellsworth."

Adam looked up to where the stranger stood. Rising, he swung Anna onto one hip and snatched his hat off his head. "Adam Friesen. Anna's papa." Another wagon rumbled up.

Wyatt Dahl jumped down. "On the days you don't need me at the farm, I've been helping handle freight over at the depot. Any chance you could help me take the lady's things inside?"

Adam nodded. When he set Anna down, she hurried back up the stairs to stand beside Miss Ellsworth. To take her hand, Adam noted. He and Wyatt wrestled the first trunk off the wagon and began to carry it up the stairs.

Aunt Jennie came to the door. As she held it open for the men, she said, "I see you've met Rachel. She's come to stay with us for a while." She waved them into the house. "Upstairs. The room to the right." She invited Adam to stay for supper. "Lizzie's got an apple pie in the oven."

"That sounds so good," Adam said, "but I promised Molly I'd bring the children there for supper."

"The baby's already there. Molly agreed to watch him so we could meet Rachel's train, and we've yet to collect him."

Adam nodded. He and Dahl hoisted the trunk up the stairs and set it down inside the door to a huge room with a door opening onto the porch on the west side of the house. The aunts were certainly treating their niece well. Giving her the largest room in the largest house in town. Then again, no one was kinder than the Meeker sisters, no one more hardworking or generous.

Adam remembered how suspicious his own mother and her friends had been when the two spinster daughters of the widowed Dr. Fred Meeker first walked into First Church. It was the very first Sunday after their father—a notorious agnostic with a reputation for hard drinking—was laid to rest. As far as anyone knew, no Meeker had ever set foot inside a church until that day. But by living humbly, practicing mercy, and serving others, the sisters won their way into hearts. Adam didn't know what he would have done without them.

Aunt Lizzie stepped into the hallway from the kitchen just as Adam and Dahl descended the steep stairs to retrieve the second trunk. She put a few coins in Dahl's hand as she spoke. He tried to refuse, but she insisted, saying something about the evening train and a crate. Apparently the railroad had failed to transport something of Miss Ellsworth's. Something important, to hear Aunt Lizzie's tone of voice. Dahl reassured her that if the crate was on the next train, he'd find it and deliver it right away. The two men finished hauling trunks upstairs and then, with a tap to the brim of his cap by way of salute, Dahl left.

Anna giggled when Miss Ellsworth handed her the smallest of three bandboxes and asked if she'd carry it up the stairs. She did so, following the tall, slender newcomer who held the other two boxes aloft as if they held priceless treasure. Once back downstairs, Anna launched herself at Adam again, this time looping her fingers through his suspenders and stepping onto the toes of his boots while demanding they dance.

"Papa doesn't feel much like dancing tonight, little one," he said. Prying her fingers out of his suspenders, he lifted her into his arms again. "Oof," he grunted. "What are the aunts feeding you? You're heavier than a sack of potatoes."

"Too heavy for you to hold?"

"Never too heavy for that," Adam said, carrying Anna with him toward the front door.

Miss Ellsworth spoke as she descended the stairs, offering her condolences for his loss.

Anna spoke up. "Rachel's mama died too. And her papa. She didn't have anywhere to live, so now she lives here, just like Brother and me."

Miss Ellsworth smiled. "I suppose it does look like I'm moving in, but the truth is I'm just visiting for a few months. I'm to be married next year."

Adam barely heard what she said. *She lives here, just like Brother and me.* Did Anna think he'd given her up? Given the baby up? A new wave of sorrow threatened. "We must not keep Molly waiting," he croaked. "Let's be on our way."

"We'll have pie wrapped for you to take home with you later," Aunt Lizzie called from the kitchen doorway.

Adam thanked her before carrying Anna out the door and down the steps. Setting her on the wagon seat, he climbed up beside her. As he guided the team back out onto the road, the now-familiar sensation of helplessness washed over him. *She lives here, just like Brother and me.*

With all his heart, Adam wanted to bring his children home. With all his mind, he knew it was impossible.

Chapter 3

Rachel ducked down to see herself in the small mirror hanging on the back of the bedroom door. Perching her hat at just the right angle, she secured it with the elegant pin Landis had given her for Christmas. She closed her eyes briefly, thankful for the distraction of Nel Berkey's quilting bee. Her paintings and easel had not been on the evening train yesterday, after all. What if they were lost? Turning away from the mirror, she looked over at Mama's quilt, smiling at the memory of how pleased Aunt Lizzie had seemed when Rachel lifted it from her trunk and spread it out upon the bed.

"I remember Katie working on that," Aunt Lizzie said, tracing one of the pyramids made up of small triangles. "No one thought she'd be able to execute such a complex pattern, but she did it beautifully."

Rachel hadn't really thought about the difficulty of the piecing until that moment. Now, as she looked at the quilt more carefully, she realized that Mama had used dozens of different fabrics, and yet they blended together. Soft golds and pinks scattered across the surface like spring flowers popping up in a mostly dormant field of brown. Rachel couldn't remember ever thinking of Mama as artistic, and yet she'd transformed dress scraps into a balanced composition for a quilt. *Maybe my talent came from Mama.*

A soft knock sounded at the door. "Rachel? Aunt Lizzie doesn't want to be late."

Oh dear. She'd lost track of the time.

When Rachel opened the door, Anna's eyes opened wide. "You look pretty."

"Thank you." Rachel grabbed her beaded bag and nodded toward the stairs. "Let's go." Aunt Lizzie was waiting by the front door. One look at her simple calico dress and bonnet, and Rachel realized she was overdressed. She paused halfway down the stairs. "I should have asked what to wear." She dropped Anna's hand and prepared to retreat. "I'll change."

"Don't," Aunt Lizzie said. "We're already late." She opened the door and waved Rachel and Anna out onto the porch. Once outside, she took Anna's hand and led the way down the steps and toward the street.

Rachel glanced back toward the house. "What about Aunt Jennie?"

"Jennie doesn't quilt. She's trying a new bread recipe and tending the baby."

Aunt Lizzie kept walking. Rachel hurried to catch up and they walked in silence. From the row of farm wagons and buggies hitched in front of Berkeys', Rachel assumed a full complement of quilters had already gathered. She took a deep breath in a vain attempt to calm her nerves.

Aunt Lizzie pointed toward the Berkeys' and smiled down at Anna. "Someone's watching for you."

Rachel looked ahead. Blond hair and a pair of blue eyes were barely visible above the top of the picket fence bordering the Berkeys' front lawn.

"May I?" Anna asked.

Aunt Lizzie released her hand. "You may."

Anna tore off like a runaway filly.

Aunt Lizzie answered Rachel's unspoken question. "Ezra Dahl. Younger brother to the boy who delivered your freight yesterday. A 'little surprise' to his mother. You'd likely think her Ezra's grandmother if you didn't know."

The children disappeared around the side of the house and Aunt Lizzie opened the gate. Rachel could hear the buzz of conversation wafting through a window that opened onto the front porch. She apologized. "I'm sorry I made you late."

"You're forgiven. Just don't make it a habit."

The moment Rachel stepped through the Berkeys' front door, conversation stopped. If Aunt Lizzie hadn't been right behind her, she would have taken a step back. Instead, she stammered an apology for making Aunt Lizzie late.

Nel Berkey rushed in—from the kitchen, Rachel assumed. "Oh my goodness," she gushed and made a show of inspecting the nosegay of silk ribbon flowers arranged around the crown of Rachel's broad-brimmed hat. "That's the most beautiful hat I've ever seen." She looped her arm through Rachel's, drew her into the room, and waved Rachel toward an empty chair. "Let me introduce everyone."

Rachel perched on the edge of the oak chair, clasping her beaded bag in her gloved hands and nodding at each woman Nel introduced. Other than Mrs. Berkey and Mrs. Dahl, little Ezra's mother, she despaired of ever remembering names, in spite of the little trick she'd learned from Mama long ago. Mrs. *Black* always carried a *black* *b*eaded *b*ag. Mrs. *Graystone* lived next door to a gray stone house. Robert *Grainger* was thin as a stalk of grain. But by the time Nel had pronounced the eighth name, Rachel had already forgotten the first.

In the momentary lull after introductions, Rachel sat looking down at her beaded bag and feeling ridiculous for wearing her most stylish ensemble to a gathering of women dressed in simple cotton day dresses. They probably thought the girl from the big city was uppity.

"You look like you just stepped out of the latest *Harper's Bazaar*," Mrs. Dahl said. She chuckled. "My George would give anything if I'd dress up on occasion. Then again, I'd give anything if he'd knock the mud off his shoes before he comes into my kitchen."

Soft laughter circled the room. Conversation ebbed and flowed, eventually landing on the topic of "poor Adam Friesen all alone out there on the farm."

"Does anyone know who's taking care of Esther's chickens?" one woman asked. "She always took such pride in that flock. Not in a sinful selfish way, mind you. But in the way that she'd brought them up herself and weren't they the best layers hereabouts."

As the women talked, Rachel deposited the beaded bag beneath her chair and began to thread a needle. Aunt Lizzie handed her a thimble. She put it on the middle finger of her right hand then hesitated, watching the other ladies quilt. One pushed the needle with the underside of her thumbnail. Another used the tip of a thimble, inserting the needle so it was perpendicular to the fabric and then, in a rocking motion, feeding stitches onto the needle before drawing the thread through the fabric. Nel used the side of her thimble and only took a couple of stitches at a time. Rachel decided to try that and hoped no one would realize she was a novice. She knew the basics, but once she'd learned to draw and paint, she'd had little interest in needlework.

"Look at those tiny stitches," Nel said, and nudged Rachel with her shoulder.

Rachel shrugged. "I didn't know if I'd remember how."

"It appears you do," Aunt Lizzie said with a smile.

The woman sitting next to Mrs. Dahl spoke up. "I was so sorry to hear about your recent loss, my dear."

Another said, "We've been praying the Lord would give you comfort. And make the journey here an easy one."

Rachel croaked her thanks. A wave of homesickness washed over her. She blinked tears away and concentrated on her stitching.

"It's good to have someone Nel's age join us," another woman said. "You'll meet more young people on Sunday. In fact"—she looked around the room at the others—"why don't we have a welcome picnic after church Sunday?"

Aunt Lizzie spoke immediately. "Jennie and I will host."

While the ladies planned, Rachel concentrated on stitching along the chalked line marching across the surface of the dark blue fabric. Friendly conversation and no small amount of good-natured teasing filled the room with a cloud of friendship and fellowship.

And the knot in Rachel's midsection relaxed.

Adam Friesen pulled out of the cemetery and headed for town, bent on fetching a load of lumber from the sawmill to continue working on pews for the new church. The promise to do the work hadn't saved Esther, but a promise was a promise. Besides that, the work kept his mind off all the things that were wrong in his world. He was nearly past the train depot when Wyatt Dahl flagged him down.

"You going to the Meekers' today?"

Adam shook his head. "Wasn't planning on it. Anna's with Aunt Lizzie at the Berkeys' quilting. I'll stop there to see her on my way out of town."

Dahl grimaced. "Miss Ellsworth's crate came on this morning's train. Aunt Lizzie asked me to check on it, but—I was hoping you'd take it over. When Pa learned I wasn't working for you today, he wanted me to see to the shoeing of one of the teams. He's not much for waiting once his mind's set on a thing." He shrugged. "No matter. I'll see to it."

Adam grunted softly. To say Wyatt's father "wasn't much for waiting" was a mild way to put it. "I'll do it," Adam said. The relief on Wyatt's face made him glad he'd set aside his own plans. He reined the farm wagon close to the railway loading dock. When he prepared to jump down to help, Wyatt waved him off.

"I can bring it out," he said. "I could almost carry it to the house. Almost." He retreated into the depot. When he returned, he was lugging a small crate, which he eased into place behind Adam's wagon seat. Adam shrugged out of his lightweight coat and draped it over the crate, lest dust sift inside. He spoke to the team and reined them about in the direction of the quilting bee. It was near on to noon. The ladies would be taking their lunch break, and his stomach was rumbling.

Ouch. Rachel pulled her left hand from beneath the quilt and inspected her middle finger. A morning's worth of miniscule pinpricks had taken its toll, and that last overzealous prick had drawn blood. Rachel looked over at Nel who glanced at the tiny drop of red.

Leaving her own needle in place atop the quilt, Nel rose. "I'm volunteering Rachel and me to get the food out for luncheon."

In the small kitchen, Nel pulled a stack of plates off a shelf while Rachel lifted away the napkins covering the contents of several baskets lined up on the kitchen table. A shout of joy in the backyard called her attention to Anna who was dashing toward a wagon pulling up to the back fence. "Looks like Anna's papa."

Nel peered through the kitchen window before snatching up a plate. "I bet Adam hasn't had a decent meal all day." She loaded the plate with food and hurried out the back door.

Rachel prepared plates for Anna and Ezra. Balancing a plate on each open hand, she backed her way through the screen door and out onto the porch. She hadn't expected a large dog to be sprawled just outside the door. With a loud "whoops!" she staggered, almost saved the plates and then failed. Both plates landed with a clatter, and the dog began to gobble food. Rachel ducked back inside for a broom, just as Aunt Lizzie and Mrs. Berkey hurried into the kitchen.

Rachel hurried to explain. "Nel took lunch to Anna's papa. I was taking food for Anna and Ezra. I didn't know there was a dog. I stumbled." She looked past Aunt Lizzie to Nel's mother. "I'm so sorry. I—I'll clean it up. Where's the broom, please? I feel terrible. The plates are in pieces."

"Goodness, child," Mrs. Berkey said. "It was an accident." As the quilters filtered into the kitchen to fill their plates and then moved into the dining room to eat, Mrs. Berkey produced a broom and dustpan. She chuckled as she glanced toward the back porch. "Give Buster a few more seconds and he'll have most of it cleaned up for you."

Broom in hand, Rachel went back outside. Aunt Lizzie followed with more food for the children. When Mr. Friesen caught sight of Rachel he left Nel with the children and crossed the lawn to the porch. "Wyatt Dahl loaded your crate into the back of my wagon just now. I'll be taking it on to the house after Anna and I have some lunch."

"Oh, thank you!" Rachel set the broom down and hurried to peer over the fence, surprised to see a coat draped over the crate.

Mr. Friesen went through the gate and climbed into the wagon bed. "I'd have had a packing blanket if I'd known I would be hauling precious cargo." Smiling, he lifted the coat. "See? None the worse for the delay."

Rachel nodded. "Thank you for taking extra care."

They walked back to the picnic table together, with Friesen sitting down beside Anna and Rachel continuing on to the house. Nel lingered at the table, but then Mrs. Berkey called for her. Rachel finished sweeping up and went back inside, where Nel was busy slicing pie.

"Cherry is Adam's favorite," she said, sliding a huge slice onto a pie plate. She'd headed for the door when her mother stopped her.

"Let me do that. You pour coffee for the ladies." She turned to Rachel. "Would you mind bringing dessert to the children?"

"Happy to," Rachel said.

"But—" Nel protested.

Mrs. Berkey cocked an eyebrow.

"Fine." Nel handed the plate over and spun away. She lifted the coffeepot off the stove and began pouring coffee with such energy it sloshed over the rims of more than one cup.

What'd I do? Why's she so upset? Rachel cut two small slices of pie for the children. "I'm sorry, Nel. I didn't mean—"

"Oh, it's all right," Nel said. "It's not your fault. Mother's just being...Mother." She sighed. "She thinks I was flirting. Goodness, I know better than that. It's only been four months. It's far too soon for Adam to be thinking of anyone else." She took a deep breath. "I was just offering to help with Esther's chickens. To find someone willing to take them until things get back to normal." She finished pouring coffee, muttering as she worked to mop up the spills. "It's not like he needs the eggs, all alone out there on the farm."

Rachel said nothing. Nel might not have been flirting, but there was something about the way she'd sprung to action when the man drove up, something about the way she said the name

Adam. And did she really think his life would get "back to normal"? *Normal* didn't exist for a widower with two children. It probably never would—*unless. Ah.* So that was it. Nel wanted to help Adam Friesen find a new *normal.*

Rachel took the pie to the children. She saw Adam Friesen with new eyes. A girl could do much worse than the broad-shouldered, russet-haired farmer whose hazel eyes sparkled when he teased his daughter. Whose strong hands revealed a man who knew the meaning of hard work.

And Anna adored her papa. There was something very attractive about a man who took time for his children.

As Rachel returned to the house, she smiled to herself. How wonderful it would be one day to see her own daughter fly into Landis's arms. They were both looking forward to having children. In fact, they'd discussed the matter extensively. They hoped to wait a few years before starting a family. After all, Landis needed time to settle into his position at the bank—but once they were ready, they would have three children. Hopefully at least one boy. Landis would be a good father. Rachel was certain of it.

Chapter 4

Rachel had just finished her own lunch and taken her seat at the quilting frame across from Hazel Mitchell (of the hazel eyes)—when a screech and a thud, followed by a cry for *Mama* summoned Mrs. Dahl. But she didn't even go outside before calling, "It's Anna."

Aunt Lizzie was quick to respond, followed by Rachel and Nel. They found Anna sitting on the ground near the swing, staring down at a jagged cut as blood dripped onto her dress.

"Oh...my." Nel went pale and stopped in her tracks.

Aunt Lizzie knelt to inspect the cut. "We need to take her inside."

Rachel scooped up the child, and they all hurried into the house. Rachel sat at the kitchen table with Anna in her lap. Finally, she convinced the child to move the hand she'd clamped over the wound so Aunt Lizzie could see it. It was a nasty cut. Mrs. Berkey retrieved some muslin, and she and Aunt Lizzie began to tear it into strips.

Nel's voice wavered. "Oh, that's awful. I'll get the doctor. And find Adam."

Aunt Lizzie shook her head. "Jennie can see to the cut. There's absolutely no need to bother Adam." Her voice softened as she said to Anna, "At least not until you have an impressive bandage to show him. You'll want to tell him how brave you were." She smiled. "Did you know that Aunt Jennie gives a special treat to brave little girls?"

Anna swiped at the tears spilling down her cheeks. "Wh-what is it?"

"All in due time, little one," Aunt Lizzie said. She cleansed the wound and wrapped Anna's thin forearm.

"It's too tight," Anna whimpered.

"It has to be tight for now," Rachel said.

"That will help it stop bleeding," Nel explained from across the room. "And it'll be quite all right once Aunt Jennie sews it up."

"She-she's gonna sew my arm?" Anna began to cry again. "She'll poke me. It'll hurt."

Rachel unbuttoned the cuff of her left sleeve and pulled it away from her wrist. "Look here," she said and pointed to a small scar. "When I was just your age, I was trying to climb a tree. I fell and this is where the doctor stitched me up. Once yours heals, we'll match."

"I wasn't trying to climb," Anna sniffed. "I fell off the swing and bumped the table."

"I knew that table was too close to the swing," Nel muttered. "I should have asked Adam to help me move it when he was here."

Anna traced the scar. "They sewed you up?"

"They did."

"Did it hurt?"

Rachel hesitated. "It did. But only for a little while." She paused. "And then I got three pieces of my favorite candy and when I went to bed that night, and my mama read to me until I fell asleep."

Anna said nothing for a moment and then asked, "It only hurt a little while?"

Rachel nodded.

"Can I sit in your lap when Aunt Jennie sews it?"

"Absolutely."

Anna spoke to Aunt Lizzie. "And if I'm brave I get a special treat."

Aunt Lizzie nodded.

Anna looked back at Rachel. "And you'll read me a story until I fall asleep?"

"I will. In fact, I brought a book of children's stories with me. I'll find it before bedtime so I can read you my favorite."

"And now we should take our leave," Aunt Lizzie said.

One of the quilters called from the doorway. "I've got us all packed up. I'll drive you. It will be my joy to help."

Joy. Rachel remembered. The woman's name was Etta Joy. Hazel Mitchell had hazel eyes. Mrs. Dahl was Ezra's mother. Of the eight women who'd come to quilting today, Rachel had only three more names to learn.

With Miss Ellsworth's crate beside him on the wagon seat and his wagon bed filled with newly sawn lumber, Adam Friesen pulled his team up to the Meekers' well, intent on watering the team before going inside. He expected Anna to hear his arrival and trip down the back stairs and to the well. When she didn't materialize, he wondered if quilting might have gone longer than expected. He could hear the baby crying—loudly. The child had strong lungs. Thanks be to God—and the Meeker sisters.

By the time Adam's second gray finished drinking, the baby had quieted. But there was still no sign of Anna. He set the bucket down and headed for the back door. When he knocked, Aunt Lizzie admitted him to a scene that wrenched his heart: Anna, her left forearm bandaged, sitting on Miss Ellsworth's lap at a table that had obviously been used to sew up a wound.

When she saw Adam, Anna held up a bandaged arm and blubbered her way through the telling of a fall and bleeding and stitches. "But I get a treat and a bedtime story," she sniffed, " 'cause I was brave." She looked up at Miss Ellsworth. "Wasn't I brave?"

"Very." Miss Ellsworth hugged her.

Aunt Jennie spoke up. "I'd have sent for you right away if it had been any more serious, but it only took a couple of stitches."

"And I was brave," Anna repeated.

Adam chucked her beneath the chin. "Can you be brave a while longer while Papa brings in Miss Ellsworth's crate?"

Anna nodded.

Miss Ellsworth looked down at her. "Is it all right if I help your papa?"

"You can help me set out some cookies," Aunt Jennie said. "If your arm doesn't hurt too much."

"It's better." Anna hopped down.

Back at the wagon, Adam maneuvered the crate to the edge of the wagon seat. "It isn't heavy," he said. "Just awkward." Miss Ellsworth steadied the crate while Adam balanced it on his shoulder. She held the door open while he carried it inside. All evidence of Aunt Jennie's doctoring had disappeared, and Anna was setting a plate of cookies on the table.

"We're making coffee," she said, in her best imitation of a grown-up voice.

Adam was heading toward the hallway to take the crate upstairs, when Aunt Lizzie spoke up. "If you don't mind, Rachel, Jennie and I would love to see your paintings."

Miss Ellsworth said she'd love that too, and so Adam set it down. Aunt Lizzie opened a drawer and produced two screwdrivers and a hammer. Aunt Jennie thrust the baby into Adam's arms.

The baby's blue eyes were wide open, and as he stared at Adam's face, his russet brows drew together. Thinking he was about to cry, Adam said, "It's all right, little one. Papa is here." When he caressed the tiny hand, the baby clutched his index finger. Adam wondered anew at the perfection of the round cheeks and dimpled chin. So taken was he with his boy, he didn't look away until he heard Aunt Jennie exclaim over one of the paintings.

"My dear, I had no idea you were so gifted."

"It's—" Aunt Lizzie paused, as if searching for a word. "It's marvelous. How did you ever manage to capture the light so perfectly? A magnificent sunrise in all its glory."

Adam looked up at the painting. *Magnificent* was a good word for it.

"I painted it for Papa," Miss Ellsworth said. "After Mama died. We were both so ... " Her voice wavered. "We were struggling." She cleared her throat. "Papa took to reading the Bible aloud at the breakfast table every morning. He started with Psalm 139—about the day of death being decided before birth. That reminded us that God had never lost sight of Mama." She stared at the painting. "And he loved the book of Job. He said it was all right to tell God we didn't understand why Mama had to die. After all, God said Job was a blameless man, and Job asked plenty of questions. Which God didn't really answer. Still, one of the things God did say inspired this painting." She quoted from the Bible. "'Where wast thou when I laid the foundations of the earth.... Hast thou commanded the morning...?'" She shrugged. "I painted a sunrise to remind Papa—and me—that God commands the dawn and everything else. I love thinking about Mama there, just on the other side of that beautiful sky. Waiting." She choked out the words, "And now Papa's there too." She set the painting down abruptly and fled out of the kitchen, up the stairs, and to her room.

Rachel stayed in her room until she heard the back door slam shut in the wake of Adam Friesen's departure. After she'd dried her eyes, she went through her trunk of books and found the storybook she'd mentioned to Anna. Finally, she descended the stairs and rejoined her aunts and the children in the kitchen. The baby was sleeping soundly in the coffee-crate-turned-cradle nestled in one corner near the stove. Anna was struggling to change the dress on a china-headed doll while the aunts washed supper dishes.

"Thank you for understanding my not wanting to come down for supper," Rachel said. Aunt Jennie had knocked softly once and retreated when Rachel pleaded for some time alone. She laid the book on the table and spoke to Anna. "Would you like some help with that?" Anna handed the doll over. Rachel admired its curly blond hair and painted blue eyes as she worked. "She's very pretty."

"Aunt Lizzie gave her to me to play with. Long as Papa can't have me at home. And after that, I'll still be able to come play with her. Whenever I want. Even if I'm grown up."

Rachel finished changing the doll's dress. Laying her aside, she reached for the book. "There's a story in here about a little girl and her doll. Shall we read that one when it's bedtime?"

"You remembered!"

Rachel nodded. She turned to look at the shipping crate and its contents, still sitting where she'd left them. Setting the book down, she rose and went first to the paintings. The dawn portrait was leaning against the still life, obscuring it.

"If you'd like, we can hang them in your room," Aunt Lizzie offered. "Unless they bring more sorrow than comfort."

"I'd like to hang them. Very much."

Aunt Lizzie inspected the still life. "This is excellent composition. The way you've set the goblet off to the side. Things are balanced but not overly so."

"You know...art?"

Aunt Lizzie shrugged. "Enough to be a bit of a snob about it."

"A *bit* of a snob?" Aunt Jennie chided, albeit with humor in her voice.

Aunt Lizzie explained. "Before we came west, our father was friends with some of the artists who eventually became part of the Hudson River School. Do you know it?"

"Know it?" Rachel exclaimed. "I adore their work!"

"Follow me," Aunt Lizzie said.

Moments later, Rachel gasped with delight when she saw the three oils hanging in Aunt Lizzie's room.

"Thomas Cole," Aunt Lizzie said, pointing at the first before moving on. "Edward Church. And that one's only a study, so it's not signed. But I do love it."

"I never would have expected—" Rachel broke off.

"To find *real* art in Lost Creek?" Aunt Lizzie chuckled. "Your pieces are very good. I hope you get to continue your studies."

"Landis promised that I could." As she and Aunt Lizzie went back downstairs, Rachel described the wedding trip she and Landis would take. "He understands how important my painting is to me. His father's banking interests often take the Groves abroad, and Landis is expected to follow in his father's footsteps. I may even get the chance to take some lessons in Paris."

The moment they returned to the kitchen, Anna demanded the promised story.

"As soon as I get my mess out of the way," Rachel said. She lifted the disassembled easel out of the crate before sweeping up packing straw and replacing the lid. Next, with her aunts' help, she carried the easel and paintings up to her room. Anna stayed behind, leafing carefully through Rachel's storybook, entranced by the color illustrations.

"It's good your two pieces are already framed and ready to hang," Aunt Lizzie said.

"You don't need to go to the trouble," Rachel said. "I can just set up the easel and use it for display." She looked doubtfully at the little space left after her three trunks had been lined up against one wall. "I'd like to store the shipping crate, though—in the barn, I suppose."

Aunt Lizzie shook her head. "Not in the barn. We'll ask Adam to take it up to the attic next time he's here.

Every morning began the same way. In the seconds after Adam woke, it was as if the past few months hadn't happened. And then he remembered. He always sat up abruptly and nearly jumped out of bed, trying to ward off the pain. He dressed in the dark and hurried outside to the well to splash water in his face and get a drink before heading for the barn, where the sweet aroma of hay and warm animals helped him battle the yawning hole in his life.

Most mornings, he pretended the children were at the house with their mother. Sometimes he even caught himself listening for Esther to call him to breakfast.

Today was different, though. Instead of fleeing the house like a frightened colt running from a storm, Adam stood peering into the small bedroom where his children should be sleeping. He closed his eyes, listening to the silence. *I have to bring them home. Somehow.* He looked up. *You command the dawn. Can You not help me to find a way to bring my children home ?*

For the first time in a while, Adam wished either his parents or Esther's were still in Lost Creek. Their relationship hadn't been a good one, but surely the arrival of grandchildren would have helped cross the divide. Esther's had moved farther west and Adam's parents lay at rest in the same cemetery as Esther. The only family left in Lost Creek was Molly, Adam's older sister.

She'd offered to raise them as her own, bless her. But Molly and Walter Bingham already had six children. Adam could not bear the thought of Anna and her brother being taken in out of duty—and eventually becoming a burden, which they surely would be to an already overworked mother. No, Adam thought. He must bring his children home and raise them up as a father should.

Fresh sorrow sent a pang through him. He'd had enough of sobbing, and so he raked his fingers through his hair and went out into the predawn light. He went first to Esther's chickens. As he opened the coop and then began to scatter grain for the emerging hens, he thought on Nel Berkey's suggestion yesterday that he let her arrange to "board them out." Nel meant well, of course. She could not know that Adam needed Esther's chickens right where they were, clucking and pecking at him when he gathered eggs. They connected him to the way life should be.

I've been thinking, Adam, Nel had said as she handed him a plate mounded high with food, *thinking of how I might help you and the children*. She hemmed and hawed for a moment before bringing up the notion of his giving up Esther's chickens. She'd even offered to drive out to the farm and tend them a few mornings a week—if it would help, she said. With Anna along, of course. And therein lay the seed of an idea.

Adam looked toward the east where the sun was just now beginning to peer over the horizon. Was it possible God would answer his prayer so quickly? Nel Berkey was willing to drive out to the farm. What if others could? It would be asking too much of Molly, of course, with all the children already hanging on to her apron strings. But Aunt Lizzie might do it. And what if Wyatt could bring Ezra with him one morning. Ezra, Anna, and Wyatt could see to the planting of the garden. Wyatt might be glad for an excuse to work out here more often. If he'd agree to take the gardening on for a share of the produce—old man

Dahl might even like that idea. So. Nel Berkey, Aunt Lizzie, and Wyatt. If each of them could bring Anna to the farm one morning a week, she would know the farm was still home. That could be the beginning of mending the canyon that ripped through their lives when Esther died.

Adam hurried to finish morning chores, finishing by picking a small bunch of Esther's daffodils to take to the cemetery on his way to town. By the time Wyatt arrived, he was waiting, the buggy hitched. He shared his idea, and Wyatt responded with enthusiasm, "I'd love to bring Ezra out here. It's something we could do together."

"You'll be doing me a favor."

"Maybe. But you're returning it, giving me an excuse to avoid Pa. He might even like the idea when he hears you'll pay in produce."

Adam talked to the Almighty all the way to the cemetery. When he nestled the daffodils against the gravestone, he realized something felt different. He still didn't understand why God had allowed Esther to die, but he felt less rage. More...something. Not exactly acceptance. He didn't want to accept life without Esther. And yet he realized that he needed to do just that—God willing, without bitterness. After all, not once in all his life had Adam Michael Friesen commanded the dawn.

Chapter 5

Rachel woke and lay still for a few minutes, listening to the steady drum of rain on the roof of the little porch off her room. Last evening, she'd left the door to the porch open to let the June breeze waft into her room while she reread Landis's letters. He'd kept his promise to write often—for a while. From April and all through May, Rachel received a letter almost every other day—and answered it immediately.

She described her room and how the aunts had helped to hang her paintings. She spoke of Aunt Lizzie's knowledge of the Hudson River School and Aunt Jennie's skill as a midwife. She recounted amusing little stories about Anna and a prank Ezra Dahl had played on the quilters, sneaking into the house while they picnicked outside and sprinkling flour over one corner of the quilt to obscure the chalked quilting design.

> *That earned him a spanking from his mother; even though I found it a simple task to brush the flour off and redraw the feathered design. You would have thought I'd sketched the Mona Lisa. At the end of the day, Nel recruited me to help her with a quilt she's planning for her hope chest.*

She told Landis about the children staying with the aunts and how they had wheedled a place into her heart.

*I didn't realize how much I would miss teaching the children's
Sunday school class at home. It makes me especially grateful for
the two little people residing beneath the Meeker roof. I do what
I can to help their days pass happily—poor little motherless
things.*

She described how the deceased Mrs. Friesen's friends had
banded together to take Anna to the farm several mornings a
week. It enabled Anna to feed her mother's chickens and gather
eggs. The child had even planted the garden with Wyatt Dahl,
Mr. Friesen's farmhand.

*I've gone with Aunt Lizzie and Anna a couple of times. It's a
short and pleasant drive into the countryside. The Friesen place
isn't anything like the impressive estate your father purchased
last year, and yet there is something about it that says home—
something that resonates deep within my heart and inspires day-
dreams of our future together.*

In one of his May letters, Landis wrote that he was proud
of her for making the best of the situation. He spoke of the new
minister who had none of Reverend Ellsworth's oratorical skill.
Even so, the church was enjoying a growth spurt with the arrival
of three families attached to Washington University. Rachel
would be pleased to know that two of the professors' families
included people Landis and Rachel's age. They'd added a lively
element to the annual spring picnic. Rachel would like them.

Rachel responded to each letter the day she received it.
When the frequency of Landis's missives waned, she did her best
not to complain. She said she missed hearing from him when
he couldn't write, but she understood. He was busy learning at
his father's side—an investment of time that would bear fruit for
their future together. Keeping busy here in Lost Creek helped

the time pass. They had only six more months to wait. She would be home for Christmas.

Rachel did not write about her dreams of a Christmas marriage proposal, although she expected Landis was even now making plans for it. At least she hoped he was. She'd offered enough hints. Often in the evenings after she slipped beneath the quilts, she held her left hand up, envisioning the ring Landis would place on her finger. She imagined standing in the glow of the fireplace in the private family parlor, the scent of the evergreen boughs adorning the mantle, the comforting warmth kindled by a cup of eggnog. Would he have hidden the ring box among the packages beneath the tree—or might he have kept it in his pocket for weeks, wanting to keep it near while she was far away? Either way, when Landis guided her around the dance floor at his parents' annual Christmas ball, an engagement ring would adorn her finger. It would make future Christmases pale by comparison. *The Christmas of our engagement.*

But an entire week had just passed without a letter from home, and as she lay in bed listening to the rain, Rachel could not shake the sense of foreboding. Rereading all those letters hadn't helped one bit. If nothing, she was more worried than ever. Landis must be ill. If there was no letter today, she would ask the aunts if she might send a telegram.

The storm raged. Rain poured. Thunder rolled. When a flash of lightning chased across the sky, Anna bolted into Rachel's room. She clutched the edge of the bed as she said, "Aunt Lizzie's already downstairs. She said she wouldn't let a little rain stop us from going to see Papa. She said not to be worried." The child cringed when thunder sounded again. "But that's *loud.*"

Rachel held up the covers. Anna dove into the bed and Rachel pulled her close. "My mama used to tell me that loud thunder was the angels marching in heaven."

Another rumble. Anna looked over the edge of the quilt toward the porch. "That's lots of marching."

Rachel chuckled. "It is, but it's nothing to fear." She slipped away from Anna and put a pillow in her place. "Hug the pillow if you feel afraid again. I won't leave the room, but I do need to get dressed. I'm meeting Nel at the mercantile today to help her plan a quilt."

Anna clutched the pillow and ducked back beneath the covers. Rachel moved quickly to dress. By the time she'd wound her long hair into a bun at the back of her head, the storm had abated. She had the telegram wording planned. She'd retrieve the mail while at the mercantile with Nel, and if there was no letter from St. Louis...

Anna pulled the covers down just enough to watch as Rachel gathered Landis's letters and tied them together with a bit of ribbon. "Are those Landy's letters?"

"It's Landis, and yes, these are from him."

"Papa says people in heaven don't get to write. We just got to know they love us without any letters."

Rachel set the letters in the top tray of an open trunk. "He's absolutely right," she said and went to the bedside and sat down. "They can't write letters, but they still love us. And someday, we'll see them again."

"When we go to heaven. They can't come back here. They're in heaven with Jesus forever. Papa said so."

Rachel nodded.

"I wish Mama could come back for a visit."

"Sometimes I wish for the same thing."

Anna sat up. "I got a quilt Mama made. But Brother doesn't. Mama went to heaven before it got finished. If she could come visit, I bet she'd finish it."

Poor child. "Maybe we can ask Aunt Lizzie to bring it back to town with her after you visit today. If your papa doesn't mind.

I'm certain the quilting ladies would love to finish it for the baby."

Anna hopped out of bed. "I bet the pieces are still in Mama's sewing basket. I better get dressed so we can fetch it!" She skittered out of the room and across the hall.

From her bedroom doorway, Rachel saw a nightgown flutter to the floor. When thunder rolled again, Anna shot back out of Aunt Lizzie's room. She'd managed to pull her dress on and was clutching shoes and stockings to her body. "Marching," she said to Rachel as she stepped across the landing and onto the top stair. "Marching. Marching. Marching." She was halfway down when lightning flashed. She flinched but kept going.

The rain stopped, Aunt Lizzie and Anna drove off to the farm, and Rachel picked her way through the puddles to the mercantile. The train hadn't pulled in yet, so the matter of a letter from Landis would have to wait. Rachel was thinking how sweet Anna would look in a dress made from the double pink calico when Nel stepped through the door.

"You'd think the mills would know there's enough double pink calico in the world," Nel groused.

"It'd make a darling new dress for Anna."

"I wasn't aware Anna needed new clothes." Nel sighed. "I do wish Adam would have said something. I've told him and told him I'll help in any way I can."

"It may not be a need. But it'd be something nice to do for her. Or with her, if she catches on easily."

"You're going to teach a four-year-old to sew?"

"Maybe. This morning Anna mentioned a baby quilt her mother didn't finish. Aunt Lizzie's going to see about bringing it back with them today. Anna's excited about helping finish it."

157

"I remember it, and believe me, Anna won't be helping. It's a sunburst with a ridiculous number of pieces in each block." Nel paused. "You should just give it to me. I'll finish the piecing, and the quilters can take on the quilting as a group—maybe as a surprise for Adam, if Anna hasn't already ruined that idea."

Rachel directed the conversation away from the Friesens and back to the reason she'd come to the mercantile in the first place. "That pink I was admiring is part of a new shipment Mr. Sutter just got in. The latest colors, he says."

Nel scanned the bolts of cloth, frowning. "I'm so tired of brown and pink. And that green makes me positively dyspeptic." She reached into her bag, drew out a piece of paper, unfolded it, and handed it over. Nine blocks featured appliquéd hearts created with a narrow band of cloth, as if the strip were a broad line of ink. Each heart was dotted with red berries—or perhaps cherries, from the size—and green leaves. Alternating blocks between the hearts featured a wreath of appliquéd leaves. And more tiny red circles.

Rachel gasped with admiration. "I had no idea you could design quilts. This is stunning."

"Oh, I didn't design it. I just copied a quilt like it that was on display at the county fair a few years ago. I've never forgotten it." Nel smiled. "With all those hearts, it's a perfect wedding quilt."

Rachel teased, "I hope you're not already secretly engaged, because this is going to take a very long time to make. Even with help."

"I have time. At least I think it'll be a while." Her cheeks reddened.

Rachel looked around to make sure no one was within earshot before asking, "Anyone I know?"

The blush deepened. Nel tapped the edge of the paper. "I want it to be a masterpiece."

"It will be. All those tiny circles…" Rachel counted the dots around the heart. "Fifty-eight to a block and nine blocks—plus more for the wreaths? That's—a lot of tiny circles." Rachel looked up from the drawing. "Are you sure you want to take it on?"

"Positive. I can do the appliqué, but I'm no artist. And the shapes have to be just right. Do you think you could draw a pattern? And can you think of something that would make it unique?"

Rachel studied the sketch. "Those hearts and wreaths and berries really should be red and green. I don't think you'd be happy with another color. It wouldn't seem right." She looked past Nel to the fabric again. "However—"

"However?" Nel followed Rachel's gaze to the bolts of cloth.

"The original quilt you admired. Was the appliqué on a white ground?"

"Of course. Just like every other red and green quilt I've ever seen."

Rachel moved down the shelves of fabric and ran her palm across a vibrant orange. "Mr. Sutter said they're calling this *cheddar*. Or *California gold*. Using this for the ground instead of white or muslin would certainly make it unique."

Nel frowned. "An entire quilt out of that? Are you sure?"

Rachel pulled the bolt of gold cloth out and set it on the counter then added a rich green and a Turkey red. Taking a pencil in hand, she sketched a swag border. "Red swags with green sprouts here, at the place where the swags join. That would provide a vibrant frame to the blocks—an element the original didn't have."

"*Vibrant.* I suppose that's one word for it." Nel cocked her head to one side and studied the fabrics Rachel had selected. "I don't know. It's…loud."

"Cheerful," Rachel corrected. "Bold. Artistic, even."

"I'm not sure *artistic* would appeal to Ad—" Nel stopped abruptly. "To someone from Lost Creek. Not that there's anything wrong with artistic. *Your* young man would probably love it."

Rachel smiled. "*My* young man thinks quilts are unhealthful. Or at least his mother does. She actually quoted something out of a magazine on the topic not long ago. An article that touted new blankets over 'old-fashioned, outdated quilts.'"

Nel made a face. "I'd wager—if it weren't a sin to gamble—she's never attended a quilting bee. If she had, she'd know they're about a lot more than quilts."

Rachel laughed. "You don't need to wager. Mrs. Grove wouldn't be caught dead with a needle and thread in hand. She has servants for that kind of thing." She stopped abruptly. "I'm making her sound horrible. She's not. She's just...not like the ladies here." She patted the bolt of orange cloth and changed the subject back to Nel's project. "Buy enough to make a sample block. See what you think."

Nel shook her head. "If I'm going to do it, I'd better buy enough for the whole thing. Ida Joy ran into trouble last year when she did a sample block and by the time she got back to the mercantile, an entire bolt of blue was gone." She pondered the fabric. "Are you sure I'll like it?"

"I'm sure *I'd* like it," Rachel said. "But I'm not the one who's going to live with it." She handed the drawing back to Nel. "Think about it for a couple of days. If you want to come back to the house with me, I can draw up the pattern for the blocks. At least we'll get that accomplished."

Nel agreed and tucked the drawing in her bag just as Wyatt Dahl stepped into the store, the mailbag perched on his shoulder. Rachel tried—and failed—to be patient while Mr. Sutter sorted mail and Nel struck up a conversation with Wyatt about Adam's plans for the farm and how good it was of Wyatt to agree to managing the garden.

Finally, the kindly storekeeper/postmaster handed Rachel a small stack of mail, atop which rested an envelope from St. Louis. But it wasn't from Landis. Rachel recognized the flowery script at once.

Mrs. Grove.

Chapter 6

*N*el broke off her conversation with Wyatt and hurried over. "What is it? You're white as a sheet." Grasping Rachel by the arm, she pulled her behind the counter and toward a tall stool. "Sit. Breathe. Shall I get you some water?" Rachel shook her head. "It's just—Landis hasn't written for some time. I've tried not to worry, but—" She pointed to the flowing script. "This is from his mother." She blinked away gathering tears. "If Mrs. Grove is writing, something's happened." She turned the envelope over, but Nel stayed her hand.

"You should wait to read it. Until you get home."

Home. If Landis was ill, she must go home. There would be so much to do. Her heart raced just thinking of it. "I can't wait. I have to know." She reached for Nel's hand and gave it a squeeze. "But—stay?"

"Of course."

Trembling, Rachel opened the envelope.

June 19, 1890
St. Louis, Missouri

Dearest Rachel,

Do you remember that day in Mr. Carpenter's office when we agreed that the earth spins and we must continue to spin with it, even when it brings us sorrow? You were so brave, sitting in that opulent office hearing such terrible news. I admired you then and I know that should I see you in the future, I would have opportunity to admire you yet again. You are stronger than you know. We all saw it during the aftermath of your mother's passing and again when our dear Reverend Ellsworth passed on. You must be strong now. And brave.

The knot in Rachel's stomach grew. This was bad. Very bad. What if Landis—*no. Don't jump to conclusions.* She kept reading.

It is one of the burdens of motherhood to accept the task of sparing their children pain. We do it out of love. I hope that one day you will believe that love is the reason I have taken on this task. I want to spare Landis—and you—more pain than is necessary; Landis, so that he doesn't have to write words that wound one he has loved, and you, because hearing our news from me instead of Landis will hopefully cushion the blow.

At a soiree we hosted at Mr. Grove's social club last evening, Landis and Miss Daisy Marcom announced their engagement.

Rachel gave a soft cry of disbelief. Nel put a hand on her arm. Rachel reread the last sentence. Landis...engaged? Who was Miss Daisy Marcom? Rachel read on.

Daisy is the daughter of a Washington University professor. The family are relatively new residents in St. Louis who joined the congregation of First Church not long after you departed the city.

Huh. Landis had written about newcomers to the church. "People our age," he'd said. Something about how they'd "livened up the spring picnic." *I'll just bet they did.* Rachel clenched her jaw. Anger welled up. She almost crumpled the letter. Instead, she took a deep breath and finished reading.

You must know that Landis was devoted to the plans the two of you had made until—well. Until God brought Daisy into his life.

God did that? Rachel snorted with disbelief.

We must all accept God's direction, even when it demands that we walk a path heretofore unknown. May He guide you through the sorrow this letter will undoubtedly bring. It has pained me greatly to write it.

Cherishing the good memories,
Wishing you the best,
Martha Grove

Wishing you the best. Rachel stared at the words in stunned silence for a moment before reading the post script.

I have personally seen to the packing of the paintings you left in our care. Rest assured that I have taken every precaution to see that they are well protected for the journey to Lost Creek. You may expect them to arrive at the depot within a couple of days of receiving this letter.

"What's happened?" Nel asked. "Are you going back? I can help you pack. If we hurry, you can meet the afternoon train. Tell me what to do."

"I'm not going anywhere," Rachel said. Blinking away her tears, she held the letter out. "Read it."

"Are you sure?"

Rachel nodded. Nel took it, and Rachel watched her friend's expression transform as she read. Concern. Confusion. Shock. Disbelief. And, finally, anger.

Finished reading, Nel held up the letter and practically hissed, "Who *is* this person?"

"Until recently, she was my future mother-in-law."

"*Was.* There's always something to be thankful for." Nel spit it out and then apologized. "I'm sorry. I shouldn't have said that." Again, she put her hand on Rachel's arm. "Let's walk. My house. Your house. Around town. Or I'll leave you alone. Just—tell me what you want."

Rachel stood on wobbly legs. "I don't—know." She stared down at the fabric still lying on the counter. *A masterpiece.* Nel wanted to make a masterpiece. Rachel pointed at the letter. "Put that in your bag." She reached for the other mail. "Let's go—" She shook her head and led the way out of the mercantile. She'd almost said, "Let's go *home.*" Would she ever have a home again?

Adam grunted with dismay as he set yet another mousetrap in the pantry. He'd been doing battle for over a week now and lost count of how many critters he'd carried out of the house. Had the varmints sent out some kind of announcement? *No one living at Friesens. Come party.*

With the trap set, he stood up, bumped a shelf, and upset a tin of something. It toppled off the shelf, and when he went to put it back, he noticed a small notebook tucked between a couple of empty crocks. He opened it. *Biscuits.* A recipe written in Esther's neat handwriting. Swallowing the lump that rose in his throat, he flipped through the pages.

And I thought she just instinctively knew how to make those biscuits. And flapjacks. Here was the recipe for the corn bread he loved. For Anna's favorite cinnamon rolls. And piecrust. His mouth watered at the thought of biscuits fresh from the oven, slathered in butter and topped with Esther's elderberry jelly. He flipped back to the first page and read through the instructions. How hard could it be?

A few minutes later, Adam slid a pan of biscuits into the oven. He cleaned up the mess and settled at the table to wait, sipping coffee and listening to the consistent drum of rain on the porch roof. After a peek at the biscuits—they needed more time—he sat back down and opened the Bible he'd taken to leaving on the kitchen table.

The book fell open to Esther's favorite, the Psalms, but Adam backed up to the beginning of Job. He'd been reading it since the day Rachel Ellsworth quoted it—choking back tears as she did so. The power the words had in Rachel Ellsworth's life intrigued him. He remembered her saying, *Papa said it was all right to tell God we don't understand.* There was plenty about his life right now that Adam didn't understand. Still, reading God's Word seemed to help quiet the turmoil.

Today, with the sound of rainfall and the aroma of freshly turned earth blowing in through the open window, as Adam read the book, he felt comforted. Rachel Ellsworth had been right about Psalm 139 too. Adam had taken to praying the last of it. *"Search me, O God, and know my heart: try me, and know my thoughts: And see if there be any wicked way in me, and lead me in the way everlasting."*

Most of the book of Job remained a mystery—except for the last part, which definitely had the power to put a man in his place. This morning, as he thought on Job's *"what shall I answer thee? I will lay mine hand upon my mouth,"* Adam nodded. He thought back over all the man had lost—his possessions, his family, and, finally, his own health. But not his faith. Never his faith. A man could learn a lot from Job's example.

When the biscuits were ready, he pulled the pan out of the oven and inverted it over the counter. He slit a biscuit open with a bread knife and slathered it with butter. The aroma of warm bread made his mouth water. He wasn't sure he needed jelly. He took a tentative bite. Then another. And, finally, he smiled.

What-d-ya know. Adam Michael Friesen, making biscuits. Good biscuits.

Wrapping the warm biscuits in a towel, he set them near the stove and headed out to the barn. As he milked the cow, he muttered names. "Ethan John Friesen. Asher Friesen. William Friesen. George Washington Friesen. Benjamin Franklin Friesen." Favorite uncles. Distant relatives. Famous Americans. Nothing resonated. Nothing seemed to be a proper fit for the russet-haired blue-eyed boy who increasingly dominated his thoughts. "Esther," he finally said aloud. "If you don't find a way to speak up, I'm just going to toss some names I like in a hat and hope for the best." He chuckled. "Or I could let Anna name him. Although I don't relish the thought of Mordecai Azalea."

He heard Aunt Lizzie's buggy turn in the drive. Milk pail in hand, he made his way to the barn door and then across the drive to wait by the path leading to the house. The minute the buggy stopped, he set the milk pail down. "I wondered if the rain would keep my butter churner in town," he teased. Lifting Anna out of the buggy, he set her down and then held out his hand for Aunt Lizzie.

"I'm sorry we're late," Aunt Lizzie said as she climbed down.

"You aren't. I was only teasing." Adam tapped the tip of Anna's nose. "Go on inside, little one. You can have a glass of milk before the churning. And a biscuit."

Anna looked up at him with a small frown. "You don't know how to make biscuits."

"I learned. You and Aunt Lizzie go on inside. I'll see to the buggy and be along." He led the little mare across to the barn, unhitched her, and turned her into a small corral before returning to the house. The moment he stepped into the kitchen, Anna spoke—around a mouthful of biscuit.

"These are good."

Aunt Lizzie echoed Anna's sentiment. "And I'll admit I'm surprised."

"I found Esther's recipe notebook this morning." He allowed a little smile. "It seems I can follow directions—at least when it comes to biscuits." He paused. "I've been thinking. If I start soup in the morning, it can cook all day to be eaten for supper. That would work, yes?"

"It would," Aunt Lizzie agreed. "But you'd need to check on it. To make certain it wasn't burning. Or that the fire hadn't gone out."

Adam nodded. "Between Wyatt and me, we could manage. Do you think?"

"I think two strapping men should be able to figure out a kitchen. I can bring soup makings with me next time I come and give you a brief cooking lesson."

"We have quarts and quarts of tomatoes in the root cellar. Potatoes and carrots too. Maybe more. Why not use what's already here?"

"Why not indeed," Aunt Lizzie said, and reached for the apron hanging on a hook by the stove.

"Beyond salt and pepper," Adam said, "I don't know anything about spices."

"You will when I'm finished with you," Aunt Lizzie said. "And speaking of finishing…Anna mentioned a baby quilt Esther had started."

Anna spoke up. "Rachel said if you say it's all right she'll show me how to sew and we can finish it. Together. And then Brother will have a quilt Mama made, just like me."

Adam nodded. "If Miss Ellsworth wishes to help you finish it, I will be very grateful." He went into the small parlor. Esther's sewing basket was still on the table beside her rocking chair. A stack of completed quilt blocks, a spool of thread, assorted fabric pieces, a pincushion, and scissors were positioned just as they had been the last time Esther sewed. Adam gathered it all up and tucked it into the sewing basket. He picked up a piece of paper that had been hidden by the quilt blocks. Going to the one window in the room, he parted the curtains just enough to see ... a list of names, all of them crossed out, save one.

Barrett Michael Friesen. Tears gathered as he looked up toward heaven. "So. You found a way." He carried the piece of paper and the sewing basket to the kitchen. He handed the basket to Aunt Lizzie, and then he swept Anna up into his arms. "Baby brother has a name."

Chapter 7

*F*eeling numb, Rachel sat at Aunt Jennie's kitchen table, her hands folded, her back straight. Nel stood behind her, one hand on the back of the chair, both of them waiting while Aunt Jennie read Mrs. Grove's letter.

"Can you believe it?" an impatient Nel finally said. "Of all the nerve."

The baby had been asleep, but at the sound of Nel's strident voice, he woke and began to cry. When Aunt Jennie moved toward the cradle, Nel waved her away. "I'll see to him. Rachel needs you."

Aunt Jennie came to sit beside Rachel. She reached for her gloved hand. "My dear, sweet niece. I am so very sorry."

The older woman's sympathy broke the dam of self-control. Rachel began to cry. Meaning to retrieve a handkerchief from the bag at her wrist, she managed only to tangle the strap and close it tighter. Frustrated, she began to yank on the strap. Aunt Jennie put a hand over hers. Rachel stilled.

"One lace-edged handkerchief isn't going to be enough, anyway," Aunt Jennie said and handed over a napkin. When Rachel began to sob, Aunt Jennie pulled her into her arms.

"How *could* he? Why didn't I guess? But no, I lost sleep over him. Envisioning poor brave Landis, wasting away but not wanting to worry me." She sat back and blew her nose. "I thought he was so—perfect. He was going to take me to Paris. He understood my art." Tears flowed again. Rachel leaned into Aunt Jennie's hug. And the baby cried louder.

Nel was standing at the sink, the screaming baby in her arms, a look of frustration on her face. "Is he hungry?"

"I'm all right, Aunt Jennie," Rachel said. "Help the poor little man."

Aunt Jennie rose and crossed to where Nel stood, taking the baby in her arms. In no time, the child was lying on a blanket near the stove, kicking happily.

"I'll make tea," Aunt Jennie said. "It's an herbal remedy." She nodded at Rachel. "It'll make you feel calmer." She'd just set the kettle on to heat when someone pounded on the back door.

"Jennie Meeker! It's Val Brooks. Lena says to come right away. Pains are getting close together."

Rachel spoke up. "You have to go. I'll be all right."

"I can stay," Nel offered.

"Thank you, dear," Aunt Jennie said. "I hate to leave, but I must." She began gathering supplies and tucking them into the carpetbag she took to every birthing.

Rachel forced more confidence into her voice than she felt. "It'll be all right, Aunt Jennie. Truly."

"Lizzie and Anna shouldn't be gone much longer," Aunt Jennie said. She looked over at Nel. "And you're sure you can stay? I don't want Rachel to be alone."

Nel promised.

Aunt Jennie pulled a small green tin down from the shelf above the stove. She handed it to Nel. "Steep two tablespoons of this in two cups of hot water. Wait until it's a very rich green color then strain the herbs out." She looked at Rachel. "Drink every drop." Taking the carpetbag in hand, she headed for the back door then hesitated at the threshold. "I'm not one for platitudes, Rachel, and I won't minimize the hurt you've been caused.

But the woman who wrote that horrible letter was right about something. You're strong. And a man who lets his mother do his dirty work is not the right man for a strong woman." She paused. "You're going to be all right, dear. It will take time, but Lizzie and I will help you. And what you said a moment ago when you were crying on my shoulder—about not having a home to go to? Nothing could be further from the truth. You have a home right here in Lost Creek with people who truly love you."

In the aftermath of Aunt Jennie's departure, Rachel scooped up the baby while Nel made the tea. When Rachel looked into his face, the baby watched her intently for a moment then gave her a toothless grin. Rachel smiled back. "Aren't you a darling boy." She touched the dimple in his chin. "Let's see another. Yes, that's it, little man."

Nel set the cup of tea on the table, and Rachel handed the baby over. She took a sip and made a face. "That's—awful." She rose to get the sugar, and the baby began to cry.

"Probably needs changing," Nel said. "I'll see to the diaper if you'll tell me where you keep the clean ones."

By the time Rachel had drunk the tea, the baby had a clean, dry diaper, but he'd added flailing and kicking to the cry. Nothing Nel tried worked. Finally, a frustrated Nel handed him back. It was as if a knob had been turned from *sad* to *happy*. Instant smiles.

"Well, I never." Nel frowned.

"It's just that he knows me better," Rachel said. "He's getting to the age."

"And what 'age' is that?"

"The one where babies tend to cling to what they know and be wary of those they don't know as well."

"Is that what it is?" Nel sat down next to Rachel and tickled the baby beneath the chin. "Well, we're just going to have to fix that, aren't we?" She cooed, but the baby boy sat staring, his lower lip jutted out just enough to ward off any new attempts at removing him from Rachel's arms.

"Why don't you get out the drawing of your quilt," Rachel suggested. "I'll get some fresh paper and pencils and see what I can do about creating a pattern."

"Are you sure?"

"I am." Rachel rose, settled the baby on her left hip, and went into the parlor to retrieve yesterday's newspaper. Back in the kitchen, she laid it out on the table. "We can trim that down to the block size, and then I'll play with outlining the appliqué pieces. We'll work on that until we have the right balance. Once that's done, we can move on to leaf shapes and circles."

With a smile and a soft sound of affection, she laid the baby atop the pallet and wrapped him in a blanket. He closed his eyes and fell asleep.

"If I didn't know better, Rachel Ellsworth," Nel said in wonder, "I'd think you knew some magic that casts spells over babies."

"Don't be silly. I'm just—I've always had a knack with children."

"Well, I wouldn't mind if it were contagious," Nel said wistfully. "Especially when it comes to two particular children."

"Now that we're going to work on your masterpiece together," Rachel said, "he'll get to know you better." She looked down at the spot of spit-up on her dress. "And be spitting up on you in no time."

Nel grimaced. "Delightful."

"You don't get the smiles without the drool and spit-up," Rachel said. "And speaking of spit-up, he's going to be hungry when he wakes up, so if we're going to make any progress at all, now's the time." She reached for Nel's drawing.

Rachel was spooning the last bit of milky grits into the baby's mouth when she heard the rattle of a harness as Aunt Lizzie and Anna drove past the house and toward the small barn at the back of the lot. They were back. Aunt Lizzie would have to hear the news about Landis.

Nel looked up from tracing a leaf. "Do you want me to go? So you can—talk about it?"

Rachel sat back. "Would you mind if I took the letter out to the barn and sent Anna inside? She can amuse her brother for a few minutes."

"Of course," Nel said. "Go. The children and I will be fine."

Rachel went outside. Anna saw her and came charging across the lawn, spouting news. "Papa named the baby. Mama wrote it down, but Papa didn't know, and when he put the quilt blocks in Mama's basket he found the paper and now the baby has a name! And Papa found Mama's recipes, and he made biscuits. I didn't even know he could do that, but they were good. And Aunt Lizzie is going to teach him to make soup. Do you want to know it?"

"Know...?"

"My brother's name, silly."

"Of course," Rachel said.

"Barrett Michael Friesen. Mama's name was Barrett before she was Friesen, and Aunt Lizzie says ladies do that sometimes so their family name doesn't get lost. Someday when I grow up and have a baby boy I'm going to name him Friesen." She stopped, frowning. "Although that isn't a very pretty name. Maybe I'll put it in the middle." Anna was still rambling on about names when Aunt Lizzie caught up to them.

"I need to speak with you for a moment," Rachel said then spoke to Anna. "Nel and I have been working on a project. You can give her all the news while I talk to Aunt Lizzie."

"Take this in with you," Aunt Lizzie said and handed Anna a lovely handled basket. "You can help Nel sort the quilt blocks."

Rachel watched Anna go and then held out the letter. "I've had word from St. Louis."

Aunt Lizzie read quickly then engulfed Rachel in a hug. "You'll stay here, of course. It will be a great blessing to us. I'm only sorry for the way it happened."

"Aunt Jennie said the same thing. About my staying here." Rachel took in a ragged breath. "I'd like that."

"It's settled then." Aunt Lizzie paused before saying, "This will be hard for you to believe, but in time you may come to realize that God allowed your heart to be broken in order to save you far greater pain later."

Rachel didn't want to think about that. Pondering the *why* of tragedy had never done her a bit of good. She'd heard Papa say the same thing dozens of times. "Instead of floundering in the Sea of Why, we must anchor ourselves in the Land of What Now." She would resist wallowing in *why* and do her best to focus on *what now*. At least part of the answer to the latter question lay right inside the back door of the house. *Help your aunts with Anna and the baby. Help Nel make her masterpiece. Finish Barrett's baby quilt. Think beyond yourself.*

Taking a deep breath, Rachel folded up the letter and led the way inside.

"Rachel! Come look!" Anna was kneeling on a kitchen chair, looking over the quilt blocks from Esther Friesen's sewing basket. She held up a round bit of cloth. "It's a sunrise."

"Sun*burst*," Nel corrected then addressed Rachel and Aunt Lizzie. "Now you can see what I meant when I said Anna wouldn't be able to work on them."

"But I *want* to," Anna insisted.

"The pieces are far too small."

Rachel looked down at the intricately pieced block, a circle surrounded by a dozen triangles interspersed with as many diamonds and then finished into a larger circle with wedge-shaped pieces. Nel was right. It wasn't a simple block. Still, she smiled at Anna. "We'll find a way."

"It's impossible," Nel said firmly. "We'll find something else for Anna to make." She picked up a circle of cloth.

Anna snatched it away. "It's *my* Mama's quilt and it's for *my* brother, and I'll sew it if I want to! Papa and Rachel said I could!" Anna grabbed a pile of pieces and charged out of the room.

Nel was fuming. "That child needs someone to take her in hand."

"She's been through a great deal for one so young," Aunt Lizzie said gently.

Nel's voice calmed. "Her poor papa must be overwhelmed. Even with folks doing everything they can to help...it just isn't enough." She paused. "Mother's said as much, and she's right. The poor man needs a wife. No one can expect him to manage alone."

No one does. Rachel thought it, but she didn't say it. Aunt Lizzie went after Anna who came back presently and choked out an apology. Together, they sorted the fabric pieces, triangles atop triangles, wedges atop wedges, circles atop circles.

Aunt Lizzie tucked them back into Esther's sewing basket. "I'll keep them here until the next quilting. I'll ask each of the ladies to complete one block." She smiled at Anna. "While the ladies are finishing the blocks, Rachel and I will teach you to stitch a perfect seam. Then you'll be able to help set them together."

"See, little one?" Rachel tugged on one of Anna's blond braids. "We found a way."

Anna shot an *I told you so* look Nel's way before retrieving the china-headed doll and sitting down beside her napping brother.

Aunt Lizzie continued to stack pieces back in the sewing basket. Then she noticed Rachel's sketch of Nel's masterpiece. She leaned closer, inspecting the drawing. "Wh-what's this?"

"It's from a quilt I saw years ago at the county fair," Nel said. "I've always planned to make it for my hope chest. I'm not certain I remembered it exactly, but—"

Aunt Lizzie traced a heart with the tip of her index finger. "You remembered very well. But it didn't have a border." She grabbed Esther's sewing basket. "I'll just put this in the parlor for safekeeping." She called to Anna. "And if you'd like to get started with a sewing lesson, you can come with me while Rachel and Nel work here at the table."

"I should be going," Nel said. She looked at Rachel. "I'm going to trust you and buy the gold fabric. If I hurry, I can get to the mercantile before it closes. Then I can work on cutting blocks and pieces this evening." She tucked her own sketch, Rachel's drawing, and the patterns for leaves and berries in her bag. Then she reached over and squeezed Rachel's arm. "I'm very sorry for what's happened to you. But I'll admit to being glad you won't be leaving Lost Creek. I've longed for a best friend. Now I have one."

Chapter 8

For the first month after receiving Mrs. Grove's letter, Rachel did well avoiding what her father had called the Land of Why. When the promised crate of her paintings arrived from St. Louis and Wyatt Dahl hauled it to the house, Rachel had him take it directly up to the attic. Just seeing the crate sent a pang of regret through her. She didn't need any reminders of what she'd lost. Best to put the paintings out of sight for now so she could focus on What Now.

An abundance of worthy tasks occupied her time. She pieced her assigned block for Barrett's baby quilt, advised a couple of quilters on new projects, and helped tend the garden. She even went along a few times when it was Aunt Lizzie's turn to take Anna to the farm. Once, she took the baby with them. When he reached for his son, Adam's hazel eyes sparkled with joy. *Hazel, with flecks of green.*

The brief flicker of attraction reminded Rachel of the promises Landis had made and would never keep, the future he'd abandoned in favor of one with someone else. A powerful sense of rejection constricted her throat and made her turn away from Adam and Barrett. She strode across the road to the garden where Wyatt Dahl was taking a hoe to the weeds. Anna ran after her, taking her hand as they walked. It was an innocent gesture, but it too reminded Rachel of Landis. She had so wanted children.

On the drive back to town, Aunt Lizzie tried to strike up a conversation. Rachel didn't have the energy for it. She knew Papa would not approve of her retreating into the Land of Why, and yet she couldn't seem to resist. Why would Landis throw her away so easily? Why didn't he at least write to her himself? Why didn't he give her a chance to fight for him? Why did good men like Adam Friesen lose the women they loved and men like Landis simply give them up?

The weather didn't help her mood. High temperatures and scorching winds sapped her energy and made her feel sluggish. By early August, Aunt Jennie was busy answering calls from mothers worried about losing babies to "summer complaint." Rachel and her aunts ate mostly cold food—boiled eggs and sliced ham, raw tomatoes and cucumbers. Anything that didn't require standing over a hot stove. Any baking happened either very late at night or very early in the morning. Windows were raised and stayed that way. Rachel took to sleeping on the little porch just outside her room, thankful not only for the screens that frustrated mosquitoes but also the chance to feel the slightest breeze.

Whys and regrets continued to roll in like waves, even as Rachel witnessed Adam's coming to terms with his loss. The quilters—who set up their frame beneath the shade tree in the Berkeys' backyard these days—spoke of how pleased Esther would be with the way Adam doted on his children. Wasn't it wonderful he'd followed Lizzie's advice in the kitchen? Husbands said the man's crops were in good shape. And he was making steady progress on the new church pews.

Rachel thought of Mr. Friesen simply as *Adam* now—probably because Nel mentioned him at every opportunity. Rachel

didn't honestly know why, but she found Nel's assumed owner-
ship of the details of Adam's life more than a little annoying. As
if she had a special claim on it. Adam this and Adam that. It was
enough to give a girl a headache.

In the predawn light of what promised to be another scorching
summer day, Adam descended to the root cellar by lamplight.
Setting the lamp on a shelf, he counted out three quarts of tomatoes. Two potatoes. A bunch of carrots. An onion. A piece of the
dried herb hanging nearest the stairs. He couldn't remember the
name of it, but Aunt Lizzie said it was good in soup. He'd soaked
the beans overnight like she said. Today, he would put soup on
to cook and be thankful he didn't have to stay in the kitchen
with the hot stove. He and Wyatt would check on it periodically,
and when they came in tonight, they'd find supper ready to eat.

Back in the kitchen, Adam added ingredients to the Dutch
oven and set it over a low fire. He was drinking his second cup
of coffee when Wyatt drove in—not alone, though. Nel Berkey
hopped down and reached into the wagon bed for a basket.

"Surprise!" she called as she stepped into the house. "The
quilters wanted to make sure there isn't any more of the fabric
Esther was using for Barrett's quilt before they put the blocks
together. I offered to check."

Adam said he didn't know.

"I didn't expect you would," Nel laughed. "Rachel has an
idea for the finishing, but I told her we should keep it as close to
what Esther wanted as possible. If there's more fabric, we should
use it."

Adam motioned toward the parlor. "If Esther had more
fabric, she'd have put it in the cupboard next to the sewing
machine."

"I'll look." Nel plopped the basket on the table. "I've brought you boys a hearty lunch. I'll just spread a picnic under the cottonwood by the house."

"You're going to stay out here. All day?"

"Of course not." Nel giggled. "We wouldn't want to start any rumors, now would we? Aunt Jennie's driving by right after lunch. On her way to the Mitchells' to check on Blanche. She had their seventh last week. You didn't hear?"

Adam shook his head. He stood there, feeling awkward and wishing Nel hadn't invited herself to the farm. He resented the idea of her pawing through Esther's fabric. It was for a good reason, but still—truth was, there was something about Nel that just didn't sit well with him.

"You go on to work now," Nel said. "Don't let me keep you. I'll look for the fabric, and then I've brought handwork to keep me busy until it's time for our picnic." She flitted into the parlor.

Adam left the house, wondering why he resented the sight of a picnic basket brought by a friend. Maybe it was because Nel hadn't asked if he and Wyatt needed lunch. She'd just assumed. Hadn't even noticed—or had ignored—the soup pot on the stove. Nel was like that sometimes. Pushy. Had been since they were young. It hadn't mattered when they were all growing up, because Adam just kept his distance. It mattered now, though. He glanced toward the house. She was going through Esther's cabinet. Helping herself to fabric. Assuming. Too much.

As for a picnic lunch, he and Wyatt had corn bread and freshly churned butter and molasses, and that would be plenty for the both of them until the workday was over and they sat down to soup. With a soft grunt of displeasure, Adam made his way to the open work area on the north side of the barn where he'd set up an outdoor workshop beneath an overhang. The pews he was making were a simple design and he enjoyed the process. Making pews was predictable. If he did things right, they'd turn out right. Being able to depend on an outcome was a good thing.

He was so deep in thought that when Nel's voice sounded from the far corner of the barn, it startled him.

"I didn't know you were a master carpenter," she said, coming over to run her hand along the top edge of a finished pew. "These are beautiful."

He didn't look up. "I'm not a master carpenter, but they're sturdy and will likely last longer than any of us. Did you need something?"

"No. I just wanted to tell you I found the fabric. Now we can finish Barrett's quilt—just the way Esther wanted it."

Adam nodded. "Anna's excited about helping with it."

"Yes. Well, it's a fairly complex design. But we'll find something for little Anna to do."

He glanced her way, frowning. "Did I misunderstand, then? I'm certain Anna said Rachel—Miss Ellsworth—had promised she could help with it. It means a lot to Anna." He held Nel's gaze, willing her to give in.

Nel glanced down at the piece of cloth in her hands. "Then of course we'll find a way for that to happen." She forced a smile and looked back up at him. "Rachel's a dear, but she doesn't know quite as much about quiltmaking as I do. She might not understand how difficult it can be for a four-year-old to learn to stitch." She brandished the gold-colored square. "But when it comes to drawing, her talent really shines. Take this for example. It's my design, but as soon as I described it, Rachel drew it up as easy as pie."

Adam glanced at the square of cloth. *A heart.* What was he supposed to say? He gave a noncommittal grunt and concentrated on the sanding.

"What do we have here?" Wyatt came up behind Nel and reached for the square of cloth. She snatched it away.

"Keep your grubby hands off it."

Wyatt made a show of holding his hands up and waggling them about. "Not grubby. Just washed them. Thought you were out here telling Adam to come to lunch." He pointed at the square of gold cloth. "Hearts, eh? Must be for someone special."

Nel drew it to herself so Wyatt couldn't touch it. "It's for my hope chest, if you must know."

"That mean you're hoping to get hitched?" Wyatt asked.

"It means I'll be prepared to make a home for—someone."

Wyatt's tone changed. "Well, *someone*'s going to be real lucky."

"Thank you. That's a very nice thing to say."

"Wasn't being nice. Just saying what is." Wyatt offered Nel his arm. "What say I help you set out that picnic you were bragging about. Adam can join us whenever he's a mind to."

Thank goodness. Nel allowed Wyatt to lead her away. Adam glanced up from his work a few times to check on the progress of the picnic. Not until things were set out and Nel and Wyatt were settled on the checkered cloth did he venture to join the party. He declined to sit down, ate while standing, and excused himself as soon as he could.

He didn't want to believe it, but it felt like there was a bit of flirtation going on from Nel's direction. Toward him. He hoped he was wrong. Nel was nice enough. She just wasn't the kind of person he'd ever want to marry. If he ever did marry again. *Huh.* He'd resisted the idea, but the truth was, Anna and Barrett deserved to have a mama. Someone to care for them right here at home. While the idea didn't horrify him, it did make him feel guilty. That was probably only normal. But Nel Berkey? There was not one tiny little spark in that direction.

It was quilting day, but Rachel wasn't going. She'd decided that in the middle of the night. Now, well after time to be up and about, she descended the stairs to the kitchen. "I'm sorry," she said to her aunts and Anna, "but I don't feel well enough to go to quilting today." She crossed to the stove to pour a cup of tea.

"Not well enough?" A concerned Aunt Jennie rose from the table. She put her palm to Rachel's forehead. "You don't feel feverish. Your appetite's been off, though. Any other symptoms?"

None I can say in front of Anna. Rachel shook her head. "I'm sure it's nothing serious. Just a headache. And I'm tired. That's all." *And sick to death of hearing Nel go on and on about Adam.* Ever since Nel had invited herself to accompany Wyatt Dahl to the farm under the guise of finding fabric for Barrett's baby quilt, it seemed that every time they were together, Nel had another anecdote to share about the wonders of Adam Friesen. Rachel had heard more than her share of anecdotes. The final blow had fallen only yesterday afternoon.

They'd been sitting on the screened porch at the back of the property, each one stitching away, when Nel lowered her voice and confided her secret. Adam Friesen needed a wife and she, Nel Berkey, was going to see to it that he got a good one. Her. It was only a matter of time. Adam probably wouldn't propose for a while yet. Although some men did. Goodness, Vernon Carter had barely managed six months before remarrying. But then Vernon had married the first woman who would take him, just to get out from under managing his four children. Adam was a devoted father. He would need more time. Nel blushed when she confided, "I'm hoping for a proposal at Christmas."

A proposal at Christmas. The phrase reminded Rachel of what she'd lost when Landis met that other girl, and it sent a barb straight to her heart. While Nel rattled on, Rachel fought back tears. Nel was oblivious until finally, Rachel claimed a headache and fled up to her room. She'd spent much of last night rereading

Landis's letters—and Mrs. Grove's cruel missive. She could face neither the quilters nor Nel's barrage of Adam-anecdotes today.

"Nel will be so disappointed," Aunt Lizzie said. "She loves it that you're helping with her quilt."

"I've had quite enough of that infernal quilt," Rachel snapped. And then brought her hand to her mouth in horror. "I'm so sorry. I just—" A sob escaped. "Nel means well, but—"

Aunt Lizzie looked at her with concern. "You've been holding something in for weeks now, dear girl. Out with it."

Rachel looked over at Anna. She shook her head. "I can't talk about it. Not now."

Aunt Jennie caught on immediately. "Take your tea upstairs and rest. Perhaps you'll feel more like talking later."

Rachel obeyed. From her perch on the little porch, she saw Aunt Lizzie and Anna leave for quilting. And then...Aunt Lizzie returning a few minutes later. Alone. The expected knock at her door came moments later.

Aunt Jennie opened the door just a crack. "Even if we can't fix whatever's bothering you, it might help if you had someone to listen. Anna's with the quilters, and Barrett's taking his morning nap. I've made a fresh pot of tea, and I just brought some of my corn-bread muffins out of the oven. Please, Rachel. Let us help."

Rachel spun about in her chair. "You baked? In this heat?"

"Well...yes. You love my corn-bread muffins. I hoped it would tempt you to come downstairs."

It had been a very long while since Rachel had confided in another woman. Since Mama died. She'd learned to keep things in. To soldier on. Goodness, hadn't she been soldiering on all these months in Lost Creek? First, ticking the weeks off until she would leave. And now...just soldiering on. And all the while listening to Nel blather about her rosy future.

"Rachel?" Aunt Jennie pleaded.

Rachel rose from the chair and went to her bedroom door. "Yes," she said, her voice wavering with emotion. "I think—maybe—maybe it would help." Once downstairs, she joined her aunts at the kitchen table. She took a sip of the tea Aunt Jennie had just poured and tried to collect her thoughts. "I can't seem to get past losing Landis. I'm beginning to wonder if I ever will." Tears threatened. She forced them back and choked out a little more. "I know you both said I would. Goodness, even Landis's mother said I was *strong*. But I don't feel strong and I'm not sure I *am* going to be all right. My future was all planned out. And so beautiful. Paris...art lessons...Landis. Children." She allowed a little sob. "Now it's... bleak. Blank."

"Blank?" Aunt Jennie chided. "You may wish you could erase us, dear child, but that's never going to happen. You're stuck with us. And with Nel and the quilters and Adam and the children and even Wyatt Dahl. All of those people care about you."

Rachel sighed. "I'm grateful, but it doesn't help. I feel adrift."

"Of course you do," Aunt Lizzie said. "You've had a terrible shock. It will take time to find your way. But you will. In time."

"How much time?" Rachel spoke through her tears. "It's been nearly a month since that letter came, and I feel worse than ever. Adam lost his *wife*, but he's managing. He's even beginning to smile again. What kind of weakling am I that I can't get over losing a man who didn't even have the courage to write his own letter saying he'd found somebody else?"

Aunts Lizzie and Jennie were quiet for a few minutes. Finally Aunt Lizzie asked, "What does any of this have to do with going to quilting? Or with Nel and her quilt? Spending time with friends is a way to move toward healing."

Rachel sighed. "I'm sure it comes as no surprise to the two of you that Nel has set her cap for Adam. Which is fine. Who could blame her? He's kind and strong and hardworking—and very handsome. But Nel's obsessed. Lately it's all she talks about. And yesterday—yesterday she was daydreaming about how she hoped he'll propose. At Christmas."

"She—what?" the aunts said in chorus.

"I've tried not to resent her. Really, I have." Rachel's tears started to flow again. "But Christmas was going to be *my* engagement to Landis. I want to be happy for Nel—but every word she says reminds me of everything I've lost." She dabbed at her tears. "I just can't listen anymore."

Aunt Lizzie spoke up. "Adam Friesen is no more going to propose to Nel Berkey than a man is going to walk on the moon. They're totally unsuited for each other. Anyone who knows them can see that. And I'm quite certain Adam sees it even if Nel can't." She paused. "But that's neither here nor there at the moment. Right now, our concern is for you." Aunt Lizzie reached over and took both Rachel's hands in her own. "It may take longer than you want it to, but trust me, dear. One day you will wake up and realize the dark clouds have parted. The sky is blue again, and you are looking forward to what the day has for you. I know it beyond a shadow of a doubt."

Rachel wanted to believe Aunt Lizzie. Truly, she did, but what could a spinster know of broken hearts and lost dreams?

Aunt Lizzie let go of Rachel's hands and sat back. "Then again," she said, "what could an old maid like me know of such things?"

Rachel looked up in horror. "I would never say such a thing!"

"Of course not. But you'd think it. What beautiful young woman wouldn't, having an old hag like me spinning tales of blue skies ahead?"

Rachel started to protest, but Aunt Lizzie held up a hand. "I don't blame you." She reached for a muffin, plopped it on a plate, and handed it to Rachel. "Eat. I'll be back in a moment." She left the room.

Rachel looked over at Aunt Jennie who only shrugged and passed the butter and jam. She heard Aunt Lizzie go up the stairs. She heard a door creak. *The attic?* "Is she going to the attic? It'll be like an oven up there."

"If she's after what I think she is, she won't be up there long."

Aunt Jennie was right. Rachel had taken one tiny bite of muffin when Aunt Lizzie returned. Rachel's jaw dropped. Aunt Lizzie had retrieved a quilt from the attic. Hearts appliquéd onto a white ground. Leaves and berries. And the quilting! My goodness... the quilting.

Aunt Lizzie draped the quilt over the back of a chair and sat down. "Nel was too young to remember who made the quilt she admired at the fair all those years ago." She swept her palm across the surface. "It was to be my wedding quilt."

"Wedding." Rachel echoed the word, trying to absorb the idea of Aunt Lizzie in love.

The old woman's eyes filled with tears. "You see, dear niece. I *do* know what you're going through. Only my young man didn't write a letter. He died. At Gettysburg." She reached over and took Rachel's hand. "We do find a way to go on, a way to happiness. My life has not been the life I dreamed of, but it's been very, very good. And I *am* happy."

Rachel sniffed and wiped at the last of her tears. "I'm so sorry you had to go through that. Sorry I doubted that you could understand."

Aunt Lizzie touched the quilt again. "I kept it on my bed for a while, but in the end, even though it is exquisite, I just couldn't bear it anymore. I felt smothered beneath it, and I knew I had to put it away. I couldn't let my loss define the rest of my life. I had to look to the future. I begged God to help me find my way back to hope and joy. And He did. Not all at once. But He did."

Aunt Jennie spoke up. "You must not give up hope, Rachel. Don't deny how much it hurts. Cry the tears. Grieve. And know that on the other side there's the wonder of dawn and a new beginning—just as you painted in that sunrise for your father." She smiled. "Maybe that painting can remind you of another verse. The one about joy coming in the morning."

"And until joy comes," Aunt Lizzie said, "you simply do the next thing. Have the muffin. Drink the tea. Get dressed. Take a walk. You do the next thing and the next and the next. And one day, after countless 'next things,' you'll realize you're feeling better and finding your way."

What treasures these women were. What storehouses of wisdom. Rachel took a deep breath. "I know you're right." She offered a wry smile and muttered, "But I still don't want to hear Nel go on about a Christmas engagement."

"And who could blame you?" Aunt Lizzie rose from her chair. "I'm going back to quilting right now, and while I'm there I'll let everyone know that you're feeling a bit better, but Jennie's insisting you take it easy for the next day or so."

Aunt Jennie nodded. "And if you need more time, I'll ask for extra help with the children for the next few days. Or longer." She reached for the quilt and spoke to Aunt Lizzie. "I'll take it back up for you."

"I can do it," Rachel said. "Just tell me where it goes." She took a deep breath. "And then...there's a 'next thing' I need to do. It's time I unpacked my trunks." *And time I burned some old letters.*

Chapter 9

As August gave way to September and harvest neared its conclusion, Adam found a new way to see his children nearly every day. He began to spend more time with the crew building the new church, arriving late in the afternoon and lingering until he had to get back home for evening chores.

It was especially nice that he could count on one of the three women at the Meekers' being part of the group of ladies who served an afternoon snack at the building site. Once they realized Adam might be there, they began to bring Anna along—and Barrett, if he'd wakened from his nap. It was another precious few moments he could spend with his children.

It was on a perfect afternoon in late September, when Adam suddenly realized that on the afternoons when he was at the building site, he'd begun to watch the road for the arrival of the "basket brigade," as the men were wont to call the ladies. And not because he was hungry, although he always was. No, he was watching for a tall, slim young woman wearing an outlandish straw hat. Outlandish for Lost Creek, anyway. But probably very much in style in St. Louis.

One day, when the men were gathered around the table created with an old door and sawhorses, a breeze caught Rachel's hat and sent it flying. Adam chased it down. When he brought it back and she reached for it, their hands touched. It was only the briefest contact, and yet that night when he retired, Adam replayed the moment in his mind. It was as if he'd seen Rachel Ellsworth for the first time. Those dark eyes. The way the corners of her mouth turned up when she thanked him. And later in the afternoon, her laughter when she plopped a chain of woven clover on Anna's head and swung the child about.

He tried to resist the attraction. Tried to focus on friendship. With appreciation for what she was doing to help the Meeker sisters. After all, it was going on eight months since Esther died. It had to be hard for them. No doubt Rachel lightened the load. Anyone could see she delighted in children—and Anna and Barrett delighted in her.

"That one"—his sister Molly said one day when she was at the building site—"is going to be a wonderful mother."

Adam pretended not to hear.

Molly stepped close and spoke quietly. "Esther was my best friend. You made her very happy. And she'd want you to be happy. She'd also want her children to have a flesh-and-blood mama."

"Can't think on that," Adam groused. "I'm not ready."

"But when you are?" Molly nodded toward Rachel who was busily serving up slices of pie to a gaggle of men. "Just don't take too long. You're not the only man in Lost Creek in need of a wife."

It might be a coincidence, but at that very moment Adam saw Rachel smile at Zeb Gruber. And then laugh at something Zeb said. *Huh.*

"And one more thing," Molly said. "In case you haven't noticed, your children favor Rachel over someone who shall remain nameless, but who has definitely set her cap for you. Initials *N.B.*"

Adam frowned. *N.B.* So. He wasn't imagining things when it came to Nel. "As to what Esther would want, when it comes down to it, isn't what *I* want what really matters? In that matter."

"You mean the matter you aren't ready to discuss?"

"Yes. That one."

Molly chuckled. "Agreed. In that matter, what really matters is what matters to you. I just thought I'd let you know that when it comes to that matter you aren't ready to discuss, what matters to me is that you're happy. And that's what would matter to Esther too." She shifted the baby in her arms to the other hip. "Glad we had this little chat." With a laugh, she hollered for the twins to round up their siblings and stepped back to the table where Rachel was serving pie.

And still talking to Zeb Gruber, Adam noted. *Huh.*

Rachel stood on the front porch looking east, where the sky blazed with pinks and peaches and oranges beyond anything she had ever painted. *"Weeping may endure for a night, but joy cometh in the morning."* Remembering that scripture made her smile even as she crossed her arms and hugged herself against the chill of the crisp, cool air.

Just as Aunt Lizzie had predicted, after many days of just "doing the next thing," it had happened. She'd begun to look forward instead of dwelling in the past. Most of the time. It had taken a new kind of "soldiering on" to move from the Sea of Why to the Land of What Now. She'd cried more tears and read more scripture and finally...finally, the pall of sadness over her life had lifted. Hope had begun to glimmer—especially in light of the day ahead.

The instant the neighbor's rooster crowed, she'd thrown back the covers and hopped out of bed, dressing quickly and hurrying downstairs and out onto the front porch so she could watch the dawn. And it was glorious.

"Thank You, Lord, for eyes to see," she whispered. "Thank You for Aunt Jennie. Aunt Lizzie. Their welcome. Thank You for new friends." She allowed a low chuckle. "Yes, Lord. Thank You for Nel. Help me be a good friend to her and a help with that 'infernal quilt.'"

If being able to smile about Nel's determination to capture Adam's heart wasn't proof that Rachel was going to be all right, nothing was. "Oh God, You are so good. Thank You for hope."

Behind her, the front door opened with a creak. Still in her nightgown, Anna came to Rachel's side. "What you doing out here?"

"Look," Rachel said, gesturing toward the sky. "Isn't it beautiful?"

Anna yawned. Rubbed her eyes. "It's all pink and purply."

"And orange and peach." Rachel moved to sit on the front step and motioned for Anna to come sit in her lap and snuggle close against the morning chill. "I've never been to a county fair before. I'm excited!" Anna's stomach rumbled. Rachel laughed and hugged the child. "Guess we'd better feed that growly bear."

Back inside, Rachel put her finger to her lips, signaling they should be quiet. Together, she and Anna tiptoed into the kitchen. Anna set the table while Rachel stirred up the fire, made coffee, and mixed a batch of flapjacks. They'd both eaten half their stacks when the aunts bustled into the kitchen with exclamations over how late they'd slept and how good breakfast smelled.

Rachel rose from the table and waved the aunts into their chairs. "I want to wait on you this morning." She poured batter into a skillet and coffee into mugs. She'd just set the coffee before the aunts when Barrett woke and began to cry.

Rachel changed his diaper, talking as she worked. "I've got grits cooking for you, little man." She picked him up, settled him on her left hip, and went to flip the flapjacks.

Aunt Lizzie leaned toward Aunt Jennie. "It would appear, sister, that we have become obsolete." She made a show of snapping her napkin and spreading it across her lap. "And if this is what it looks like, I'm all for it."

Once Rachel had set a plate of flapjacks before her aunts, she settled Barrett in his high chair. Tying a towel about his midsection for extra stability, she dished up grits, added milk from the icebox, and sat down to feed him. When she realized the aunts were both smiling at her, she cocked her head. "What?"

"It's good to see you doing 'the next thing' with a real smile on your face," Aunt Jennie said.

Anna asked for more flapjacks. Rachel fed Barrett and refilled the aunts' coffee cups between pouring and flipping more flapjacks. Finally, she poured herself a cup of tea and sat down.

"Rachel's never been to a fair before," Anna said.

"A *county* fair," Rachel corrected. "Papa and I went to the Centennial with a group of church members."

"If you went to the Centennial," Aunt Lizzie warned, "don't get your hopes up for today."

"The Centennial was overwhelming. There was too much to see and too much to do, especially when we only had one day there."

"Well, you won't be overwhelmed today," Aunt Lizzie said.

"But you will have fun," Aunt Jennie added quickly. "Last year's quilt exhibit was quite fine. There's to be a baseball game in the afternoon and a dance this evening—if we last that long."

Aunt Lizzie glanced Anna's way. "I don't suppose anyone here will care about it, but I have it on good authority there will be pony rides for the children."

Rachel wiped the baby's face and set him on the pallet. "Anna, could you entertain your brother for just a few minutes while I do the dishes?"

Aunt Lizzie rose to help. When Rachel tried to protest, she waved her off. "Breakfast was lovely, and I am sufficiently impressed with your homemaking skills. But now I want to help so we can get going. Get the big picnic basket out of the pantry, won't you?"

A knock sounded at the back door. Rachel went to answer it. *Adam?*

"Papa!" Anna squeezed past Rachel and practically climbed him as if he were a tree.

Rachel waved him into the kitchen. "We weren't expecting company."

"What a nice surprise!" Aunt Lizzie exclaimed. "We didn't hear you arrive." She looked past him, obviously expecting to see his buggy.

"I pulled up out front," Adam said. "Over chores, Wyatt asked to borrow the buggy. He's hoping to surprise Nel Berkey and squire her about for the day." He glanced Rachel's way. "Wyatt's idea gave me an idea. What better way to spend a day than to gather up a passel of kids and friends?" He looked to the aunts. "If you don't mind riding in the bed of a farm wagon, I'd be pleased to drive you all. I must get home this evening to do chores, but if you decide to linger, Wyatt can bring you home. He was set on staying for the dance." He put Anna down. "I'm hoping to keep the children with me overnight. I've been wanting to see how that would go."

Aunt Jennie spoke for them all by asking Rachel to fetch some quilts to make a pallet in the back of Adam's wagon. "We can make the wagon bed comfortable for the drive, and then we'll be able to rig up a nice little napping spot beneath the wagon when it's nap time."

"I won't need a nap today," Anna declared firmly. "We're going to have *fun* all day."

Adam tweaked her nose. "We'll have fun before and after your nap."

Anna made a face, but she didn't challenge him. "Me and Ezra will want to ride the ponies. I hope we can find him."

"Oh, we'll find him," Adam said. "Ezra's riding with Wyatt and Nel. Whoever gets there first will save a spot for the other and set up camp as close to the entrance as they can get, claiming some shade near that little creek that runs through the fairgrounds." He crouched down to Anna's level. "Think we can be first?"

"Yes!" Anna said.

"You wearing your nightgown?"

"No!" Anna shot out of the room and up the stairs to dress.

Rachel called after her to be sure to bring her bonnet. "And speaking of bonnets," she said, "I'd best be getting mine."

Upstairs in her room, Rachel opened the bandbox holding her straw sailor hat. Settling it on her head just above the rather loose bun she'd created on rising, she reached for a hat pin. Instead of the elegant pin Landis had given her, she chose Mama's. Simple. Serviceable. And an excellent choice for a girl from Lost Creek, Nebraska.

Chapter 10

When Adam drove the wagon through the county fair entrance, he caught sight of Wyatt and Nel right away, settled exactly where they'd all hoped to locate in a spot of shade near the creek running along the edge of the fairgrounds. The couple sat on a blanket, with Wyatt pointing at something on a gold square of cloth spread across Nel's knee and listening to what she was saying with rapt attention.

As the morning progressed, Adam was surprised by many things. While Nel was holding her nose and trying to pull them all away from a livestock exhibit, Rachel Ellsworth seemed genuinely interested in learning the differences between a Hereford and a Shorthorn. Adam would not have expected that from a big-city girl.

After being excited about pony rides, Anna hesitated when confronted with a shaggy little beast that kept stomping one of its hind feet and tossing its head. Adam had never realized his daughter could be tentative about trying new things. She steadfastly refused to climb aboard, until Adam promised to walk alongside with his hand on the saddle, all the way around the temporary corral.

And then, as he walked alongside Anna's pony, Adam saw Rachel smiling up at Zeb Gruber and it made him feel—surely not jealousy, but something. He remembered Molly's comment that day at the church building site about him not being the only man in need of a wife. He didn't like seeing Rachel smile at another man.

And then there was the surprise over what he didn't feel when he took Barrett in his arms and let the ladies lead the way to the quilt exhibit. The quilters had finished Barrett's baby quilt. There it hung, pinned to a clothesline above the blue ribbon winner that was spread out across a stack of hay bales. Even he could appreciate the skill it had taken for Esther and her friends to wrangle all those tiny pieces into place. Dark blues, light blues—scraps of Esther's dresses, probably. The surprise was the absence of the awful sense of loss at the pit of his stomach. He felt ... proud. And thankful. Proud of Esther. Thankful for the friends who'd completed the quilt. Thankful for the healthy baby boy in his arms.

When Anna took his hand, Adam looked down with a smile. "It's beautiful, little one."

"And I helped."

"She certainly did," Rachel said. "She sewed that last border on all by herself."

"I didn't think she could do it," Nel Berkey said. "But Anna proved me wrong. She did a fine job. We only had to re-stitch a very little bit."

Adam nodded. There were no tears to hold back. Only a gentle kind of sadness and a whisper of regret. He'd finally escaped the darkest part of grieving. He looked from Rachel to Nel and back again. "Thank you for making this happen." He pulled Anna to his side and gave her a one-armed hug.

After the quilt exhibit, the group meandered around the fairgrounds without a specific aim. Until Wyatt came trotting up to recruit Adam for a tug-of-war.

Adam shook his head. He jostled Barrett. "I'm busy."

"You aren't going to get out of it that easily," Nel said and pulled the baby right out of his hands.

Barrett protested. One of the aunts took him and settled him down.

"It's First Church against Lake Street," Nel said. "We can't let Lake Street win two years in a row." She tucked her hand beneath Adam's arm and tugged.

Adam looked over at Rachel in dismay, but she only shrugged. "Don't look at me. From what I know of church rivalries, they're not to be trifled with. Besides, I've seen you wield a hammer. Why not use those brawny forearms for something fun?"

"Rachel's right," Nel said. "The boys need your muscles."

Adam allowed himself to be pulled back toward the creek. On the opposite bank, half-a-dozen men he recognized as members of Lake Street had already assembled. First Church was definitely underrepresented.

"Those guys haven't been building a new church in their free time," Wyatt said. He raised his arms and flexed his biceps.

Someone on the other side of the creek jeered. "That all you got? Let's show 'em, boys." He strutted about like a circus performer preparing to lift a heavy barbell.

Wyatt took the challenge. "Come on, men. Let's do this!" He marched to the edge of the creek and grabbed the rope just this side of the white flag that marked its center.

The small crowd of onlookers began to shout encouragement, some to one team and some to the other. In a lull, Adam heard Anna cry out. "Yay, Papa!" He glanced over to where she stood beside Ezra Dahl, both of them jumping up and down with excitement.

Adam bent down and dusted his palms. Seeing the move, Wyatt let go of the rope and followed suit. Zeb Gruber showed up. He paused to say something to Rachel before joining the men. He tried to shoulder Wyatt out of the way.

"Strongest should be the front man," he said.

"Actually"—Wyatt said and let Zeb have the spot—"now that you mention it, the strongest men should be last in line." He moved back to join Adam at the end of the rope.

The front man on the opposite team shouted, "Ready for your baptism, First Church? Full immersion is the only way, you know."

The rope was stretched, the white handkerchief at its center poised mid-creek. Clutching a red kerchief, the official raised his hand high. The crowd quieted. Waited. And boom. The hand came down. The other team was strong. So strong, in fact, that for all of a couple of minutes, Adam thought surely Zeb was going to get that full baptism Lake Street had threatened.

"Hold!" someone cried from the crowd. "Come on, First Church. Hold!"

Adam didn't want to just hold. He wanted to win. Planting his feet, he collected himself, and then, with a shout and a mighty surge, he and his teammates pulled. Together, they dragged the Lake Street team into and across the creek.

Cheers went up even before Adam lost his footing and fell backward. He landed atop a clump of tall grass. Wyatt fell on top of him and rolled away, and the two men lay on their backs, looking at each other and laughing.

And for Adam, that was the biggest surprise of all. He was having fun. That odd feeling he hadn't been unable to identify this morning? *Happiness.* He'd forgotten how it felt.

After the men's tug-of-war victory, everyone accompanied the aunts back to the picnic spot. Adam lowered the wagon tailgate and the ladies set out a spread—fried chicken, canned peaches, sliced tomatoes, boiled eggs, fresh bread, and pie.

Barrett was already asleep in Aunt Jennie's arms. Aunt Lizzie and Rachel spread a quilt in the shade beneath the wagon. When lunch was over and it was time for the baseball game, Barrett was still asleep.

"You go on," Rachel said to Nel, Adam, and Wyatt. "Anna and I will stay here and mind the baby." She reached for Anna's hand and jiggled it. "We may even take a nap ourselves." Anna sank down and stretched out, with Rachel's lap for a pillow.

"It would appear, gentlemen"—Nel said, looking from Wyatt to Adam—"that I have you all to myself for the afternoon." Linking arms with Wyatt on her right, she wound her left arm around Adam's and proceeded to lead the men away.

Rachel reached over to stroke Anna's blond curls, smiling at the expression of happy exhaustion on the child's face. Whatever happened for the rest of the day, the county fair had been wonderful. She closed her eyes, listening to the murmur of the crowd, the swishing of horse's tails as the animals grazed nearby, a distant cheer as something wonderful happened in the baseball game. She was dozing when she sensed rather than heard a presence. She opened her eyes just enough to see a scarred boot.

"Looks like it wasn't just Anna who needed a nap." Adam settled on the blanket.

"And what of the baseball game?"

"Not a good one. Lake Street was ahead by five runs over the Country Boys in the second inning."

"Faulty pitching or a slow shortstop?" Rachel opened her eyes, satisfied to see surprise on Adam's face.

"You know baseball?"

"My father was a huge fan. The St. Louis Brown Stockings. We went to as many games as possible. And I learned a little in spite of the fact I was more interested in the fresh roasted peanuts than the game."

"There's a peanut vendor on the far side of the grounds. Say the word and I'll deliver to this very spot. It's the least I could do after you volunteered to stay here while we went off to have fun."

"And did you?" Rachel asked. "Have fun?"

"Surprisingly, yes."

"I'm so glad," Rachel said. She moved to get up.

"Please stay," Adam said, touching her arm. "I'd like it if we could—talk."

A pleasant little sensation rippled up Rachel's backbone. She felt herself blushing even as she settled back down.

Adam crossed his legs and leaned forward, elbows on knees, fingers laced and cradling his chin. "I know you grew up in St. Louis. Your mother passed a few years back. Your father was a pastor. That first day I met you, you made it clear you wouldn't be staying in Lost Creek. But now...some fool didn't have the sense to keep you, and here you are." He gestured about them. "Experiencing the glories of the York County Fair." He studied her. "How about it, Rachel Ellsworth, are *you* having fun?"

"I am." She said it without hesitation, and then she grinned. "Although I'm still not clear on the advantages of the Hereford over the Shorthorn. Or vice versa."

He laughed. "That's quite all right. I didn't know the difference between patchwork and appliqué until you explained it at the quilt exhibit."

"I guess we're even then."

He nodded. Studied her. Seemed about to say something more and then looked away abruptly. "It's time I made my way home. Evening chores are calling. Do you mind gathering Barrett out from under the wagon?"

Rachel slipped out from beneath a sleeping Anna and reached for the baby. She stood up with Barrett in her arms. "He's going to want to eat the minute he wakes."

Adam nodded. "I'd still like to take them both with me, but if you think it's crazy, I won't do it."

"Let me see if I can get him awake enough to give him his supper before you drive out. If you have cold biscuits or crackers at home, that'll do for a snack later—or breakfast tomorrow. And it's messy, but he can drink from a cup now."

Adam nodded. "We'll manage."

In the next few moments, Adam hitched the team, Anna woke, and Rachel fed the baby. She'd just settled him on the pallet in the wagon bed, braced between a couple of rolled-up quilts, when Nel and Wyatt returned.

When Nel realized Adam was leaving, she protested. "But there's to be a dance tonight."

"I'm no dancer." Adam nodded over at Wyatt. "But Wyatt will keep you spinning till dawn if you let him."

Nel peeked into the wagon bed. "You're taking Barrett?"

"I am. I want to see if I can handle the little man overnight." Adam lifted Anna up onto the wagon seat then turned to speak to Rachel. "I'll likely drive them back to town right after morning chores tomorrow. Maybe deliver a couple of church pews in the mix. After that, Wyatt and I have to get to the corn shucking." He climbed up beside Anna. "Wyatt, thanks for driving the ladies home. And ladies, thank you for a nice day." He touched the brim of his hat, chirped to the team, and drove away.

"We should plan a shucking bee," Nel said as she watched Adam drive off. She grabbed Wyatt's arm. "A shucking bee for the men, a quilting bee for the ladies, a community supper, and a dance to finish it off."

Rachel listened in stunned silence. What presumption. What gall!

Wyatt shrugged. "If you're going to take the Friesen place over, it's Adam you should be talking to, not me."

"Adam won't mind. He just said he'd welcome help."

Wyatt looked doubtful. "Far as I remember, he said he and I had a lot of work to do. Didn't say anything about asking for help."

"What farmer doesn't welcome help from his neighbors?"

Nel chattered away about where they'd set up the supper and whether or not they should clear out the barn or Adam's workspace to make way for a dance. All the while she talked, Rachel was watching Adam drive away, little Anna at his side. She put her hand to the place on her arm Adam had touched a few moments ago. She remembered the look of surprise on his face when she revealed a knowledge of baseball. And his calling Landis a fool for not keeping her. She thought about how easy it had been to say yes to his question about whether she was having fun. And she wondered what it would be like to be filling the empty space on the wagon seat.

Chapter 11

"She...what?" Adam kept stirring the grits he was making for Barrett as he looked over to where Wyatt sat at the table, drinking coffee. The two had agreed that Wyatt would take care of morning chores—no matter his being gone half the night dancing and then driving the women home.

"You heard me," Wyatt said. "Nel's got the idea you'd welcome her planning a shucking bee for Saturday. And you know how Nel is. A shucking bee became a party—a quilting bee for the ladies, a community supper, and then a dance. I wouldn't be surprised if she comes out sometime today to ask where you want the dance—in the barn or under the overhang where you've been building those church pews."

Adam slid the bubbling grits off to the side and put another pan on, preparing to scramble eggs. He plopped a dollop of butter in the pan and cracked nearly a dozen eggs before saying anything.

"Help with the shucking wouldn't be so bad. Would it?"

"Of course not. But the rest of it?" Adam slid the iron skillet to the back of the stove beside the pan of grits before serving himself. "Help yourself," he said to Wyatt and sat down to eat. He waited for Wyatt to join him before asking, "How was the dance?"

Wyatt took a swig of coffee. "I surprised her. She didn't know I could dance."

Adam nodded. He took a bite of the biscuit, chewed, and swallowed before taking on the real topic at hand. "I need to have a talk with Nel."

"About?"

Adam gestured with his fork. "Bee this and bee that. And a dance." He shook his head. "Don't want it." He looked over at Wyatt who seemed to be studying him.

"You don't want Nel either. Do ya?"

"Nel and I have always been friends."

"That's not what I meant."

Adam sighed. Barrett was awake. Anna would be too before long. Rising from his place at the table, Adam went into the children's room. When he bent over the baby's crib, Barrett looked up at him and smiled. Reached for him. Adam lifted him into his arms, soppy diaper and all.

"Papa? I'm hungry."

Anna peered at him from beneath the covers, only the top of her blond head and her eyes visible.

"Go on out to the kitchen," Adam said. "Wyatt will help you get something to eat while I change Barrett's diaper. *Diapers. Do they get boiled with the rest of the wash ... no. That'd be a different pot entirely, wouldn't it?* He pondered laundry for the two children while he readied Barrett for the drive back to town. When he returned to the kitchen, Anna was at the table eating.

"Thanks for helping," he said to Wyatt. He put grits in a bowl and poured milk with his free hand then settled Barrett on his knee at the table. *Oops. Need a bib.* He retrieved a dish towel, setting Barrett on the table just long enough to tie it around the baby's neck.

Wyatt sat back with a big smile on his face.

"Enjoying yourself?" Adam asked as he sat back down and spooned grits into the baby's mouth.

"You do all right," Wyatt said. "Can't say as I'm all that surprised. Nel has plenty to say about what a wonderful father you've turned out to be."

Nel again. Adam caught Wyatt's attention and nodded toward Anna. They'd need to measure their words carefully now that four-year-old ears were listening. "As to that matter," Adam said, "I should probably settle it once and for all after I drop the children at the Meekers' this morning."

Wyatt grinned. "I hope that means what I think it does."

Adam caught a dribble of grits with the spoon and returned it to Barrett's mouth. "If you hope it means there's not going to be any planning of festivities without first checking with me, and if you hope it means there's not going to be any assumption of a future that might include a partnership of any kind between myself and a certain person, then your hope will not be disappointed."

Wyatt took a bite of biscuit. Chewed and swallowed. Finally, he nodded. "Then you wouldn't be opposed to my pursuing a ... er...partnership."

"I'd encourage it."

Wyatt reached over and tousled Anna's gold curls. "You hear that, little one? Wyatt's gonna help your pa." He chuckled. "In fact, how about I help by doing the dishes so you can leave right away?"

Adam rapped on the Berkeys' front door midmorning. When Mrs. Berkey appeared at the door, he snatched his hat off his head and stepped back. "Good morning, ma'am. I was hoping to have a word with Nel."

"She'll be delighted to see you," Mrs. Berkey said. "Please come in."

"Thank you, but I'd just as soon speak to her out here on the porch."

Mrs. Berkey looked back into the house. "It's Adam, dear. He's asking to speak with you."

A flurry of words ensued, but Adam couldn't hear them clearly. He did, however, hear footsteps ascend the stairs just inside the door as Nel hurried up to her room.

"Can I get you a cup of coffee while you wait?" Mrs. Berkey asked.

Adam shook his head. "No, ma'am. Thank you. I had coffee at the Meekers' just now when I dropped the children off."

Mrs. Berkey smiled. "And how did things go last night?"

"Fine. Just fine. Wyatt did morning chores so I could mind the children and—"

"Adam!" Nel squeezed past her mother. "Thank you, Mother." She pulled the door closed behind her.

Adam stepped back lest Nel brush into him in her eagerness to join him on the porch.

"I'm sorry I kept you waiting." Nel made a show of smoothing her already perfect hair. "I wasn't about to let you see me until I'd changed out of my morning wrapper."

"Wyatt told me about your plans for the bee."

Nel smiled brightly. "I hope you're pleased."

This was going to be harder than he'd expected. "I'd be a fool not to be pleased when friends want to help."

"There's no reason to think *my* willingness to help will ever end. I care too deeply about you—and the children, of course—to ever—"

He'd practiced this speech all the way to town. He had to get Nel to hush long enough for him to deliver it, so he blurted out, "Nel. Stop."

"Stop...what?" She looked sincerely surprised. And confused.

Just deliver the speech. Adam took a deep breath. "You planned a party without talking to me first." Nel opened her mouth to

say something, but Adam held up his hand. "Just listen. I practiced this speech all the way to town. Let me talk."

Nel crossed her arms. "All right. Talk."

He nodded. "You were a good friend to Esther and you've
been kind to my children and me. I hope that never changes. But
you can't be planning quilting bees and the like at my place. It
sends a message to folks about you and me that's not true." He
paused. *Oh no. She's going to cry.* "I hope those tears mean you're
understanding what I'm trying to say."

Nel nodded. She looked away.

"I appreciate you as a close friend. But that's all we are ever
going to be." He waited for the words to sink in. "Do you need
me to say any more? Because I need this to be settled between
us, once and for all." He waited. It felt like he waited a long time.

Finally, Nel took a deep, wavering breath. She sniffed and
cleared her throat. "What—what did I do wrong? I mean … for
you to change your mind about me. About us."

"I didn't change my mind. My thoughts never went beyond
friendship. So. If you've talked to anyone about this shucking
bee, you need to tell them it's canceled."

She pursed her lips. "Well, goodness, Adam. It's only ten
o'clock in the morning. I haven't said a word about it to anyone.
Except Wyatt."

Wyatt. The name landed in the middle of the conversation
like a gift, and Adam grabbed it. "Now there's a good man." He
watched Nel's reaction to the hint. It took a minute or so, but
finally she uncrossed her arms and relaxed against the railing. He
relaxed a little too.

"A good man—and a good dancer." With a little nod, she
crossed the porch to the front door. Opening it, she stepped
inside. And she did not look back.

A week after the county fair, Rachel was playing hide-and-seek with Anna in the backyard when Nel stopped by. After all the work the quilters had done to help with the county fair, they'd decided to take a brief hiatus from their weekly meetings at the Berkeys, and so Nel and Rachel hadn't seen each other. "I've missed you!" she said, when Nel came within earshot.

"Bet you haven't missed my big mouth," Nel said.

"What?"

"All that talk about marrying—making you listen. When the only reason you moved to Lost Creek was because of *not* marrying. Why didn't you just tell me to shut up?"

"It wasn't that bad."

"It was awful for me to do that without a thought of how it must have made you feel. I am so sorry."

"You didn't mean to hurt me. I know that." She changed the subject. "How's the quilt coming?"

"Only five hundred and forty of those infernal circles to go. That's actually what I came about."

A little voice sounded from the barn. "Rachel! You gonna find me or not?"

"Oh my goodness." Rachel wheeled about. "Excuse me. I forgot I was supposed to be 'seeking.' " She raised her voice. "I'm coming!" She hurried to the barn and made a show of not finding Anna who always hid in the same spot. After an appropriate delay and a few *where-is-that-child-now?* mutterings, Rachel peered behind the stack of hay bales in the corner. "There you are!"

Anna squealed with delight and tore out of the barn and toward the outhouse.

"Looks like it's a good thing you found her," Nel laughed.

"Can you stay? I'll make us some tea and we can catch up."

"I'd like that. If you have time."

"I have all the time in the world. Aunt Jennie's been called to a lying-in, and Aunt Lizzie is delivering supper to a family over on the west side of town." As she talked, Rachel retrieved Barrett and the quilt he'd been lying on. Anna exited the outhouse and they all headed inside.

Nel exclaimed over the fall bouquet in the center of the kitchen table.

"Papa picked them," Anna said. "He said Rachel likes sunflowers."

Rachel hurried to add, "Everyone loves sunflowers. After all, they're the last wildflowers we'll be able to enjoy before winter sets in."

"But Papa said *you* like them," Anna insisted.

"Anna, why don't you go get your sewing basket? You could show Nel what you're working on." After Anna left, Rachel explained. "We made up a little sewing kit that could be just hers. She's been doing a very nice job stitching a little four-patch doll quilt."

Nel was uncharacteristically silent. Finally, she said, "Did you know Wyatt Dahl was such a good dancer? I had no idea until the county fair."

Relieved that *Adam* wasn't the first name out of Nel's mouth, Rachel said, "No...I...I didn't. Know. Until then."

Anna came back with her sewing.

"I think he's probably the best dancer in the county. And strong? Oh my goodness! When he won that tug-of-war—"

"My *daddy* won the tug-of-war," Anna said, as she placed her sewing basket on the table and sat down.

"Well, yes, of course your papa helped. All the men on the First Church team helped." Nel shot a look that said *but we both know the truth* Rachel's way before peering into the sewing basket. "Is this what you're making?" She held up four rows of little quilt blocks.

Anna nodded. She pointed to one of the fabrics. "There was just a tiny piece left from when Mama made Barrett's quilt, and

Rachel said we should put it in there, so one day when I have my own little girl and she sees it, it'll be a remember of my mama."

"A *remember*," Nel murmured. "That's beautiful."

Anna set the project out on the table, took up the next row of blocks, and settled down to pin them in place.

"Don't you want to do that for her?" Nel asked. "She'll never get it straight."

Rachel smiled. "*Straight* isn't the most important thing right now."

Nel pondered that for a moment before saying, "Anyway. Where was I?"

"Wyatt. Dancing."

"Oh. Yes. Well, there's more I'd like to talk about but another time. What I really came about was to see if you'd be willing to help with my quilt again. If I promise not to fill the air with a bunch of nonsense."

"I didn't think it was nonsense." *But I'd like it very much if that were true.*

"It was. And it probably hurt you. And I'm sorry." Nel took another sip of tea and stood up. "I should go now. Wyatt's mother invited me to supper with the family and I can't wear this old thing to meet the parents, even if I do already know them. So. About sewing together. What day is good for you?"

She's meeting the parents? Wyatt's parents? Rachel stammered a reply. "How's M-Monday afternoon? But it'll have to be here, unless I can bring Anna and Barrett with me if the aunts are busy."

"Monday." Nel nodded. "Thank you." She reached out to touch one of the sunflowers and murmured, "I hope you appreciate what these mean."

Rachel didn't know what to say to that. Nel was probably reading far too much into a bunch of wildflowers. On the other hand, a girl could hope.

Chapter 12

Adam stirred the fire in the stove and then went to peer out the kitchen window at the dormant landscape. Wyatt was late. Again. He'd agreed to come early a couple of mornings a week so Adam could have the children at home overnight, but Adam's attempt at establishing a regular routine wasn't working. At least it was for a good reason. Wyatt was spending a lot of time with Nel, which alternately relieved one problem and created another. Nel was no longer forcing her way into Adam's life. But Wyatt wasn't as reliable now that he had a reason to spend more time in town. *Ah, well.* Winter would be here soon, and once snow was drifting over the roads, the children would probably have to stay in town anyway. Best not to make an issue of it.

Turning away from the window, Adam prepared breakfast. As expected, a half-awake Anna stumbled into the room moments before Barrett woke. The children were almost finished with breakfast when Wyatt came inside with a troubled look on his face.

"What's wrong?"

"I don't like the looks of that cut on Bo's pastern. Took me a minute to even get him to settle enough to let me check it. There's heat running up the cannon almost to his knee."

Adam frowned. The horse had caught his hind foot in the fence the day before, but he'd remained calm and pulled it back.

The injury hadn't seemed that bad. But it wasn't like Bo to be hard to handle.

"I'll stay here with the kids if you want to check it yourself."

"Anna," Adam said, "you help Wyatt with Barrett if he needs it, all right? Papa's just going to check on Bo. I won't be long."

Wyatt had been right about the big gray's unusual restlessness. When Adam tried to check the injury, the horse tossed his head and backed away. When he finally succeeded in checking the wound, what he discovered wasn't good. The cut was worse than he thought.

Back inside, he rummaged in Esther's fabric bin for something he could use for bandages. He'd ripped a mound of strips when Anna came into the little parlor. "Bo cut his foot. Papa's going to have to take care of it. I'll ask Wyatt to take you back into town."

"But *you* always do that."

"And I want to do it today, but I can't. You'll be fine with Wyatt."

Wyatt was more than willing to return to town. And was it all right if he took time to surprise Nel and stop by the Berkeys'?

Anna stomped her foot. "I don't *want* to ride with Wyatt. We'll be good, Papa. You can even take us out to the barn."

"It's too cold for that today," Adam said. He looked over at Wyatt. "After you drop the children, you can take lunch before driving back out here."

Anna thrust her lower lip out. "I want to stay home."

"You love it at the Meekers'."

"I love it better at home."

Adam knelt down. "I'm glad you do, little one. And I like it better when you're here with me too. But with Mama gone..."

"You said Mama's not coming back. You could get us a new one."

"Where'd you get an idea like that?" If Nel had been putting ideas in Anna's head—if she'd only been pretending to give up the ridiculous notion—

"From Aunt Molly."

"Molly?"

Anna nodded. "Aunt Molly said maybe someday you'd get us a new mama. She said our mama in heaven would prob'ly think that was a good idea. And I think so too. So Barrett and me can come home."

Well. That was a little better. Molly was interfering, but only because she loved Anna and Barrett and wanted the best for them.

"I'm sure Aunt Molly means well, but new mamas aren't something you just order up from the catalog." He forced a little laugh.

"I know that," Anna said. "Besides, Rachel's already here. Me and Barrett like her just fine. And you like her too. Else why'd you bring her sunflowers?"

Adam was suddenly aware of Wyatt, leaning against the door, his arms folded, a knowing smile on his face. The man was enjoying this entirely too much.

"We'll talk about this another time," Adam said. "Right now, you need to get dressed so Wyatt can take you back to town." After hesitating a moment, Anna trotted out of the kitchen and into her room. Adam glared at Wyatt. "Not a word."

"Did I say anything?"

"No, and you'd better not." Soon, Wyatt was headed back into town with the children and Adam had turned his attention to Bo. Mostly. *Rachel's already here. Me and Barrett like her just fine.*

The image of Rachel Ellsworth hovered on the fringes of the rest of his day. And while Adam could not quite envision her in Esther's house, he had no trouble at all envisioning her in his arms.

After Wyatt brought the children back to town—along with news of Bo's injury—Rachel could not seem to keep from worrying. Adam needed those horses. What if Bo didn't recover? When a couple of days went by and there was still no word, Rachel worried more. Thoughts of Adam seemed to hover over nearly everything she did. When nearly a week went by without his coming to town, even the aunts began to worry. And then cold, dreary weather settled in.

Anna was nearly inconsolable. "Will Papa visit today?"

"We don't know, little one."

"Why can't he come?"

"Because he has to take very good care of Bo. You know how important the horses are to the farm. They do so much work for your papa. But he'll come as soon as he can."

When Adam missed church on Sunday, the aunts and Rachel planned to drive out together right after lunch. But then a storm moved in, bringing cold winds and sleet that coated the road.

"I'm sorry, little one," Aunt Lizzie said to Anna, "but if the wind picks up any more, the buggy could slide right off the road. It's too dangerous for us to go today."

Anna burst into tears. Aunt Lizzie eventually managed to convince her to join in a game of jackstraws.

Rachel mixed up a batch of bread dough. She was kneading—furiously—when Aunt Jennie joined her. "I hate it when winter announces itself with an ice storm."

Rachel gave the dough a punch. "Poor Anna was really counting on a drive out to the farm today."

"I don't think you have to worry about Adam," Aunt Jennie said.

"I'm sure you're right. I just can't seem to think of anything else." She shook her head. "It's strange."

Aunt Jennie chuckled.

"What's so funny?"

"I wouldn't call it strange at all."

"What would you call it?"

"I'd call it falling in love," Aunt Jennie said.

Rachel protested. "That's not it. I've been in love and this—this isn't the same."

"Are you sure you've been in love?"

"Of course I am. His name was Landis. Landis Grove."

Aunt Jennie nodded. "I remember the name. What I'm asking is...was that love or a habit? Everyone assumed you would marry, so you assumed it too."

Rachel pondered the comment. "I don't...know," she finally said. "I suppose I'm afraid to find out. Afraid he doesn't feel the same way."

"He does."

"How do you know? How will *I* know?"

Aunt Jennie smiled. "Have patience. When he finally decides to speak his mind, Adam won't leave any room for doubt. And in the meantime...enjoy every breathless moment."

Freezing rain coated the world in a glimmering sheet of ice. Tree branches broken by the weight crashed to the earth. More than once in the night, Rachel was awakened by a sound like cannon fire. Trees splitting, Aunt Jennie said. At last, warm air moved into the area and the ice began to melt.

"Papa will come!" Anna clasped her hands and hopped up and down with joy.

"Or," Aunt Lizzie said, "we could go to him. Would you like that?"

In less than an hour, the aunts, Rachel, Anna, and Barrett were in the buggy, sloshing along the muddy road. Anna could barely contain her joy. The moment Aunt Lizzie pulled the buggy to a halt, Anna dashed for the house, flung open the door, and went inside. She returned just as quickly, announcing that Papa wasn't inside.

Rachel hurried into the barn ahead of the others. She found Adam, sound asleep atop a row of hay bales just outside a stall. When she put her hand on his shoulder, he started awake and sat up, blinking against the sunlight shining in through the door.

He squinted up at her. "What's the matter?" He lurched to his feet. "The children—"

"—are fine. It's you we're worried about."

Anna skittered up the aisle. The aunts peered inside. Seeing Adam and Rachel, they retreated after saying they'd see to getting a meal started in the house.

"We were so worried, Papa," Anna said. "Why didn't you come to church Sunday?"

"The ice," Adam said. He looked toward the stall. "And Bo." He stepped to the stall door. "No-no-no—" He jerked the stall door open and knelt beside the giant gray horse, lying on its side in the straw.

When Anna took a step toward him, Adam held up his hand to ward her off. Rachel reached for Anna's hand, and together they backed out of the stall. *Poor Adam.* The man was clearly exhausted. Losing one of his team would be—but wait. At Adam's touch, the horse flicked an ear. Lifted its head.

"Hey, boy," Adam murmured, his voice low and gentle. He grasped the halter and encouraged the horse to rise. With a mighty surge, the huge animal was on his feet. He shook from head to tail, tossed his head, and moved to the corner of the stall where a bucket waited, wedged into a corner shelf. He lowered his great head, snuffled, snorted, and turned his head to look at Adam.

Rachel burst out laughing. "I don't know a lot about horses, but I know disappointment when I see it."

Adam looked up toward heaven. "Thank you!" He looked at Rachel. "He's hungry. He hasn't eaten in two days. I've been nursing him day and night...nothing I could do...I'd nearly lost hope." He looked back over at the giant horse. At Rachel. Down at Anna. "It's good to see you. So good." He scooped Anna up and gave her a hug. "He's going to be all right! Bo's going to be all right!" And suddenly he was including Rachel in the hug, whirling about and lifting her off the ground.

He set her down quickly and apologized. "I'm sorry." His face turned red. "I smell like a horse." He took the bucket out of Bo's stall and strode away, returning with grain.

The bell that hung just outside the farmhouse door rang. Aunt Lizzie shouted, "Breakfast in twenty minutes!"

"That's just time for me to get the rest of the stock fed."

Anna spoke up. "Rachel and me can feed the chickens."

Adam looked doubtful, but before he could speak, Rachel agreed. "We certainly can." She motioned for Anna to lead the way. At the doorway, she glanced back at Adam. His hair was a mess. And he *did* smell a bit like a horse. And she loved him.

Chapter 13

Rachel's life took on the rosy hues of sunrise after Adam picked her up and swung her about in the barn. Adam smiled at her and she blushed. He drove into town on Sundays and offered her his arm and they walked to the newly finished church together.

On the first Sunday in December, after they'd all slid into a pew in the usual order—Rachel, Aunt Lizzie, Aunt Jennie, Anna, and Adam on the aisle holding Barrett—Adam leaned down to speak to Anna and stood up. Anna followed him down the aisle to the back of the church and back up the side aisle, where he slid in next to Rachel. She could feel herself blushing furiously, even as the aunts slid sideways toward the center aisle. Midway through the first hymn, Adam handed Barrett over. And it felt right.

Rachel spent many December evenings sequestered in her room sketching the gifts she would present to her new family on Christmas Day. One of Anna and Barrett for Adam. Another of their beautiful home for the aunts. And one of Nel with her wedding quilt draped across her lap, for the future Mr. and Mrs. Dahl had announced their engagement at Thanksgiving.

Snow fell in spurts throughout the month of December, and it stayed cold. Anna squealed with delight when Rachel took her coasting. Lost Creek didn't offer much in the way of real hills, but they still had fun. Barrett took his first steps, toddling across the parlor carpet one weekday morning to the applause of an appreciative audience.

When snow began to fall in earnest two days before Christmas, Anna worried. "What if Papa can't come to town?"

Rachel didn't know how to allay the child's fears. She felt them too. But the snow stopped and Adam arrived on Christmas morning in a borrowed one-horse sleigh. Anna hopped up and down with glee. They rode to church, with Rachel sharing the front seat with Adam and Anna and the aunts and Barrett snuggled beneath an old buffalo robe in back.

The service was glorious. Rachel's heart soared as they all sang "Glory to the newborn king." The pastor's sermon focused on the hope that was central to the coming of God's Son. Rachel bowed her head. *Thank You for bringing me to Lost Creek. Thank You for never leaving me. For holding on to me, even when I struggled to hold on to You.*

The pastor read from Romans. "Now the God of *hope* fill you with all joy and peace in believing, that ye may abound in *hope,* through the power of the Holy Ghost." He quoted Christmas carols in the message. *"Joy* to the world, the Lord is come. *Peace* on earth, good will toward men. O little town of Bethlehem … the *hopes* and fears of all the years are met in thee tonight." Joy. Peace. Hope. All of it fulfilled in Christ.

Rachel's heart brimmed with happiness. How good of God to bring her here to Lost Creek and give her a new home, a new hope, and a new future.

Back at the house, after Adam helped the aunts and Anna down, Rachel waited for him to lift her down too. But he didn't. Instead, he said, "I'd like to speak with you about something. Do you mind taking a ride?"

Before Rachel had a chance to respond, the aunts had commandeered Anna and the baby and scurried inside.

Adam settled the buffalo robe over Rachel's lap and then walked around and climbed up beside her. "It was a nice service," he said as he reined the horse onto the road.

"It was."

"I hope you aren't too cold."

"I'm fine."

"I probably should have taken time to heat some stones to keep your feet warm."

"How far are we going?"

"Not far." He didn't even look at her. "I suppose you've had many a sleigh ride before this. In St. Louis."

"Not that many."

He went on like that. Talking as if they'd just met. As if they were strangers. What was going on? Rachel looked back toward town. "I should be helping with the meal."

"I spoke with the aunts. They'll understand. I want to show you something."

"So you said. May I know what it is?"

Adam shook his head. "Not until we're there."

"Where? At the farm?"

"Just past it. But still on my land."

Rachel looked up at him. Square jaw clenched. Eyes on the road. Hands holding tightly to the reins. Not relaxed. Not at all. "You're making me nervous, Adam. What's this about?"

"Christmas."

As if that explained anything. She clasped her gloved hands beneath the buffalo robe and settled back. *Christmas. Really?* They glided right on past the farm. Rachel looked up at him again. "Adam?"

"Just a little farther. I'll tell you everything in less than a mile."

Steam rose from the horse's haunches. A dot appeared on the horizon ahead. As they approached, it resolved into a line of cedar trees. Past the cedars, a house. Larger than Adam's house. And older, from the look of it. He reined the horse about and the sleigh crashed through a low drift. He pulled up alongside a wide porch that led up to the front door. Tying off the reins, he hurried around the sleigh, but he didn't offer to help Rachel down. Instead, he stood in the snow beside the sleigh and motioned toward the house.

"This is where I grew up. My father built it. It's been let go a bit, but it's a good, solid house." He paused. "Not fancy. Just... solid." He pointed at the windows. "Parlor to the left, kitchen behind it. Dining room back there. Three bedrooms upstairs. Something like the Meekers', but not as fancy."

Rachel looked over at him, confused. Why were they here?

"Esther and I lived in the hired man's house. We moved there after we married. My parents lived here. Until they died."

She still didn't know why he'd brought her here.

Abruptly, Adam turned around. He held out his hands, palms up. Rachel took them, expecting him to help her down from the sleigh. But he didn't. Instead, he said, "Anna wants to come home to stay. She wants a new mama. Molly says Esther would want her children to have a mother."

Rachel's heart sank. She was getting a Christmas proposal after all. But not the kind she'd been hoping for.

Adam gave a low sound of frustration. He let go of her hands. "That's not—not what I wanted to say at all. I had it memorized. And here I am babbling on about my parents and how Anna wants a mother and..." He looked behind him at the house. "This house. I brought you here because it's the best I have to give, and it's not enough. It could be a good house, I think. But it's nothing like what you're used to. And I want to give you so much, Rachel."

Her heart skipped a beat.

"Anna's mother and I found our way to love, eventually, but it wasn't—it wasn't—this." He motioned between the two of them. "It wasn't what I feel for you." He reached out to trace her cheek. "I can barely breathe sometimes, just looking at you. I can barely sleep some nights, just thinking of you."

When he went to drop his hand, Rachel captured it between hers and held on.

"I've never been in love this way. I want to give you—so much." He swallowed. "I love you so much, sometimes I think my heart will burst. This house isn't enough. But we could make it enough together. Do you think?" He waited, his breath rising in the cold air. His lips parted.

"I think," Rachel said, "that any house in the world would be enough, Adam. As long as you are in it."

He gathered her in his arms. Words fell away. Hope surged. Love reigned.

A Patchwork Love

Chapter 1

Omaha, Nebraska, 1875

*I*t took every ounce of Jane McClure's waning faith to put her last two coins into the horse-drawn trolley driver's hand. Normally she and ten-year-old Molly would have walked to the train station this evening. But Molly had developed a slight cough as the temperature plummeted, and Jane was determined that she not "come down with anything." Mr. Huggins was kind but a bit remote when it came to Molly, and nothing must stand in the way of their enjoying a pleasant holiday together—as if they were a family. He'd enclosed two tickets in his recent letter—a letter that sounded … *hopeful*. He'd even mentioned how much Molly would enjoy seeing the Christmas decorations in Denver's department store windows. For Mr. Huggins to be thinking of how to please Molly was a good sign. And so Jane was spending the last of her money for a ride to the train station. Out of the cold. For Molly's sake.

The driver waved them on board the empty car with a teasing comment about the chilly fog descending over the city. "Just look at it, won't you?" He waved around them. "The perfect atmosphere for magic!" He winked at Molly. "Tell the truth now, miss. You're a princess and this old car is soon to become a golden coach." He called out to the gray horse. "Hear that, yer majesty? It's a golden harness for ye, and a velvet cape for myself!" The horse shook its head and whickered, as if answering the old man in the battered top hat.

Molly giggled and led the way on board, sliding into a seat near the driver. Jane plopped their two carpetbags on an empty seat and sat down, tugging Molly's knit cap down over her ears.

"All right, ladies," the driver called out, "next stop, Omaha City's train station—with stops along the way for other fares, of course." With a tip of his hat and a curious smacking sound to the horse, he took up the reins, and they were off.

When Molly put a mittened hand to her mouth to suppress a cough, Jane scolded herself, even as she concentrated on the familiar scenery passing by the plodding car. *I should have put the last of that wood in the stove this afternoon.* Why couldn't she seem to conquer her fear at the prospect of using up the last of things? It had wound itself into the fabric of her every day in recent weeks. Three bits of wood in the woodbox meant they wouldn't freeze. Even one coin in her threadbare change purse meant they weren't destitute. And as long as there was a bit of cheese and a package of biscuits in the cupboard, hunger couldn't win.

But the cupboard's bare now. That's the last of the cheese and biscuits in your bag. Of course using the last of the food made sense today. They wouldn't be back for at least a week, and food must not go to waste. But wood for the stove was different. She'd be able to build a fire when they got back. On the other hand . . . if things went perfectly, perhaps they wouldn't have to come back. Should Mr. Huggins's hopeful tone bear fruit, perhaps they'd be wiring Mrs. Abernathy to pack up the few things in their rooms and ship them to Denver.

Molly coughed again and snuggled close. Jane hugged her bony shoulders. "Quite the adventure we're having, isn't it? Money for a ride to the station *and* passage to Denver." She forced anticipation into her voice. "Mrs. Abernathy says Denver is 'big and bustling.' And Mr. Huggins said he's looking forward to showing you the Christmas displays in the department store windows."

Molly sniffed. "Wicked," she said, and shrugged a bit of distance between herself and her mother.

"I beg your pardon?"

Molly repeated the word. "Mrs. Abernathy said that Denver is big and bustling... and *wicked*." She cleared her throat. "I don't know why we have to go."

The ever-present knot in Jane's stomach tightened. She hadn't realized just how worried she'd been of late, until Howard Huggins sent those train tickets, and she nearly cried with relief. "Well..." She paused. "It would be rude not to accept such a generous gift. And won't it be nice to see someplace new? Someplace... exciting?"

"I suppose so." Molly sat back, then murmured, "I wish Sarah hadn't moved away. She said she'd write." She peered up at Jane. "What if her letter comes and we're gone?"

"Mrs. Abernathy will save it, and it'll be waiting when we get back. Probably tucked under the door." *If we come back.*

With a "Whoa" and a tug on the reins, the driver pulled the team up alongside the walkway leading to the train station entrance. Grabbing hers and Molly's bags, Jane thanked the driver and headed down the steps with Molly close behind. She'd just let go of the bar by the step when she realized that the evening mist was beginning to freeze. One foot found purchase. The other did not. Grabbing for something—anything—to keep from falling, Jane turned back toward the horse car, but she was too far away. As she fell, she shouted a warning at Molly. Molly took care, but Jane lost the battle to stay upright.

For a moment, everything faded away. When things began to unscramble, Jane realized she was sitting in a most unladylike position, legs sprawled, bonnet askew. Molly crouched next to her, frightened tears shining in her blue eyes. Blinking, Jane concentrated on Molly's terrified "Mama! Mama!"

"It's all right...I–I'm...all right." Jane reached up to straighten her bonnet, grateful to see that Molly was holding on to both their bags. It wouldn't do to lose the only decent things they owned to some thief taking advantage of the ice and the evening shadows.

"Here now, miss."

A hand cupped her elbow, and the aroma of stale tobacco smoke wafted down as the driver tried to help her up. Kind eyes shone from beneath his bushy white eyebrows as he asked, "You all right?"

"I—I think so," she said. But when she tried to stand, she wasn't sure what hurt more, her right knee...her left ankle...or the elbow the driver held while helping her back to her feet.

"I told one of the porters they needed to spread sand out here. I could feel the temperature dropping long before it did. My knees always give warning, and they've been killing me all day. But did anyone listen? And now...now they've caused a lovely lady to be injured."

"Really...I'm all right." Was she bleeding through her last pair of good stockings? Had she torn anything? She wasn't bent on deceiving anyone, but she saw no need to let Mr. Huggins see *destitution* when she and Molly stepped off the train. Thank goodness she'd packed a mending kit. Mr. Huggins had to know she wasn't well off. He'd insisted on seeing her back to the boardinghouse one evening during his brief visit to Omaha a few weeks ago. It was obvious from her lodging that Jane had suffered a setback. Still, Mr. Huggins had continued to write. And as the weeks wore on and their situation grew more and more desperate...well. This trip simply had to work out.

Her heart pounding, Jane suppressed a groan as pain shot up both legs. She forced a bright smile. "Thank you for being so kind. Please don't let me make you late for your next fare. We'll be fine." She reached for the larger of the two bags and forced another smile for Molly's sake. *Please, God, You know I don't have the fare to pay for a ride back to the boardinghouse. We have to get on that train.*

The driver looked doubtfully toward the station, then back at the trolley, where three people had now taken seats.

"I'll be fine," Jane repeated as she reached for Molly's hand. "We'll take our time."

"See that you do," the old man said, sliding the sole of one boot across the pavement. "It's slick enough to go coasting without the sled." With a nod and a tip of his hat, he climbed aboard.

Jane let go of Molly's hand long enough to straighten her bruised elbow. "Did I tear my sleeve?" she asked, grateful when Molly inspected it, then shook her head. She shifted her weight to her right leg and tested her left ankle. The ankle seemed all right. The knee was another matter. In fact, it nearly gave way. With a quick little gasp, she put her hand on Molly's shoulder to steady herself. The look of panic on the child's face strengthened her resolve.

"A twisted knee is *not* going to keep us from our adventure." Jane took a deep breath, noticing for the first time the pools of light dotting the slick surface as night fell and the new city gaslights lit up. "We have to take small steps on the ice anyway. Just go slow. I'm sure I'll feel better once I've loosened it up a little. It'll be warmer inside. That will help, too." Leading with her left foot, she clenched her teeth and limped her way toward the station.

Once inside, she was afraid to pause. They had to get on that train. She could ice her knee and wrap it and do whatever else might be required once they rolled out of the station, but she could not let a little thing like a silly fall keep her from the promise represented by Mr. Howard Huggins. If this trip worked out, it could mean an end to Jane's constant worries. They'd have enough. Enough food. Enough fuel. No more days struggling to keep Molly from realizing her mother had skipped a meal to feed her. No more excuses about being tired and needing to turn in early, when the real reason for heading for bed was a lack of fuel and a need to get warm.

Mr. Huggins might be a bit shorter than Jane and a bit portly and a bit—well—*quite* bald, but he was forward-thinking enough to believe in education for women. In fact, he'd said there was a very good boarding school they could visit with Molly in mind "if things worked out." And Jane was determined to see that "things worked out." Mr. Huggins might not be a knight in shining armor, but he seemed kind, and a woman could learn to love. Friendship was more important than passion anyway.

Pushing against the pain, Jane led the way through the station and to the track, pausing just long enough to look up at the board indicating that the train to Denver was on—of course—the far track. She peered in that direction. Less than a city block. Surely she could walk that far.

"We shouldn't go," Molly said. "You're hurt, and Mr. Huggins doesn't even *like* me." Her voice wavered. She tugged at her scarf, then used it to cover her mouth while she coughed.

"Mr. Huggins," Jane said with more certainty than she felt, "is actually rather fond of you. It's just that he hasn't been around ten-year-old girls. He doesn't quite know how to—Well, he's a bit shy."

Molly tipped her head and met Jane's gaze with a doubtful eye.

"You aren't the only one in the world who's shy, Molly. Even grown-ups can be shy."

"I'm not *shy*," Molly protested. "I'm just...quiet around people I don't know."

"Well, then. You should be even more excited about this trip, because once you've had the opportunity to get to know him, I'm quite certain you'll discover that Mr. Huggins has many admirable traits. And he will discover that *you*"—Jane tapped the tip of the freckled nose—"are *wondermous*." When Molly giggled, Jane smiled and nodded at the far track. "Let's make our way to the train before you turn into a *frozen* wondermous." She clenched her teeth and willed herself to walk.

Somehow they made it onto the train, although Jane couldn't help letting out a grunt or two with the effort of climbing aboard. To make it up the last step, she placed her carpetbag at the top of the stairs, grasped the railing with both hands, and hopped up so she could land on her good—or at least her less injured—leg. She managed to make a joke that put a smile on Molly's troubled face and then hobbled to the first seat they came to in the emigrant car, where they'd be until night after next.

Mr. Huggins might want them to come, but he hadn't seen his way to providing berths in the sleeping car. That had been a disappointment, but Jane reminded herself that thrift was an admirable quality. After all, if Stephen had been a bit thriftier, his widow and child might not have found themselves pinching pennies until they—*Stop resenting poor Stephen, God rest his soul. He thought that investment was a good idea.*

As passengers filtered onto the car and settled in for the long ride ahead, Jane entertained Molly by whispering stories. The tall man with the ridiculous mustache was a prince in disguise. The portly middle-aged woman had once trained elephants in the circus. As for the gentleman across the aisle who had tipped his hat and made Jane blush—well. Jane didn't know what to say about him, until Molly nudged her and offered the opinion that he seemed much friendlier than Mr. Huggins. By then Jane's throbbing knee was challenging her forced good cheer.

"You are simply going to have to trust me in the matter of Mr. Huggins. I've said all I'm going to say on that subject." As the train whistle blew, announcing their departure, she reached into her bag and withdrew the book she'd been saving for the long trip. "Would you like me to read to you?"

Molly shrugged. "I guess."

"I beg your pardon?"

"Yes, ma'am."

"That's better." Jane traced the gilt oval on the dark cover. "I've been saving this until you were old enough to enjoy it."

Molly gazed down at the book. "Where's it been?"

Jane smiled. "At the very bottom of the little trunk I keep under my bed." She paused. "I was seventeen when this book was new." She cleared her throat. "Your grandmother and I took turns reading it to one another through a very long winter when the snow piled up against the windows and we huddled next to the stove trying to keep warm." The memory of that horrible, hungry, snowbound winter still made her shiver.

The train picked up speed, and finally they were leaving the bluffs along the river and heading out onto the Nebraska prairie. The flickering light in the train car and the rhythmic rocking helped Jane ignore her throbbing knee. She'd check it later when Molly was asleep.

Opening the book, she began to read. " 'Christmas won't be Christmas without any presents, grumbled Jo....' "

Chapter 2

Molly dozed off somewhere in the middle of the March girls' Christmas performance of an "Operatic Tragedy." Jane realized the child had fallen asleep only when a soft snore sounded and was then punctuated by yet another cough—this one accompanied by a significant amount of rumbling in Molly's chest. A woman a few seats away glanced at Jane with a frown. Closing *Little Women*, Jane slipped it into her carpetbag, then slid over and pulled Molly closer, offering her lap as a pillow.

She glanced around the train car. Most of the passengers who hadn't disembarked at various stops along the way had headed for the dining car with murmured comments about the roast beef or a "nice cup of tea." When Molly coughed again, Jane wished tea were an option for them. Mrs. Abernathy had given them an early supper at the boardinghouse. If they were very careful about portioning out the cheese and crackers, they'd be only hungry and not ravenous when the train finally pulled into the station in Denver. Jane could only hope that Mr. Huggins would be amenable to a late welcome supper. In the meantime ... there would be no hot tea ... and no real treatment for her swollen knee either. She could, however, get a look at it in the necessary.

Tucking her carpet bag beneath Molly's head for a make-shift pillow, Jane grasped the edge of the seat to keep her balance, then hopped the few feet to the necessary, hoping the handful of passengers still in the car wouldn't notice the ridiculous performance. Once inside, she lifted her foot and braced it on the rim of the commode as she leaned back against the wall and pulled her skirt up to see ... *Oh dear.* She hadn't bled through her stockings. She'd ripped a hole large enough to expose her entire knee. Not only had it ballooned in the last couple of hours; it was also beginning to turn several shades of purple and green. Try as she would, Jane couldn't straighten it. *Probably the swelling.* Looking at it seemed to make the pain worse. Trembling, she closed her eyes and leaned against the wall, moistening her lips and closing her eyes. *All you have to do is make it to Denver.*

Somehow she managed to hobble back to her seat and retrieve her mending kit. She was trying to gather courage to move again when a porter came into the car. His mellow voice was kind as he held out a pillow and blanket "for the young lady."

Jane shook her head. "That's very kind, but we can't—"

"Courtesy of the Union Pacific," he said with a wink.

Jane could have hugged him. Instead, she snuggled the blanket around Molly.

"Name's Henry, ma'am," the porter said. "You need anything else, you let me know. I'm on all the way to Denver." When Molly stirred and coughed, he glanced her way, then back at Jane. "Tea with lemon and honey? Be happy to bring some on my way through next time."

"That's very kind of you, but we—" She swallowed the words *don't have any money* and forced a smile. "We'll be fine." She busied herself smoothing Molly's blanket and blinked away desperate tears. The porter went on his way.

As the evening wore on, Jane learned that most of the people in the car had rented sleeping berths. Only one seedy-looking couple at the far end of the car had unfolded their seats to arrange makeshift sleeping quarters on the train car. Once again, Jane fought the temptation to wonder about the extent of Mr. Huggins's devotion. Why couldn't he have arranged for a berth? She and Molly would be on the train for two nights.

As the train swayed and the lamp the porter had turned down on his way through the car cast only the faintest glow, Jane once again made her way into the necessary. Removing her gloves, she laid them on the edge of the wash basin and lifted her skirt, fumbling beneath her bustle in a vain attempt to untie the ribbon holding her petticoat up.

The train swayed and she nearly lost her balance. She finally gave up and, taking her mending scissors, felt her way to cutting off one leg of her drawers, which she then cut into strips. Tying the strips together, she bound her injured knee as best she could, happy that the effort did seem to ease the pain a bit. It would help keep the swelling down. At least she hoped so.

Sacrificing her drawers was humiliating. But then, who would know? She supposed it was better to sacrifice drawers than a petticoat. Now that she thought about it, the drawers were definitely the way to go. An observant man might notice the absence of a petticoat. Was Mr. Huggins observant? The thought made Jane blush.

Someone knocked on the door. "You baking a cake in there? There's other people on the train, ya know."

Jane opened the door and apologized. It took all her will-power not to cry out in pain as she attempted to take a normal step into the aisle. The other woman didn't notice, merely brushed past Jane and slammed the door, quite literally almost in her face. Blinking back more tears, Jane hobbled back to her seat. Grabbing the pillow the porter had left behind, she used it to cushion her knee as she settled opposite Molly on the bench vacated by passengers who'd disembarked at the last stop.

Leaning her head against the frosted window, she closed her eyes and fell instantly asleep.

Jane started awake. *Gray light.* She glanced over at Molly, still fast asleep, only the top of her head showing from beneath the blanket supplied by the kindly porter. What time could it be? She gazed about the car. Had the others gone to breakfast? Her stomach growled at the thought. She moved gingerly, all thought on her injured knee as she lowered her feet to the floor. Was it her imagination, or did her knee hurt less? *Please let it be better. Please.*

She swiped at the window, wondering what stop they were at now. *Snow.* Bending low, she whispered at Molly's still form, "Someone is frosting the world with white, princess. It's snowing!"

Molly stirred. With an audible sigh, she tugged the blanket down and peered over the edge at Jane, croaking, "Snow?"

Jane nodded as she reached for the carpetbag tucked beneath their seat. "Snow and breakfast, if you're hungry."

Molly shook her head. Turning onto her side, she snuggled back out of sight. Jane broke off a bit of bread and had popped it into her mouth just as the porter made his appearance, bearing a steaming mug of tea.

"For the little lady," he said, then offered it to Jane. "Or her mama, since the little lady is obviously not ready for breakfast." He nodded toward Molly. "I was glad to note a distinct absence of coughing as I passed through in the night."

Jane nodded, even as she declined the tea.

"Might as well drink it. You'll be doing me a favor, actually. Someone in the next car ordered it, then changed their mind and decided to head up to the dining car. Said to just toss it out." He looked down at the cup. Shook his head. "Never did understand how a body could add cream to a perfectly good cup of black tea." He held it out. "Shame to let it go to waste." When Jane finally relented, the porter nodded. "Next stop is Grand Island. They put on a good breakfast if you're interested."

"Thank you, but we've brought everything we need."

The porter nodded again and continued on his way. Jane settled back to stare out the window at the empty landscape and the swirling snow, sighing with pleasure as the warm tea coursed down her parched throat.

Molly was still asleep when the train stopped at the place called Grand Island. Peering through the snow, Jane could see evidence of neither an island nor anything grand. When she said as much to the porter, he laughed.

"Can't speak to the idea of 'grand,' but there is an island in the middle of the river. Lovely when it's warm." He cocked his head at the still-sleeping Molly. "That little miss is quite the little bedbug, isn't she?"

"She was coming down with a cold when we left home. Hopefully she's mending so she can enjoy the sights in Denver."

The porter nodded. "I might ask you to move up to the Pullman if no one climbs aboard at the next stop. There's no reason for the two of you to be back here all alone, and to tell the truth, it'll lighten my load if I only have to keep one car warm. Word from up ahead is we're headed into quite a storm. Thermometer's dropping fast at Kearney Junction."

Jane glanced out at the snow drifting softly to the earth.

"I know. It doesn't look like much, but there's nothing to stop the wind out here, and things can change fast." The porter smiled. "Nothing to worry about. Even if we have to stop over at one of the stations and wait for the storm to blow by, the UP takes good care of its folks." With a tip of his cap, he was on his way.

The train headed into the storm.

Molly woke not long after the snow began to fall in earnest, grimacing as she stretched her arms above her head.

"It's about time you woke up." Jane smiled and nodded outside. "It's still snowing."

Molly swiped a hand across the window to clear the steam away. "Wow." She looked back at Jane, her cheeks red, her eyes bright with . . . something besides excitement.

Instinctively, Jane pressed her palm to Molly's forehead. "Tell me how you feel."

Molly frowned. When she opened her mouth to answer, her words were cut off by a dry, raspy cough. She grimaced. "My throat hurts. And . . . everything."

"Everything?"

Molly nodded. "Everything hurts."

And just like that, money and Mr. Huggins and the snowstorm became the least of Jane's worries.

True to his word, the porter checked back with them after two more stops and suggested they move to the Pullman. "We've only two more passengers," he explained, "and they're getting off at Gibbon. Shame to have that big fancy car and no one enjoying it."

"I appreciate it," Jane said. "Really, I do. But Molly isn't feeling well, and I—well, I slipped on the ice at Omaha, and

I'm afraid I'm about as useful as a lame horse at the moment. I'm sorry to make you walk the length of the train just because of us, but I don't think—"

"How about I carry the young miss, and you lean on my arm?" The man didn't wait for Jane's reply before scooping Molly up. "She's light as a feather. Reminds me of my little gal waiting at home." With obvious practice, he shifted Molly to his right shoulder so that his left arm was free to assist Jane. He smiled. "I guarantee you'll love the Pullman."

Clutching their bags with her left hand, Jane tucked her right hand beneath the man's arm and hung on. When they traversed the open space between the cars, she shivered. The thermometer was most definitely dropping. She glanced at the landscape, but swirling snow obscured everything.

The porter opened the door to the Pullman. Jane stared in amazement at the opulence—the brass fittings, the plush seats, the velvet drapes, the painted murals up above. Molly barely woke as the porter settled her in one of the overstuffed chairs while he made up a berth, then moved her once he had it ready. With Molly settled in, he stood back with a satisfied smile. "That's better, don't you think?"

"It's wonderful," Jane agreed. "I don't know how to thank you."

The porter smiled as he moved a chair close to Molly's berth so Jane could stay close. "You just did, ma'am. If my wife and child were headed into a blizzard alone, I'd hope someone would see to their needs. 'Do unto others'—isn't that what the Good Book says?"

A stern male voice sounded from the front of the car, some-one demanding the coffee he'd asked for "long ago."

With a little salute, the porter headed off, leaving Jane to wonder at her good fortune, even as she worried over Molly's red cheeks, the fringe of damp curls about her face, and the occa-sional whimper that sounded as she slept.

Chapter 3

The grumpy passenger who'd demanded so much of Henry's attention disembarked at Kearney Junction midmorning. From where Jane sat by Molly's berth, all she could see of the train station was a dark smudge in a world of white. Moments after the train headed out, Molly began to toss and turn. The porter brought more tea with honey, insisting that the UP would have his head if he didn't offer comfort for an ailing child. "So please, ma'am, let's not have any more arguments about the matter," he said, and Jane relented. When Molly grimaced with each swallow, Jane's stomach clenched a little more.

A few minutes later Molly whimpered for Katie, and Jane produced the rumpled rag doll with growing concern. Molly had been going through an I'm-too-grown-up-for-dolls phase. They'd only stuffed the doll in her carpetbag at the last minute. Now Jane sighed, alternately grateful for the comfort the beloved doll could give and worried over just how sick Molly was going to get.

Moments later, when Jane handed Molly's empty teacup over, Henry said, "Next stop is Elm Creek. There's not much there save the store and the railroad eating house. But we can wire ahead for you and have the doctor at Plum Creek meet us. We'll pull in there about 1:30 this afternoon if the storm doesn't cause any delays."

Jane shook her head. "I haven't any way to pay a doctor. Unless—" Did she dare presume on Mr. Huggins to wire money? She swallowed and looked into the porter's kind, dark eyes. "Surely she'll be feeling better by then."

Henry nodded. "The young ones have a way of bouncing back. I'm sure the good Lord can be trusted to undertake for the little miss."

How Jane longed to be as certain as the porter seemed to be of God's taking notice of one child on an empty train. She settled back in her chair, newly aware of her throbbing knee as she fought her fear with prayer. *I haven't asked You for anything in a long while. But this—this is important. Please let Molly get better quickly. Let us find a doctor who won't take advantage. And let Mr. Huggins understand. We need his help. Please let him see that. Let him care.*

Molly coughed again. Jane began to hum, then to sing, directing the words of a favorite lullaby toward Molly, who opened her eyes for a moment and smiled. "I like that one," she croaked, then closed her eyes.

Jane's stomach roiled with hunger. Breaking off another crust of bread from the increasingly stale loaf in her bag, she chewed and washed it down with the rest of the lukewarm tea Henry had brought her when he brought Molly's. She'd just reached for the copy of *Little Women*, thinking to calm her own nerves by reading ahead, when, with the screeching of metal on metal, the train ground to a halt.

Frowning, Jane set the book aside and leaned toward the window, looking first this way and then that. Seeing nothing but a wall of white, she rose and limped to the door. She'd only cracked it open when the roar of the wind and a blast of snow made her yank it shut. With a shiver, she rubbed her arms and sat back down, but not before pulling her coat down to use as a lap robe.

Molly stirred. "Are we there?" She lifted her head, frowning as she glanced at the window.

"It's snowing even harder," Jane said. "I think we must be at the next stop, but I can't tell."

"I'm c-cold."

"I'll see if I can get you another blanket." Jane rose and hobbled toward the front of the car, searching the compartments overhead as she moved along. Finally she located a thick red-and-black-striped blanket. Shaking it out, she made her way back to Molly. She'd just tucked it around when someone stepped into the car—someone new, Jane thought. He was taller than the porter, his face obscured by a turned-up collar, a bushy mustache, and the flaps of his hat pulled down to cover his cheeks.

His black eyes glittered as he glanced to where Molly lay, peering at him above the edge of the blankets. He nodded at Molly, then turned to Jane. "S. C. Parr, ma'am. Henry's readying a place for you and the little miss up in the dining car. Sorry to make you move again. Won't be as comfortable up there, but we'll do our best. Crew's on its way to clear the tracks, but it could be awhile. Soon as the storm stops, I expect the stationmaster at Elm Creek will get word as to what to expect. Until then, we've enough food to get by for a few days. Fuel's scarce, but we won't freeze. Henry'll be back to fetch you soon as we're ready to hunker down."

Jane frowned. She glanced out the window. "Hunker... down?"

"Yes, ma'am. We've hit a wall. Of snow, that is. Drifted up so high there's no way through. At least not right now. As soon as the storm blows past, we'll get out with our shovels and get to digging out. Crews will be heading our way from the west as well. I don't imagine we'll be stuck longer than a day or two. Hopefully not even that long."

Jane's heart began to pound. "But—my daughter—the porter was going to see about a doctor at Elm Creek."

"I know, ma'am. And we'll do what we can about that as soon as possible. In the meantime, you enjoy whatever accommodations the UP can provide—*gratis*."

Jane thanked him, just as Henry stepped into the car with an armful of blankets. With a nod, the other man was gone.

"Got things set up for you," he said, and handed Jane two more blankets. "Wrap yourself up good. Thermometer's dropping faster than a frog falling down a well. Don't you worry, though. We'll be toasty up in the dining car." He grinned. "Toasty and well fed. Mr. Parr said to use up whatever we want." He scooped Molly up and headed for the door. "I'll come back for your bags, ma'am. Soon as we get the little miss and you settled up by the best stove on the train—aside from the boiler, that is." Before opening the door, he put a blanket over Molly's head.

Jane hobbled after Henry as best she could. When the car door opened, snow blasted into the Pullman. The wind roared. Henry didn't have to tell Jane to hold on tight. Even so, she felt compelled to lean against the wind whistling between the two stalled cars. Once in the dining car, she ventured another look outside, shivering at the thought of anyone caught out in the blizzard.

As promised, the dining car was warm and inviting. Henry stretched across a table to lay Molly as gently as possible on one of the cushioned benches. Jane thanked him and slid onto the opposite bench as Henry retreated to get their bags. It wasn't quite noon yet, but as soon as Henry returned, he began to light the elegant brass lamps hanging overhead. The glow of lamplight did little to make it feel warmer. Jane pulled her own blanket around her shoulders, newly aware of her numb feet and fingers. How far had the thermometer dropped? How cold would it get?

Molly whimpered, and Jane moved to her bench, doing her best to gather the child in her arms, all the while trying to ignore the frisson of fear that ran up her spine.

As the storm raged and Molly slept, Jane alternately worried and read. When the wind finally died down, she limped to the doorway and peered out, gasping at the realization that the train was virtually buried in a drift. It was impossible to see beyond the edge of the platform connecting the dining car to the coal car ahead.

The crew worked to dig them out, and as the afternoon wore on into evening, they managed to clear away the snow so that Jane and Molly could see out the windows on the north side of the car. Only an occasional shadow stained the white surface of the earth, albeit without giving a hint of what might lay beneath the drift. As the light faded, snow began to fall again.

Molly woke and croaked a request that Jane read to her, but as Jane opened the book, she cocked her head. "You hear that?" She sat up and swiped at the frosted window, peering outside.

Could it be? Jane slid over to the window on her side of the table and squinted into the distance.

Molly coughed even as she smiled. "Sleigh bells!"

A dark dot of something came into view, gliding across the snow like a low-hovering raven flying toward the stranded train. As Jane peered at the spot, it grew, transforming into the discernible outline of a sleigh pulled by a massive black horse. The driver could have been animal, vegetable, or mineral, so swathed was he—or she—in a fur coat and hat. It was hard to tell where the coat left off and the hat began, thanks to a wide gray scarf wrapped 'round and 'round the driver's neck and head. Jane wondered at the driver's ability to see much through the narrow slit at what Jane presumed to be eye level.

Molly waved as the sleigh slid past the dining car. A pile of blankets next to the driver moved, and one red-mittened hand returned the wave. Apparently the driver wasn't alone.

The car door opened, and Henry stepped inside, followed by a woman with merry blue eyes shining above the scarf she was pulling down from her face as Henry spoke. "Looks like the good Lord has answered our prayers for the little one." He nodded at the woman. "Mrs. Gruber's son was at a neighbor's when the storm hit. He saw the stranded train on his way home—"

"—and so," the woman said as she plopped a basket on the table, "I bake." She pulled a blue and white cloth aside to reveal three loaves of bread.

The driver—presumably Mrs. Gruber's son—stomped in behind them, still swathed in the gray scarf.

"My son, Peter," the woman said as she reached for the basket he was carrying. Relieved of his burden, the man said something to Henry about talking to the engineer and retreated back outside, leaving his mother to reveal the contents of the other basket—a pie of some kind and a plate of cookies. Pulling off one red mitten, the old woman reached for a cookie. She hesitated, looking to Jane for approval. "Is all right, *ja?*" She nodded at Molly.

Jane nodded. "Yes, of course."

But Molly had already hunkered back down beneath her blankets. When Mrs. Gruber held the cookie out, Molly shook her head. "Thank you," she coughed, "but I'm not hungry."

The old woman tilted her head and stared down at Molly. Depositing the cookie back on the plate, she stepped closer and leaned down, putting her palm to Molly's forehead. She turned back to Jane. "To the house you must come." She paused. "Better

I make the child. Ve haf tea. And herbs." She pointed at the horizon to the north. "Just there. Is warm, Peter's house. We bring you back when the train is ready." She glanced at the porter. "The whistle you blow, and Peter brings back. Is gut, ja?"

Jane didn't give Henry time to answer. "That's very kind of you, Mrs. Gruber, but we should stay with the train. We'll be fine." She nodded at the baskets of food. "Especially now that you've brought supper." The aroma of whatever was in that pie was making her mouth water.

"Is nothing," the old woman said with a wave. "Better I have at home." She looked at Henry. "You should all come. Eat." She went to the door and shouted for Peter. Her son reappeared, tugging at his gray scarf as Mrs. Gruber waved him into the train car. She babbled in German and gestured toward Molly and Jane.

The man's voice rumbled through his scarf. "We don't live far. Come where it's warm, Mrs.—?"

"McClure," Jane said. "Jane McClure." She glanced at Molly. "And this is Molly."

The man chuckled and glanced at his mother, who smiled and said, "Is good name, Molly."

Mr. Gruber's voice warmed with obvious pride as he said, "Mother's brought several hundred children into this world. She's an excellent nurse." His dark eyes crinkled at the corners as he said to Jane, "She already has an onion plaster planned to break the fever. And there's syrup for the cough." He shrugged. "It tastes terrible. But it works."

The old woman broke in. "When train whistles, Peter brings you back in sleigh." She patted Molly on the head. "Your Molly will be better."

Jane cleared her throat. "I ... I don't have ... " She swallowed. Shook her head. "I can't pay for medical care."

The old woman put her palm to her chest. Sighed. Shook her head. "Not to pay." She tucked gray curls back beneath her knit cap, then pulled her mittens back on as she appealed to Henry. "You must to say. Ja?"

Henry spoke up. "I've been riding these rails a few years now, ma'am. Porters hear things, just as a routine part of the job." He smiled. "Mrs. Gruber has quite the reputation in Buffalo County. Healing hands, folks say."

As if on cue, Molly coughed. And coughed. And coughed, whimpering with the effort and murmuring about a sore throat. Jane swallowed. Was it her imagination, or was her own throat a little sore as well? The woman smiled and nodded. And her son—what little of him Jane could see—he had kind eyes, at least. She relented with a nod. "All right then. Thank you." When she reached for her coat, her knee twinged. With a soft grunt and a grimace, she shifted her weight.

Mrs. Gruber caught her hand. *"Vas ist?"*

"It's nothing," Jane lied. "I slipped on the ice at the train station."

The old woman arched one eyebrow. "Also ve vill see to this 'nothing.'" She spoke again to her son. Jane helped Molly don her coat and then shrugged into hers. While they gathered their things, Henry reassured Mrs. Gruber that the train crew would gather soon and enjoy the feast she'd provided before the pie got cold.

As Jane reached for their carpetbags, she twisted her knee just the wrong way. Pain shot up her thigh, and though she pressed her lips together to prevent it, Mrs. Gruber apparently heard her soft cry, for she said something to her son, and before Jane could utter a protest, the man had swept her off her feet and headed up the aisle of the train and out to the sleigh. Over his shoulder, Jane saw Henry scoop Molly up and follow in their wake. Mrs. Gruber trundled behind them with the two carpetbags.

In no time, Jane and Molly were settled behind the driver's seat, swaddled in layers of fur hides and comforters. Mr. Gruber helped his mother aboard and then climbed up beside her, even as Henry called out reassurance from the platform between the train cars. "You rest well, ma'am. Soon as the snow stops, we'll start digging out. There's sure to be a crew on the way to help. You'll be in Denver before you know it."

Denver. Jane gazed back at the train as the sleigh glided across the snow to the rhythmic jangle of the sleigh bells attached to the black horse's harness. She should have asked to send word to Mr. Huggins. Would the Union Pacific give notice to people coming to meet the train in Denver? Surely they would. Still, Jane wished she'd asked Henry about sending Mr. Huggins a telegram. Then again, telegrams cost money. And she had none.

Chapter 4

With a whimper about her head hurting, Molly climbed into Jane's lap as Mr. Gruber drove the horse across the frozen landscape. Not until the sleigh came to a stop did Jane take note of anything but Molly's whimpers, her restlessness, and the heat from her feverish body. Mr. Gruber helped his mother down first, then came to the side of the sleigh where Jane was seated. When he opened his arms, Jane handed Molly over.

As the man headed for the house, Jane took note of what little of the place she could see. Did these people live in a cave? Snow obscured nearly everything, save a length of pipe emerging from a drift and the shoveled path to what appeared to be a very heavy wooden door. There had to be a barn, but Jane couldn't see it. The world around them was a blank slate of white.

The child was too thin—just like her mother. They both had that pinched look about their eyes, the look he'd seen on too many faces in the cities he'd marched through on that fabled "March to the Sea" masterminded by General Sherman. Peter had been little more than a boy all those years ago, but some of the things he'd seen still haunted him. There'd been so much hunger. So much need.

Peter offered to carry the woman inside if she would just wait while he took the child in, but she shook her head and climbed down with a soft grunt. As she followed him inside, Peter wondered what lay hidden behind those gray eyes of hers. The pinched look and the lightness of the child didn't match the fineness of their clothes. And people on Pullman Palace cars didn't carry threadbare carpetbags. Ah, well. Whatever the mystery, *Mutti* would soon have the child feeling better. Thank God for Mutti and her way with people … and her gift for healing.

The minute Peter stepped inside, Mutti waved him toward her room. "Take her there. I get featherbed. In here we set up cot."

"Let me climb up and get the featherbed," Peter said, ducking into Mutti's room to deposit the sleeping child on her bed. He hesitated only long enough to pull the bottom half of a tied comforter up from the foot of the bed to cover her. It would keep her warm for the few minutes until Mutti had things arranged.

Intending to climb to the loft, he hurried back into the main room, but Mutti had already shed her cape and bonnet and mittens and was halfway up to the loft above. Peter knew better than to scold her. Mutti didn't appreciate reminders of her advancing age. She seemed to have read his mind though, as she shot him a warning glance. *Don't say it.* She was already to the top of the ladder before the child's mother had so much as unbuttoned her coat. When the woman hesitated, looking about the room, Peter pointed to the free hook next to Mutti's cape.

She hesitated. "But that's for your coat."

"I have to see to things outside," he said. "My Molly doesn't take kindly to being made to stand in the cold once she's home." When she looked confused, Peter smiled beneath his scarf. "The horse. Her name is Molly, too."

They both started. Mutti had pushed the featherbed off the ledge above. It landed with a thud at the base of the ladder. "If lingering you are, Peter, let me hand down some quilts."

Mrs. McClure quickly removed her coat and hung it on the hook Peter had indicated earlier. "I'll take them." She headed for the ladder.

He couldn't help but notice the woman's narrow waist as she limped across the room to where Mutti waited, a stack of quilts just showing at the edge of the loft above her room. *The limp.* He'd forgotten. Something about a sore knee. If he stayed inside to help, he was going to have to unwrap the scarf and— He glanced up at Mother and saw understanding—and with it, sadness in her eyes.

"You may go," she said, her voice gentle. "We will be fine here."

With a nod, he headed back into the cold world outside.

Jane held her hands above her head as, one by one, Mrs. Gruber dropped three quilts and then sheets and two pillows down from the loft. Finally Mrs. Gruber lowered a bundle that proved to be a folding cot. As Jane bent to unfold it, she thanked Mrs. Gruber again. "This is so kind of you."

The old woman backed her way down the ladder, but once her feet were on solid ground, her wrinkled face folded into laugh lines as she said, "To have guests makes blizzard into blessing." She put her palm to her chest. "You must to call me Anna, please."

Jane nodded. "All right, Anna. And I'm Jane." She smiled. "I understand your son's horse and my daughter share a name."

Anna chuckled. "Is good name, Molly. Fine horse, beautiful child." Just then the Molly in the other room began another round of coughing. Anna followed Jane into the bedroom, where she bent down and pulled out what proved to be a trundle from beneath the bed. "We make this up for Molly"—she hesitated and pointed at Jane's knee—"or for you. Whichever is better. You decide."

Jane frowned as she glanced toward the middle room. "But we just—" She hesitated.

Anna nodded. "The cot is for me."

"I couldn't possibly—"

"You must," Anna insisted. "Your Molly needs rest and quiet. Peter is up very early. I must cook for him. Is better for all." She bustled into the other room.

Jane went to Molly's side, murmuring comfort as she helped her out of her coat. "You have a fever." She bent to make up the trundle and had just pulled Molly's nightgown out of her carpetbag when Anna appeared in the doorway.

She held up a huge shirt. "Please to put this on." She showed Jane the deep V at the front, explaining that the nightshirt was one of Peter's castoffs and would make things easier when it came time to apply the poultice she would cook in the next few minutes. "So," she said, "you make ready, and I make poultice and tea." Without waiting for Jane to answer, she retreated back to the main room.

With a grimace, Jane moved about the trundle, spreading a clean sheet across the featherbed. "I'll help you with the nightshirt, but you're going to have to climb down to the trundle yourself, sweetheart. I'm afraid I don't trust my knee to pick you up."

Molly sat up, blinking and putting her hand to her head. "My head hurts. It's too bright."

Jane turned to look out the window that was, now that Molly had mentioned it, letting in more light than she would have expected. The sun must have peeked through the clouds. Jane rose and went to the window to pull the plain muslin curtains closed, smiling as she noted the embroidered design on the simple fabric—a crane of some kind, from the long neck and storklike legs. As she reached up to draw the curtains closed, a shadow fell across the snow. Jane leaned forward just in time to catch sight of Peter Gruber leading his Molly around the rim of a mountain of snow that Jane realized must be hiding the barn. She smiled at the picture of the massive black horse following its owner like an overgrown dog.

When the mare stretched out her neck and nipped Mr. Gruber's shoulder, he batted her away. She dodged his hand, then lowered her head and butted him between the shoulders, sending him headlong into the snow. Jane could have sworn the horse was laughing as it stood, bobbing its head up and down as it watched Mr. Gruber flounder his way back to his feet. Gruber's booming laughter sounded through the window as he shook the snow off and bent to pick up his scarf.

With a sharp intake of breath, Jane stepped back from the window and dropped the curtain. She glanced back at Molly. Maybe she wouldn't notice. *Of course she'll notice. Unless he's only inside when it's dark, she'll notice. And ask all sorts of embarrassing questions. Children just do that. They don't mean anything by it, but—*

The poor man. Such terrible scars. Just the thought of the agonies he must have endured made Jane shiver. She would make certain to speak of it to Molly. In some way to prepare her to be polite. And kind. Wondering if it had been a mistake to come here after all, she limped back to the bed and finished helping Molly change.

Peter's laughter died the instant he noticed movement at his mother's bedroom window. Snatching his hat out of the snow, he clamped it on his head, then grabbed Molly's bridle in mock anger. "Come along, you. Just look what you've done. They've only been here a few minutes, and you've managed to frighten our guests." His eyes stung from the cold. He turned his face away from the window. The woman had let go of the curtain, but maybe she was still in there...peering at him through that tiny crack where the curtains didn't quite meet the window frame.

He shook his head as he headed into the barn. Even after all this time, a little thing like a curtain moving brought everything back. Would he never escape it? He'd come here to do just that— to build a life away from the memory of rejection and from the pity he'd never asked for. Mutti called the scars his "Medal of Honor." He wouldn't mind them so much, if only a few more of the boys in his regiment had gotten up that hill behind him before the rebels realized there was a sharpshooter in the trees. All the while he was tending Molly, Peter fought the memories of the shouts...the rebel yells...and the searing pain of the minié ball that had changed everything. Forever.

Once Molly was unharnessed and standing in her stall, contentedly munching on the mash Peter had mixed for her, he pulled his scarf back up over his nose and ventured back to the house, keeping a wary eye on the bedroom curtain as he walked the shoveled path between the barn and the soddy. After he opened the front door, he leaned in just far enough to make certain his mother heard him call for her, keeping the scarred side of his face turned toward the door.

"Come in and close the door," she scolded as she looked up from where she stood at the stove, stirring something oniony. Mrs. McClure wasn't in the room. Still, Peter only stepped in far enough to pull the door closed against the cold. "I need to shovel a path to the necessary. Then I'll check the harness. And Molly seems a bit off her feed. I may stay out in the barn for a while to keep an eye on her. Don't worry if I don't come in right away."

"It's too cold for you to be outside for long."

"I've got that little stove in the tack room. I'll work in there. It'll be fine."

Mutti tilted her head and peered at him, a question in her eyes. She glanced at the room where the sick child and her mother must be resting, then looked back at him and shook her head.

He cleared his throat. "Do you need me to move the child?"

"She is settled in my room." Mutti pointed at the cot. "I sleep here."

Peter nodded, relieved that he wouldn't have to dance about trying to avoid guests bedded down in the main room. He could rise early and find things to keep him busy out in the barn until the train signaled its departure.

Mutti leaned over the pot to inspect the contents as she spoke. "As soon as I have seen to the poultice...and to Jane's knee...I start our supper." She ladled some of the concoction into a crockery bowl and reached for the squares of flannel on the table. "Go," she said, shooing him out the door. "Tend to things in the barn. But there will be a meal served at the usual time, and coming after you by lamplight I will not do."

He nodded. "Just light the lamp in the window. I'll come right in."

Chapter 5

Molly had just donned Peter Gruber's nightshirt and, with a little shiver, settled back beneath the covers when Anna bustled into the room, bowl in hand. "Please to make ready for poultice," she said to Jane, as she moved to the opposite side of the high bed.

It didn't make sense for Anna to have to stoop to tend Molly. "I'll sleep on the trundle," Jane said, then shoved it back beneath the bed with a grunt. She pulled Molly's covers down, unbuttoned the borrowed nightshirt, and held it open while Anna spread a gooey concoction across Molly's pale skin.

Molly made a face. "It stinks."

Anna nodded. "Ja. Is gut. And soon better you will be." She laid a double layer of soft flannel over the poultice, then nodded to Jane, who buttoned up the nightshirt. Anna pinned through the nightshirt to hold the flannel in place, and together the two women began to pile on the comforters.

"I'm hot," Molly protested.

"You have fever," Anna said. She produced a small bottle from her apron pocket and, pouring what looked like black sludge into a teaspoon, enticed Molly to take it. "This tastes not good," she said. "But it will help stop the coughing. You can rest while I make soup for our supper."

Molly shuddered as she swallowed. Her eyes opened wide. "It's awful," she croaked, and a tear slid out of the corner of one eye. She glanced over at Jane. "I want Katie."

Even as Jane searched both their carpetbags, she suspected the truth. "Oh, sweetheart. I'm so sorry. Katie's still on the train." Tears threatened to spill down the child's flushed cheeks. Jane rushed to reassure her. "I'm certain that kind porter, Henry—he has a little girl just about your age. He'll know how important a special doll is. He'll take good care of Katie."

Molly sniffled. "I don't want to go to Denver. I don't like Mr. Huggins, and I don't care about the department store windows and—and I want to go home." She began to cry. "Why can't Christmas be like always? Just you and me... and not some... *stranger.*" She began to cough again.

Anna stepped in with another teaspoonful of the dark sludge, and although Molly protested taking it, once it was down, both the tears and the coughing quickly subsided. She closed her eyes, and when Jane was certain she'd fallen asleep, she followed Anna into the main room. Anna had set the poultice bowl on a battered worktable positioned against one whitewashed wall. A couple of shelves above the table were laden with an assortment of colorful tins, small boxes, and blue-tinted Mason jars with zinc lids. Anna reached for a green tin as she said, "Is gut for her to sleep." She pulled a chair out from the dining table and motioned for Jane to sit down.

For some reason, Jane felt the need to apologize for Molly's outburst. "What you must think."

Anna shrugged. "Is of no importance." She pointed at Jane's knee. "Please to show me."

When Jane hesitated, Anna glanced toward the door. "Peter will not come until he sees in the window the lighted lamp." Her voice sounded sad. "If he comes at all." She sighed. "He is … how do you say it … *shy*." She took the bottle of cough syrup out of her apron pocket and set it on the lower of the two shelves.

"I saw his face." Jane blurted it out, then hastened to explain when Anna turned back to her with a concerned frown. "Molly was complaining about the bright light in your room when the sun came out earlier, so I went to pull the curtains closed. The horse—Molly shoved him, and Mr. Gruber stumbled into a snowdrift. The scarf fell away." She took a deep breath. "It'll be all right. I won't let Molly be rude." She shook her head. "I can't imagine what he's been through."

Anna nodded. She glanced toward the barn, and her eyes filled with tears. "The worst wounds you cannot see." She seemed about to say more, but then she cleared her throat and motioned for Jane to lift her skirt while she retrieved a footstool. When she set it down, she patted the needlepoint surface.

With a grimace Jane lifted her foot onto the footstool and raised her skirt. When Anna touched a bit of the lace edging that had been one leg of Jane's bloomers, she felt herself blushing. "I … uh … had to make do on the train."

Anna chuckled. "Ja. That I see. Is gut." She headed into the room where Molly was resting and returned with a sewing basket in hand. *"Fräulein* Molly sleeps." She put one wrinkled hand to her bosom and inhaled deeply. "She breathes like so." Opening the sewing basket, she handed Jane a pair of scissors and motioned to the makeshift wrapping. "Snip and undo, please. I have many ointments, but I must see to know which is best."

Jane obeyed, snipping the makeshift wrap with trembling hands. Focusing on the knee seemed to make it hurt more. Or was she nervous about having mentioned Peter Gruber's scarred face? As Anna poked and prodded the swollen joint, Jane said, "I didn't mean to be rude. About Mr. Gruber. I only meant to say there's no reason for him to—" She broke off. "It's his home, after all. He shouldn't be out in the cold because of Molly and me."

Anna grasped Jane's ankle and, ever so gently, helped her straighten her leg. "He does not stay out because of you." Gently, she guided Jane to bend her knee. "He hides because of someone else." When Jane grimaced and let out a little moan, the older woman nodded and let her rest the leg. Rubbing her hands together, Anna cupped Jane's knee between her palms. The warmth felt wonderful, until Anna began to poke and prod. With each painful intake of breath or "Ouch!" Anna alternately nodded or apologized. Finally she let go and crossed the room to the shelf. Taking down a blue tin, she dipped two fingers in and spread something thick and golden over Jane's swollen knee. "My Peter is hero," she said as she worked. "Many men lived because of him. But he did not get away." Her voice wavered. She shook her head. "What they did to my beautiful boy."

"It must have been terrible," Jane said.

Anna nodded. "But worse was to come." She paused. "People don't see hero. They see only ... what they see." She continued massaging Jane's knee. "He was beautiful man, my son. And he was to marry."

Jane sat quietly, no longer thinking about her sore knee.

"But after," Anna said, "she could not see that man she loved. She was like everyone else. Everyone who sees only with eyes."

Jane frowned. "She abandoned him?"

Nodding, Anna finished wrapping Jane's knee. "I only tell you because—" She lowered her voice. "The child must not be frightened if she sees. He is good man. Only hiding inside. Like in folktale. What is seen hides truth. You understand, ja?"

Jane nodded. As Anna finished wrapping the knee, she said, "That's what I keep telling Molly about Mr. Huggins. That we mustn't judge by appearances. That he's kind." She paused. "We've been corresponding for some weeks now, and he sent tickets so that we could join him for Christmas. But Molly—" She broke off, took a deep breath. "I'm sure it'll be fine. She's just—we've had a bit of a hard time recently. Once she sees the possibilities—how much better things could be for her ... " Jane's voice trailed off. Did she sound mercenary?

Anna's eyes shone with kindness. "Mothers do what is best for their *kinder.* Sometimes the kinder don't understand. But still, we try to do what is best."

Jane nodded. "Exactly. I'm only trying to do what's best for Molly." With a grimace, she rose to her feet. "My knee feels so much better. Please let me help you with supper." She smiled. "Working in the cold used to make Molly's father ravenous. I imagine Mr. Gruber is no different." While she helped Anna with supper, she spoke of Stephen. His battle scars, his plans, his dreams ... and his death.

By the time the lighted lamp appeared in the window, Peter's stomach had stopped growling and begun to hurt. He'd shoveled the path to the outhouse first, then retreated to the barn, polishing the tack and brushing Molly until her coat shone. He'd combed her mane and tail until they rippled like corn silk, trimmed her hooves, fed the sow in the corner stall, shoveled out the chicken yard, and practically given himself a stiff neck hunkering in the henhouse to repair a couple of broken nesting boxes. He'd just begun to think about attacking the drift obscuring his bedroom window when the lighted lamp appeared. With a final look around the barn to make certain all was in order for the night, he made his way inside.

As quickly as possible, he shuttled into his room, laying coat, hat, scarf, and mittens across the foot of the narrow mattress. Taking a seat on the ladder-back chair by his bed, he pulled off his boots, sighing with relief as he pulled on fur-lined moccasins and wiggled his numb toes to get the circulation going again. That little stove in the barn wasn't nearly as efficient as he'd claimed it was.

He dipped his hands in the bowl atop the little washstand beside the door, swiping them across his face and shuddering before reaching for a towel to dry off. Reaching for his comb, he glanced in the mirror. Did he always do that? He hadn't noticed before, but did he always turn his head so that all he saw was what he wanted to forget? Odd that he chose to look at the bad side first.

He turned his head, almost surprised to see the unscarred side of his face. He remembered Priscilla's giggle. *"Why, Peter Gruber. You know why I had to have that dance. You were the handsomest man there, and I always dance with the handsomest man."* She'd laughed after saying it, and he'd told himself that silly talk was just the way girls were these days. Priscilla loved him. She was just—coy. That's all it was. Except that wasn't "all it was." He hadn't learned it until she'd come to the hospital. Mutti had been there for weeks. Priscilla, on the other hand ... Priscilla had waited. And then ... then she'd written the last letter.

Facing himself in the mirror, Peter compared sides and reminded himself to be thankful for Dr. Warren's skill with reconstruction. He hadn't been able to rebuild a cheekbone, but he'd done miracles nonetheless. Peter was luckier than a lot of men he'd seen during that long, nightmarish stay in the hospital. Movement in the doorway caught his attention, and Peter stepped back. Away. Dodging the light.

Mutti's voice was kind, but a note of something sounded beneath the kindness. Care. Wariness, even. "The child still sleeps," she said. "I have told Jane not to wake her. You come now." She held out her hand. "Join us." She turned back toward the main room. "I have put another lamp in the child's room.

I will be able to see better in the night." She forced a chuckle. "We have only candles for supper. I hope you can see your way."

Dear Mutti, trying her best to make things easier for everyone. Lowering the light so he could hide. He peered into the room, ever mindful of keeping the wounded side of his face turned away. Mrs. McClure was already seated, her foot propped up on the footstool.

"She wouldn't let me help her," she complained, pointing to the footstool. "But she obviously didn't need help." She leaned down and inhaled the aroma of the bowl of soup before her. And then she looked up at him and smiled. "If you're like my Stephen always was, you're hungry enough to eat a bear." She paused. "I hope you won't let the presence of strangers chase you out of your own home, Mr. Gruber." Her voice wavered as she met his gaze. "You've been so kind. I don't know how Molly and I will ever repay you."

Peter sidestepped to hold Mutti's chair as she sat down between Mrs. McClure and him. Once she was seated, he slid into his own chair, careful to position it so that "the bad half" was at least in the shadows.

Mutti reached out, inviting Mrs. McClure and Peter to take her hands. When they did, she bowed her head, praying in German. Peter wondered if their guest knew what was being said, if she knew that Mutti was invoking God's healing hand on the sick child in the other room. It worried him a bit to hear how Mutti prayed. As if she was much more concerned about the child than she'd let on. He kept his head bowed, but finally managed a glance toward the other end of the table. Was Mrs. McClure taking the obvious opportunity to inspect his face?

She wasn't. In fact, Mrs. McClure seemed to be praying, too, moving those lovely full lips—He stopped midthought, scolding himself for noticing. He closed his eyes, waiting for the "Amen."

Chapter 6

Everything changed in the night. With a strangled cough, Molly began to sputter and cry, and Jane leaped to her feet, staggering momentarily on the trundle. She gazed at Molly, who lay wheezing, her eyes wide with fear as she struggled to breathe. Anna rushed into the room and turned the lamp up while Jane rolled the trundle out of the way. Leaning forward, Anna lifted Molly's chin so that the girl would look at her. "Calm, *mein liebling*," she said gently. "Stay calm for just a moment. Anna will make better soon."

When Anna patted Jane's shoulder and directed her to climb up and hold Molly, Jane felt steadied. She pulled Molly into her lap, and together they leaned against the high headboard. Jane stroked Molly's dark hair, whispering comfort. "Shhh … shhh … it's all right. Anna knows what to do." Molly's chest heaved with the effort to breathe while, out in the next room, Anna rattled about. She was stirring up the stove—Jane heard one of the round covers rattle as Anna slid it out of the way. And then Mr. Gruber's voice.

"What is it? What's wrong?"

Oh no. They'd awakened him. His deep voice sounded closer as he crossed the room to where his mother stood. "Here. Let me."

Jane didn't know what Mr. Gruber was doing, but at some point a cold blast of air indicated he'd opened the front door. "Is this enough?"

"Another washtub full," Anna replied. "Melt it all while I warm up the poultice." She paused. "A tent over the bed would be good."

"I'll get the old wagon cover."

The moments crawled by. Was it her imagination, or was Molly's breathing easing up a bit? *Please, God ... please.*

"Mama ... " Molly pulled her arm free. "Don't hold so tight. It hurts." The words came out clearly, but then another attack of sputtering and coughing wracked Molly's thin frame, and she began to cry. "It hurts ... it hurts." She put her hand to her throat.

Jane began to rock back and forth in a vain attempt to comfort herself as much as Molly. "Show Mama where it hurts." Molly lifted her chin and touched a spot just beneath her jawline. Terror rising, Jane felt beneath Molly's chin and was nearly swallowed by dread. *Swollen glands. Sore throat. Croupy cough. Fever.* It might be nothing, she told herself. Just a cold. Admittedly a bad one, but not—that. She wouldn't let herself think the word. If she allowed the word into her conscious mind, she'd be of no use to Molly, because she'd be too terrified to think clearly. "Shhh ... shhh ... it won't be long now, and Anna will be here with more medicine. Remember how much better it made you feel?"

Molly nodded.

And Jane held on.

Peter scaled the ladder leading up to the barn loft and dragged the old wagon cover out of the corner, hoping that once he got it down where he could take a look, it wouldn't be so covered with bird or mouse droppings that they didn't dare use it. Back down below, his hands trembled as he unfolded and spread it out in the darkened walkway before lighting a lamp so that he could look it over. Once he'd lit the lamp, he bent low to inspect the canvas, relieved that a good brushing was all it would take to make it usable.

When his Molly thrust her great head over her stall door, Peter patted her soft muzzle on his way to the tack room to retrieve a broom. He swept the canvas cover briskly, then turned it over and cleaned the other side. Finally, back outside, he did his best to shake the dust off, mimicking Mutti when she hung sheets on the clothesline between the house and the barn—the clothesline now buried in a pile of snow.

While he worked, Peter was surprised to find himself think-ing about God. *Surely You didn't bring them to Mutti to have the child d—No.* He wouldn't even think it. He would string the wagon canvas from the rafters and create a tent. Steam would relieve the child's breathing, and she would get better. There was no need to be morbid. He would not think the word that had come to mind. He would not. And yet, as he remembered the sound of that cough, as he carried the wagon cover back inside, another word forced its way into his conscious mind. A word that rep-resented a scourge to parents and, sometimes, to entire families. A word that had populated Buffalo County cemeteries with far too many children.

Diphtheria.

When Jane moved to settle Molly in the bed so she could help put up the tent, Mr. Gruber shook his head. "You're doing what's best. No one comforts like a mother. Mutti and I will take care of this. You stay with the child."

So Jane remained beneath the covers, holding Molly, rocking her, humming, as Mr. Gruber positioned chairs around the bed. Anna helped him by standing on a chair and holding the canvas up while he rigged rope to the rafters above, and in moments Jane and Molly were surrounded by a stained canvas tent.

Anna ducked beneath it and into view, and while she directed him, Mr. Gruber positioned a small table on either side of the bed. "We will put pans of hot water here," Anna said. She made circling motions with both hands. "We need steam, but you must be very careful so that no one is burned, ja?"

Jane nodded, and Anna disappeared. When she returned with more of the poultice, Jane unbuttoned Molly's nightshirt while Anna applied more of the stinking concoction. This time Molly didn't complain about the smell. In fact, she struggled to inhale the aroma, coughing and sputtering but fighting less. Anna had her take two teaspoons of the stuff in the brown bottle and left again.

"I have the hot water." Mr. Gruber's voice sounded from the other side of the canvas.

"We're settled in," Jane said, wrapping her arms around Molly, thankful for the shadows in the darkened room. Even if Molly opened her eyes, she wouldn't notice the poor man's scars.

In moments, Mr. Gruber had positioned two pots of steaming water beneath the tent. And finally Molly took a deep breath without coughing—without that horrible, terrifying, strangling sound.

Molly stirred and croaked, "I want Katie."

"I know you do, sweetheart, but remember—"

"Who's Katie?"

Mr. Gruber's rumbling voice caught Jane off guard. "I didn't mean to eavesdrop," he said. "Mutti had me bring in another lamp."

Anna ducked beneath the tent, lamp in hand, and asked Molly to open wide.

Molly shook her head. "It hurts."

"Ja." Anna's voice was gentle. "This I know. If you let me see, I will know how to help it not hurt so much. Peter will hold the lamp high, and your Mutti can still hold you. Is gut, ja?"

Molly looked up at Jane. She nodded reassurance. With a sigh, Molly agreed.

Mr. Gruber appeared on the side of the bed where only the handsome side of his face would be reflected in the lamplight. Anna reached forward to cup Molly's face in her hands, then directed Molly to lift her chin while she inspected the swelling. Jane couldn't interpret the old woman's expression. She wasn't certain she wanted to. While Mr. Gruber held the lamp high, Anna produced a mirror. Molly opened her mouth wide, and Anna peered inside, all the while using the mirror to reflect light so that she could get a better view.

Red tonsils. Gray membrane. Dear God ... don't let her see a gray membrane ... please.

Anna put the mirror away and motioned for Mr. Gruber to withdraw. Jane thought her heart might pound out of her chest while she waited to hear what the old woman had to say.

Anna smiled down at Molly. "Red is why it hurts so much. And spots. You have spots."

Molly raised her hands, as if looking for spots on her skin.

"Nein," Anna said, and took Molly's hands in hers. "Not on skin. Inside. I can make it better, but that medicine tastes even worse. Still, you must take, ja?"

Molly swallowed, grimaced, and nodded.

Anna smiled then and looked at Jane. She brushed her own throat with the tips of her fingers. "You must to stay with us until Fräulein Molly is better."

Jane's voice wavered as she asked, "Did you see—is there— her throat. It's only red?"

Anna nodded and said something about God answering prayer and sparing them the worst. She also said that Molly needed at least a few days of bed rest before she and Jane continued on their journey.

Of course Anna was right, but still, Jane felt tears gathering. She hated feeling so helpless. It was one thing to accept overnight lodging when a blizzard stopped a train in the middle of nowhere, and quite another to impose on strangers for—how long? How long would it be until Molly could travel? And what of Mr. Huggins? Would he wait? Would he understand? And yet, what could she do? *Nothing.*

Anna put one hand on Jane's shoulder and gave it a little pat. "She sleeps," she said, and nodded at Molly.

Jane slid out of bed, and Anna helped her elevate Molly's head with pillows.

Putting her finger to her lips to indicate silence, Anna handed Jane a blanket to wrap up in and motioned for her to come out into the other room. Once there, she waved Jane into a chair and said, "I make tea."

"No, *I'll* make tea while *you* sit," Jane said, but just as she moved to lay the blanket aside, the door opened and Mr. Gruber appeared, bearing yet another huge tub of snow to melt atop the stove. Jane clutched the blanket around her nightgown and stayed put.

Ducking beneath the canvas tent, Peter replenished the steaming water and paused to look down at the sleeping child, thankful that her breathing seemed to have eased a bit. They would have to stay for at least a few days, of course. That would be awkward, especially once the child started feeling well enough to pay attention to—things. He reached up and traced the worst scar with his fingertips, wondering what it would have been like if he and Priscilla ... if Priscilla hadn't—The child began to murmur in her sleep. She was dreaming, talking about something pleasant. She smiled and murmured the name *Katie*. Katie again. Who was Katie?

As Peter stood gazing down at the sleeping child, it hit him. He could have had a daughter just this age by now. Would she have had dark hair like his, or would it have been blond like Priscilla's? A shadow played across the surface of the tent around the bed, bringing Peter back to the moment. Mutti's voice sounded from the other side of the canvas. "Is everything all right?"

Peter ducked back into the room. "It's fine. She's dreaming. Murmured something about her friend Katie."

"Her doll," Mutti said. "Left on the train. Twice she has asked now."

Back in the other room, Peter avoided making eye contact with Mrs. McClure as he headed for his own room.

"We are having tea," Mutti called softly. "You should join us."

Peter shook his head. He didn't want to have tea with a beautiful woman tonight. Not when she was trapped and when good manners would require her to pretend that she wasn't revolted by the sight of him.

"Thank you," he said, "but I want to get an early start in the morning. I'll hitch the sleigh and head to the train first thing." He paused in the doorway, speaking over his shoulder. "If you'll write out a message, Mrs. McClure, I'll ask the porter to see that it's sent on to Denver as soon as they reach the next station. So your family won't worry. Just leave it on the table. I'll leave at first light." He didn't wait for her to answer. But once in his room and out of sight, he stood at the window for a while, looking out on the landscape, listening to her voice as Mrs. McClure and Mutti talked. Mutti reassured her that she didn't think they were fighting diphtheria, and that she and Peter counted it a blessing to help others.

A blessing to help others. Mutti said it with such conviction. Of course she believed it with all of her gentle, God-fearing heart. Peter had believed it once, too. Before the "blessing" of helping others had cost him the chance to build a life with Priscilla.

Chapter 7

*I*n spite of Anna's reassurances and remedies, the night wore its way through one episode after another of Molly waking, coughing, crying, needing more steam and more of whatever it was in Anna's brown bottle, and finally, in the gray light of dawn, a newly prepared poultice. Weariness creased Anna's already-wrinkled face as she spread the warm goo. Jane began to worry for the old woman's well-being, but when she pleaded with Anna to please rest for a while and let Jane tend Molly, Anna shook her head.

"A mother should not be alone when her child suffers."

"At least sit down for a while," Jane pleaded. As soon as Molly was resting comfortably, she followed Anna into the main room, pleased when the older woman pulled her rocking chair close to the doorway and sat down with a sigh.

"Do not forget," Anna said, pointing to the table where a piece of paper and a pencil waited. "Peter will need your message for Mr. Huggins."

Anna leaned her head back and closed her eyes, and Jane settled at the table. Composing a telegram that displayed just the right sentiment proved difficult. She must not hint at the near-panic she felt when she wondered if Mr. Huggins's interest would wane if they didn't meet again soon. She wanted to show interest. But how to do so without appearing shamefully forward? Finally she wrote a letter across the top half of the page Anna had torn from her household ledger book, knowing that the process of writing it out would help her compose the shorter version Mr. Gruber would telegraph to Denver.

> *Dear Mr. Huggins,*
>
> *By now you have received word that the train is snow-bound. We have been assured that all appropriate measures are to be taken to clear the tracks as soon as possible. Unfortunately, Molly has taken ill, and I am advised by the kind woman who has taken us in that she should not travel for a few days. While I at first feared diphtheria—just writing the word makes me shudder—Mrs. Gruber assures me that Molly's symptoms will continue to improve, and that we should be able to take up the journey in a few days.*
>
> *Please know that Molly and I are desperately disappointed at this unfortunate turn of events. We sincerely hope that the delay will not force a change in your plans. While we will miss the pleasure of spending Christmas in Denver, we hope that the idea of welcoming the New Year with us is anticipated with the same warmth displayed in your invitation for Christmas.*

Jane read the letter over and over again. If only she could send that. It sounded so much more positive in tone. Taking a deep breath, she underlined the essential information and ended up with the telegram.

> MOLLY ILL *Stop* FEARED THE WORST BUT NURSE ASSURES SHE WILL RECOVER SOON *Stop* HOPE TO ARRIVE IN A FEW DAYS *Stop* ANTICIPATING OUR TIME TOGETHER *Stop*

Jane stared at the last line. Was it too forward? *Is it even true? A* twinge of guilt raised its head. *I am anticipating it. Just because it isn't a romantic anticipation doesn't mean it's a lie.* She decided to leave the last sentence. Next came the matter of how to sign the thing, and that caused more than a little consternation. Finally she decided to use her Christian name, hoping that Mr. Huggins would take note of that, too. He had yet to depart from addressing her as *Mrs. McClure.* Perhaps he needed permission. She would give it. *Jane.*

She set the pencil down and sat back, looking over at Anna and smiling at the image of the older woman fast asleep in the rocking chair. Rising with a soft grunt, Jane hobbled past Anna's sleeping form and into the bedroom. When Molly stirred and whimpered, Jane climbed up beside her. Beneath the pile of comforters, with her arms around Molly and the child's head on her shoulder, she closed her eyes and fell instantly asleep.

Jane woke with a start to the aromas of coffee and fresh-baked bread. Molly stirred when she slipped out of bed, then settled back into a deep sleep. When Jane put her palm to Molly's forehead, relief washed over her. She might still have a slight fever, but *slight* was a good word. And while rumbles and rattles still accompanied each breath, Molly wasn't struggling like she had in the night. Jane closed her eyes for a moment and listened, then sent a fleeting thanks toward heaven.

When she ducked beneath the canvas tent and looked out the window, she realized that someone had put the lamp out. A band of gray light shone below the hem of the embroidered curtains. What time was it? Just as she reached for the blanket draped across the foot of the bed, she heard it. *The train whistle.* What could that mean? Surely a crew hadn't reached the train yet. They couldn't possibly be ready to leave.

The telegram! Clutching the blanket around her, Jane hurried into the other room. A blast of warm air greeted her as Anna opened the oven door. When Jane glanced at the table, Anna said, "The note Peter has taken to the train." She hoisted a loaf of bread out of the oven and inverted the pan over a plate. "The whistle is for to say all is well. He has delivered your message and is on his way back." Wrapping the fresh loaf of bread in a towel, she placed it on the open oven door. She crossed the room and donned her cape. "I go for eggs. Peter will be hungry when he returns." And with that, she hurried outside.

Jane got dressed, then returned to the main room where she set the table and sliced the warm bread, pausing often to step into the bedroom and listen for Molly. Finally, when she'd done everything she knew to help prepare for breakfast, she lingered in the doorway between the two rooms, noticing for the first time that the framed needlework above the table really was lovely, and wondering what it said. The only word she recognized was *Gott*. She knew that German word because one of Mrs. Abernathy's boarders had a penchant for profanity. She smiled in spite of herself, remembering the confrontation one day when Mrs. Abernathy stood, hands on hips, glaring up at the lumbering boarder and telling him in no uncertain terms that if he insisted on using the Lord's name in vain in *any* language, he could find another place to live.

The needlework featured what looked like a castle tower. Pink and burgundy flowers gathered along the base of the stone wall and then meandered around the edge of the sampler. Now that she thought about it, as Jane gazed around the room, she realized that the soddy epitomized the word *cozy*. It was so different from Mrs. Abernathy's drafty, two-story frame boardinghouse. Different, too, from the rooms Mr. Huggins had described over his mercantile store in Denver.

Anna returned in a swirl of cold air, her blue eyes bright as she produced several eggs from the pocket of her cape. "It snows more," she said, closing the door and scurrying over to stand by the stove while she took off her cape and mittens. She thanked Jane for setting the table and had just gone into the next room to check on Molly when Mr. Gruber returned. At least Jane thought it must be Mr. Gruber, although from all appearances it could have been anyone, so encased in crusted snow was the person who staggered in the door.

Jane glanced out the window. Another wall of white. "You drove into that?"

Mr. Gruber nodded once. He stepped closer to the stove but then hesitated and turned into his room instead.

"Wait," Jane said. When he looked back her way, she shrugged. "Please. You've been so kind to us. Stay by the stove where it's warm."

Anna bustled in and, grabbing her son's coat sleeve, pulled him closer to the stove, muttering like a hen clucking over a wounded chick. She dragged the rocking chair over, and as soon as Mr. Gruber had shrugged out of his coat, she directed him to sit down. Jane took her own coat off the hook and hung Mr. Gruber's where it would dry more quickly, then headed into the bedroom to deposit her coat over the sewing rocker by the bedroom window.

When she returned to the main room, Mr. Gruber was leaning toward the oven, soaking up the warmth as his mother unwrapped the stiff scarf wrapped around his head and neck. Once again he'd positioned himself so that only the handsome side of his face was in view. His cheeks were so red Jane wondered aloud at frostbite. She poured coffee. Mr. Gruber cupped the mug in his huge hands, then took a sip and sighed with pleasure.

"Sit back," Anna said, kneeling before him while she helped with his boots.

"They hope to be dug out by the end of the day," he said. "This round of snow shouldn't last long. There's a thin line of blue far to the west." He glanced up at Jane. "The porter promised to send the telegram as soon as they reach the next stop." He smiled down at his mother. "And they said to thank you for the meal." He paused. "I was in such a hurry to get inside, I left your baskets in the sleigh."

"Is no matter," Anna said as she set her son's boots on the open oven door. "Soon we have bread, eggs, and griddle cakes. Is gut, ja?" She moved to the rustic narrow table positioned beneath her medicine shelf and began to mix batter for griddle cakes.

Mr. Gruber stood up and stretched, then crossed the room in his stocking feet, talking to Jane over his shoulder as he reached inside his coat. "Your Molly talks in her sleep," he said and held up the rag doll he'd tucked in the inside pocket. "I heard mention of a Katie."

The look on Jane McClure's face as she took Katie from his hands was something Peter would savor for some time to come. Somehow he got the courage to actually turn around and look at her. If he was testing her, she received high marks, because she looked him in the eye and smiled. A real smile, not one of those conjured expressions people managed out of a sense of duty to *not* notice.

She held his gaze for a moment before glancing down at the well-loved doll and then back up at him. "Thank you. So much." She paused. "I've been dreading having to tell her that Katie was on her way to Denver without us. You have no idea how relieved I am that that won't be necessary. You're very kind to have remembered."

Kind. No one had said that of him for a long while. And for some reason, it made him want to retreat before the inevitable happened and she could no longer stomach looking him in the eye. He nodded and headed for his own room, pausing at the door just long enough to say, "The porter said that your Mr. Huggins would likely be reading the telegram by Christmas Day."

"Will they deliver a telegram on Christmas Day?"

"He seemed to think so, especially in light of the train getting stranded."

"Mama!"

All eyes looked toward the bedroom where Molly lay.

"I'm here," Jane called back, limping into the room, the doll in hand.

Mutti stood still for a moment, her head tilted. At the child's joyous exclamation over the doll, she smiled at Peter. He nodded at the room. "Go and see after her. I can fry griddle cakes." Mutti headed in to check on the child, and he slathered butter on a slice of bread, eating it while he used his free hand to flip griddle cakes, stack the finished ones on a plate, and pour out more batter.

The women were still in the other room when the cloud cover gave way and sunlight poured in through the window. The temperature might not be climbing, but the sunshine made it feel warmer. Mutti bustled back into the main room just long enough to snatch two bottles off her medicine shelf. She nodded at his unspoken question. "She is to be well. It takes time." She pointed at the stack of griddle cakes waiting on the table. "Eat. We will join you soon."

But they didn't. Mutti joined him, but Mrs. McClure stayed in the other room with her child. Which was only to be expected. For many reasons. When he'd finished eating, Peter hauled in two more tubs of snow to once again make steam rise inside the canvas tent. The child thanked him for bringing Katie "home," speaking from the other side of the canvas wall in a raspy voice that ended in a sputtering cough.

"You're welcome," Peter said, then retreated to the main room where he helped Mutti wash the dishes. By the time Mrs. McClure emerged from the bedroom, he was donning his coat to retreat to the barn. He needed to retrieve the baskets from the sleigh, he said. And he had things to tend. Both were true, even if the real reason he wanted to escape was the desire to savor the first genuine smile he'd received from anyone but Mutti in a very long time.

Chapter 8

Molly finally asked for something to eat Thursday afternoon. Anna soft-boiled the egg she'd kept out of the flapjack batter, and Jane made toast and tea. Molly grimaced with the first swallow of toast and opted for the egg and tea. After eating, she settled back against the pillow and asked Jane to read more about Jo and Meg. While Anna heated up more water and sent more steam into the tent, Jane climbed up beside Molly and read until the child fell asleep. When she ducked back out from beneath the sheet of canvas, the sun had begun to set. Once again Anna lit the lamps in the windows. Then she asked to examine Jane's knee.

"It's much better," Jane said as she sat before the stove and unwrapped her leg.

Anna perched on the footstool at Jane's feet and repeated the poking and prodding, nodding with satisfaction when Jane only winced. "Is gut," she said, then reapplied ointment. When the front door opened abruptly, Jane started and stood up so that her skirt would fall back into place.

Mr. Gruber, his arms full of firewood, kicked the door closed behind him and crossed the room to the woodbox. He bent to deposit the wood, and by the time he'd turned back around, Jane had snatched the bandage off the floor and muttered something about checking on Molly.

"If all goes well tonight," Anna called after her, "Peter takes down tent tomorrow, ja?"

That night Molly held Katie close and slept so soundly that, midway through the night, Jane slipped out of bed, pulled out the trundle, and crawled beneath the pile of comforters with a sense of gratitude and a weariness borne of the ever-present concerns of recent days.

Moonlight spilled in the window as Jane lay listening to Molly's even breathing and trying to imagine where they would have been this night if Molly hadn't taken ill. She wondered at the kindness of Anna Gruber and her son. *Thank You. I haven't spoken to You in a while, but thank You for taking care of us. Thank You that Molly didn't have*—She still couldn't even think the word. *Thank You that she didn't have that.* She wondered at the tragedy that had ravaged Peter Gruber's handsome face and the heartbreak he'd endured. How could a woman turn her back on a man she loved? How many men had had that happen to them after the war? How terrible for Peter.

And he didn't look that horrible. Not really. If you looked past the scars and into those beautiful eyes—Thinking of Peter's dark eyes reminded Jane of the expression in them earlier this morning when finally he'd let her look him in the face. She'd caught a glimpse of caution. Wariness, as if he was testing her.

It made her think of that time she'd encountered a stray dog in the alley behind Mrs. Abernathy's. The poor thing had stood its ground over a ham bone, watching her. Wary, although now that she remembered, it hadn't bared its teeth. Not once. It had just watched her. And when she spoke kindly to it, it lowered itself to its haunches, the hambone between its front paws. Not exactly relaxed, but not so defensive either. When Jane said, "That's a good dog. I won't bother you," the dog had thumped the earth once with its tail. And never stopped watching her as she returned to hanging out the day's assortment of kitchen towels and linens.

Mr. Gruber's gaze earlier reminded her of that dog. Wary. Hoping for the best but accustomed to being kicked and chased off. She was so glad she hadn't looked away. So glad she'd concentrated on his kindness in bringing Katie back from the train and seen beyond the scars to those beautiful eyes. Stephen had had brown eyes, too, but not like Mr. Gruber's. Not that dark, not set beneath finely arched eyebrows, not separated by an aristocratic nose.

Molly muttered in her sleep. Jane tensed momentarily, then realized it wasn't anything to worry over. Her breathing was even, and she didn't cough or sputter. She must be dreaming. Jane rolled onto her side and burrowed into her pillow. Her last conscious thought was the somewhat troubling realization that she couldn't remember the color of Mr. Huggins's eyes.

Peter woke with a start and sat up in bed, listening. Listening. Swearing softly under his breath at the realization that his campaign against unwanted residents in the house was about to begin again. He and Mutti had waged war on field mice after the first cold snap in the fall, setting traps in the loft and engaging in more than one chase involving brooms and the two of them in their nightclothes—chases that had ended in success and with them both out of breath and laughing at their ridiculous antics. Mutti wanted a cat. Peter agreed it was a good idea. He had word out to several of the neighbors in case any Christmas litters appeared in barn lofts nearby.

Another rustle out in the main room convinced him he'd better get up. He'd have to wake Mutti, but she wouldn't mind. She defended the soddy against unwanted invaders with the passion of a Prussian field marshal. Quietly, he slid out of bed and pulled on his pants. He padded to the doorway and peered into the main room, thankful for the faint moonlight reflecting off the whitewashed walls. What he saw made him smile.

The child had her back to him. She'd moved a kitchen chair over to the shelving on the far wall—that must have been what he heard—and was standing atop it, reaching for a biscuit tin. He stepped into the room, doing his best to move silently, lest he startle her and make her fall. The hem of the borrowed nightshirt she was wearing touched the seat of the chair. One of the sleeves had come unrolled. As she extended her arm to reach for the biscuit tin, several inches of sleeve dangled past her outstretched fingers.

When Peter was close enough to the chair to keep her from falling if she startled, he whispered softly, "It's good to see that you're hungry."

She didn't look his way, just stood with her hand stretched toward the biscuit tin. She was cradling her doll in the other arm.

"I'm afraid that's not what you think it is," he whispered, coming to her side. Still, she didn't answer. Her eyes were open, but—*Ah.* She was sleepwalking.

He reached to the higher shelf and a cracker tin that did, indeed, contain crackers. Opening it, he offered her one, shoving the dangling sleeve back up her arm to free her hand. She took the cracker, then stood motionless.

"Shall we give Katie a cracker as well?" She nodded, and Peter gently pried open her hand and put a second cracker in her palm. "There," he said. "Ready to go back to bed?"

Again the child nodded. This time she looked toward the window.

"It's still nighttime. Tomorrow, when you wake up, you can have a nice breakfast. Katie, too. All right?"

He intended to help her down off the chair and walk her back to bed, but when he touched her arm, she tucked the doll between her upper arm and her body, put the crackers into that hand, and with her free arm, reached up, clearly intending for him to pick her up. When he did, she curled up in his arms and laid her head against his chest. She sighed, and he felt her relax in his arms. Sound asleep.

There was nothing to do but put her to bed. How he would explain it to Mrs. McClure if she awoke to find him standing over her, he didn't know, but as it turned out, she was sound asleep in the trundle. As he crept around the foot of the bed to the opposite side and ducked beneath the canvas curtain to put Molly back in bed, her mother didn't stir.

Peter settled the child back against the pillows and, pulling the covers up, tucked them beneath her chin. He crept into the main room, replacing the chair at the table and then pausing to put the lid back on the cracker tin and return it to the high shelf. He'd just headed back toward his own room when Mutti stirred.

"Vas ist?"

"It's nothing, Mutti," Peter said quietly. He stepped closer. "The child was up. Sleepwalking, I think. Hungry. I gave her some crackers and put her back to bed." He chuckled. "I heard a rustle. I thought we were going to have another war against mice."

He heard Mutti's low laugh. "Another dance with a broom, ja? Let us hope not, at least not until our guests depart."

"Let us hope," Peter agreed.

"She is pretty, ja?"

"She's a beautiful child. Those dark curls. Thank God she's going to be all right."

"I speak of Jane. She is pretty. And kind. It's nice having her here." Mutti sat up in bed. "We must to have special Christmas, ja? For the child."

"They might be gone by Saturday."

"Nein. Molly must rest a few days at least."

Peter sighed.

"She is child, Peter. She must have Christmas. A tree, ja? If you take the sleigh out to the river, you could find something."

He could almost hear Mutti's thoughts skittering about as she gathered ideas and made plans. He knew her so well. She was making a paper chain in her mind. Already tearing out another page of her ledger book to make *Scherenschnitte* snowflakes. And making *springerle* cookies. How he loved springerle. He could almost smell them baking, imagine the aroma of anise oil in the air. Mutti was right. Why not give a sick child a happy moment? Why not, indeed. He didn't know about a tree though.

"It's only two days away, Mutti."

"And what? You have so much doing in this snow you can't take the sleigh to look for a little tree?"

She was right. Again. He chuckled. "You can't see my face, but I'm smiling. And yes. I'll drive out tomorrow and see what I can find. I'll keep it in the sleigh until you come out and approve it."

"That's my Peter," Mutti said. "It will be wonderful surprise. You will see."

Peter padded back to his room and slid beneath the covers, shivering when his bare feet touched the cold sheets.

It was still dark when Jane woke—to the sound of Mr. Gruber leaving the house, she realized. Probably headed out to feed the livestock. *Livestock. I wonder what they have in the way of livestock.* She hadn't paid much attention to the length of Mr. Gruber's absences from the house. In fact, she didn't really know very much about him except what Anna had said about his injury and subsequent heartache. She didn't know anything at all about Anna, except that she was Peter's mother and she'd apparently only come to live with him since he was injured. Where had she been before that?

Hearing Anna in the next room, Jane rose and dressed. "How can I be of use today? I feel like I've been something of a pampered guest, and I'd like it if there were a way to repay you for all your kindness."

Anna reached for a small basket hanging on a peg below the "medicine shelf." "Bundle up and gather eggs while I knead dough." Anna leaned into her kneading. "Inside the barn look to farthest wall. You will see the door to the chicken coop."

Unwilling to admit that she knew next to nothing about chickens and had never gathered eggs, Jane donned her coat and headed out to the barn by way of the trench Mr. Gruber had dug in the snow, which was nearly up to Jane's waist, thanks to the way the wind had drifted it between the house and barn. When she stepped inside the barn, the black horse thrust its head over a stall door—so suddenly that Jane dodged away.

"She's just saying hello," Mr. Gruber said. "She's very gentle. Never bites or kicks." He raised his head to glance at the horse. "Do you, Molly-girl? You never bite or kick?"

When the horse whickered, Jane laughed. "It's as if she's talking back."

"She talks back all the time," Mr. Gruber said. "She's a *she,* after all. Can't let a man have the last word." He glanced Jane's way, and his grin disappeared. "I do apologize, Mrs. McClure. I didn't mean anything by it."

Jane smiled his way. "That's perfectly all right, Mr. Gruber. I didn't take it to mean much of anything." As she made her way toward the door at the opposite end of the rows of stalls, she passed several pigs huddled together in the deep straw in one of the larger stalls, and a dun-colored cow obviously expecting a calf. In the next stall, Mr. Gruber sat milking a second dun-colored cow. He nodded at the basket in Jane's hand. "I see Mutti has put you to work."

"I offered," Jane said, nodding at the door just beyond the little room. "That opens into the chicken coop, right?"

Mr. Gruber nodded. As Jane walked past, he said, "Don't let Solomon worry you. He's all bluster and no fight."

Solomon? Jane didn't have to wonder long who Solomon was, for the instant she opened the door to the coop, a large bird began to flap its russet-colored wings and march toward her. How on earth could a chicken sound threatening? But this one did. Jane turned away from it and went to the four rows of nesting boxes to her left, all save one inhabited by a rust-colored hen, looking perfectly content and almost cozy. Jane hesitated. The blustery bird fluttered up off the earth, menacing enough that Jane ducked and raised her arm to shield her face.

"Stop that, Sol!" Mr. Gruber stepped into the coop, and the rooster settled and sauntered away. At least it seemed to Jane that he was sauntering.

"Thank you," she said primly, and turned once again to the nesting boxes. She hesitated. How did one get the hens to vacate the premises so their eggs could be collected?

"You've never gathered eggs before." He sounded surprised. Amused. Before she could respond, he brushed past her and slid his hand beneath one of the birds.

"No eggs," he said, but when he checked the next box, he withdrew an egg and, with a smile, handed it over.

So they don't bite. Jane followed Mr. Gruber's example, but the second she began to slide her hand beneath a hen, it clucked madly. Jane snatched her gloved hand away just in time to avoid being pecked. *Thank goodness for gloves.*

"You don't have to be afraid. They don't know you, is all. They're mostly bluster and very little bite." He paused. "But if you *are* afraid, just hand me the basket, and I'll take care of it. Mutti never has to know."

Was he teasing her? He'd said more since she'd come into the barn than he'd said the entire time she and Molly had been here. Jane lifted her chin. "I believe I can handle a few clucking hens, Mr. Gruber." She glanced toward the barn. "And besides, weren't you milking a cow?"

He nodded. "I was, and I apologize if I seemed to think you aren't up to handling the ladies." He nodded at the nesting boxes, then sidled around her, pausing at the door. "Just keep an eye on the rooster. He's been trained to attack if his ladies are threatened." He swallowed. "Killed a big bull snake once."

Jane glowered at him. "Are you teasing me, Mr. Gruber?"

He shrugged. "Well, something killed the bull snake. Maybe it was the dog."

"You don't have a dog."

"We did. It ran off. But I haven't seen a bull snake about, so you needn't worry about that."

"Just because I grew up in the city doesn't mean I'm afraid of snakes. And for your information, I am not. Unless, of course, they rattle."

"I'll still gather the eggs if you'd like."

By way of an answer, Jane slid her hand beneath another hen, ignored the creature's clucking and fussing, and was rewarded with not one, but two eggs. She glanced his way. "Anna said to tell you that breakfast will be ready soon." She quickly investigated the rest of the nesting boxes. She was tempted to glance back to see if Mr. Gruber was watching her but didn't want him to see her do so.

"Well, look at that," he finally said. Jane looked his way. He was pointing at the rooster, who'd settled on his perch. "You've won Solomon over." He retreated into the barn and bent to retrieve the milk pail. "Your Molly can have fresh milk if she feels up to it this morning."

Jane pulled the door to the coop closed behind her. "She had a good night. I have high hopes." Mr. Gruber swept his hand toward the house, like a gentleman showing a lady the way to a coach. With a smile and a nod, Jane led the way inside, hoping that the friendly man she'd just been joking with in the barn wouldn't go into hiding inside the house.

Chapter 9

*J*ane had just stepped inside and set the egg basket on the floor when Molly called out, "Look, Mama! I'm helping make biscuits!"

And indeed she was. Her nose smudged with flour, Molly—still in Mr. Gruber's nightshirt—stood at Anna's worktable near the warm stove, pressing a biscuit cutter into the sheet of flattened dough spread on the table before her.

"She is so hungry," Anna explained with a smile, as she crossed to where Mr. Gruber was standing. Taking the milk pail out of his hand, she called out to Molly, "And now Peter brings you fresh milk, just as Anna promised."

Molly had been concentrating on her biscuit-making, but at the mention of fresh milk, she looked up. And over at Mr. Gruber. And—

Jane hurried to get her gloves and coat off as she spoke. "Fresh milk, Molly. Isn't it wonderful?" Feeling a knot form in her midsection, she bustled over to where Molly stood and put a hand on her shoulder. *Please don't. Don't say anything.* But Molly said something. A word that made Jane cringe.

Her eyes round with surprise, Molly blurted out, "You're my monster!"

Mr. Gruber's hand went to his scars, and he turned away.

"Oh ... Molly," Jane said under her breath.

"No...really, Mama." Molly put the biscuit cutter down. Mr. Gruber was headed into his room, but Molly called out, "I dreamed about a monster. A *good* monster."

Mr. Gruber stopped.

"He gave me a cracker." Molly turned to look up at Jane. "And Katie. He gave Katie a cracker, too." She pointed at Anna's medicine shelf. "Out of that."

Jane looked up. There was, indeed, a cracker tin on the shelf above the row of bottles.

Mr. Gruber turned back to face Molly. He dropped his hand from his cheek. "You were sleepwalking." He glanced at Jane. "I thought I heard a mouse skittering about in the night. Molly was up on a chair, reaching for"—he glanced meaningfully at his mother—"the wrong tin." He shrugged. "I gave her two crackers and carried her back to bed. That's all."

Molly nodded. "That's what I said. There was a good monster, and he helped me. In my dream." She frowned and looked at Mr. Gruber. "But it wasn't a dream?"

He shook his head. Swallowed. "No. The monster is...real."

Molly's brow furrowed as she inspected the man's face. "Does it hurt?"

He shook his head. "No. Not in the way you mean."

"What happened?"

"Molly—" Jane tried to stop it, but Mr. Gruber glanced her way. Shook his head.

"It's all right." He smiled at Molly. "The war. Do you know about the war?"

Molly nodded. "A lot of people got killed. And the slaves got free. But people still don't let them ride on the trolley car."

"You know a lot."

"Papa told me about it. Sometimes, when it rained, he limped. And he had a scar, but you couldn't see it. He showed me once. It was on his leg." She reached down and patted her shin. "He said I almost didn't get born because he almost didn't come back to Mama."

Jane spoke up. "One of Stephen's best friends saved his life. Keig was the best shot in the company, and one day they were taking heavy fire, but when the retreat sounded, Keig stayed behind." She looked into Peter's dark eyes, forcing herself to meet his gaze as she said, "He was very heroic. He gave his life saving several of the men in the company."

"Papa said Keig was why I got born."

Jane felt the heat rising in her cheeks. "I doubt that it comforted Keig's widow very much, but Molly's right. Because of him, Stephen came home." She cleared her throat. "In fact, I know of at least a dozen children who never would have existed if not for his sacrifice." Her voice wavered, even as she wondered how many children were alive thanks to Peter Gruber's scarred face.

For a moment, the room was quiet, and then Molly spoke again. "Can I touch it?"

There was nothing to do now but let it play itself out. To Jane's amazement, Peter Gruber motioned Molly over and knelt down. She put her palm to his ruined cheek and traced the scars. Finally she said, "I'm sorry you got hurt." She sniffed. "You're a *good* monster."

It seemed to take Peter a long while to respond. He blinked, but a tear escaped and trickled across the scars. He took Molly's hand and kissed it. "I'm glad you know you don't have to be afraid of me."

And then the spell was broken. Molly said she was cold and headed back toward the cookstove. Jane scurried into the bedroom to retrieve a blanket and settle her in Annas rocking chair. Peter poured a mug of warm milk for her, then set the table for breakfast, while Anna finished cutting biscuits and slid them into the oven.

Soon they were gathered around the table eating breakfast together, like prisoners who'd inhabited cells alongside one another but never seen each other's faces. And now that they'd been set free, they could get acquainted and talk about normal things.

As the morning wore on and Molly began to wilt, Mutti administered more tonic and Peter carried Molly back to bed for a nap.

"You have a nice house," Molly said, while Peter stepped up on chairs and untied the ropes that held the wagon cover up to the rafters.

"Thank you." Peter smiled down at her, then went back to untying the rope he'd looped through the iron hooks in the rafters above the bed. "Do you know about sod houses?"

Molly shook her head.

"I plowed up the prairie to make bricks. And then I stacked the bricks to make these walls."

Molly looked around the room. "It doesn't look like dirt."

"That's because I plastered the inside. If there wasn't so much snow, you would have seen the sod bricks when we drove up to the house."

"Won't it wash away when it rains?"

Peter paused. "That's a very astute question."

"What's a stoot?"

Peter chuckled. "*Astute* means you're perceptive. You ask good questions." He paused and moved the chair to take down the last rope. "And you're right. This house will eventually wash away, even though the eaves are wide to protect the walls from rain, and even though I have boards at the corners to keep cattle from rubbing against them. They like to do that. It's a way for them to scratch their own backs, and with so few trees growing on the prairie, the house is a constant temptation. However, I'll have a new house built long before this one is in danger of washing away. One more like the houses you're used to seeing in town."

"Where will you get the bricks?"

Peter shook his head as he looped the rope he'd used to tie up the wagon cover and laid it in Mutti's sewing rocker. "The new house won't be brick. I'll order lumber from the sawmill and hitch my Molly up to the farm wagon and haul it back here."

Jane grabbed one edge of the wagon cover, and together they folded it up.

"We had a brick house," Molly said. "But then my papa died. We had to sell it and move."

Peter hoisted the wagon cover over his shoulder. "I'm sorry to hear that."

"It's okay. The boardinghouse isn't so bad. Sometimes I miss Sonja though."

Jane spoke up. "It's time for you to settle in, young lady."

Molly burrowed deeper beneath the comforters. But she kept talking. "She was our housekeeper. But after Papa died, we couldn't keep Sonja anymore. She got another job with someone else. We do our own housework now. And Mama helps Mrs. Abernathy cook for everyone."

Jane's cheeks blazed scarlet. Peter wished Molly a good nap, gathered up the rope, and headed for the main room. He paused before heading back out to the barn with the wagon cover. With a glance behind him, he stepped closer and lowered his voice as he said, "I don't want you climbing that ladder again, Mutti. Think about what else you need to bring Christmas to Molly, and I'll retrieve it as soon as I get back inside."

Christmas! Dismay colored over Jane's enjoyment of the last hour spent gathered around the table with Anna talking about life growing up in Germany—she'd worked the motto hanging over the table as a young wife before she came to America. *Ein' feste Burg is unser Gott*, it said. After translating the motto—it meant "Our God is a strong tower of defense"—Peter had waxed poetic about his mother's apple butter and talked about the three varieties of apple trees they'd planted behind the house.

"Will they survive the blizzard?" Jane asked.

"If they don't, we plant again," Anna said. "Someday we will have an orchard. Fields of wheat. Many cattle. And more horses."

Peter had reached over to squeeze his mother's hand and said, "You'll have to forgive Mutti. She seems to think we're going to work miracles out here on the prairie."

Anna pretended to be indignant. "Is not miracle. Is hard work and God's blessing. Both will come. You will see."

Anna's love for her son and her faith in God were both so strong. Jane wanted the moment of joy to last, but as Peter headed outside and she helped Anna clear the table, all she could think of was that she had nothing to give Molly for Christmas. Mr. Huggins had said they would all go Christmas shopping together in Denver. And here they were—snowbound.

Anna put her hand on Jane's shoulder. "Please don't be sad. To Denver you will soon go. As for Christmas—snow cannot keep the Christ child away."

"Of course not." Jane forced a smile. "It's just that we were supposed to go shopping in Denver. I don't have anything to give her."

Anna pondered for a moment, then said, "Perhaps we make new dress for Katie. Would Molly like such?"

"She'd love it. But do we have time?"

Anna headed into Peter's room, waving for Jane to follow her. Feeling like an intruder, Jane stood back while Anna rummaged in Peter's dresser drawers. Jane couldn't help noticing that Peter Gruber's bed was neatly made up. And he had plants growing on the wide windowsill. In fact, one was about ready to bloom. Jane was trying to decide what the flower might be when Anna held up a blue work shirt and said, "We make blue dress? I have small piece of lace in my sewing basket. With nice buttons—"

"But I can't let you cut up one of Peter's shirts for a doll dress," Jane protested.

"Is old shirt." Anna held up one sleeve and pointed out the frayed cuff. Without waiting for Jane to agree, she headed back to the main room. "Peter goes now to find Christmas tree." She laid the shirt aside. "And we make springerle. Later, we sew." When Jane repeated the word *springerle* as a question, Anna pointed to the two rectangles of carved wood hanging on either side of the framed motto. "Please to take those down, and I will show you." She smiled as she bustled about. "Put on apron, Jane. We have much work to do!"

Peter squinted through the layers of his scarf as his horse pulled the sleigh toward the river. It was going to take a miracle to find a suitable anything to use as a Christmas tree in all this snow, but he was determined. Short of risking freezing to death, he'd find a way to make Molly smile on Christmas morning. He was, after all, a *good* monster. The idea made him smile briefly—until he remembered the other reason December was meaningful.

He'd proposed to Priscilla in December. And, as always, memories of Priscilla brought a flood of other emotions. Rejection … loss…grief…and loneliness. He frowned and willed himself to remember little Molly's voice saying, *"You're a good monster."* And thinking on that, Peter realized that he didn't want to wallow in the past anymore. Something about the way Jane

297

McClure was able to smile and banter with him and the way Molly had touched his ruined cheek—something about all of it made him feel hopeful.

As his Molly plodded along, head up, ears alert, Peter replayed the scene in his mind, smiling beneath his scarf and savoring the idea that someone had finally said the word *monster* aloud and made it part of a memory he would treasure. At least for a little while today, what that minié ball had done to his face hadn't really mattered all that much. In fact, as they sat around the breakfast table listening to Mutti talk about life in Germany and God's goodness and her hopes for an orchard, it was as if it hadn't even happened.

That first night when he'd stood looking down at Molly, he'd wallowed in regret when he realized that he and Priscilla might have had a child her age by now. But today, Jane had spoken of another soldier whose sacrifice had played a part in precocious Molly McClure's existence. What children would never have been born if Peter Gruber hadn't stayed up in that tree? Would he wish them out of existence to melt his scars? Given another chance, would Keig have saved his own life and let his friends die? Peter shook his head. He knew the answer to that. In battle, some men stood their ground, and some ran. He'd been the first kind in battle that particular day. Funny that he'd spent so much time running ever since.

Molly pulled up abruptly, tossing her head and snorting. Peter looked about, realizing they'd come to the riverbank. He guided her to turn east. There was a low place not far ahead, and if he remembered right, a few small cedar trees grew along the edge of a low rise. Maybe, just maybe—yes. Exactly as he'd hoped. The wind had driven snow across the top of the rise, accumulating more slowly in deep drifts along the opposite side of the clump of trees. He could still see the tip of the tallest one. Now, if only he could manage to dig one out.

Suddenly he was floundering in waist-deep snow again, laughing and flailing with his arms, until he struck gold. Or green at least. A small cedar tree. He returned to the wagon for his ax, and in a few minutes, red-faced and breathing hard, he'd put the tree in the sleigh and headed home. About halfway there, he had an irresistible urge to sing.

"Stille Nacht ... heilige Nacht ..." Something broke inside when he got to the last verse and the line *"Da uns schlägt die rettende Stund. Redeeming grace..."* He hadn't felt like the recipient of grace in a long while. And yet, thanks to Molly McClure, he realized it had always been there. He'd missed it, ignored it, refused it. And yet God offered it. Even to monsters.

Peter began to talk to God.

Chapter 10

Molly woke from her nap, ravenous and thrilled with her first taste of springerle. But she was coughing a bit and said her throat felt "scratchy," so after a dose of Anna's tonic, the challenge became how to keep her quiet so she would let her body rest and recover.

"Tomorrow is Christmas," Anna said gently. "You must to rest so it can be special. We have surprises." She leaned close. "Even Peter has surprise."

When Molly looked at her with doubt in her eyes, Jane smiled. "Anna's right. We have all kinds of plans for you. In fact," she teased, "now that I think of it, you really should go to bed at once so that we have time to prepare."

But fueled by promises of surprises, Molly had no interest in retiring. She wanted to go out to the barn and see the animals. They managed to stave off that idea with the news that Peter had harnessed Molly to the sleigh and headed off on an errand.

Molly's expression was hopeful. "Is he telling Mr. Huggins we aren't coming?"

"Of course not," Jane replied. "Because we are going. As soon as Anna thinks you're well enough." She retrieved *Little Women* from the other room and proposed to read another chapter.

" 'What in the world are you going to do now, Jo?' asked Meg one snowy afternoon, as her sister came tramping through the hall, in rubber boots, old sack, and hood, with a broom in one hand and a shovel in the other. 'Going out for exercise,' answered Jo with a mischievous twinkle in her eyes."

"That's what *I* want to do," Molly muttered, tossing Katie onto the table with a decidedly rebellious attitude and kicking her foot back and forth in a restive rhythm.

Jane pretended not to hear and kept reading. " 'I should think two long walks this morning would have been enough! It's cold and dull out, and I advise you to stay warm and dry by the fire, as I do,' said Meg with a shiver.

" 'Never take advice! Can't keep still all day, and not being a pussycat, I don't like to doze by the fire. I like adventures, and I'm going to find some.' "

Before Molly could comment on her obvious desire for adventure, Anna spoke up. "I am thinking poor Katie is cold with no blanket of her own." As she spoke, she laid some scraps of cloth alongside the doll. Smoothing them, she looked over at Molly. "What would you think if we make Katie a quilt of her own?"

Molly looked at the fabric. "I don't know how to sew except for buttons and hems."

"I'm afraid I haven't done my duty in that regard," Jane said quickly. "I—I just—"

Anna waved the explanation away. "Is no matter. Perhaps God knew that Molly would need ... *diversion* ... one day." She looked over at Molly. "What do you think? What colors for Katie?"

Molly leaned forward. She pointed to a tiny black-and-white check that reminded Jane of the apron Anna had loaned her earlier in the day.

Anna nodded. "Is gut." She rummaged in her sewing basket, then stood up. "One moment." She went into the bedroom. Jane heard the sound of scraping, as if something was being pulled out from beneath the bed, although of course only the trundle was beneath the bed. Anna returned with a bit of red cloth. "Is nice for accent, ja?"

"Red's my favorite color," Molly said.

"Then must be Katie's, too." Anna smiled. She laid two pasteboard squares atop the fabrics and handed Molly a pencil. "You must draw around square on fabric then cut on line. Are these colors gut?" Molly nodded. "Of little square, twenty-four dark, twenty-four medium. Of big square, you make six light."

"How do I know if it's dark or medium or light?" Molly frowned. "Some of them could be either one, couldn't they?"

Anna quickly sorted the bits of cloth into three piles. "Dark, medium, light. You see?"

Molly nodded and, taking up the pencil, began to trace. When Jane offered to help her, Molly shook her head. "I'd rather you read about Jo's adventure."

The sunlight was fading when Peter Gruber finally came through the door. He wasn't quite as frozen as he'd been after going to the snowbound train—or maybe he just didn't seem as cold, for the first thing he did was cross to the worktable where dozens of springerle cookies lay cooling. "There is no aroma on the earth better than this."

He inhaled with pleasure and had just reached out to take one when Molly said, "We aren't allowed." She turned around in her chair and looked over at him. "We have to wait until after supper."

"Is that right?" He unwound his scarf then and looked to Anna, pressing both his hands together as if in prayer. He said something in German that Jane didn't understand, but it made Anna laugh.

"All right, all right." She held up two fingers. "Two each for you and the little one. But only two."

With a wink in Molly's direction, Peter pulled off his mittens and immediately popped two cookies into his mouth.

"You didn't even look to see the designs!" Anna scolded.

"I know the designs," Peter said. "I made them. Ja, Mutti?" He scanned the cookies on the table and selected two, which he carried over to Molly. "Two flowers for a lovely girl."

Jane looked up at the carved molds she'd rinsed off and returned to their place of honor on either side of Anna's embroidered motto. "You carved these?" She reached up to trace the intricate design of a stag, then a prancing horse. "They're gorgeous."

He bowed. *"Danke."* Then he clomped across the floor to the stove and, sliding past it to the rear of the room where Anna's cot was set up, took off his coat and sat down on the cot. Once again, she helped him with his boots, insisting that he stay put while she hurried into his room to bring out his fur-lined moccasins. He slid into them with an audible sigh, murmuring something to Anna. He waited until Jane looked his way and nodded a yes as he gestured with his hands.

Jane realized he was telling her how tall the tree was. When Molly looked his way, he pretended to be scratching his ear. Jane suppressed a smile.

"Something's going on," Molly said.

"What could be going on?" Jane grinned.

Molly rolled her eyes. "Christmas."

Peter came to the table and sat down. "Would you like some help with that?"

"Men don't sew," Molly said.

"Men do so." Peter reached into his mother's sewing basket, pulled out a spool of thread and a needle book, and in no time he was stitching two squares of fabric together.

Jane didn't hide her amazement. "You sew, you carve—do you cook, too?"

"As long as it only requires flipping flapjacks." He finished stitching the squares of fabric together and showed Molly how to finger press along the seam.

Molly took a bite of her second cookie. She looked at Jane. "Mr. Huggins doesn't do anything," she said. "He just stands behind a counter and takes people's money."

Later that night, Jane hung the last snowflake atop the little tree Peter had dragged home from the river. She and Peter had worked half the night making paper chains and Scherenschnitte snowflakes and tying calico bows on branches, while Anna fashioned a new dress for Katie out of Peter's worn blue shirt. When she finally held it up—with an apology that it wasn't nicer—tears sprang to Jane's eyes. "It's beautiful," she said, then looked back at the tree. "Everything is so beautiful."

Peter stifled a yawn. "If I feed the livestock now, I can sleep a bit longer."

"I'll help," Jane said. Peter looked surprised. "You said your horse doesn't bite, and I refuse to let that raging lunatic of a rooster intimidate me." She crossed the room and took down her coat and scarf.

"I will roll out the dough for cinnamon rolls," Anna said. "We have enough butter for a good batch."

"You should get some rest," Jane protested. "I can do that when we come back in. I don't even want to think about how many hundreds of cinnamon rolls I've made in that boarding-house kitchen in the past couple of years. I'm happy to do it—if you don't mind the sounds of someone else in your kitchen while you rest, that is."

Anna hesitated for only a moment then nodded. "Danke." She was in bed before Peter and Jane left the house.

Out in the barn, Jane inhaled the aroma of fresh—and not-so-fresh—straw, following Peter's lead as he moved from one stall to the next, cleaning out his Molly's stall, breaking the ice in her water tank, and tending to the other animals. When he settled on the milk stool to milk the cow, Jane headed into the chicken coop and gathered eggs, happy that Solomon had apparently decided she didn't present any threat to his harem.

It seemed that they were back inside the house in no time at all. They entered to the sounds of Anna's soft snoring. Jane smiled as she hung up her coat, donned an apron, and rinsed her hands in the bucket of water Anna kept beside the stove for washing. She dusted the worktable with flour and began to roll out the dough for their cinnamon rolls, then spread it with butter and sprinkled cinnamon and sugar over the entire surface. In only a few minutes, two pans of rolls were rising atop the warm stove. It wasn't until she'd cleaned off the worktable and rinsed her hands again that she realized Peter hadn't gone to bed after all.

He was standing in the doorway to his room, watching her with a look of—something—on his face that might have worried her if a new boarder had expressed it. At the moment, it only made her catch her breath.

"I didn't mean to startle you." He held up his coffee mug. "I thought I might steal another cookie and some coffee, if there is any."

Jane lifted the coffeepot to check. "A cup, anyway." She grasped the handle. Peter crossed to where she was standing, and she poured the coffee, blushing for some foolish reason.

"Danke," he said.

His tone made her look up at him. "I–I'm afraid I don't know how to say 'You're welcome' in German."

"Bitte."

She nodded. "Bitte, then. Really, it's nothing."

"You're wrong about that," he said. "It's everything. To have a woman as beautiful as you look at me without wincing. To have a child see through this"—he touched the scars—"and call me a good monster."

"You're not a monster. You're a good man."

He nodded. "But I'd forgotten that. Until you and Molly came into our lives."

Anna coughed. Jane started and, with a little laugh, set the coffeepot back on the stovetop. She nodded toward Anna's cot. "I refuse to be responsible for her response if she catches you stealing her springerle." She reached behind her to untie the apron, and for a moment she thought perhaps he would put his arm around her and draw her close. For a moment, she wished he would. But instead, he grinned like a mischievous boy as he lifted the lid of the wooden box where Anna had stowed the springerle.

Anna's voice sounded in the darkness. "Only two, Peter."

Chapter 11

"Is it Christmas yet?"

Jane opened her eyes. Molly was leaning over the edge of the bed looking down at her.

With a groan, Jane glanced toward the window. Gray light. "I believe it is. But you have to wait here until things are ready. We were up very late—actually until early this morning. Peter and Anna may wish to sleep a little longer." When she pulled her stockings on beneath the covers, she was suddenly aware of her new ability to bend her knee. With a quick thanks to the heavens, she rose and wrapped herself in a blanket. She paused at the foot of the bed before heading into the kitchen. "Promise me you won't peek."

"I won't. But I might get dressed. Is that okay?"

Jane gathered up Molly's things and handed them over. "That's perfectly all right. I'll be back in a bit." She tiptoed into the main room, glad when it seemed that both Peter and Anna were still asleep. As quietly as she could, she stirred up the fire in the stove, grateful for the warmth that emanated into the room as she stood, transferring her weight from one foot to the other in an attempt to keep them from going numb with cold.

"It's too cold for stocking feet."

She jumped at the whispered comment. Peter held out a pair of fur-lined moccasins.

"But where—?"

"There's a pile of cured hides beneath my bed. I guessed at the size, but at least you won't freeze." He anticipated her protest. "It took all of twenty minutes to cut and stitch a pair. They're very primitive."

Jane slipped one on. "They're wonderful." And suddenly she was newly aware that beneath the blanket wrapped about her, she was in a nightgown. And her hair was down. She felt heat crawling up the back of her neck. "I just wanted to get the rolls in the oven. I—I'll get dressed now."

Molly called again. "Is Christmas ready?"

Peter smiled down at her. "I think Christmas had better get ready."

"I hate to wake Anna. She must be exhausted."

"Anna is fine," the old woman said with a chuckle. "She can nap later."

Jane looked over at Anna's cot. Only a pair of merry blue eyes were visible above the edge of the woman's comforters. She'd been pretending to sleep. And obviously enjoying whatever it was that was going on between her son and Jane.

Jane shrugged deeper into the blanket, holding on tight as she headed into the bedroom to get dressed. When she glanced back to see if Peter was watching her, he was.

Almost.

As Peter lay in bed Christmas night, that was the word he finally landed on to describe the day. Almost perfect. Of course Molly had no intention of making Peter feel the way he did as he lay in the dark, trying to talk himself out of the emotion that had been born inside of him and grown steadily. Today had been the first day in years when he could simply be a man enjoying life without any need to hold himself apart in order to escape notice.

The aroma of Jane's cinnamon rolls had lingered all through the presentation of the tree and the new doll dress this morning. Molly had clapped her hands with joy over both. She said the tree was almost as big as the last one she remembered at their old house. When Mutti presented a tray of her springerle for an afternoon snack, Molly said that even Sonja couldn't make cookies as good as Anna. They were almost the best she'd ever eaten.

In the afternoon, Peter and Molly played checkers while Jane and Anna napped. And then, when Molly insisted that she was almost well and begged to see the animals, Peter bundled her up and carried her out to the barn. She loved every minute of it. Molly the horse's stall was almost as big as the stalls where Papa kept his team when they lived in the other house. That barn had been brick. And Molly didn't call it a barn. She called it a stable.

As the day went on, Mutti's stew bubbling on the stove filled the air with savory aromas, and while Jane made biscuits, Peter once again took up needle and thread and joined Mutti and Molly as they stitched some more pieces of the doll quilt together. After supper Peter read the Christmas story by lamplight, first from Mutti's German Bible and then from his own English Bible. And they sang carols—Mutti in German and the rest of them in English.

The day had been perfect. *Almost.* Except for Peter's realization that Jane McClure had known fine things and was likely hoping for fine things again, and that he, Peter Gruber, with his ruined face and sod house, could not give them.

Mutti was right to say that it had been a blessing to help the McClures through a difficult time. But as he lay thinking back over the day, Peter told himself that it was also good that Molly was feeling well enough for them to go. She and Jane deserved to be blessed by the generosity of a man who offered prosperity in a bustling city where Molly would get the best of schooling and Jane—Peter closed his eyes.

The memory of Jane McClure looking at him without revulsion would grace his life forever.

Standing beside the bed, Jane smiled down at Molly as the child said her prayers, thanking God for the tree and the doll dress, for springerle and cinnamon rolls, for Molly the horse and Solomon the rooster, and, it seemed to Jane, for everyone and everything in the sod house. In spite of the nap she and Anna had taken this afternoon, Jane was exhausted. Poor Anna had nodded off while Peter read the Christmas story from his English-language Bible this evening.

When Molly finally pronounced her "amen," Jane stopped fighting her own weariness. Molly settled beneath her covers with Katie at her side, and Jane quickly undressed and followed suit. She'd just closed her eyes when she heard Molly say, "And please make it snow again. A lot. So that we can't leave tomorrow."

It was quiet for a few minutes, and Jane had almost fallen asleep when Molly leaned over the edge of the bed. "Did you hear that last part, Mama?"

"I did."

"Do you think God heard it, too?"

"Of course."

"Do you think it made Him mad for me to ask for snow?"

"Why would it?"

"Because I want snow so I don't have to do what you want." She was quiet for a moment. "Did it make you mad?"

Jane took a deep breath. "No, Molly. I'm not angry. But we can't stay. Mr. Huggins is waiting."

"Do you like him better because he doesn't have scars?"

Jane took another deep breath and let it out slowly. What or who she liked didn't matter. Mr. Huggins was offering them—something. And for all his kindness and gentle ways, Peter Gruber was not. "Do you remember what I said on the train when we left Omaha?"

Silence. Finally, a muttered, "You mean about having to trust you about Mr. Huggins?"

"Yes."

"I remember."

Molly tossed and turned for a moment. When she'd finally settled down, Jane said, "I love you more than you can possibly know, Molly."

"I love you, too, Mama."

In spite of her weariness, Jane lay awake for a long while, trying her best to look forward to Denver.

"Peter."

Peter woke with a start and sat up. Mutti sat on the edge of his bed trembling. His first thought was of Molly or Jane, but then Mutti put her hand to her chest. She covered her mouth with the other hand and coughed. "I am afraid that I am unwell."

He reached out to take her hand. She leaned in, and he felt her forehead.

She nodded. "Ja. Is fever." She coughed again. "I am so sorry."

"There's nothing to be sorry about." He slipped out of bed and guided her to lie down. "Rest. Everything will be fine. Do you need anything?"

"In the green tin," she croaked. "Make tea. And don't— don't tell Jane. She must not worry."

Peter paused. "I'll tell her you were tired, and I insisted on you resting in my room. She'll understand."

"I want to go to the train. To say good-bye."

"I'll bring the tea. We'll see how you feel in the morning."

Peter had commenced making the herb tea as quietly as possible when Jane appeared in the bedroom doorway. Obviously she'd expected to see Mutti bustling about. She hadn't bothered to wrap herself in a blanket. When she saw Peter, she took a step back.

Before she could ask, Peter said, "Mutti's worn herself out. I talked her into sleeping in my room and letting me bring her some tea to help her sleep." He looked away, but not before taking in the vision of Jane's thick hair cascading around her shoulders. "I'm sorry I woke you."

"It's all right. Can I do anything to help?"

He shook his head. "She'll be fine." He concentrated on pouring hot water into the waiting mug. When next he glanced up, Jane had retreated to bed.

Mutti protested when Peter insisted that he move the cot in where he would hear her if she needed anything, but he did it anyway, and he was glad. As night wore on, she began to cough more, although she smothered each cough with a pillow. Finally, when Peter insisted that there must be more he could do, she directed him to make a different kind of poultice.

"No onions," she croaked. "It will wake our guests."

And so he crept about, wincing with each sound, grateful that Jane didn't reappear in the doorway while he followed Mutti's instructions. She applied the poultice herself, tapping on the edge of the bowl when it was all right for him to retrieve it. Then she insisted he keep it on his own nightstand so there'd be no evidence of anything but tea-making out in the main room when Jane and Molly got up.

"Don't look so worried," she said as she leaned forward so that Peter could put more pillows behind her. "Is gut. I will be fine."

But she wasn't fine. She slipped into a heavy sleep, and her fever raged.

Jane leaned down and lay the back of her hand against Anna's pale cheek, then looked up at Peter, standing next to her. "We can't leave. Not today. Not until we know she's better."

Molly's voice sounded from the doorway. "I didn't mean for it to happen this way." Her voice wavered and tears spilled down her cheeks. "When I prayed that we could stay, I didn't mean—"

Peter went to her. Crouching down so he could look into Molly's eyes, he said gently, "Of course you didn't. This isn't your fault. You mustn't think any such thing."

Molly's lower lip trembled, and she looked down at the floor. "I was sick. And she took care of me." A tear slid down her cheek. "Maybe I brought it."

"The only thing you brought into this house that matters, Molly McClure, is joy and laughter. Because of you, Mutti and I had the best Christmas we've had in years. Because of you—" He broke off. Tapped his ruined cheek with his forefinger. "Because of you, I won't let this keep me from having a good life." He took her in his arms and held her close while she cried. "You must believe me. Mutti is going to be all right. And this isn't your fault. People get sick. We're both so glad you came to us." He let her go. "Do you know what you could do to help Mutti get better?" Molly shook her head. "You could finish the doll quilt while your mama helps me take care of her. It will make her feel happy to know you like it so much that you really are going to finish it."

"I was always going to finish it," Molly said. "I just didn't have time."

"Well, now you do. Spread your things out on the table, and I'll light the lamp. And you and your mama can tend Mutti while I drive to the train and send another message." He glanced at Jane. "If you're sure—"

"I'm sure," Jane said. "We're staying."

She wrote another telegram. This time the words came easily.

FRIEND TAKEN ILL *Stop* MUST STAY TO HELP *Stop*
APPRECIATE YOUR UNDERSTANDING *Stop*

She hesitated again about the signature. If only she knew how Mr. Huggins had responded to the delay. Perhaps there would be a response waiting when Peter delivered this new message. Something that would give her a hint as to what he was thinking. But for now it was impossible to know. And so she signed the telegram *J. McClure.*

Anna was still sleeping when Peter finally bundled up and headed off to deliver Jane's telegram to the train station. Molly begged to go with him, but when Jane sent a pleading glance his way, Peter seemed to understand.

"I would love nothing better than to take you for a ride. But we must take care that you don't relapse. Do you know what that word means?"

Molly sighed. "It means I have to stay here."

Peter smiled. "It means we don't want to take any chances that you would get chilled and get sick again. We need you to be healthy to help with Anna." He paused, then said, "Is gut, ja?"

Molly shrugged. "Is gut." She grimaced. "But not really."

Jane handed Peter the piece of paper with the message written out. He folded it without reading it and tucked it in his shirt pocket. Then he donned his coat and hat. "I wish we had at least two real bricks," she said. "I could heat them in the oven to keep your feet warm while you're gone."

"You know about such things?" He seemed genuinely surprised.

"Sonja used to do it for us," Molly said.

Peter nodded. "Of course. The servant."

Something about the way he said it made Jane feel odd. Why did mention of Sonja annoy him? She retrieved a couple of blankets from the cot in his room, rolled them up, lowered the oven door, and set them down. "These will warm up while you hitch up the sleigh. Give a shout when you're ready to leave, and I'll bring them out. You can put them under the lap robe—" She broke off. The way he was looking at her made her feel foolish. "I only meant, we can't have you taking a chill. One patient at a time is enough."

He nodded. "Danke."

When Jane heard Peter's voice calling, "Ready," she grabbed the warmed blankets and hurried outside. He'd driven the sleigh near the door. As she handed up the blankets, words tumbled out. She jabbered all the while Peter was wrapping his legs and pulling the lap robe around them. *Be careful. Hurry back. Thank you for doing this. I'm so sorry to be extra trouble. Be careful. Hurry back.*

Finally he interrupted. "Jane. It's all right. Of course I'll hurry. If your Mr. Huggins has sent a message, you'll be reading it before you know."

Chapter 12

Molly stitched, Anna slept, and Jane worried. What if something happened to Peter out there in the cold? She wouldn't have any idea what to do without him. What if Anna was truly, desperately ill? Henry, the porter on the train, had indicated that Elm Creek didn't have a doctor. How did people stand living in a place where they didn't have a doctor? And Mr. Huggins. How would he respond to the news that Molly was better, but they still weren't heading to Denver? Would he understand? Was Jane ruining her only chance to give Molly a better life by lingering?

"Mama!" Molly's frustrated tone drew Jane back to the moment.

She held out a bit of patchwork. "My thread knotted up, and I can't make it work."

Jane took the sewing into her own hands but went to the doorway leading into Peter's room to look in on Anna before checking Molly's sewing problem. Anna was still sleeping, so Jane retreated to the table. She unthreaded the needle and used it as a tool to loosen the knot in the thread. Problem solved, she rethreaded the needle and handed the patchwork back to Molly.

"You don't have to work on that every minute if you don't want to."

Molly didn't even look up. "I want to show Anna when she wakes up." She bent to the piecing. "Anna said to make the stitches small and to back a stitch every third or fourth one."

"It's called a 'backstitch,'" Jane said.

Molly ignored her. "Anna said it makes the seam hold better."

Jane nodded. "She'll be very pleased to see your progress. Are you certain you don't want any help?" Molly was certain, and so Jane rose and stirred up the fire, hesitating for a moment when she realized that she wasn't quite certain what to cook. She decided on potato soup when she found some shriveled potatoes in a crock along the back wall. And onions. Anna had quite a supply of onions, which was no surprise, seeing as how she had such a firm belief in smelly poultices. Jane set to peeling potatoes and peeking in on Anna and counting the minutes, all the while wondering when Peter would return and what would happen when Mr. Huggins heard the news.

Jane stared down at the telegram Peter had brought back from the station.

Regrets *Stop* Plans on hold *Stop* Hope to hear good news soon *Stop*

He'd signed it *H. Huggins,* which made her regret the *Jane* she'd sent his way. Did he think that too forward of her? At least she'd signed today's differently. She thanked Peter and tucked the telegram in her apron pocket. He hung his coat and things up and hurried to Anna's bedside.

When Jane heard low voices, she went to the doorway and peered in. Peter sat on a chair leaning forward, clasping one of Anna's hands between his while she smiled at him. At the sight of Jane, she looked up, but when she opened her mouth to speak, she began to cough. Peter hurried into the other room and returned with a mug of water. Anna took a sip, grimaced with the effort of swallowing, and then spread one wrinkled hand across her chest as she explained what was needed to make another poultice—this one with onions.

"I know how to do it, Mutti," Peter said, patting her hand gently. "And you want the syrup in the green bottle—not the brown one, right?" Anna looked surprised, even as she nodded her head. Peter said he'd see to the tea as well, kissed her on the cheek, and motioned for Jane to follow him into the main room. Once there, he handed her the green bottle and a spoon. "If you'll get that down her—take a mug of water with you—I'll handle the poultice and the tea."

"Can I help?" Molly had set her sewing down and was watching them.

Peter smiled. "You may." He reached for a small washtub. "Step outside the door and fill this tub with clean snow and bring it back inside. Then you can help me make Mutti's special tea."

When Jane went back to Anna, the old woman waved the teaspoon away and took a sip directly from the green bottle, then grimaced and drank down the mug of water. "Don't look so sad," she said. "Grubers are strong people. I will be fine. Mostly I am only tired. And I have—" She lifted her chin and stroked her throat with her fingertips, then coughed.

"At least you don't sound like you're congested the way Molly was." Jane paused. "Do you think we should put another steam tent up?"

"Nein." Anna took a deep breath to prove that her lungs were clear. "I breathe good." She reached for Jane's hand and put Jane's palm to her forehead. "See? Is only little warm, ja?"

When Jane agreed, Anna settled back with a smile. "All will be better in a few days. Maybe a week. Maybe a little more. We will see." She motioned to the main room. "Now go. Help Peter."

Peter had Molly cut a square of cheesecloth and spread it on the worktable. Next, he reached for the cracker tin on the medicine shelf. "This is what you were after in your sleep that night." He took the lid off and held it so Molly could see the contents. When she took a whiff of the herbs and made a face, he chuckled. "I agree. It makes a powerful tea, but it's not something to be savored as a midnight snack." He took a generous portion of the dried leaves and put them in the center of the cheesecloth, then directed Molly to get some of Mutti's strong thread and help him make a tea bag. "We steep this until the water is a horrible shade of green, and then we take it in to Mutti." While he talked, he was heating water on the stove.

Jane came out of Mutti's room, went to the onion bin, and came back to the worktable. "She said they don't need to be peeled. I don't honestly remember seeing her make the poultice for Molly, but somehow that doesn't seem right."

"I know, but that's how she does it." Peter reached for a knife. "If you'll mind the teapot, I'll do the honors."

They worked together for a few minutes, and finally Molly looked up from the mug of tea she'd been watching. "It looks pretty awful," she said, and leaned down to take a whiff. "And it smells worse."

Peter leaned over to take a look. He nodded. "Yes, I believe that's just about terrible enough to effect a cure."

"Can I take it in?" Molly asked as Jane lifted the herbs out of the cup and set the sack on a saucer.

"Of course." Peter nodded. "Thank you for helping."

As soon as Molly got to the doorway, Anna called out a greeting, followed by a few dry coughs.

"It doesn't sound too bad," Jane said. "I mentioned a steam tent while you were gone, but she said it wouldn't be necessary."

"She said as much to me," Peter agreed. "But I'm still going to bring the wagon cover back in and the ropes. Just in case she's proven wrong in the middle of the night."

Anna administered her own poultice as before, and when Peter coaxed her to eat a little supper, she proclaimed Jane's potato soup delicious. As evening wore on and Jane mentioned reading to Molly before bedtime, Anna asked if she would mind reading at the bedside so she could enjoy the story as well.

Peter brought Mutti's rocker in for Jane and set it by the window. He turned up the lamp so she could see to read. Mutti insisted that Molly climb up and sit at the foot of her bed. Peter was about to step into the other room when Mutti called for him to stay. "Get chair. Stay near." She paused. "Bring springerle for Molly." She forced a weak smile.

After everyone had retired, Jane lay awake for a while. It struck her suddenly, right before she fell asleep. Mr. Huggins hadn't mentioned Molly in the telegram. She rose and went to the sewing rocker by the bedroom window where she'd put her day dress and the apron, then dug the telegram out of the pocket and held it up to the low-burning lamp. Of course telegrams were by nature brief and to the point. *Regrets*. It occurred to Jane that, while she hated the idea that Anna was sick, whatever she was feeling about not being able to catch the train today, *regret* did not apply. *Relieved* was a better word for how she felt when it came to not being able to leave for Denver.

Plans on hold. At least Mr. Huggins had made some plans and was still hoping they would be realized. That was reassuring. Wasn't it?

Hope to hear good news soon. Jane sat back in the chair and looked toward the bed where Molly lay asleep. *Good news.* Yes. It would be good news when Anna was feeling well—well enough for them to say good-bye.

Jane sat for quite a while in the dim light of the lamp, thinking. Staring out at the snow. Finally she rose. On her way back to bed, she folded the telegram and tucked it into the side pocket of her carpetbag.

It was three long days and three longer nights before Anna finally asked Peter to help her out of bed and into the main room to sit at the table with everyone for breakfast. Molly proved herself a willing and able nurse, making tea according to Peter's instructions, shuttling toast and medicine bottles to Anna's bedside, and sitting with Anna while Peter tended the livestock—except for the chickens. Jane had taken over the chickens, surprised to find that she enjoyed the chore. She admired Solomon's spectacular iridescent tail feathers and even named the hen that seemed particularly resistant to the idea of giving up her eggs to an interloper.

"The one with the gold eyes," Anna said, when Jane called the hen a "she-donkey."

"How did you know?"

Anna chuckled, although the laugh cost her a few minutes of coughing and a grimace as she commented on how sore coughing made an old woman's ribs. She glanced toward the door before speaking and then motioned for Jane to come close. "I never have liked that hen. Maybe we have her for supper when I'm feeling better, ja?"

For all of Anna's pain and coughing, it appeared the old woman had been right and that her illness wasn't going to be serious. She never needed the steam tent. Jane was thankful, but as the days wore on and Anna stayed abed, she began to wonder again about Mr. Huggins. She could almost sense dark clouds gathering in the west and a storm about to break.

A week after Peter had gone to send the second telegram, Jane's imaginary dark clouds became real. A loud knock on the door made everyone jump. Anna, who'd joined them at the breakfast table, clutched her blanket close as Peter rose to answer the door.

"Sorry to bother," a voice said, "but I've a letter for a Mrs. McClure. It's marked urgent." Peter swung the door wide enough for the speaker to step inside.

Jane rose. "I'm Mrs. McClure."

The man rummaged inside the oversize fur coat he was wearing and finally withdrew an envelope. He held it out, speaking to Peter as he did so. "Hope it isn't bad news. The sender addressed it to the telegraph operator at Elm Creek and enclosed two dollars as incentive to get me to deliver it right away. Said I was to wait for a reply."

Jane opened the envelope with trembling hands.

Jane—I take the liberty of addressing you informally, in light of the telegram which brought such disappointing news. I have thought of little else but how to understand the situation since receiving your brief notice. While I do not wish to appear unsympathetic, it does seem that you have more than repaid the kindness of strangers. It is my utmost hope that you will relieve my nagging questions by directing the bearer of this letter to respond with a telegram stating the time of your arrival—which I think

it reasonable to expect within the next two days. You said you
were looking forward to welcoming 1876 in my company. We
are several days into the new year. Have I been wrong to think
that you shared my hopes for a mutually beneficial future?

Respectfully,
Howard H. Huggins

"It's from *him*." Molly was the first to speak, and she didn't try to hide her resentment.

"Is everything all right?" Peter's voice was gentle. Concerned.

Jane swept her hand across her forehead as she stared down at the letter. "Yes. Of course." She looked up. Forced a smile. "I think so." Her voice wavered. "I'm not sure."

"Not meaning to rush you, ma'am," the letter carrier said, "but I'd rather my team not stiffen up waiting in the cold."

Jane nodded. And then, quite suddenly, she felt weak in the knees and once again took her seat at the table.

"I'll get you a pencil and paper," Peter said, then offered the man waiting a cup of coffee. "I'll take it," he said, "but if you don't mind, I'll wait outside with the team." He grasped the mug Peter offered and spoke to Jane. "Try not to take too long, ma'am." And he was gone.

It seemed like all the joy had gone out of the room. Jane stared down at the letter. Cleared her throat. Took the pencil and paper Peter offered.

Anna sighed. "Peter," she said, "help me back to bed. I think—I think I have fever again." She sighed, grunting softly as Peter took her arm and helped her back to bed.

As soon as they were gone, Jane forced a smile as she said to Molly, "He wants us to come soon. He's—well, he's tired of waiting, and he wants us to come no later than day after tomorrow."

"But Anna's still sick," Molly said. "And I don't have my quilt finished. She has to tell me how to finish it."

Peter's voice sounded from the doorway. "You don't have to answer it now. I'll send the driver away. When you have an answer, I'll take it to Elm Creek."

"I can't ask you to—"

"You didn't ask," Peter said. "I offered."

Jane lay the pencil down. "Thank you."

He was out the door almost before she finished the second word. When he came back inside, Jane rose and picked up the letter. "If you don't mind, I think—" She looked toward the room she and Molly had been sharing.

Peter spoke to Molly. "How about you stop pricking those dainty fingers of yours and try to beat me at checkers?"

Molly shrugged. "I can't beat you."

"You did beat me, just last night."

"Only because you let me."

"You think I let you win?"

"I know you did."

"Why would I do a thing like that?"

"Because you're a good monster," Molly said. She looked over at Jane. "Mr. Huggins wouldn't ever let me win," she said. "He doesn't even *like* to play checkers." And with that, she jumped up and ran into the bedroom.

Anna called for Peter, and Jane was left alone with the letter.

Chapter 13

"What is it, Mutti?" Peter hurried to the bedside. When he reached out to see if she had a fever, she waved his hand away.

"Is nothing," Mutti said. "I must rest." She hunkered down and turned her back on him.

"But you just called for me."

Mutti nodded her head. "Is small house. Jane must be alone for a while."

Peter sat down in the chair by the bed. Leaning forward to rest his forearms on his legs, he stared down at the floor, agonizing over what might happen if he didn't speak up, terrified to risk it.

Mutti turned over in bed. She pulled the covers down below her chin. "You are going to let them go?"

"Please don't worry," Peter said. He reached for her hand and gave it a squeeze. "I'll take good care of you."

She sighed. "For that I do not worry. I worry for you."

He frowned. "I'm not coming down with whatever it is. My throat's fine. My lungs are clear."

Mutti rolled her eyes. "Lungs clear. Brain clouded." She paused. "You love her. You think I don't see?"

He took a deep breath. "I have nothing to offer. She had a fine house with her first husband, and this Mr. Huggins will likely provide her with another."

"And what is a fine house without love?"

He met her gaze. "And what is life with a monster?" He stood up. Mutti opened her mouth to say more, but he held up his hand. "Please. You're going to say it doesn't matter. But it does." Surprised when tears threatened, he drew a ragged breath. Forced a smile. "Molly calls me a good monster, and I'll never forget that. Between the two of them, they've healed something I didn't think could ever be right again. Those are good memories. And I don't want them ruined by the memory of yet another beautiful woman looking away when I declare—when I ask—" He broke off. "Sleep well, Mutti. I love you very much."

There was no point in his trying to sleep. Peter didn't even try. Instead, he headed outside to the barn. He hung a lantern on a nail by Molly's stall and brushed her sleek coat until it shone. He mucked out stalls. Finally, when he ran out of work, when his feet felt like two blocks of ice, he headed into the little tack room. He closed the door behind him and started a small fire in the woodstove before perching on a bale of hay and propping his feet up on a crate.

He woke with a start to Solomon's crowing. With a groan, he stood up, stretching before opening the door to the tack room and peering across the way through the little window that faced the house. The snow was beginning to melt. The clothesline was no longer buried in a snowdrift. He left the door open to the tack room and made his way past the stalls and out into the fresh air. The sky was getting lighter in the east. In the west, it was still dark. A sliver of moon hung low in the clear sky. If he was going to take Molly for a sleigh ride, he'd better get it done today. He'd bring her out after breakfast and—He gulped. Jane was lighting the lamp in the bedroom window. He looked back at the barn. And finally up to the sky. *I'm afraid. God.... I'm so afraid.*

He turned toward the house. He hadn't felt this way since that long-ago day when he perched in a tree and watched gray uniforms emerge from a cornfield. Everyone told him he'd been brave that day. Maybe he had. He'd wanted to defend his friends.

What was a man worth if he wasn't willing to try just as hard to save himself? Taking a deep breath, Peter whispered, "Help," and headed inside.

It was still dark when Jane rose and lit the lamp in the window. Without bothering to do anything about her hair, she slid her bare feet into the moccasins Peter had made for her, then grabbed a blanket and headed into the other room. *Peter.* She'd heard him leave the house. He hadn't come back inside. The idea of him sleeping in the barn spoke volumes. Whatever flights of fancy she'd entertained, whatever she thought she'd read in his dark eyes, obviously she'd been wrong. He was avoiding her.

She laid Mr. Huggins's letter on the table, then lit another lamp and tiptoed to Peter's room to look in on Anna. The old woman was sleeping peacefully. Whatever vestiges of illness she was fighting off, it was obvious she no longer needed special care. Mr. Huggins was right. It was time to go.

Back in the main room, Jane heated water. She didn't want to disturb Anna by grinding coffee. She would settle for hot water until everyone was awake. Then they'd have a proper breakfast, and she'd tell Molly what she'd decided they must do.

She sat for a moment staring down at the letter, praying desperately for peace. Finally it came. Taking up the pencil, she wrote the letter that Peter would take to the depot today. Tears slid down her cheeks as she signed it, then folded it and slipped it into the envelope. Swiping them away, she clutched the mug of warm water between her palms and looked around the room. She gazed up at the sampler. For a moment, she closed her eyes. *Please be my strong tower today.*

Molly was going to be so angry about not having time to finish her doll quilt before they left. She would promise the child that they would have a cabinet photo taken of her with Katie and the finished doll quilt so that Anna could see it. Maybe that would help. Certainly Anna would enjoy a memento of their brief friendship.

The door opened, and Jane sprang to her feet. Peter moved slowly, unwrapping his scarf, removing his hat, hanging everything up before he said a word. When he did, it was to nod at the envelope on the table. "I was hoping..." He paused. "You've written your answer."

Jane nodded.

"I wanted to..." His voice trailed off again.

"You must be so cold." Jane set the mug of warm water down. "Did you sleep at all? Annas resting. I haven't heard her cough once. I'll make coffee. And breakfast. Just let me get dressed." She headed for the bedroom.

"Don't go."

She turned to face him, afraid to say anything, afraid she'd heard what she wanted to hear, not what he'd actually said.

"Did you hear me, Jane? I said, 'Don't go.' "

"I heard."

He looked away. "I have a medal for bravery. For what I did that day." He drew his palm across the scarred cheek. "But I'm not brave. I'm terrified right now. Terrified to talk and afraid that if I don't I'll lose—" He closed his eyes, then finally looked her way. Shook his head. "Molly's right. I am a monster. I know that. Stephen McClure gave you so much. You had a servant, for goodness' sake. And this Huggins fellow? I can't compete with any of it." He took a deep breath. "But I love you, Jane. Heaven help me. I love you, and I love Molly. But if you can't love me back, I understand. Really, I do."

Jane swallowed. Couldn't he hear her heart beating? See her trembling? She nodded toward the letter. "I did my best to explain—to apologize. I never intended to mislead him. I just—I just wanted what was best for Molly." She paused. "We lost the house, Peter. Stephen made some terrible investments, and then he died, and we lost it. I had to sell it to pay all the people we owed money. I paid them, but—" She began to cry. "Things got hard. And I was so lonely. I answered an advertisement in the paper. And Mr. Huggins—" She gave a short, throaty laugh. Shook her head. "Poor Mr. Huggins. I told him we would be catching the train for Omaha."

"Omaha?" Peter frowned.

Jane nodded. "However desperate my situation, I could never marry one man when I was in love with another." Her voice wavered. "I didn't think you—" She cleared her throat. "You didn't kiss me. That night when you could have. You made a joke instead of kissing me."

"You wanted me to kiss you?"

She nodded. "I love you, too, Peter. I just—"

Whatever she was going to say slipped her mind as he pulled her into his arms.

"Molly." Jane tickled the sleeping child's cheek. "It's time to get up. Breakfast is ready."

"I'm not hungry." She was lying with her back to Jane, and she didn't budge.

"Peter's taking us to post my letter to Mr. Huggins. He said you wanted a sleigh ride, and it's a beautiful day. He thought you'd want to go along."

Molly shrugged. "I want to stay here. With Anna. I want to finish Katie's quilt."

"I know. But you need to trust me—"

"—in the matter of Mr. Huggins," Molly groused. "I know." She finally rolled onto her back. And sat up. And looked from Jane to Peter and back again.

Jane leaned into Peter, and he put his arm around her as he said, "I have a question for you, Molly."

Molly grabbed Katie and held her close. "All right. Go ahead."

"I want to ask your mother to marry me. Is that all right with you?"

With a shout of joy, Molly launched herself into Peter's arms, wrapped her arms around his neck, and planted a kiss, first on his good cheek and then on the bad one.

Anna spoke from where she was standing in the doorway. "What am I seeing?"

Jane let go and went to her side. "You shouldn't be out of bed. Let me—"

Anna shooed her away. She glared at Peter. "You have asked?" Peter nodded. She looked at Jane. "And you have said yes?"

Jane nodded and glanced at Molly. "We both have."

Anna raised both hands to the heavens. "Praise be to Gott!" She smiled and shook her head. "So sick I was of being sick." She looked at Peter. "I thought never would you ask."

"Mutti," Peter scolded. "You were *pretending*?"

Anna shrugged. "Maybe a little." She forced a cough, then turned toward the kitchen, waving for everyone to follow her. "Come. We have springerle for breakfast today, ja?" She grinned at Peter. "All you want."

More From Stephanie Grace Whitson

Love at First Light

In 1868, as part of the Ladies Cemetery Improvement Society, a well-to-do young woman who feels unlovable encounters a disfigured warrior who has given up hoping for anything beyond a life in the shadows. When their unusual connection blossoms into love, Isobel and Gideon are faced with the challenge of their lives. After being jilted at the altar, can Isobel ever trust another man? After being vilified and avoided, can Gideon ever let Isobel actually see his face?